Alex Keegan h
selling and as a
sixty-thousand-p
psychology and sociobiology. He took up writing
seriously after being involved in the Clapham Rail
Disaster and now lives in Southampton with his wife
and their two young children. A committed runner
and a UK top-thirty veteran sprinter, Alex Keegan
has worked as an athletics coach and as Race Director
for five major road races.

Alex Keegan's first novel, *Cuckoo*, was published in
1994 and is also available from Headline.

Also by Alex Keegan

Cuckoo

Vulture

A Caz Flood Mystery

Alex Keegan

HEADLINE

First published in 1995
by HEADLINE BOOK PUBLISHING

First published in paperback in 1995
by HEADLINE BOOK PUBLISHING

10 9 8 7 6 5 4 3 2 1

There is a real Caz Flood. All the author has borrowed is
the name, and that with permission. Absolutely nothing
in the novel relates to the real Caz Flood.

ISBN 0 7472 4825 7

Printed and bound in Great Britain by
Cox & Wyman Ltd, Reading, Berks

HEADLINE BOOK PUBLISHING
A division of Hodder Headline PLC
338 Euston Road
London NW1 3BH

For
Munchkinella
and
the most patient solicitor in Britain
Oliver McMurrough

One

December. Another Monday! Early. Cold. Crisp.
Black. Brighton's quiet roads washed with morning
street-light as Detective Inspector Tom MacInnes
drove slowly towards the central police station in John
Street. Alongside him, bright-faced, her eyes darting,
Caz Flood stared out, her face lit intermittently
by the flashing yellow of sodium, her blonde hair
loose over her shoulders.

The DI was lost in thought as he steered his Sierra
through the quiet streets. He was breathing slowly.
He was thinking about a serious villain, now off on
his toes, the shit still flying. He was thinking about
the spunky young copper sitting next to him. He was
thinking about himself when he was still approaching
thirty. He was thinking how much this girl was like
him.

'How's it feel, Caz?'
  'I think, pretty good, Tom. A little strange, maybe.'
  'A lot's happened. You take your time.'
  'I wish!' Caz said.

1

After a traumatic burglary, a brush with drowning and a week in hospital, the Detective Constable had moved in temporarily with the Inspector. She was still sleeping over at his flat, camping out on his sofa, and he had suggested that it would be politically sensible if he dropped her on the corner near the station. As his car drifted away, he could see her in his rear-view mirror, long and slim, her head high, just taking a deep breath. As he turned left, she was approaching the double doors at the front of the building, a spring in her step.

Two

The nick! Caz could smell it! It was so good to be back. She pushed through the doors and padded quietly past the empty front desk. Her green eyes reflected back from the glass-fronted cabinets in the entrance as she took in the older crime posters and a new one, a 'wanted in connection' video-fit of Jeremy Avocado. She walked down the cream corridor towards the charge room.

The DI had said she was to grab a coffee and to go through to DCS Blackside's office sharp at nine o'clock. He'd already told her that Avocado was still on the run and that she'd been pulled off the case, but he'd also said there would be plenty of other things for her to do. When she had asked him what, Tom MacInnes had said, 'Wait till Monday, Flood!'

There was no one in the locker room as she dropped off her rolled-up running gear, but there was a yellow Post-it note stuck on her locker door. Blackside wanted to see her in the War Room as soon as she turned in. So much for Tom's nine o'clock! She grinned, flashing even white teeth, and went straight upstairs.

It was still a tad early for the likes of Sergeant Moore, and in for half-eight was the average for DC Saint and Jim Greaves. Tom MacInnes thought seven twenty-five meant a pretty long lie-in, and Norman Blackside's idea of fun was to see the sun come up through his office window. At this time of day it was still deathly quiet; quiet enough to hear the walls.

As Caz walked, her thoughts were filling the silence. She was thinking about the failure to arrest Jeremy Avocado, a prime suspect in a recent case, almost certainly responsible for six deaths. She was trying to decide what the escape might mean to the DI and to the DCS. Blackside was supposed to be leaving soon, destined to be one among the gods at Scotland Yard. She didn't know whether Avocado's slipping the net would go down as a black mark for the DCS or be seen as just one of those things.

As she reached his War Room, she was thinking that he'd probably ride the storm. She pushed back the doors. Inside the room, there was a darkness and a silence she could feel. She hesitated. Right then, she should have guessed.

The first thing Caz heard was an off-key chorus of 'Yellow Submarine'. Then there was a click and the lights flickered on. The first thing she saw – she guessed it had to be Billy Tingle – was some long wally dressed in a frogman's outfit. The rest of the lads were wearing snorkels and masks. Someone had hung a mobile over her desk and little coloured fish on wires chased themselves in circles. On her chair was a nine-inch lump of glistening grey blubber. She presumed it was octopus. 'That's the sick squid I owe yer!' Greavsie said. Then the masks were off and the lads were cheering her in.

She grinned and looked for Moira Dibben. Moira looked back and made the sign for 'dick'eads' at the mêlée of coppers. Caz sat on a desk's edge and looked at the crew. She was grinning. 'You are *such* a bunch of arseholes,' she said.

A couple of the lads' faces turned as the doors opened again. DI MacInnes and DCS Blackside were standing there. Norman Blackside's impressive bulk dominated the slight figure of the DI but they both looked genuinely pleased to see their detective back in the fold. Tom MacInnes looked faintly sheepish, as if keeping the surprise secret from her had embarrassed him. The DCS had a brown-paper packet in his hand and he shouted for hush.

'OK, lads, OK. Enough is enough!' His dark voice took instant command. 'Six o'clock tonight in The Grapes and we can wet DC Flood's head yet again. The first round is mine, the second one is Tom's. Let's remember we've still got work to do.' He turned formally to Caz.

'Detective Constable Flood. On behalf of the murder squad and the rest of the station, I have been asked to make a small presentation. After spending fifteen minutes or so alone in the back seat of a micro-light aircraft followed by another three or four minutes down with the fishes, the lads were keen to buy you some khaki knickers. We couldn't find you any, so instead we got you this.' He offered the bag and Caz stood to take it. 'We strongly suggest you read this well, DC Flood. It may come in handy some time. Meanwhile, you should know you've been put up for a Police Medal.' There was a loud cheer from the lads. Caz opened the bag and removed a book.

It was *Teach Yourself Flying*.

Three

Caz walked in to the Chief Superintendent's office smack on nine o'clock. He was sitting behind his desk. MacInnes sat to his left side in a less substantial chair. 'Flood, it's good to have you back,' Blackside said. She sat down opposite him. 'We've got a job, needs a woman. For now, you're off the Avocado case.'

Caz waited calmly.

'In the two weeks that you were out of it, we've had a bit of grief. You know about Avocado? Well, to add to our troubles, it looks like we've got a serial rapist on the patch. Ten days ago there was a nasty rape in Worthing; a married lass on her way home. She was attacked as she opened her front door and bundled inside by her assailant. I won't give you the details, you can read the file later. WPC Dibben spoke to the victim in the General. The bastard really hurt her, then he branded her. He said so she'd never forget him.'

'Where, Sir?'

'Read the file.'

MacInnes spoke. His voice was more lightweight than Blackside's, but just as assured. 'This Friday we had ourselves another one. We think the same MO. The victim was single, aged thirty-two. Found in her bedroom. From clothing and shopping we think the rapist surprised her the same way as his first attack. We think she was hit from behind while she was opening her front door but we can't be sure. This one's not regained consciousness.'

'We've turned up three similars,' Blackside said. 'An attack in Southampton three months ago and two more in Richmond. The first was October last year, the second was April.'

'Shortening gaps, Sir.'

'And escalating violence, Flood. In the first Richmond case there was just a sudden physical attack which knocked the victim down. The assailant ran away before doing anything. Richmond Two was just a rape.'

'*Just* a rape?'

'No added violence, Flood. Vaginal entry only. Nothing else.'

'I'm sorry, Sir.'

'Don't worry about it, Flood.' The DCS paused, thinking hard.

MacInnes broke in, as if bailing out the Chief Superintendent. 'We're pretty sure that all five attacks are by the same man, but there seems to be no pattern and, as yet, no connection between the women. Three of them were single, two of them were married; the youngest was twenty and the oldest forty-one.'

'So what do you want me to do?' Caz asked Blackside.

'Catch the bastard, Flood!'

'I know that, Sir, but what—'

'There is one vague connection,' Blackside said slowly. 'Ever heard of the Richmond and Kingston Running Sisters?'

'Yes, Sir. They're a sort of all-female self-help joggers group. They go out together. Safety in numbers, that sort of thing.'

'Well, your Richmond pair knew each other vaguely. They were both in this "Sisters" outfit and knew each other by sight. After the second attack, South London tried to push the connection but got nowhere. We figured that as you were a runner and female, maybe you could come up with something.'

'What about forensic, Sir? Presumably we've got semen et cetera?'

'There was no rape on the first incident but we got forensic samples on the second and third. He's a non-secretor, but we're having DNA profiles done.'

'And the last two women, Sir?'

'Don't know yet. Waiting for the labs. Couple of weeks.'

'OK, Sir. The files?'

'On your desk in five minutes.'

Caz stood up to leave, then asked about personnel. Blackside told her to sit back down. 'We're up to our eyes here, Flood; you know that. Avocado is still out there on the loose and we can't pull anyone off that team for this. I can let you have Moira Dibben for a fortnight and we'll see where we go after that.'

'What about South London and Southampton, Sir?'

'Southampton is a DI Denham, a Sergeant and two DCs. The DS is Peter Mason, based at Shirley. He's your contact when you ring, but be warned, Flood, they're spread a bit thin down there at the moment.'

'And Richmond, Sir?'

'That's gone pretty cold. They had a reasonable squad on it at first but neither of the women would help much. One of yours, a DS Griffin, came on to the case but she got nowhere too.'

'Jenny Griffin, Sir. I've met her once.'

'Yes, well. They know we're having another go, and they'll be whatever help they can, but they're all on other cases too so don't expect much.'

'Not even from Griffin?'

'Not even from Griffin.'

She left and went to see Moira.

Moira Dibben was in the computer room, close to one of the four Holmes terminals but swivelled diagonally away from its black and green screen. She was shoeless and massaging one of her dark-stockinged feet. She glanced up briefly then turned back to her problem. 'Can you believe I went *walking* yesterday, Caz?' She was talking to her stockinged toes. 'We went up to the Downs. Billy said we only walked six miles. I reckon it was nearer twenty! It wasn't for charity or anything, just because it was a nice day. I think Billy bloody Tingle is completely and utterly mad!'

'Maybe he's recently had a knock on the head,' Caz suggested lightly. 'P'raps he's still in shock.'

Moira giggled. 'Billy's healthy enough!'

'You mean fit.'

'Do I?' Moira asked. Then she asked, 'What can I do you for, boss?'

Caz grinned. 'How'd you like a fortnight out of here, Moira?'

'You're kidding me!'

'Nope!' Caz said.

'Then I'm yours. Just tell me who I've gotta kill.'

Caz tucked the files under her arm. 'OK, Moira, get yer shoes on and follow me.'

They went down to the canteen via the back stairs to avoid as many of the male uniforms as possible. It made no difference that Moira and Billy were an item or that Caz was going out with Val – the quick looks, the touched shoulders, the unrequested jokes and the uninvited remarks from the pit would be feet thick. In the nick, you measured harassment by the square yard. It didn't change. If you stuck it long enough you grew a thicker skin. If you couldn't take it, you got out. The guys'd tell you it was just fun. It was tough being a copper and you have to let off steam, don't you?

They arrived unscathed. Caz asked after Moira's boyfriend.

'Billy's not daft, Caz. I reckon he booked today off to recover from the walk. He went home straight after your little welcome.'

They heard a quick rush of men's laughter in the corridor.

'You really like him, don't you, Mo?'

'I do,' Moira said. She was smiling with soft, dark brown eyes. 'Compared to that lot out there, my Billy is an angel.'

While Moira got the coffees in, Caz grabbed a table near the only window. There were a few uniforms still sitting around, night-shifters stuck at the nick finishing arrest paperwork. Every one of them looked grey-eyed, dark-faced and short-tempered; ready to go home and crash straight into bed, probably without a shower. They ignored Caz, but nevertheless she went for an isolated table; two girls on a rape case and for certain someone would take an interest.

She'd deliberately left the case notes for later. Before she read the official reports, she wanted to hear Moira's side of things, her impressions from the victim interviews, the subtleties and the nuances of their interactions. What she didn't need was the emotional emptiness of a bare statement, nor the rounded-down sterility that came from ball-point pen on white.

They were brewing up behind the bar, steam spitting from stainless steel. Moira stood patiently. She was a tallish size twelve with shining black hair, faintly dusky, with a hint of South American that made her exotic as well as noticeably beautiful. Caz could only guess at why Moira had chosen to be a copper, but the greater mystery was how she'd ended up with Billy Tingle. Love being blind was one thing, but deaf, dumb and mortally stupid was another. Billy and Moira bewildered Caz. But then these things usually did.

'Very black and bloody 'ot!' Moira said. 'Sorry it took so long. Night shift finished off the urn!' She sat down opposite Caz. Light slanting in from outside lit one side of her face. 'What's it all about then, boss?'

Caz told her. The Worthing rapes.

'Oh, shit,' Moira said, meaning it. 'I think I'd rather work Holmes.'

'You don't mean that, Moira. No one wants to work Holmes.'

'You were in hospital,' Moira explained. 'Just about everyone was out looking for Jeremy Avocado. John Street was a complete riot. It was absolute bedlam, double shifts, overs, everything. Blackside managed to use up December's overtime in three days! We were working in sixes and we checked out every marina and berth from Sheerness round as far as Bournemouth. It was on the telly, you know, wanted in connection with a number of deaths and all that. They put a temporary stop on Blackside's transfer to the Yard and I heard that there was Special Branch at every airport. Most of the boys who were qualified here booked out pistols, and they had Region in. Some of them were carrying machine guns!'

'Hechler and Kochs?'

'You tell me, Caz, I haven't a clue. The point was, the Avocado thing was so big they didn't have anyone for the rapes in Worthing. They pulled Greavsie and me out, but only short term. Jim was only with me for one day. I had to do the follow-ups.'

'MacInnes said there wasn't even a whisper of Avocado.'

'Not the faintest. Thin air job. Your friend Jeremy just disappeared off the face of the planet.'

'OK, Moira, tell me about the first attack.'

'She was a secretary, twenty-five, married to a bloke who worked away on oil rigs. His company flew him out as soon as they knew. Nice bloke. He's taken her away for a few days – see if it'll help.'

'When will they be back?'

'I'm not sure. Just a couple of days, they said. We could hardly stop them.'

'I suppose not,' Caz said. 'Tell me what happened.'

'She was coming home with a bit of shopping. Got pushed through her own front door just as she was opening it and the bastard did it to her in the hall. You don't want me to describe it to you, do you?'

'I'll read it, Mo. What did this woman—'

'Her name's Jackie Engels.'

'What did Jackie say about the attacker?'

'She said he hardly spoke. When he hit her, she fell face down. She thought he was pretty heavy, maybe worked out. He grunted something about God. Jackie said he sounded a bit slow. Either he had some sort of speech problem or he might have been sub-normal. She just wasn't sure.'

'And it wasn't just rape?'

'No, it wasn't. He really hurt her, Caz.'

'And what's this thing about him branding her?'

'Jackie said he said, "Remember, God sent me." Then he burnt her shoulder. She said it was really hot. The mark's about an inch long and about quarter of an inch wide. Doesn't look like anything. Why do blokes do that, Caz?'

'Do what?'

'Hurt us. Isn't the rape enough?'

'To tell themselves we're worthless, Moira. They can do it to us because we're nothing. If we mattered they'd have to feel guilty.'

Four

Blackside had promised Caz that the rape files would be on her desk in five minutes; the fact that she didn't *have* a desk was relatively trivial. When she and Moira returned to the War Room, Jim Greaves gave them a shout. They could get this lot out of his way as soon as they liked; he had enough on his plate as it was. 'DI says you'll have to nick yourself a corner of the computer room or borrow one of the cells for a couple of days.'

It was Hobson's choice, and Hobson wanted the cell. They took the computer room. Looking out, Caz felt odd watching the organised chaos of the search for Avocado. The activity was just a window away, but for now she was glad to be out of it. She knew Avocado was very unlikely to be found. Let the lads burn shoe-leather and adrenaline. She had a rapist to catch.

Moira mimed 'Drink?' and Caz nodded absently. The five files were each no more than half-an-inch thick, not nearly thick enough, and only one of them looked dog-eared enough to indicate any serious work. Caz grimaced. This was going to be a tough one. She began to read.

The thinnest file was on the first attack, a youngster called Brown. Reading between the lines, it looked as if DS Griffin had either thought that the girl was making it up, or she was hard-pressed by her other 'outstandings'. The nearby door-to-door had been minimal, and no one had seen anything. Six months later, when one Mrs I. Stubbs, forty-one, was attacked, the Detective Sergeant had quietly unearthed the older file.

The older case had virtually died and the trail was cold. A re-interview with Brown had brought up the 'Sisters' connection but nothing else. She had simply wanted to forget that anything had ever happened.

The Southampton attack was in the following September, on a history teacher from a local college. She had lived alone, in a quiet estate of semi-detached Barratt houses, but now her file was marked 'gone away'. The initial battery was identical to the two Richmond cases but the severity and diversity of the sexual attack was much worse. Miss Fleet had been semi-conscious and had seen or heard nothing, but she had added at a second interview that perhaps she had smelt something burning, something hot. She had not been branded. It was one scar less.

Moira had got back from the canteen and was now reading the files, one file behind Caz. As she took the third and Caz moved on to the first Worthing attack, she let out a little puff of breath and cursed quietly.

'Drink your tea, Moira,' Caz said formally, 'don't let it get to you.'

'It's not the attacks,' Moira sighed, 'it's these case files. It looks like no one cares a damn about these women.'

'You don't know that, Moira. Richmond One was a dead-end no-hoper, and Richmond Two wasn't a lot better. We do our best. I'm sure Jenny Griffin did her best, but you know what it's like, there's just too much to chase. We can't do it all.'

'I just wish—'

'We all do that, Mo, but in the end it doesn't catch villains, does it?'

'No.'

'Hard graft does. Plus a little bit of luck and the appliance of science.'

'Yes, boss!' Moira said. She managed a weak smile. 'I just hope Jane Daily comes out of her coma OK. She makes five. If she was in the bedroom she may have seen and heard a bit more than the others. So far this is . . .'

'Dead water?' Caz suggested.

Moira nodded. 'And he's out there now . . .'

Information on the last attack was sketchy. It was by far the worst of the five and the victim was still in a coma. As well as the sexual assault, Jane Daily had received a broken jaw, a cracked cheekbone and the fractured skull that had precipitated the severe concussion and her current comatose state.

Caz felt sick and coldly angry. This wasn't a rapist, it was a wild animal. Daily's doctors were calling her coma 'protective' and she was now expected to pull through, but Caz knew for certain that if this animal was not caught soon he would eventually kill. What made her sick and fearful was the almost complete lack of real information. She had nothing to check, almost no one to see and no real sense of direction. All she could do was start again and hope that something had been missed. She turned to Moira. She needed some action, something to make her feel productive.

'Get hold of Jenny Griffin, Mo. See if we can go there this morning.'

'This morning?'

'Or sooner, With Jackie away, there's not a lot we can do here until we can talk to Daily.'

Griffin was in the field, almost literally, looking for a persistent flasher who had been causing problems in Richmond Park. Moira wasn't doing too well trying to arrange a meeting and she handed the phone to Caz just as a DCI came on the line.

'Who's this?' It was a hard, abrupt, northern-sounding voice.

'DC Flood, Sir. John Street, Brighton.'

'Well, I've already told your girl, Griffin's out. She's not contactable.'

'This is urgent, Sir.'

'Everything's urgent.'

'But this really is, Sir. Very. We've got serial rape and attempted murder already.'

'DS Griffin is out. I just told you.'

'When will she be back in?'

'End of shift.'

'Thank you for your co-operation, Sir. You've really been most helpful.' She appeared to be smiling but as soon as she had put the phone down she hissed 'wanker' at the receiver.

Moira chuckled and said, 'Don't let it get to you, boss!'

'You're right,' Caz said. She pushed four of the cardboard files together while she thought. She looked again at the phone, hand-signed 'wanker' at it, then she made a decision. 'That's it! Come on, Moira, we're out of here!' Moira asked where, and Caz told her as they scuttled through the War Room. 'Richmond Park, Mo. We're looking for a man in a dirty raincoat.'

They could go through the rigmarole of booking out a car or they could use Moira's motor. Caz said they didn't have the time to mess about; it was Mo's little Ford or they were walking.

Richmond was a good hour's drive; they were bound to talk about men. Moira mentioned the dark DC from Woking who'd been drafted in during the Avocado fiasco. He wasn't bad-looking. If she wasn't with Billy, well, she probably would have said yes when he asked her out. 'But I didn't. I told him about Billy. He just said, "so what?" Blokes!'

'It takes all sorts,' Caz said.

Moira drove with her hands at ten-to-two on the small steering wheel, and kept glancing in her rear-view mirror as if she was still on her driving test.

'You're a bit careful,' Caz said.

'Yep,' Moira snapped, 'with my driving, and with my men!' She tooted her horn and flashed her lights as she passed a white Mercedes van. 'Anyway,' she said, softer this time, 'how is it with you and Valerie now? You two sorted yourselves out yet?'

'Don't ask!' Caz said.

'I already did!' Moira retorted. 'So you might as well tell me. We've got to talk about something; it's a fair way to Wimbledon.'

'Richmond.'

'That too,' Moira said. She was staring at the road.

Caz was quiet, listening to the wind whistling round the car.

Moira glanced across. 'Well?'

'Well what?'

'You and Valerie, what's the score?'

'I'd say about even at the moment. He's in Portugal and I'm kipping on the DI's couch.'

'I heard you were stopping with the DI.'

'I said. On his couch.'

'I know!' Moira's voice sailed quickly up and down. 'Come on, tell me about you and Valerie. Are you and him . . . or what?'

'I think it's "what". To tell you the truth, Mo, I'm not absolutely sure. He's gone off for a few weeks to go hang-gliding and to work things out in his head.'

'I thought you two had made up?'

'We did, sort of. But I think now, with his best friend dead, and all that went on round the Avocado

21

case . . . well, he's not sure that he likes me.'

'*Likes* you! I thought you two were a lot heavier than that.'

'I didn't say he didn't *love* me, Mo. He says he's not sure what I am – whether there's any point in us being together. I know what he means.'

'Blokes!' Moira said.

'If you like,' Caz said.

She was trying to be cheerful but her mind was somewhere else.

Five

They parked in a side-street close to one of the ornate gates to the park. It was 'residents only' parking, so Moira stuck a POLICE sticker on the dash before locking up. 'Let's go!' Caz said. Now she was doing something, there was a little more fire in her face.

She still hadn't decided what exactly they *were* doing, but she knew that she wouldn't just sit around in John Street waiting for a phone call. She was more than half-pissed by the attitude of the Richmond DCI, but what really made her seethe was the feeling that earlier she'd kept from Moira – the feeling that Jenny Griffin had let the cases slip away. She wasn't holding back now. She was telling Moira as they entered the park, 'We all know about case loads, Mo, but this one should have been different. There's never any slack, but when it's one of ours—'

'A copper?' Moira sounded surprised.

'I meant a woman.'

'Oh,' Moira said.

At this time of the day they had to be lucky to see the park deer, but as they walked along the tarmac sweep of a footpath they could see about thirty spotted does grazing near a massive oak tree. A huge, magnificent stag faced out from them, his head high, grey-white antlers displayed defiantly. Sunlight flashed off bone.

'Isn't he gorgeous?' Moira said.

'Ah, it's all show,' Caz tittered. 'He's a medallion man really.'

'And are all those, you know, are they his, know what I mean?'

'You mean, his girlfriends?'

'Yeah.'

'Of course,' Caz said, speaking with authority. 'He's the biggest and the strongest guy in the neighbourhood and you've got to admit one thing, he is *bloody* handsome.'

'He's magnificent!' Moira said.

Caz told her she meant sexy.

'Do I?' Moira said. There was a little flutter in her voice.

Caz chuckled. 'Why Moira, do I detect a touch of pink in your cheeks?' She paused. 'What time did you say you were meeting Billy tonight?'

'I wasn't,' Moira said slowly. She looked again at the stag. 'But I think I might give him a ring later ...' Caz was grinning. She licked a finger and drew a 'one' in the air.

Moira was in 'half-blues', a civilian overcoat over her uniform skirt. The black stockings and sensible shoes would shout 'copper' to any serious villain but not to a pervert, Caz reckoned; they were too single-minded. Caz wore her favourite Levi 501's, a white Tee, a leather jacket and Asics trainers. As usual she was comfortable but ready.

Four or five hundred yards away to their left, a steady stream of traffic passed through the park on its single road. The two policewomen drifted towards that. Caz had persuaded Moira to relax and drop her shoulders. By walking tall, she said, they gave off too much strength; by slumping, they looked more like victims. They weren't likely to bump into Freddie the Flasher, but it made good sense to keep their options open. The art was to be alert without looking so. Caz had forgotten to mention to Moira that she was bait.

It was eleven-thirty and the temperature had finally crept above zero. The white of the overnight frost was molten now, giving way to a black shine on the tarmac and a dark green sheen on the grass. Caz twitched her nose, sniffing at the air. The weather was exhilarating – sharp yellow light in their faces, energising cold round their ears. 'God, what a day!' she gasped. Then she said she wished that she was running, right now.

'You're completely mad!' Moira said. 'You and Billy Tingle both. The two of you are loopy. I just cannot understand this big thing about being fit. What's so wrong with being laid back? I *like* my lie-ins.'

'Don't you ever simply feel so bloody *good*?' Caz asked. 'Haven't you ever seen some mountain and just simply *had* to run up it?'

'Nope.'

'Have you never seen some forest trail that just called out to you?'

'Nope!'

'Or a long beach with hard flat sand that's just *screaming* to be run on?'

'Nope.'

'Oh what?' Caz said, disbelieving. 'How'd you cope with the fitness test?'

'It's only once a year. I go jogging for a couple of weeks beforehand. I just do enough to get through.'

'Well how do you feel? Doesn't it make you feel good when you work out?'

'Is this a trick question?'

'No, it's not!'

'Well, I feel shitty if you must know, Caz. I get hot and sweaty, my legs ache like hell, and as soon as I start running, I want to pee. I hate running and I think that anyone who likes it is *very* sick!'

Caz was exasperated. She shook her head and muttered, 'Oh, my Gawd!'

'And what exactly is *your* problem?' Moira said.

'Problem?' Caz fired back. 'P-rob-lem! Are you *serious*? My God, woman, have you taken a look at this superb body? Did you say problem? I am a finely honed athlete and I'm spending the next fortnight with a couch potato-ette!'

Moira waited, trying to think of a sharp reply. None came to her so she waved an upturned hand with a single pointed finger and coughed, 'Huh!'

From the bushes he saw the two of them, younger

ones, their hands flying about them in conversation. He was in a Nike shell-suit and a pair of New Balance trainers. The shell-suit was purple, white and lilac with the Nike International logo splashed across the back. The trainers were soft and comfortable, grey, with deep black rubber soles and a large silver 'N' on the sides. When he had picked them up in the shop, the salesman had said they were high-mileage shoes, so he bought them. Not that he ever ran very far; the only mileage he ever did was this little jog – to the park, and then to some bushes. And if he went to the toilet and came out, it wasn't his fault if he'd not put it away properly, was it? It was just a mistake. He was just a jogger.

Really, he preferred older women or young girls. Women like these frightened him a bit, but he was getting cold now so he stepped out, the front of his suit trousers pulled down. The first woman had thick dark hair. He grinned awkwardly at her as he stepped in her way. He saw her hesitate, her jaw drop slightly. For a split second he thought, 'This is the one, she likes me.' But then her eyes darkened and she shouted, 'Caz!'

The dark one moved towards him first; she was closer. He turned to run away, but as he did so she caught his arm. She was not as big as him and he thought about hitting her, but then the other one, the blonde one, caught his arm and shouted something nasty at him, something about his thing. Then she said, 'You're nicked, pal!' and he fell down, his face pressed into the grass. He wanted to tell them.

It was a mistake. He was just a jogger. He was just out jogging. He'd just been going to the toilet and they had surprised him.

Someone was kneeling on his back and he felt something cold snap around his wrists. He wanted to tell them but they sounded angry. Then he heard some people running, heavy people, and lots of shouting. The weight on his back went away but when he went to lift his head a foot pressed him back down toward the floor. He could smell dog-mess. He started crying. Then he heard someone else. 'Who the *fuck* are you?' a man's voice said. It was very loud and very angry. The foot pressed him down.

A woman's voice answered. 'And who the fuck are *you*?'

'I'm Detective Sergeant Cole, Richmond.'

'Well, I'm DC Flood, John Street, Brighton, and King Kong there—' the foot pressed down again, 'is WPC Dibben, same nick.'

'So what the f—' The man stopped himself. 'What are you two doing on our manor?'

Someone else ran up, with lighter feet. A woman's voice, out of breath. 'Is it him? Is it him?'

'I presume so,' the man's voice said gruffly, 'and this pair just collared him.'

'Let me guess.' The breathless one again. 'Caz Flood, right?'

'Hi-yah, Jenny!' the other woman said. 'Have you met Moira Dibben?'

'No, I bloody well have not!'

'Moira, you can take your size fives off the maggot

28

now.' The voice lowered. 'Mo, come over here. Come meet Jenny Griffin.'

He felt the foot lift from his neck. Slowly he turned over. Three men and three women stared down at him, bright blue sky behind them. They all looked disgusted. He was still tearful. He wanted to explain but he couldn't speak.

Then the women turned and walked away.

Six

'We're not interested in the arrest, Jenny. We don't fancy the paperwork.'

'Is that right?'

'Yeah, the bloke is yours.'

'Well, thank *you*, Flood! You come trampling all over our patch, nearly put paid to a week's observation . . .'

'We weren't trampling anywhere. We were on our way to Scott Street.'

'Then what the hell were you doing in the bloody park?'

'Walking. We left the motor over the other side and took a wander through. The parking's crap in central Richmond and we didn't want to hang about at the nick. We had a lot of time to kill, so we decided to stretch our legs.'

'So why Scott Street? Haven't you read the file?'

'What there is of it, yes. We both have. It's a shut door.'

'So what are you trying to do, Caz? Make me look stupid?'

'No.'

'Well, you're going about it a bloody funny way, *detective*!'

Caz went formal. 'I'm sorry, Sergeant. I was asked to come up here and it was cleared by both our Supers. We have a nasty serial rapist on our patch; and he looks an awful lot like the same John who warmed up on yours. Now we've got five cases, my DCS has asked us to go back over all the old ground to see what's common across the cases. No one's having a pop at you. You couldn't have done much more on Richmond One. Some slightly neurotic girl says a man's knocked her over and then ran away? We'd've been the same.'

Jenny Griffin huffed. 'Hindsight is an exact science!'

Caz went with her. 'And even more so when it comes from a DCS!'

'Who, of course, *has* to be a man.'

Caz left it. Man-hating would do for now. At least it gave them common ground. She smiled and touched the chain-smoking sergeant on the arm. The sergeant's body was full of tension. 'Hey,' Caz said softly, 'we got any coffee?'

They weren't at the nick. After the arrest of the flasher, Jenny Griffin had dragged them to an unmarked Transit van that had been the control for the observation. The van was deliberately scruffy, but the windows were one-way dark glass and inside was tape equipment, a video camera and two auto-focus Canon EOS 1000's sporting long lenses.

Jenny had bundled them angrily inside and the first thing that had hit them was the smell. It was a cross, somewhere between a sports changing room, a brothel and a public lavatory. Caz had done observations before, she knew the smell. Moira hadn't. As she stepped inside the van, she let out an involuntary 'Yuch!!'

There was a short vinyl-topped bench to one side and a square of rubber matting near the cameras. The Brighton women sat together on the bench. Griffin unfolded a black-backed director's chair and sat opposite them, her head an inch from the ceiling. Moira was still turning her nose up and Griffin sighed. She looked downwards towards a small hole in the floor near the back door, then back up at Caz. 'For God's sake, tell the girl, Flood!'

Caz was staring at the floor by Griffin's feet. She explained. 'Moira, this is an ob van. Once yer in, you don't get out. When you have to go, you have to go. You use the hole. Do you understand?'

'And,' Jenny added, 'if you're sharing the van with some big lout like Kingy Cole or Bernie Evans it's even more fun. For some reason blokes think farting is obligatory when they're in here.'

'Nerves,' Caz said.

'What about that awful perfume?' Moira asked weakly.

'Awful?' Griffin said. 'That's mine!'

'Oh, I'm sorry . . .'

'Don't be,' Caz said quickly. 'Jenny's taking the mick. You use a cheap one to cover up the other smells.'

'Oh,' Moira said. She felt like a child.

Griffin straightened up. 'Well, aren't you going to ask?'

'What about?' Moira said.

'Aren't you going to ask me about going to the lav?'

'I didn't like to.'

'Neither did I!' Griffin let out a measured laugh.

Caz spoke to the floor. 'When you gotta go, Mo, you gotta go . . .'

'And these macho bastards wouldn't *dream* of looking the other way!'

'What, Jenny? But I couldn't . . .' Moira sounded pathetic.

'Sometimes you have no choice,' Caz said gently.

'Yeah,' Griffin said. 'It's either sit on your dignity or squat in the corner.'

Moira was still unconvinced. 'But, I just couldn't . . .'

'It happens, lass, believe me.'

'Well, I think it's awful.'

Jenny relaxed and smiled. 'It's not always that bad, Moira. A *few* of the guys are almost civilised. When you've been through the hoop at least once, they'll find ways to give you a little bit of privacy. Besides, do a few obboes with animals like Kingy and you soon learn to train yer kidneys.'

'What about the DCs? Do they . . . I mean . . .?'

'Piss in the corner? Jesus, child, of *course* they bloody do! Don't be so naïve! It's quite funny. I hide in this van from six o'clock every morning for a week, trying to catch a flasher, and there are great big policemen waving their dicks about *in* the van every half an hour! *They* think it's funny.'

'Romantic, isn't it?' Caz said.

Jenny did have coffee, not café noir or cappuccino, but Nescaff – straight out of a flask and made with long-life milk. The surroundings weren't perfect either, but, hell, this was a war zone. 'Cheers!' Caz said.

They drank their coffees. The taste reminded Caz of long-gone late nights at university. Jenny explained that the arrest of the flasher was on video-tape, so even if they wanted to, there was no way they would be able to drop Brighton's involvement. She pressed buttons while she talked and a flickering image wound back on a monitor screen. Then she told them to take a look.

The four-by-three-inch colour screen was a liquid-crystal device. On it, Moira and Caz watched themselves in some sort of heated discussion. The detail was just enough to show Moira give Caz the finger before it showed Caz glance ahead, hesitate, then bend down to tie a shoelace. The detail was not sufficient to show that the lace was already properly tied.

Then the flasher stepped out from the bushes. He had pulled his track-suit trouser-front down and was exposing his penis. The footage showed his face clearly from two hundred metres on times ten magnification. The offending member was less obvious, but obvious enough for a conviction.

The only sound on the film was the creaking from within the Transit van but Moira's head could be seen, first moving fractionally backwards, and then tilting upwards as she shouted silently. Caz could be seen to glance up and a professional watcher might have suggested that she hesitated, even deliberately, as she observed her colleague move quickly in to arrest the man. It would have been hard to decide on how crucial the second officer's intervention was. The best bet was to award the pull to the WPC.

'So with evidence like that, we can't take the collar, can we?' Jenny didn't sound the happiest of sergeants.

Moira chipped up, 'Couldn't we have contacted you, Jenny? Maybe offered to be bait, or something? You know, while we waited for you to come off duty?'

'And how exactly did you contact us, through control?'

'Why not?'

Jenny paused. 'I suppose I could have a chat to the desk.'

'There, y'see?' Moira was grinning. 'No harm done!'

'Best leave it now, Mo,' Caz said seriously. 'Leave it to Sergeant Griffin.'

'Yeah, do that!' Jenny said.

They waited, watching the older woman. She looked as though wheels were moving behind her eyes. Suddenly, she perked up and said, 'Right!'

The change of attitude Caz took to mean 'OK, ask

me about Brown and Stubbs.' So she did. What could Jenny recall about the Richmond attacks?

'God, this coffee is shit!' she said first. Caz grinned. Moira raised her eyebrows, she thought the drink was all right, actually.

'Brown was a bit of a joke – at the time,' Griffen said. She shifted in her seat. 'She was just twenty, if I remember, the sort of girl who'd be really pretty if she made an effort, but didn't. You know the type?'

Caz nodded. Moira was pouring more coffee.

'She was just a bit overweight, a sort of floppy twelve or a small fourteen. She told me she'd just started running a couple of months before – before the attack, that is. She was in baggy trousers and a sweat-top when I went to see her. Said she'd started jogging and had joined this "Sisters" organisation.'

'The Richmond and Kingston Running Sisters?'

'Correct. Anyway, there was almost nothing to go on. She wasn't marked; she wasn't even distressed. She was one of these dizzy young things, living on her own, you know?'

'Not particularly credible?'

'Absolutely. It's not that you don't want to give them the benefit of the doubt, it's just that when there's so much clear-cut crime out there . . .'

'I know.'

'And what exactly were we looking for? I got the community PC to ask around and I door-to-doored the houses either side, but there was just nowt. Oh, one neighbour said there'd been a TV engineer's van in the street, but when we tried the obvious companies we drew a blank. The witness thought it was an Escort van or maybe a Vauxhall. She didn't remember the colour.'

Caz had written three words in her notebook. 'And that was it?'

'For then, yes. I'd've file-thirteened it if Stubbs hadn't been attacked.'

'Tell me about it.'

'Different kettle of fish altogether. Mrs Stubbs was returning home from shopping. She was hit on the back of her head as she opened her front door and raped in her hall. Apart from the first blow – and the rape itself – she wasn't attacked in any other way. She never saw or heard anything; she may even have been unconscious during the rape.'

'Do you think so?'

'It's hard to say. Mrs Stubbs was upset, of course, but she wasn't hysterical. I think it's quite likely.'

'Nice bloke.' Caz said.

'Aren't all rapists?'

'Sorry.'

'I suppose you want to know about this Richmond and Kingston thing, the connection between Miss Brown and Mrs Stubbs?'

'You could say that.'

'Well, as far as I could see, there is none. Coincidence!'

'So how did you find out?'

'When Mrs Stubbs went home after the medical, I went with her. There were two pairs of running shoes in the hall, his 'n' hers. I asked. She said that her husband ran marathons and that he'd persuaded her to take up jogging. She was too slow for him, so she had joined this Sisters outfit. It's a bit of a loose organisation but basically it's a get-together system for women so they don't have to run on their own.'

'And Stubbs knew Brown?'

'Not really. When we showed her a photograph she thought she knew her vaguely. We went back to see the Brown girl. She remembered Mrs Stubbs because her husband had run in the London Marathon.'

'And no other connection?'

'None at all.'

'The Sisters, they're set up and run by women, yeah?'

'Absolutely, not a man in sight. We spoke to a few men, boyfriends or husbands of some of the members, but there weren't many. Quite a few of the club – if you can call it that, it's fairly informal – quite a few are single women, anyway. I guess ladies with male partners run with them if they can.'

'Unless they're too slow. Like Mrs Stubbs.'

'Unless they're too slow.'

They climbed out of the back of the van, once Moira had finished off the flask of coffee but not before Jenny Griffin had offered her the chance to use the hole in the floor. Moira said she'd take a rain check.

There was no way to avoid Richmond Central and some paperwork. Caz agreed to give Jenny the extra ten minutes she needed to see if she could fix the desk. Then the older sergeant climbed into the

Transit's cab and the two younger women strolled back through the park, wasting a little time.

The sun was as high as it gets in a British December and a limp yellow blob shimmered above them in a peculiar haze. Water vapour drifted up from the trees in a thin mist and there was a sniff of electricity in the air. They were talking – about the arrest, the arrangements once they reached the nick, and the attacks on Brown and Stubbs. Men were scoring very low in popularity – other men, that was, not theirs.

'So what'll you tell Billy tonight?' Caz asked Moira. 'Does he worry about you being a copper?'

'That's just started. He keeps saying things like, "don't take a chance unless you have to and then don't." '

'But *he* can, right?'

'He's a man!'

'Oh, I didn't realise!'

Moira laughed. 'Those blokes today. That DS Cole and his two mates. Did they even speak, those other two?'

'Not a word. I think they were either too shocked or too choked!'

'So they should be!' Moira said. 'If I'd been alone this morning, anything could have happened.'

'I don't think so, Mo. You looked to have everything under control.'

'Oh, sure! I was bloody terrified! It was just that I was even more angry than I was scared. Some stupid little pervert waving his willy at *me*!'

'I doubt he's stupid, Mo, though you were right about little. He'd lasted a fair time playing his little games. They're not *all* dozy on the South Circular you know.' Caz suddenly grinned. 'Well, not *that* dozy!'

Seven

They would have liked a quick in-and-out of the nick at Red Lion Street, but they should have known better. Fourteen years of Conservative rule and more than five of the Crown Prosecution Service meant paper, lots of paper. The police station was old, three-storeyed, red-bricked and, Caz made a guess, built around the turn of the century. Getting the arrest paperwork done was horse-drawn too, but were they down-hearted?

'Me?' Caz said. Her fourth coffee was in front of her and she needed to go to the loo. 'No, 'course not. I *love* the CPS!'

The flasher's name was Pryer and he had no priors. Twice now she had mis-spelled the name. She was muttering '*Previous* convictions! *Previous* convictions!' when she made her third mistake.

This time she *really* lost it. 'Oh, sod it!' she snapped. The screwed-up form hit the bin at ten feet.

'Shot, Flood!' Griffin said from the doorway. 'You been practising?'

'You know how it is, Jen, lots of arrests . . .'

'Our DCI wants t'see you both. Congratulations are in order, it seems . . .'

'The desk?' Caz said.

Griffin smiled and made a circle of thumb and finger.

'Oh, brill!' Moira said. She'd been worried all afternoon.

Jenny Griffin's DCI was called Lank and was at least six feet six, even taller than Norman Blackside. But that was just height. Whereas DCS Blackside was huge with a filled-out bull-like build, Lank was like his name – stretched, long and thin with a long, pointed face and *those* eyes.

Once they were out, Moira commented, 'Did you hear him? The creep! God, I hate blokes that do that! "Oh, well *done*, PC Dibben. Excellent *collar*, PC Dibben. And while you're here, do you fancy a quickie, PC Dibben?" Yech!'

Caz sighed. 'They come from a more primitive age, my love. I'll bet he's signing stuff outlawing sexual harassment as we speak.'

'Well, *I* don't like it!'

'Oh, wow! You think *you* got problems? You heard him, Moira. "I'm coming down to Brighton shortly, DC Flood. Perhaps you could show me some of the more relevant places, you know, where the drugs are pushed, that sort of thing?" He means night-clubs, Moira. That means late night.'

'Well, complain.'

'What about? He hasn't done anything yet!'

They took another half-hour to finish up the arrest reports and to tidy up the finer points of the story with Jenny Griffin, then they were gone. As they left, the DS whispered, 'Take care, Flood', flicking her head meaningfully towards the senior officers' windows.

'Right on, Sarge!' Caz said and flounced out of the doors, trying to look cool.

Seconds later she was back, her head bowed, a sheepish grin. 'Oops!' she said, smothering a giggle. 'Car's out back!' She strutted through with Moira. DS Griffin was still doing paperwork and hardly looked up.

They'd been told that Jill Brown was rarely home before six o'clock. They were there for five-thirty, prepared to wait. There was a light. They rang the door-bell at the top of three steps. There was a distant shout. Seconds later, a bright-faced and bouncing girl answered, pulling back the door and grinning while she danced lightly from toe to toe. They were looking for Miss Brown?

'Yes? That's me. No one else lives here.'

'Uh, we were expecting someone . . .'

'Not quite so thin, eh?' Brown flashed a huge, infectious grin. 'I wasn't this thin a year ago. I'm a runner, you know. Good, isn't it? Gets you really fit, it does. I used to be a jogger but now I'm getting really quick. D'yer want t' come in?'

'Don't you want to ask us who we are first?' Moira said, faintly bemused. She still hadn't closed her mouth.

'Don't be daft!' Brown laughed. 'Yer filth aren't yer? Fancy a cup o' tea?'

Jill Brown bounced even while she made the tea. Like an over-enthusiastic boxer she pranced on her toes; while she filled a kettle, while she plonked out three mugs, while she disembowelled the fridge, while she grabbed sugar from a cupboard. Her life seemed to be full of tings and clatters.

'Sugar?' Caz said, a little bit surprised.

'Gotta keep me weight up. I did a fifteen miler yesterday and it's club night tonight!'

'Oh, give me strength!' Moira hissed.

'D'you say something, love?'

'No. I'm not into being fit, that's all.'

'Well, you should be. You look pretty strong and you're not too heavy. Look at me. When I started I was ... well, let's just say I wasn't skinny. Now I've got so much energy, and fellahs, well there's no problem there either!'

'Getting blokes never was my problem,' Moira said. She said it slowly, even heavily.

The kettle boiled, over-full, its lid tinking. Jill Brown slapped water into the mugs, oblivious of any danger. 'No,' she said, 'looking at you, I don't suppose it was.' She was bubbling more than the kettle. Advice now. 'You know, you've got a great face. You could do with a bit lighter make-up though, round the eyes there. With your skin you want to show off those eyes.'

They sat round steaming coffee mugs. Moira's was

silly but Jill and Caz both held mugs sporting a race logo.

'The Sixth Totton 10K!' Caz said, turning her mug to read the blue print. 'When was that, last October?'

'My first race. Two weeks before, you know . . .'

'How did you do?'

'Fifty-six something, I think. I didn't have a clue then. I started off far too quick and had to walk in the middle.'

'And the Eighth, I see.' Jill's mug was the same shape and colouring as Caz's, just a different logo and a different cartoon advertising the run.

'And the Seventh!' Brown said with energy. 'I ran fifty-one dead in April. In this one', she raised her drink to show the blue writing, 'I broke forty-six minutes.'

'You're improving fast, Jill. You're not overdoing it are you?'

'Not according to me coach, I'm not. He says I'm a natural. He reckons I'd be quicker but it's taken all this time to get the weight off. I'm doing steady mileage now, right through to February, hills once a week but nothing too intense. I've got into the London Marathon and I don't want to get injured.'

'I'll give you my telephone number. I run a bit. If you want any advice . . .'

'Shit!' Brown suddenly sat taller. '*That's* who you are. You've done Totton's yerself, haven't you? What's yer name, Kathryn something?'

'Don't mix me up with Kathryn Bailey, she usually wins the race and she's a lot faster than me! I'm

Kath Flood. I was second in April this year.'

'What was your time?'

'Thirty-four forty. My PB is thirty-four oh-one.'

'Oh, Jees, I wish!' Brown gasped. Her hands were waving. She slurped at her coffee and choked. 'Oh, bloody 'ell. Sorry!' There was liquid on her chin.

Caz waited. Then she said, 'Don't worry about it Jill – it is Jill, yes?'

'That's me. Jill Brown, up and coming athlete and never been raped.'

Moira looked straight into Caz's face but she bit her tongue.

The DC's hand raised slightly, waving the PC quiet. 'Wanna tell us about it, Jill?'

'It hasn't changed since the last time.'

'We know that, Jill, and we know it's been more than a year.'

'Two Totton 10Ks. More coffee?'

'Let me,' Moira said. When she stood, too quickly, her chair tipped up.

Jill leaned nonchalantly to pick it up. 'Skip the sugar this time, duck.' She smiled. For some reason, Moira flushed.

'I came home after work. It was Monday night. Someone fairly big whacked me from behind as I opened my door. That was it. The stupid bastard legged it before I saw a thing.'

'Why do you say he was big?'

'I dunno. He just was big. He *felt* big. Maybe there was a shadow. Maybe it was a sixth sense or something, but I'm sure he was a big bloke.'

'Did you know it was a man, then, or did you just presume so when the detective sergeant interviewed you after the other attack?'

'Fuckin hell!' Brown said suddenly. 'If a great bastard bloke jumped on *your* back don't you think *you'd* fuckin' know? Of *course* it was a bloke! Jesus!'

'Hey, hey.' Caz sounded calming. She glanced up, Moira was stopped in mid-pour, her beautiful mouth unflatteringly dropped open again. Caz spoke more slowly. 'Listen, Jill. You might not believe me, but it's often what people *sense*, not what they actually see and hear, that matters.'

'Well I sensed he was big. All right?'

'Don't bite my head off now, Jill, but would you like to guess how big?'

'Over six foot two, and at least two hundred pounds.'

'What?' At the sink, Moira's face was fly-catching again.

'I had a fellah a few months ago. He was big and he—'

'Would you say six-three?'

'Maybe. I just feel he was big, you know? At least as big as my fellah was.'

'That's brilliant, Jill!'

'And he had rough fingertips.'

'Like a workman, do you mean? Like a farmer?'

'No. It was the finger*tips*. He touched my neck. The ends of his fingers were dead hard. Like corns, almost. Why didn't I remember that before?'

Caz knew why. Because she hadn't been asked. She

47

stayed serene. 'It happens, Jill. Long-term memory is a funny thing. That's why it was worth us disturbing you. Really, you've been magic.'

'Coffees!' Moira plonked down mugs.

Jill Brown smiled. 'Yeah, right! Anything else? Only, I gotta get changed for club soon . . .'

Caz sipped. It was Blend 37, a small step up from Jenny Griffin's flask.

'Only one little thing, Jill. Take your time. Close your eyes, maybe. There was a television repair van seen in the street. Can you remember seeing one?'

Jill's eyes were shut. Coffee vapour curled round her face. 'I can't think . . . I was coming home. I go out before me morning post arrives. I was hoping the Totton results would've arrived. I opened the door and . . . yeah, fuck me! There was an Escort van at the far end of the street.'

Caz asked, 'The company?' It was a forlorn hope.

'I don't know. It was head-on to me and it was a bit scruffy. It might've been a Rediff van. It might've been but I just can't be sure . . .'

'I checked Brown's file, Moira. DS Griffin spoke to Rediffusion, Radio Rentals and Granada. Their nearest guy was six streets away. All their engineers are on radio phone-ins and we can tie them up pretty tight. I don't see any way one of them could have done it.'

Moira was starting the car. There was something in Caz's voice, so Moira said, 'But?'

'I was just thinking of Avocado. He had a cast-iron

alibi too. We should take a look at any of the techies who even *theoretically* could've laid into Jill Brown – and cross-match those with the Stubbs attack. See if anything comes out the other end.'

'Jill Brown was a bit of a surprise.'

'Yeah, and you showed it. You'll have to do something about your floppy jaw, Mo, you'll end up catching something.'

The Stubbs address was quite close, yards as the crow flew but ten minutes when you're new in town and don't know Richmond's one-way system. The house was quite ordinary, a late-thirties semi with tile-hung bays and plastic replacement windows. As they pulled up outside, three 500-watt security lights popped on, bathing the drive and the manicured lawn with blue-white sudden light like a night-time kick-off for a football match. Up on the wall, beneath the eaves, was a British Telecom security alarm, linked directly to the telephone exchange. Moira took it all in and shivered.

Deadpan, Caz rang the bell.

Eight

There was almost certainly someone home. The front, round-bayed room was in darkness but the sound of a television mumbled at the back of the house. Light cracked under a door at the end of the passage.

Caz rang again. This time for just a little longer. Deep from in the house they heard the muffled shout of 'George!', and then a darker male response. Light splashed from an opened kitchen door and heavy boots came towards them. 'Oo is it?' There was aggression in the voice – frustration, simmering anger.

Caz glanced at Moira and with her eyes said, 'This one is mine.' She pushed at the letterbox rather than shout. 'Police. Mr Stubbs?'

'Yeah, what d'you want?'

'We'd like a word, Mr Stubbs. It's cold out here.'

Latches unlatched, a chain rattled, the door split from its jam no more than an inch. A slice of musty light escaped. 'Where's yer warrant card?'

Caz already had hers out. She flicked it open.

The man wasn't impressed.

'And her, the looker,' he said. He nodded a grizzly face at Moira. 'Let's 'ave it!'

Moira fumbled in her handbag. Caz couldn't see her face but she could feel her going red. She was muttering apologies, scrabbling in her things.

'Can we come in, Mr Stubbs?'

'When I've seen the darkie's ID,' Stubbs snapped. Luckily, Moira wasn't listening too closely. She brandished her warrant card.

He looked and grunted, 'I suppose yer berra come in, then.' He unchained the door and swung it back. 'She's in there,' he said, dismissing them. 'If you want me, I'll be out the back.' Then he shouted harshly, 'Irene! It's the law!'

Irene Stubbs was in the back room. Her husband roughly gestured them in as he stepped through into the kitchen and closed the door behind him. Before the door closed, Caz saw his little world: a small black-and-white portable TV, a smoking ashtray, two six-packs of lager and the evening paper, open on the racing page.

Mrs Stubbs was sitting in a large deep-backed brown leather armchair that almost swamped her. Its fat, squared arms looped up from the back and her hands lay lifelessly on their flat tops where the leather had frayed. Across her legs and tucked in at her sides was a floral-printed duvet. She looked cold, but that seemed incredible. Opposite her was a gas fire with all four of its burners alight. It was orange with heat. The room baked.

The television was too loud for comfort and Mrs

Stubbs was staring at it with grey, empty eyes. She looked at least sixty and the soft focus of her stare made her look half-blind. When she spoke, her face never moved.

'I don't remember anything,' she said. They could hardly hear her.

'I wonder, could we . . .?' Caz nodded towards the television. There was a remote control on a small rubbish-cluttered table next to Mrs Stubbs. The woman picked it up and pressed 'mute'. The sound stopped suddenly. They could hear the fire hissing in the grate and the tinny burr of the other television scratching through the wall from the kitchen.

Mrs Stubbs looked up briefly, flicking her eyes over both of them and making two instant decisions.

'I still don't remember anything,' she said. Then she turned her face back towards the box in the corner and stared at the soundless news.

The heat in the room was unbelievable. Moira looked like she was about to wilt. She smiled at Mrs Stubbs and then asked could she take off her coat? They both could, Stubbs said. And they might as well sit down too. They didn't have to worry about *him* in the kitchen, she told them, he would stay in there all night.

Moira chose the armchair nearest the window and furthest from the fire, another solid brown monster from the fifties that matched Irene's chair. Caz was left to choose either cushion of the two-seater settee nearest the fire. Both cushions were warm to the touch. She wanted to sit on the sofa's arm but knew that she had to come down to the woman's level. She laughed and said it was a little warm.

'Not for me it isn't!' Mrs Stubbs said.

'I know it must be very difficult, Mrs Stubbs . . .' Caz said softly. Irene simply stared. 'We would rather not . . .' she paused, 'intrude, but . . .' Caz wasn't sure she was being heard. She reached out slowly, touching the woman's hand. 'Mrs Stubbs?'

Irene Stubbs moved her head slowly. She turned away from the blue and yellow light of the television and towards the soft pink of the policewoman's hand on hers. Then she looked up at Caz. A deep look of distress in her eyes came and passed. Caz felt a charge moving between them where their fingers lightly touched. She couldn't move.

'What's your name?' the woman said softly.

'Kathy Flood,' Caz said. 'My friends call me Caz.'

'That's a nice name.'

When Caz touched Irene Stubbs she had meant to briefly gain her attention and then to withdraw her hand; but now, like a rabbit before a snake, she felt transfixed. Seconds passed. She could feel the buzz of the house, Irene's blood pulsing. She thought she could feel her pain. Not knowing what else to do, she left her hand there, then she let herself soften, allowing herself to properly touch Irene. She felt the heat rise out of the woman and she felt her cry before she looked into her face.

'You touched me,' Irene said. There was nothing else except the hiss of the fire. 'George hasn't touched me, not once, not once since the . . .' Caz looked up to see the woman's tears, first a trickle then a free-flowing, painful release. 'He hasn't touched me. Not once. He says he can't. As if it's *my* fault. As if it was me that did something wrong.'

'Can we get you anything, Mrs Stubbs?' Caz asked gently. She leaned lower, trying to look into Irene's face. 'Would you like a cup of tea?'

The woman sniffed. 'No. I'm all right. Really I am.' She looked up. There was a flicker in her eyes, almost a smile as she looked at the detective. 'You can keep hold of my hand, though,' she said softly. 'I don't mind that.'

'No problem, Irene,' Caz said quietly. 'And forget the questions. They're not important. D'you want a tissue?'

Irene nodded.

'I've got one!' Moira said. She produced a small pack from her bag.

'Thanks!'

Moira seemed relieved to be moving. 'It's OK, Mrs Stubbs.'

'Oh, Irene, please.'

'It's OK, Irene, you're welcome to a few tissues.'

Mrs Stubbs blew into her handkerchief. 'Thanks, I really appreciate—' She stopped quite suddenly and sat up. 'Do you find it hot in here?'

Moira's white shirt was open at the neck. She coughed. 'Well it is a bit, Mrs Stubbs. But it's all right if—'

Irene looked at Caz. 'Could we turn the fire down, Miss . . . er . . .?'

'Kathy, Irene. Yes? I said? My friends call me Caz.'

'Oh yes,' Mrs Stubbs said slowly. She looked up. 'Would you turn the fire down, Caz? I think it's too hot in here.'

To adjust the fire, Caz would have to let go of Irene's hand. She hesitated, but Irene understood. She smiled and pushed gently up from the arm of the chair. When Caz bent down near the flames to find the control, she could feel the fire's heat licking at her face. She clicked the power back three notches, and for an instant felt almost cold.

'That's a bit better!' Irene said.

Caz sat forward on the sofa, her hands together, her elbows on her knees. She was leaning towards Mrs Stubbs but no longer holding her hands. Then she thought, bugger it, and reached out to touch her again. The woman gave her hand a little squeeze and looked up with brightening eyes. Caz thought for a minute. 'Irene, you've never had counselling, have you?'

The hand stiffened slightly. 'No,' Irene said. 'I didn't want to go out, and George . . .' She looked at the kitchen wall. 'George said he didn't want anyone coming here.'

'When was the last time you got out, Irene?'

'The week it happened.' She stopped briefly, then she steeled herself, suddenly sounding totally different. 'I haven't been outside the house since the week I was . . .' She stopped again, sat up and pushed off the duvet. 'I'm sorry, detective, I have not been out since the week I was raped.'

They locked eyes. Caz saw Irene's colour – like

hers, green. On an instinct she said, 'What's wrong with tonight, Irene?'

There was an achingly long wait, Irene's eyes reflecting choices being made, alternatives being weighed. She looked up with a hesitant smile. Caz's instincts had been right. No, there was nothing wrong with tonight, Irene said, but if she was going out, she would need to bathe first. Could they wait? Of course they could wait, they said. Did she need help?

'No, thank you, I'm fine!' Irene said. 'Just give me half an hour, would you?'

She got up, wobbling for a second, then stiffening her sinews. The duvet fell to the floor. As she went out into the hall, she banged hard on the kitchen door. 'George! I'm going out. While I'm gone you can clean the sitting-room!' She leaned back to speak to Moira and Caz. 'Twenty-five minutes, all right?'

Then she was gone.

Caz waited for Irene's footfall to fade away. Then she heard the blump of old plumbing being called into action. She turned and spoke to Moira.

'Put the telly back on, Mo, and make it loud. I'm going through there to have a word with the Ayatollah!' Moira's jaw control had gone again and her mouth had dropped open. Caz put her fingers under her chin and flicked it shut. 'Emmerdale Farm, Mo,' she said. 'Now.'

She knocked the kitchen door and went in without waiting. George Stubbs looked up from the paper that he couldn't see.

'Is she really going out?' he asked Caz.

'When she's had a bath, George.'

He put his can down and looked at Caz. 'Jesus! What did you say to her?'

Nine

Irene Stubbs came down the stairs after forty minutes. She was ten minutes late, but she had taken a year off her age for each one of them. Her face had taken some time – she said she was out of practice – and it had taken a while to find something that fitted. 'Six months in that back room will take a bit more than a hot bath to shift.'

The kitchen door was open and George's television was off. He sat on a kitchen stool with a can of Carlsberg in his hand and an awkward boyish sulk half-hidden on his face. Caz and Moira were at the door of the sitting-room. Caz smiled at George. He looked up at his wife.

'You don't look half-bad, Reen,' he said.

'No, I don't, do I?' Irene replied.

They went off in Moira's Fiesta, Caz squeezed into the back, sitting sideways with her feet up on the upholstery. Moira tried vaguely to complain but Caz told her to keep her eye on the road.

'Where'll it be, Irene?' Caz asked. Irene suggested a nice pub on the river.

'OK, driver!' Caz snapped. Moira pointed a finger at the roof.

They were sat down in the lounge bar just before eight o'clock. The place was filling up slowly. Irene explained, 'It's a popular pub, this, but it won't get too crowded tonight. It never does on a Monday.'

'It'll do for me,' Moira said.

'And me!' Caz said. 'Cheers!' They waved their glasses at Mrs Stubbs.

Irene hesitated, then she picked up her glass. 'Cheers!' she said. 'I'm glad to be here. Thanks, but don't you even think for a second that I'm not scared half to death.'

Caz went serious for a moment. 'He'll be caught, Irene. I promise.'

'I believe you,' Irene said.

When she began to talk, Irene Stubbs was quiet, almost whispering, still a little nervous and still unsure. She sipped at her gin and tonic and gradually her voice grew stronger, her back stiffer. A little more sparkle came back into her face. She even began to crack lightweight jokes.

She had worked for a small company doing just about everything – typing, filing, reception, even a bit of sales. She told them, 'They were quite nice. They said I could come back whenever I wanted to, but I just couldn't. I sent in my notice two weeks after. After.'

Caz knew what Irene meant by 'after'. God, how she wanted this animal!

'You know, it's funny,' Irene said. 'You never think it could happen to you, do you? I've seen people on the telly say that. Everyone says it, don't they? Well, now it *has* happened and it's happened to me. I don't know why I went the way I did, it wasn't like me at all. I'm one of those pick yerself up, dust yerself down people, you know? Start all over again . . . But not this time. I think it must've been because of me and George.'

'Because he didn't . . .' Moira said gently.

'Because he didn't want t'fuck me you mean? All right, he didn't want to make love to me if you prefer it that way. It's all right, love. After it happened, George suddenly didn't want me any more.'

'I'm sorry, I—'

'What're you sorry for, luv? Sorry that my old man – he was the only one, you know – you're sorry that he couldn't cope? It ain't your fault is it?'

'You're right, I—'

'Stop apologising. It's OK. You and your mate came along just when I needed it, so thanks. There's nothing to apologise for, right?'

'Right!' Moira said. Caz could see she didn't really believe it.

Irene smiled. 'I reckon it's my round, don't you, girls? No, don't get up. Same again?'

Caz looked up towards the bar. Irene had ordered the drinks. Now she was laughing at something the barman had just said. From one perspective, the transformation in her was amazing, but from another, it was predictable. That was what Caz had seen in Irene's eyes. She turned to her mate. 'D'you know, Moira? Two thousand years ago that lady would've been stoned to death. She wasn't a virgin when she was attacked, so being raped would have been her fault. Maybe things have improved just a bit.'

'A bit,' Moira said, 'but not a lot. Her old man's a pig.'

'George's problem is that the goods are sullied. He can't hack it.'

'He's a complete bastard.'

'No, he's not, Mo. He's a baby.'

'How can you say that? You saw their house! You saw how he was.'

'Moira, believe me, he's a child. He's suffering. Once he'd started with all that macho shit, he couldn't stop. Sometimes all it takes is a single word, or a touch, but sometimes it just doesn't happen. You fall off something and you can't get back. They were stupid, they didn't get counselling when they should have, but believe me, anyone can end up where they were.'

'Are,' Moira said.

'I said were. I meant were. They're on the way back. It'll take a while, but they'll make it. Look at Irene now. Does she look like a victim? I bet they had a really good sex life before the attack. She said George was her first and I bet she was his, too. That's half their trouble, Mo. Someone burst their balloon. Coping with a rape is like coping with adultery. It doesn't matter how much you rationalise it, what happens inside is primitive.'

'She's coming back.'

'I know. In more ways than one. Trust me, Moira. I think they'll be OK.'

Irene returned and sat down with a bump. 'Two G & T's and an orange juice, right? Mine's the big one. Cheers, girls!'

Caz and Moira grinned and raised their glasses again. 'Cheers, Reen!'

'Stopped talkin' about me now, 'ave yer?' Irene asked as she grabbed her glass. When Moira flushed, she said, 'Hey, it's all right. I was only joking!'

'No, we were,' Caz said. 'We were saying we were glad you were out.'

'Me too,' Irene said. 'I'm nervous as hell, but I'm glad I'm here.'

'One step at a time, eh, Irene?'

'Yeah, right. But this step was the hardest.'

'But you took it!' Moira said.

'Yeah, I did, didn't I?'

Irene raised her glass and looked at Caz through the liquid. She waited a second, then she lowered the glass, put her finger into the tonic and spun the lemon. She didn't look up. 'I wasn't unconscious, you know. I can remember the rape, all of it.' They stared. 'I can remember every second.'

There was no need to say anything. No need to prompt her. There were no questions that needed to be asked. They listened to Mrs Irene Stubbs, now forty-two, as she peeled away skin, as she burned bridges, as she cast out her demons, as she got back in touch with Reen again, the girl who picked herself up, dusted herself down, and – yeah – started all over again.

'George was on two-till-ten, and I'd been to Asda on my way home from Jenks. It wasn't a full shop. I was just getting some milk 'n' bread and some mince. I was going to do a lasagne for George; George likes a lasagne and they keep well when he's on shift. I just whop 'em in the microwave for three minutes when he comes 'ome and they're ready before he's finished his wash.

'I finished work at half-five so it would've been just after half-six when I got home, the latest, quarter-to-seven. I've got an old Astra and I parked that on the street. George's Sierra is a lot newer than my Astra so we stick that in the drive; it's a bit safer. Most of my neighbours park their cars in their drives or put them in the garage overnight, but there were two cars and a couple of vans at the top end of the close.

'The cars were an H-reg Sierra and a G-reg Montego, and they were parked very close to each other. I remember that, because George's Sierra is H-reg, and I thought the two cars were together somehow, like they were a couple of rep's cars or something. One of the vans was from the water board, L-reg. The other one looked like a TV van, but it was old, it was an F.'

Both Caz and Moira were breathing shallowly,

trying not to disturb Irene's recall. Behind them and around them, another world was moving, tinkling glasses, the electronic buzz-buzz-phutt of the games machines, the pheet-pheet of the till behind the bar, laughter and the occasional raised voice.

'You'll ask me later, so I'll tell you now. My memory was always good. When I try to remember it's like I'm watching a film. When I was in school I could just read a page and then repeat it word for word.

'There was definitely no one sitting in either of the cars or in the vans. One of them had a pair of fluffy dice in the back window.' She paused then nodded, as if agreeing with someone who'd just spoken. 'That was the Sierra. It was cream, might just've been white. The Montego was darkish, probably brown or maroon. The light's funny in our street, so you can't be sure just driving past.

'I parked the Astra by the lamppost outside my next-door neighbour's house. Not for security, it's just easier locking the car. If there was anyone nearby he must've been hiding because I never had a care in the world. I reckon I can sense things pretty well and nothing felt funny.

'My shopping was on the passenger seat. I locked up my side, walked round, got it out and locked the door. Then I went to go in.

'George is really good normally. He usually leaves the porch light on for me so that if it's dark when I get home I can see to get my key in. The light wasn't on, but I never thought anything of it. I just thought

George had forgotten. He does sometimes.

'I've got one of those tiny torches on my key-ring. I used that. I put the key in the lock, undid the door and then I heard him come rushing. He must've been a fair few yards away, 'cos there's nowhere in our drive that you could hide. He must've been quick too. I heard him coming but I didn't have time to do anything.

'I almost managed to turn round – I still had the shopping in my hand – but as I did, he hit me with a hell of a force and slammed me into the front door. I hit the little stained-glass window it's got. I didn't realise it then but I'd cut my forehead. I fell forward, the front door went flying and I was on my face in the hallway. It was all so sudden that I wasn't scared. It was more like I was watching a film with me in it.

'Now I know what he was up to, but then, when it was happening, I was sort of dazed. We were still in the doorway. If he'd tried to do it me there I guess he might've been seen. He couldn't shut the front door, and he said, "Get up, you cow!" and grabbed me by my hair. I'd half got up when he slammed me back down again on to the floor. He must've kicked the door shut and he was very quick. He said to keep looking at the floor. He said if I looked at him he'd kill me. I didn't say a word then, but I'd already seen him in the hall mirror.

'And then he did it. That was nothing. I remember I was more scared he would, you know, bugger me. When he didn't, it was a kind of relief.

'That was it. When he'd finished, he said "Ta!" He

65

grabbed me by the hair again and slammed me into the floor. It split my eye open. I wasn't knocked out, but I pretended I was. I grunted and tried to go limp. I just hoped he'd go quickly. I felt him get up off me but I never moved. I just stayed where I was for ages. I heard the hall clock chimes at seven and I decided he'd gone. Then I got up. How's that?'

Moira was stunned. Caz was little better. Irene had *seen* him, the rapist?

'Big. Heavy. He was like a boxer or a wrestler. He had a boxer's squashed-up nose. He was definitely over six feet tall and he was muscular. He had big fists and pudgy fingers. He had some sort of khaki waistcoat on.' She shut her eyes and conferred again. 'One of those shooting things, those jackets that don't have arms and they've got places for sticking cartridges, here and here.' She touched her chest. 'Know what I mean?'

'Was he black or white, Irene?'

'Didn't I say? He was white, and he was – what was he? He didn't have a beard or a moustache ... but he looked so smooth, you know, it was like he didn't produce hair. D'you know, like a boy?'

'And his hair? His eyes?'

'Blue eyes, I'm almost sure, but I guess they could've been green or grey.' She shut her eyes again and waited. 'They weren't green.'

'And his hair, Irene?'

'I think he was a Duncan Goodhew. You know, bald. He was wearing a bobble-hat, but I just get the feeling there was nothing underneath. D'you know what I mean?'

'Irene, my love, you are *definitely* in the wrong job.'

There was more, but Moira said she needed a drink. It was her round and she went to the bar to get herself a brandy, finally breaking her personal drink-drive rule.

While Moira was at the bar, Irene said, 'It wasn't the sergeant's fault, you know. It was just something in me. That night, you know, I was ashamed. It was easier to say that I was knocked out than to talk about it. Once I'd lied the first time it became automatic. I don't think I would've lied to you. It wasn't that I didn't like her... I didn't *dislike* her. It was just that she and I, well we never... it just didn't happen, you know? We just didn't click.'

She remembered the bobble-hat, too. It was definitely wool; it had lost its bobble and it had black-and-amber stripes. Caz was fighting down a surging forensic excitement. Three hours ago she could have written off the sad lump of woman in the corner of that little back room. Now she wanted to stay friends with this other, stronger, brighter person. Her next investigative success could wait. Right now she wanted to stay mellow; allow herself another hour with Reen. 'Forget the Mrs Stubbs,' Irene had said. 'Forget Irene. I'm Reen to my mates, Reeny when we've had too much to drink.'

Moira came back, apologising for her golden sin with a dark, guilty look, her eyebrows pushed forward, shading her face. When she sat down she said that she'd got Reen a double. Bill, the barman, had said she always had doubles. He'd also said it was great to see her back in the pub. She was one of the best.

'Oh, yes,' Irene said. 'He likes me, all right. Given half a chance, Bill would have me round the back. I put him straight ages ago. I told him I'm a one-man woman. Mind you,' she paused, then winked, 'when everything's all right, blokes like Bill are useful. They stop husbands like my George from taking us for granted.'

They bought no more drink but some sprightly man bought Reen another gin. He was forty-plus and pot-bellied, but light on his feet. His glasses were circular and gold-rimmed and he had a polished-pink bald head.

'Bloody good to see you, Reen!' he said. He grinned, left the drink, and walked away to sit alone at the bar. Caz knew straight away that he was a real and decent man. He'd done just enough, and then left, giving Irene the time and space he thought she needed.

'His name is Phil,' Irene said quietly. 'He's a nice man. We sparked around a bit when we were seventeen, eighteen, before I met George. Phil's wife died just over a year ago. Cancer. He looked after her like a baby. I never thought a man could care that much.'

There was only one other loose end. Caz wanted to ask about the Kingston & Richmond Sisters, but the moment wasn't right and she knew she had to leave it. As they left, Irene went over to Phil, put an arm on his shoulder and a hand on his bald pate. Caz saw him break out in a full-face smile and he waved to them all as they left. Irene waved back as they went out to Moira's car. She was still improving. Caz hadn't reckoned with her new razor-sharpness.

'You didn't ask me about my jogging, did you?' she said as they got in the car. 'Kingston and Richmond? Doesn't it matter now, or did you just forget?'

Caz chuckled lightly. 'Now, don't get cheeky, Reen, or we may just go back to calling you Mrs Stubbs. I forgot, all right?'

'It's all right, but just so's you know, I started training with the club in September last year, running once a week. The woman who organised the sessions was really sweet. I missed a bit in the winter, but then about a dozen of us decided to train up for a race in the April, down Southampton way.

'It's very popular because they hold it every six months and it's very well organised. They have photographs, mugs, T-shirts, everything. A few of our girls ran in the October one and they said it was the best race they'd ever been in. So twelve of us trained up and got a mini-bus together. I did fifty-five minutes.'

'You ran in the Totton 10K, Irene?'

'It's Reen! Yeah, how did you know?'

Caz felt cold race up through her, like vomit disgorging. She could hear Jill Brown. *I went off far too quick and had to walk.*

Jill Brown had done fifty-six minutes. Two weeks later *she* was attacked.

From her seat in the back of the Fiesta, Caz felt the steering and the back wheels twitch as Moira's ten-pence dropped too. She thought, 'Watch the road, Moira', but said nothing. They were both listening to Irene. The rape was behind her now, like the Fiesta's tyre-marks in the road. Rene was going to take up running again, she said. Her optimism added lights and shades to her voice. Now she sounded almost melodic as she planned out the next few months. She only faltered when she mentioned George. The hardest bit, she said, would be George. Caz thought different, but then Caz had spent ten minutes in the kitchen talking with Irene's husband.

They arrived back at the Stubbs' house. The front-room lights were on, splashing out on to the lawn through open curtains. They saw a man rise as the car stopped. It was George, but he looked cleaner and maybe younger. The house looked different too. They heard Irene say, 'I don't understand . . .'

All three got out of the car. George had come to the door.

'Will I see you again?' Rene asked.

'It's a promise!' Caz said. 'How about the London Marathon?'

Irene kissed her, then she said, 'The London? Bugger that fer a lark!' She kissed Moira lightly on the cheek, then she walked away.

George pulled the front door wider and Irene stepped inside. He was still stiff, but he hadn't forgotten his time in the kitchen with the young detective. Moira climbed back into the Fiesta. Caz waited to wave. She was right, they came to the window. A top vent was open and she could hear the voice of Barry

Manilow drifting out over the garden. She saw Irene's hand raise and wave lightly. Beside her, George raised his arm; harder, hairier, a man's arm. It wasn't actually a wave, but Caz knew what it meant. Then he lowered his arm, slowly. Caz waited until it was on Irene's shoulder then she grinned and waved back. For tonight, shoulder wasn't bad. No, shoulder was OK. George and Rene Stubbs had a long way to go, but they'd started. She felt pretty good.

But Barry Manilow? Jesus! Moira revved the car. Caz opened the door and dived in. 'Fer fuck's sake Moira!' she said. 'Get me outa here quick! Any minute now they're going to play "Copa Cabana". I'll bet it's their song too!' They tooted as they pulled away. They were going to drive too fast all the way to Brighton. If they got stopped they could always pretend they were coppers!

Ten

It was nearer twelve o'clock than eleven when they swept back into Brighton. It had been a long day, but unbelievably successful. Caz asked Moira, wasn't anyone expecting her?

'Nope, I'm on my own in a three-bedroomed Wimpey. I had a house-mate for a while but she did grass and I had to tell her to go.'

'I don't think Tom MacInnes does pot.'

Moira laughed. 'It's hard to imagine.'

'A steady diet of Whyte and Mackay maybe, but no drugs.'

'Not that alcohol's a drug, eh?'

'Oh, absolutely not!'

The rule was, if Caz was going to arrive after midnight she had to ring Tom by eleven. It was now twenty-to-twelve so she was still within house-rules. 'The DI's been really good to me, Mo. After my burglary, he let me crash at his place, and when I came out of hospital he just took it as automatic I'd move in.'

'No one ever said Tom MacInnes wasn't a decent bloke, Caz.'

'For a DI you mean?'

'I mean, for a bloke. MacInnes is all right.'

'So not all men are rapists then, Mo? That what you mean?'

'No, it ain't. I went to a talk once up at Sussex University. It made a lot of sense. They said all men were rapists.'

Caz sneered at Moira. 'Well, if they said it, it must be true! So all men are rapists, right? Every last one!'

'Except Billy of course. And your Valerie. And I don't think that guy Phil is one either, or George Stubbs.'

'And the DI? Tom MacInnes?'

'Not him either.'

Caz was knackered but she grinned despite herself. 'I just want to check this out, Moira. Tell me if I've got it right. All men are rapists; that's all except for the ones you know?'

Moira didn't respond. Instead she hunched forward, pretending to be driving more studiously. 'Drunks out this time've night, Caz. Can't be too careful.' She stared ahead as they moved evenly towards the sea.

Light flip-flapped past them. Caz thought about getting a bit angry, but she was spinning downwards towards sleep. She spoke slowly. 'They're absolutely right, Moira. All men are rapists. All Pakistanis live twelve to a room. Essex girls fuck anything that moves and black men have got rhythm and big dicks.'

'Which street is it?' Moira said.

'Drop me outside the old aquarium. I'll walk.'

73

They arrived. A few pale lights vaguely lit the pier. Wind swept off the sea up on to the promenade and cut into Caz as she opened the car door. Caz liked Moira. It was almost pumpkin time, time to go, but she had one last crack at educating her. She put one leg out on to the road and turned to speak. 'All men are rapists, Mo. And all women are typists.'

'You what? I'm not a typist.'

'I know.'

'So what you on about, then?'

Caz sighed. 'Mo, all nobody are anything.' She was so tired her eyes were almost closed. 'These things are so easy to say, that's the trouble with the world. Everybody generalises!'

'You what?'

'Oh, never mind. Ask me tomorrow, Mo. Thanks for the lift.'

With that, the detective was gone. She didn't look back but walked into the darkness between two buildings. Moira shrugged and put the Fiesta into gear. She was tired too, and faintly confused. She had completely missed the joke. She wondered where Billy was.

Caz let herself in through the street door, an over-wide, thickly-painted blue one with a never-used heavy brass knocker. Tom lived in number four, a flat on the first floor. She closed the street door behind her, then went up the silent, dark stairs without using the lights. The stairs were bare. The vault echoed with loneliness. When she got to his landing, she put her left hand up to the door of the flat, feeling for the brass lift of the Yale lock, then slipping her key through her fingers as quietly as she knew how. There was a good chance Tom would be asleep and she didn't want to wake him.

The door moved silently back, kissing the carpet just once as she pushed it open. She could hear music – very low, sombre music, the heartaching drone of a cello playing lightly. She didn't recognise the tune, only its darkness.

She felt intrusive as she whispered, 'Hi, Tom.'

'Glad you're in, Caz,' her DI said.

He was sitting in his favourite high-backed chair, faded brown leather, rich and old like a library. He had a chunk of cut glass in his hand, more Whyte & Mackay, a little water from a tiny carafe. Scattered around him were sheets of scribbled-on A4 paper. Most were flat, a few screwed up in frustration. The room was dark, lit only by a reading light, perched awkwardly near his books. Just enough light reached out to reveal Tom, showing his red eyes and a drawn, thin face. He looked more tired than her. 'It's Jeremy Avocado,' he said.

'Is there any more of that?' Caz asked. She was looking at the second glass on the table. MacInnes waved her to it.

'They're winding back the hunt,' he said heavily. 'He's away. The first one I ever missed – you know that, Caz?' She knew the myths, not the truth, but she said yes. Then she said, 'It's not over, Sir. He'll come back.'

Caz sat down. Her chair was opposite all his books. He said there was more light if she needed it. She flicked on a table-lamp as MacInnes spoke again.

'I find it hard to believe I missed him, let him go. I guess it must've been because we were worried about you. That's a mistake you know, Caz. Get the thing done first. Don't let yer personals get in the way of the job.' He gathered up the papers and shoved them roughly into the bookcase. 'D'you wanna tell me about your day? I got a phone call about Pryer's arrest.'

Caz was tired. 'I'd rather do it in the morning, Tom . . .'

MacInnes looked a little pained. 'Well, if that's the case, I'll say goodnight to you, lass. See you in the morning.' He said it as he stood, but there was a flicker of something in his voice. Shit! He wanted to talk. Wrong call.

Caz thought about changing her mind and calling back the DI, but the moment had passed. She had made a mistake but it was done now.

She said goodnight.

MacInnes shuffled away.

Eleven

It took Caz seconds to make up her bed, unrolling
her night wrappings from behind the sofa and releas-
ing them to cover the couch in a single sweep. She
was too tired to go to the bathroom and in seconds
she had stripped to her underwear and slid between
the sheets. She lay flat on her back, stretching her
legs, staring at the patterns of light on the ceiling and
thinking of the patterns of her life.

Amex had given Valerie three weeks compassion-
ate leave and suggested that he extend his usual
Christmas fortnight into a long month. He had come
to the hospital to see her and they had sat in silence,
holding each other tightly but both afraid to speak.
Eventually, Valerie had broken the silence. He said
he would stay until she had left her convalescent bed
but then he would get away for as long as he could.
He would fly a bit dangerously in Portugal, play some
cards and drink a little too much wine. When he
came back they would eat at Armando's and talk
about the future, their future. Then he said he loved
her but wished that he didn't. She didn't cry.

77

She recovered quickly. They made her stay in the hospital for five days but by the end she was causing havoc. Hero or not, Caz was a pain in the butt and they were glad to see her go. On the Saturday, she ran in a cross-country league race. Instead of her usual third behind Sue Dilnot and Kath Bailey she had to fight hard for sixth place with two veteran runners in front of her. Valerie was waiting at the finish. Caz showered and changed, then she drove him to Gatwick in his Daimler-Jaguar. He wouldn't even let her park.

No drama, he said. 'Just look after the car until I get back, OK?' He said she could use it for the month he was away. She said she daren't. They would call her Inspector Morse.

Caz was in pain when Valerie walked away. She could still sense him, feel him, smell him. She touched the leather where he had been sitting and could still feel the heat of his body. Her hands returned to the steering wheel, ready to drive from the airport, but then she stopped herself. She decided to forget their agreement, parked the car and went to find him. In the bustle of the departure lounge she felt like a leaf on water, and she realised she wasn't yet well. She watched him from a balcony as he bought a book, then she watched him again as he went through passport control an hour early.

She cleaned his car on the Sunday, then backed it into her garage, ousting her MGB. The lads could have called her Morse, she wouldn't have cared, but she couldn't face being in the Daimler for the next

thirty days. The car had far too much of Valerie.
Better that it simply did not exist for a while. Without
was not as tough as missing, and tomorrow she was
back to work. She'd live.

She thought about Irene Stubbs and the fire that
some people had, some hadn't. She pictured Jill
Brown's face, *'yer filth, aren't yer?'*, and wondered
how she would do in next year's London Marathon.
She thought of a saddened, shrunken Tom MacInnes,
briefly about Avocado, about black-and-amber hats.
Then she took a last mouthful of Whyte & MacKay
and told herself to go to sleep. Her eyes closed.

She was in the same position when they opened
six hours later. She figured on a sharp run, towards
Roedean and back. She wanted to get fit. Later, she'd
ask about self-defence classes. The 'Duncan
Goodhew' worried her. It was not going to be an
easy arrest.

She slipped out of the building and crossed the
road. She was dressed in a white hooded 'Boss' top
and stark black Lycra leggings etched with reflective
silver streaks. There was a light wind and sea-salt
floated over the road. She sucked air. Short of time,
her stretches were perfunctory and she was quickly
away, building through an eight-minute-a-mile jog
and changing up into sub-seven miling. This was
nothing near her best, but she could sense a lack of
the deep strength that came only from a period
of training that was injury and virus-free. Still, it was
dry, and four quick miles was four quick miles.

She returned, hot from the run but more wasted

than glowing. The DI was up and active and he bawled at her that she had about ten minutes if she was bumming a lift to the station.

'No problem!' she said, and dived through to the loo. Shower water hissed, then her head popped out, flashing blonde hair. 'Hey, Tom! Don't suppose there's a chance of a quick bacon buttie, is there? I can eat it in the car.' He turned to speak to her but she disappeared quickly before he could say no.

She had to be fast so she made the shower cold-to-cool, rinsed her hair, stepped out and dried herself roughly. She was not particularly kind to her locks and brushed them back wet before tying them back into her 'works' pony. Then she scooted across the parquet floor to where her case was stored and broke records to come out dressed. Today she went military in a Lee Cooper fawn shirt, brown silk tie and loose-bag khaki trousers wrapped tight into her waist with a thick brown belt. Eight minutes! Not bad.

She appeared with her trainers still in her hands. Tom MacInnes shook his head, bewildered. He held out the sandwich. She wanted to give him a big kiss. Instead, she giggled and told him to hurry up, they didn't have all day.

Caz was ready to talk about Richmond, but the DI said it wasn't worth it – they'd be at the station before she'd finished her bacon buttie. She followed him downstairs.

The DI's Sierra was parked close-by in a green-gated lock-up. MacInnes undid the padlock, passed it to Caz, and stepped inside, pushing back the gates as he went. While Caz held the gate, he circled his car quickly, glancing under the wheel arches and beneath the engine. This was the second time Caz had seen him check the car. This time she asked. 'An old habit!' MacInnes said, 'I worked in Diplomatic Protection in the eighties. Takes twenty seconds, so I reckon, why not?' He got in and drove out. Caz pulled the gates behind him and locked up. For some reason, she felt chilled. Maybe some day she wouldn't want to do this job.

The DI did his usual and dropped her on the corner. She walked in and down to the locker room. At least today there wouldn't be forty pratts in snorkels waiting for her upstairs. When she went up it was to write the notes she should have written last night in a Richmond pub.

By nine o'clock Caz was finished, her notebook was up-to-date and her head was clear. Today she would need to speak to Miss Amanda Fleet. The file gave a new address for her in Chester, more than a stone's throw or a quick drive away. Caz was hoping that if she had to, she could swing a favour from the locals up there.

Fleet's old address was in Redbridge, a wriggling little village that followed the Itchen river and stared out across marshland. Before, Blackside had described it to Caz simply as 'Southampton', but now it had an altogether different, altogether more sinister geography. The road from Lyndhurst and the New Forest to Southampton by-passed Totton, crossing the Itchen river on the Redbridge flyover, a notorious rush-hour hot spot. As the crow flew or a rapist slithered, Redbridge was just half a mile from Totton.

Twelve

Moira came through at two minutes past nine. She had gone via the canteen and produced two coffees. 'Sorry I'm late, Caz,' she said as she got rid of the most painful one, 'I bumped into Billy in the corridor and, you know . . .'

'Why, what time is it?' Caz said innocently.

They ran through what they knew and ran over their Jenny Griffin line just to be certain. With a bit of luck neither Blackside nor MacInnes would bring it up and it wouldn't be an issue.

'No, Mo,' Caz said again. '*I* contacted control, when we got to Richmond. You were just a good little PC following orders. And it was your collar. I helped you cuff him. Got it?'

After Jill Brown and Irene Stubbs, it had been presumed that the rapist was local to Richmond, maybe on the periphery of the Sisters, another jogger in the park. The first attacks were in October and then late April, but then there was the Redbridge assault. Amanda Fleet had been attacked in September, fifty miles away. A classic shortening fuse – but was their man from Richmond, moving out, or from Totton, and previously playing away from home?

Caz thought out loud. 'Could it just be a coincidence they both ran in the Totton? They had similar running times. Our man had to know them already. If he didn't, he must've picked them up while they were in Totton, watched them for the best part of a fortnight, and *then* attacked them!'

Moira looked up. 'Or he attacked two women from his own locality, then popped down to Totton and just did another one on spec.'

'I can't see it,' Caz said. 'But we need to speak to Jackie Engels as soon as we can. And get hold of Amanda Fleet.'

'You're not going to make us go to Chester, are you?'

'Not if I can help it, Moira.' Caz dropped a file in front of her. 'We've got a phone number for Fleet. We might as well try it. Let's keep a trip to Cheshire low on our list of things to do. I'm going to go through and see the guvnor – let him know what we know. If you get Amanda, find out what you can – but has she ever jogged, run in a race, anything like that? Do a good job and you won't have to pack your case.'

They would hit records as well. They now had a good description to go with the repeated MO. More than half known sex offenders re-offended, and it wasn't impossible that this one could slither out. It was worth a try, but instinctively, Caz thought it unlikely. Something in the background felt far too

calculated, too detached. This animal may have
sounded slow but he had to be intelligent. That made
him all the more evil and all the more dangerous.
Arresting him wouldn't be like cornering a burglar.
If it wasn't very violent it would be a miracle. Some
of the lads weren't exactly renowned for their deli-
cacy when arresting rapists. Only child molesters and
murderers came lower on the list.

Caz knocked on Norman Blackside's door and heard
his voice boom, 'Come!' The word bounced off the
walls. As she pushed the door, she thought it would
be nice to be following Blackside in when they finally
ran this man to ground. She remembered the first
time she'd ever seen the DCS. He had strode in then,
like a great mediæval knight. Then, he could have
been George vanquishing the dragon, Arthur defeat-
ing the beast. Now he looked mild and welcoming.
'Ah, DC Flood!' he said, dropping the decibels.
'Caught him yet?'

Caz smiled an awkward, thin smile. Maybe the
DCS wasn't joking. She almost said 'Why, Sir, have
you caught Avocado?' but she bit her tongue.

'Here's my report, Sir. Yesterday was a good day.
We have a highly detailed description of the attacker.
He has a very distinctive appearance. I think he is
choosing his victims by some sort of system and I
think, because of his noticeable appearance, he isn't
doing anything close to home.'

Blackside flicked open the file. He was reading
while Caz talked.

'I think we can presume for now that our man is south of the M4 corridor, Sir. Profiling would normally suggest that he's from Richmond – the early attacks close to his home or place of work, somewhere he's familiar with. The sudden switch to Southampton and then Brighton is way off the scale, though. Very unusual. I would be tempted to stick him in Basingstoke, Guildford, Woking, somewhere like that. That would put him not much more than an hour from any of the attacks. He could be from somewhere further out – in the Downs or over towards Tunbridge Wells – but that would involve a lot of travel and again that's not classic profile. I think he drives an old ex-Rediffusion van, probably Foxtrot registration. We have other strong leads, Sir, and there's a good chance we'll know who the bastard is before the week's out.'

'You got all that in a day, Flood?'

'With the help of WPC Dibben. Yes, Sir.'

'You must've trod in dog-shit to have that much luck.'

'I'm sure you're right, Sir. It was probably my sympathetic personality.'

'Or female intuition, eh lass?' It was DI MacInnes at the door.

'We don't have that these days, Sir. Remember? We have computers!'

Blackside spoke again. 'What've you done with records?'

'Nothing yet, Sir. Dibben is talking to the third victim right now. As soon as I've finished in here I'll speak to her, then get straight on to PNC. If this guy is on file he should jump off the screen and give himself up.'

'But he won't be?'

'I don't think so, Sir. We didn't get a match on the MO database at the Yard. We might get a few losers who look a bit like our man but if he's already in the pot I'll be genuinely surprised.'

Blackside sent Caz away, telling her to come back and see him or DI MacInnes before she went out again. As she stood up, he grinned. 'I don't have to tell you how well you did, do I, Flood?'

'No, Sir. Thank you, Sir.'

'Right. Well piss off then!'

Caz strode back along the corridors head high, pleased with herself. Being mates with a DI and on the DCS's hot list wouldn't be doing her any harm, and if they pinned down the Rediffusion Man quickly, she'd be putting herself a long way ahead on brownie points. She was in good heart when she reached the War Room.

Before she went in, she took a deep breath. The War Room was all-male and she always prepared herself for the worst. But today was different, the room was sullen and the guys lethargic. She wasn't thinking. *She* was on a high, part of an investigation that was getting somewhere, but she had forgotten what it was like to be knee-deep in one that was doomed.

Jim Greaves was sitting with a phone in his hand,

the other hand over the mouthpiece. He said good morning with a slow, plaintive voice. 'Hi, Jim,' Caz said. She tried to take the lift out of her voice. She was so glad that Blackside had pulled her off the Avocado case. There was nothing more depressing for a copper than having to go through the motions on a no-hoper. There wasn't a DC in John Street who didn't think that Jeremy Avocado had long since legged it to foreign parts. She felt a little sympathy for Jenny Griffin.

When she walked back into the computer room, Moira was in good spirits too. Girls two, Boys nil! Amanda Fleet was living with her sister in a house overlooking Chester racecourse. She had just popped out, the sister said, but she'd be back at ten o'clock. 'Apparently she's come out of it not too bad. The move away helped. The sister said she's sure that Amanda will talk to us.'

That meant they had time for a quick coffee. Caz gestured with a flick of her head and Moira followed her out. Stepping from their room back into the War Room was like going from light to darkness. The six DCs left holding the fort were slow-moving, slow-talking automatons, depression winding back their metabolism. Caz almost considered using the word 'zombies', but then some spark called out, 'Hey, it's Cagney and Lacey!'

'You what?' Moira said, laying on the indignation a little bit thick. 'Flood may be a Cagney but I'm *far* too good-looking to be a stand-in for Mary Beth!'

'How about Dempsey and Makepeace?' the DC

said, but they ignored him; his heart obviously wasn't really in it.

The canteen was little better. Despondency is contagious and even the tea-ladies were less chatty than usual. Caz and Moira grabbed their coffees and sat down. It was to be a working break. 'Your victim. Jackie Engels?' Caz said slowly. She was staring across the room. 'Could she have been a runner?'

'She could have been,' Moira said. 'She wasn't anorexic, like you or Liz McColgan, and I didn't ask at the time – but yeah, she might've been.'

'So all you're saying is she wasn't a dump truck?'

'You've a nice way with words, Caz.'

'Was there any evidence of running? Shoes, tracksuits, that sort of thing?'

'I can't remember, boss. I don't usually ask rape victims to list their hobbies!'

'I know, Mo, and I'm not getting at you.'

'Good!'

'But now I'd like you to do me a favour.'

'Which is?'

'Imagine you were forced to bet on whether Jackie ran or not.'

'How much?'

'A drink. How would you bet?'

'Then she's a runner.'

Caz went quiet. She was tilting her coffee mug in a slow circle, tempting the liquid to the edge without a spill. She looked distant, lost in thought, as if she was communicating with a far planet. 'Thanks,' she said slowly. Then she deliberately spilled an

ounce of the coffee on to the table. She started to
write in the mess, then she spoke again. 'How can a
six-foot-two gorilla, bald as a coot and dressed like
a mercenary, attack five women at their front door
and yet not be seen by anyone? Doesn't that worry
you, Moira?'

'What're you saying? You don't believe Irene
Stubbs?'

'I don't know what I'm saying, Mo. I'm just worried
and I don't know why.'

Upstairs, they got through to Amanda Fleet. She was
fine, she said. No, she said, she didn't mind them
calling.

There are things you can and things you can not
ask over the telephone. Caz wanted to know only
two things. Their early conversation was routine –
did she recall anything now that she hadn't recalled
then? Did she have any comment to make on the
events now? Two noes.

'Miss Fleet. Is it all right to call you Amanda?'

'Yes, I'd like that.'

'Amanda.'

'Yes?'

'Have you jogged at all? Have you run in the
Totton 10K?'

'I'm sorry, what did you say?'

'I asked you if you'd done any running. If you'd
ever run in a race.'

'I thought about it once. The only time I ever did
was that Race Against Time. D'you remember? They

had sponsored runs all over the world? The Bob Geldorf thing?'

'You ran in that?'

'If you could call it running. It was twice round Southampton Common. I got round, but it took ages. I'm thin but I'm not very fit.'

'And you've never run in the Totton or any other races?'

'No.'

Caz asked about the smell of burning. Could she remember anything more? What was burning? As she spoke she was aware this was only half an interview. She was also aware of how long it would take to get to North Wales and just how tight funds were.

'I was very groggy. I'm not sure what I remember. He had . . . you know, and I was barely conscious. I heard a click and then I thought I smelt something. My eyes were shut tight. I thought, if I didn't see him, he might not kill me. There was a click and then I just had the feeling of something hot.'

'What kind of a click?'

'I'm not sure. Maybe like an old-fashioned light switch. It clunged.'

'Clunged?'

'Like there was a spring.'

Caz was shaking her head. She paused. 'Why did you say you had the feeling there was something hot? Did you actually feel heat?'

'I think he may have had something to burn me with. I think it may have been by my face. I can't say because I wouldn't open my eyes.'

'But you felt it?'

'And smelt it. Like it was oily or metally.'

'I don't understand.'

'It smelt like a car overheating, something like that.'

Before she put the phone down, Caz promised Amanda that she would catch her attacker. Amanda said thank you, but she didn't have the confidence of Irene Stubbs. Nevertheless, they would do nothing less than find this monster. It wasn't just the job now, it was something else, something to do with sistership. 'I promise you,' Caz said. The phone went dead. Without even looking up, Caz telephoned Jenny Griffin at Richmond.

'Yes. DC Flood, John Street, Brighton. Urgent call for DS Griffin.'

There was an echoing wait, then the sergeant came on the line.

'Jenny! We're getting somewhere. Thought you'd want some info.'

'You could've faxed it, Flood.'

'You don't want me to, Sarge.'

'OK. Rattle it off. D'you have the rapist's name yet?'

'One sec, Jenny.' Caz put her hand over the mouthpiece and turned to Moira. 'Mo, we're going to need to speak to your Jackie as soon as poss. We can't hold back any longer and we're going to have to go over to Southampton. See if you can get DI Denham or Peter Mason down there.'

She turned back to speak to Jenny Griffin. 'We've

been lucky, Jenn. We've got a description and I've got some witnesses you might want to chase.'

'*I* might want to chase?'

'Hear me out, Jenny.'

'Fire away.' There was barely concealed anger in the voice.

'There were two cars in the street the night Irene Stubbs was attacked. An H-reg Sierra, cream or white, with fluffy dice in the back window, and a G-reg Montego, dark-coloured, probably brown or maroon. We've reason to believe the two were together. Maybe someone was selling double-glazing in the close around that time.'

'Fer fuck's sake.'

'And there was a water-board van, L-reg. That should be easy to trace. And I think you should take a look at the Stubbs' porch light.'

'Their light?'

'It's been well over six months, but there's a decent chance it's the same bulb. Have it checked for prints. The animal unscrewed it before Irene got home. If there's more than one set of prints on the bulb we might have our man. Not likely, but you never know.'

'You're not making me feel great, Caz. We all need friends.'

'I'm sorry, Jenny. Irene Stubbs suddenly opened up when we went to see her. She likes me. What's more, she has a photographic memory. She's given us a brilliant description of the animal.'

'Which is?'

'I'll fax it when I know you're by the machine. Six

foot two or three, heavily-built, bald, clean-shaven, fat fingers and coarsened skin. Wore a black and amber bobble hat. She also said he moved quickly and she'd recognise the voice again.'

'*Fuckin' hell!*'

'We weren't trying to mess with things, Jenny. We certainly didn't expect Irene Stubbs to come out like that and give us everything. When we knocked the door she was a zombie. Don't ask me to explain.'

'Forget it, Flood. Is that it?'

'Not quite. We think the animal is driving a second-hand Rediffusion van. That ties in with the earlier witnesses and something Jill Brown said. The reg is almost certainly Foxtrot. I thought maybe you'd like to chase it?'

'I would. Plus a million other cases.'

'D'you want it or not, Jenn?'

'I want it. Do I have to thank you?'

'Catch this shit and I'll buy you a Chinese.'

'One for us. All right, Caz. Just be careful, eh? I'll go to the fax now.'

Detective Sergeant Peter Mason needed absolutely no encouragement to meet the two policewomen from Brighton. What they were investigating hardly mattered, all that mattered was that they were skirt. 'Any time,' he said over the phone. 'How's this arver?'

Mason worked out of Shirley Police Station a mile or so from Southampton centre, but he arranged to meet them first-off at the bottom of the M271 in a little close underneath the Totton by-pass. 'I can show you where it went down and we'll take it from there.'

When Moira put the phone down she shook her head. 'This DS talks like he's some copper off the telly, but I don't think he's sure which country!'

Caz fancied yet another coffee but it wasn't half an hour since the last one. She was in danger of becoming a caffeine junkie. It didn't surprise her; plain-clothes drank too much, smoked too much and worked all the wrong hours. On a big case, twenty-hour days weren't unknown. It looked good but Caz knew it was inefficient in the longer run. The trouble was, being sensible about your time didn't always look good. Brownie points came to the bleary-eyed midnight cowboys. The fact that they were useless the following day seemed to slip by the average DCI, but then of course, *they'd* all been DCs once. They'd lived it rough 'n' ready and toughed it out with ciggies and coffees through the long nights. Maybe when they did let their hair down they drank a few too many shorts, but what the hell, they'd earned it, hadn't they? They deserved their parties.

They were keyboarding the new information into the Holmes database. Under 'cars', Caz entered the Montego's details and the cream Sierra. The Rediffusion van had now been clocked four times. The description of it went on to the system too. Then they went to access the police computer at Hendon to see if the animal was already in the pot.

A Holmes system had not been set up for the original attacks in Richmond. A single rape would never warrant the expense. The Southampton attack had at first been seen as a one-off. Hampshire Intelligence would have got a routine bulletin on Richmond Two and appended to that, eventually, would have been the minor assault on Jill Brown.

But all rapes are bulletined within the incident county and to bordering counties – along with serious assaults, murders, and major armed robberies. And that meant paper. A lot of paper.

Caz spoke to Moira. 'What frightens me, Mo, is a force-hopper. An animal that moves from force to force to commit crimes is close to undetectable. If our rapist had hit Dorset instead of Hants we might never have picked up number three. It's the *sequence* that gives us our chance. Isolated incidents are almost impossible to solve without a huge slice of luck.'

'D'you think the animal is that clever, Caz?'

'No, I don't. I think he's targeting runners. They happen to be spread around a bit, that's all.'

'We've only actually got two definite runners.'

'Three, if you include Fleet. Four if your instincts about Jackie are correct.'

'It could be coincidence, Caz.'

'I read somewhere, Moira – it might've been in a James Bond book – some bloke said, "once is chance, twice is coincidence, three times is enemy activity". No *way* is this chance.'

'If you say so, Caz. Coffee?'

Caz thought again about drugs, but said yes. 'And while you're doing that, I'll be getting an enquiry out to all the force intelligence officers south of Luton.

The animal may have been on their patch too. Better safe than sorry. Let's see if anyone knows a bald gorilla.'

Caz sent faxes to Portsmouth, Basingstoke, Woking, Guildford, Andover, Salisbury and Newbury, all marked urgent. The other stations she mailed. Another forty stabs in the dark. Why the hell wasn't there an FBI-style central intelligence unit? Did people really believe they would lose their freedoms to Big Brother if they had one? Which freedoms? What about the freedom to walk the streets free from the fear of rape?

'D'you want this coffee out here, boss, or are you coming back through?'

'I'm done here, Mo. Just going through the motions.'

They drank from plastic cups. Caz was muttering. 'You've got a really big bloke, stark bald, dressed like something out of *The Terminator*. No one sees him. Why?'

'Because he hides? He's invisible?'

'These are all domestic streets. They're not dead quiet. No one sees him.'

'It's dark.'

'Not really. Half-past six in April isn't dark. I know because I've trained in the evenings. Amanda Fleet was attacked when it was light.'

'You're making him sound like a ghost!'

'Oh, don't say that, Mo. That's what worries me.'

'Caz, you're not serious. He's a ghost?'

'No, he's not a ghost. But he knows he won't be seen. How can he know that?'

'He can't.'

'And that doesn't worry you, Moira?'

'All rapists worry me, Caz.'

Thirteen

On an impulse, Caz decided to take Valerie's Daimler 250 on the run through to Southampton. Moira had already said she didn't want to put more miles on her Fiesta and Caz wouldn't trust the MGB, so it was either the Daimler-Jag or sign something out. She sighed, thinking of him. She could hear him telling her off for mis-naming the Daimler yet again, but Caz had always called them Daimler-Jags and now she couldn't make herself politically correct.

It was strange sitting behind the wheel of the Daimler, sniffing to smell the leather and hoping to smell Valerie. He had said he didn't think he'd write; better, he said, for them to keep clear heads while he was away. Secretly she hoped that he'd break his promise and drop her a line.

They stuttered along on the A-roads from Brighton to Chichester but picked up from there, surging forward once they reached the M27 motorway that skirted Portsmouth. Moira thought the car was lovely and kept touching the walnut dash. Caz warned her, once more and she'd have to polish it!

Caz asked if Moira was seeing Billy tonight. She was. She said yes and then she asked what Caz would be doing.

'Mooching around, I guess. I'll probably go to my running club, do a session, have something to eat and crash early.'

'Sounds great!' Moira said. Caz presumed she was being sarcastic.

'It's OK, Moira. I need time to get my head together after the Avocado thing. Val will be back in the New Year. I can suffer being lonely until then.'

'What about Christmas?'

'I haven't decided. I might go see my father. I don't know yet.'

The Daimler moved smoothly with a satisfying thrumm under the bonnet. They were on the M27, climbing away from Portsmouth, mud and marinas to their left.

'Caz, if you and Val work it out, will you be moving in?'

'Definitely not!' Caz said quickly. 'I value my independence far too much for that.'

'It's just that I've got room at the inn. You could move in to my place.'

'Cheap?'

'Fair.'

'What's fair?'

'Forty quid a week, share the food, share the bills.'

'I don't have to sleep with anyone?'

'Nope!'

'And you pay me forty quid a week?'

'Very funny.'

'A rent book?'

'Even funnier, Caz.'

'Seems a bit expensive.'

'God, you're hilarious!'

'Give me some time to think about it.'

'No probs.'

Caz said yes as they passed Eastleigh Airport. Then she said, 'Corns!'

'What?' Moira said.

'The animal. He had rough fingertips, like corns. Where the hell would he get something like that?'

'How does "I haven't got a clue" sound?'

'Familiar, Dibben.'

'We aim to please.'

They were passing Rownham's Services. Caz was signalling to pull off on to the motorway spur. 'Maybe Mason will have some idea. I bloody hope so.'

DS Mason was waiting for them, standing next to a silver Saab 9000 as they swung left off the round-about beneath the main Southampton-Lyndhurst road. He was a tall man and stood noticeably upright. He was losing some hair, but looked the kind of ruggedly handsome bloke who really didn't give a damn. 'Sexy Rexy,' Moira giggled as she undid her belt. As they opened their doors he flashed them both a huge white grin and stepped towards their car.

'Peter Mason,' he said. Another grin. 'You're going

t'be Caz Flood. The other beauty is Moira Dibben, right?'

Caz tried not to smile but it just happened. 'Right first time,' she said. They shook hands, then Mason leaned past her to shake Moira's. He was clever enough to brush Caz as he politely said hello to the WPC.

'I hear you're getting somewhere with our rapist. Got a line on the perp?'

Caz baulked. 'I presume you mean a description of the alleged rapist.'

'Yeah, that 'n' all. You got one?'

'We've got one.'

'OK, Ducks.' (He did say 'Ducks'?) 'You can tell us all about it while we walk over to Fleet's. It's not far. The parking is easier over here so we'll leave the motors where they are. That all right with you?'

'Lead the way, Peter.'

They walked through a small close and down an alleyway between a woven fence and a long rush of thorns. Mason was talking about running. 'I have got the right Caz Flood, haven't I? Second in the last Totton?'

'I'm usually thereabouts. If I wasn't a bobby, I could do better, but the job doesn't let me train at a high enough intensity.'

'I know the feeling. I've been trying to break forty minutes for two years. In the last Totton, I did forty-oh-two. I could've hung myself.'

'It'll come,' Caz said. 'You just have to keep trying.'

'I've been telling myself that for two years!'

They arrived at the close. Fleet's was the third house on the left, the nine houses of the close arranged in a neat horseshoe, with numbers four and six on the shoulders, and a larger house on the top curve opposite the opening to the cul-de-sac. All the houses were occupied except Fleet's, up for sale, and another, also empty, with an identical estate agent's board tacked up outside.

'Morris Dibben?' Caz said with a wry smile. 'Any relation, Moira?'

Moira snapped quickly back. 'Do I look the sort of girl who'd have an estate agent in the family?'

Caz didn't respond. 'So what can you tell us, Peter, about the Fleet case?'

'If you've read the file, you know that Fleet was knocked on the 'ead early in the evening. We reckon at about five o'clock, so it was in broad daylight. All the residents of the close were working, so there was no one around. Number seven was unoccupied at the time; had been for a while. A couple had lived there. The chap worked at Fawley oil refinery, that's eight or nine miles from here. His firm moved him away three months before the attack on Miss Fleet. He's in Aberdeen now on about ten grand a year more than he got at Fawley. The locals from up there had a little chat with him for us. They said he seemed like an ordinary bloke. Clean as a whistle.'

They were stood in the driveway of number three, a pleasant if ordinary three-bedroomed detached house. There were signs of the builder's paintwork lifting already. There was no porch. Caz walked

103

towards the front door, pretended to be opening it with a key, and stood there. She felt the soft hairs on her neck rise and her back run cold. She spun round quickly, dropping as if she were defending herself. She looked straight into the doorway of number seven and pointed. 'He was in there.' It was a fact.

They got hold of the estate agents. A squawky female voice answered and said it would be impossible to get anyone there before four o'clock. Peter Mason said, no problem, they would just break in. There was a clatter of telephones and seconds later someone male and pompous came on the line. Peter explained. It was an investigation into attempted murder; they would have to enter the premises now. The voice harrumphed, but they were promised a key within ten minutes.

'They're on their way,' Mason said. 'Exceedingly helpful types.'

Mindful of Jenny Griffin, whom she at least knew a little, Caz gently asked if they had looked at the house opposite? DS Mason did not seem fazed. 'The first door-to-door was uniforms but there was nothing doing, all the locals were still at work when the felony occurred.' Caz saw Moira wince behind him. 'Checks were made of all the adjoining properties but nothing was discovered. I'm sure number seven was seen to be secure.'

She left it, playing safe. 'It's just a thought, this, Peter, but do you know if Amanda Fleet ran or jogged around here?'

'She did a bit. She recognised me from one of my regular training routes. She said she was planning to run in the Totton 10K herself.'

'Planning! Which one?'

'She didn't say. I presumed she meant October's. The eighth.'

'Are you sure, Peter?'

'No, I'm not. It was just one of those casual things that get said when you're trying to be nice. This would have been a couple of days after her rape.'

'How can I find out if she entered?'

'That shouldn't be too hard. The 10K is run by Totton and Eling Lions and Totton Running Club. Last I heard, the race director was a bloke called Clive Parker. He works for an insurance company in town. I'd say he was a very methodical chap, about forty, forty-five. He should have records of entries.'

'Brilliant!'

'Mind you, you should know: two thirds of race entries come in the last month, so it's two-to-one against you before you've even breathed.'

'Always presuming Mr Parker kept the entry forms!' Moira said.

'Oh, cheers, Mo!'

'That's all right, boss,' Moira said, cheekily. A car scurried into the close. She turned. 'Ah, here's your secret agent.'

'Estate agent,' Caz said.

Moira nodded. 'That's what I said, diddle I?'

It was a large car, something foreign. A tiny, weasly man emerged and came bobbing towards them. 'Mr

Mason?' The DS growled a yes. 'I have your – I understand you need the – your keys, Sir?'

'Thank you, Mister . . .?'

'Weedle.'

'Did you say Weedle?'

'That is correct. W-double E-D-L-E.'

There was an awful pause. Weedle attempted to grow slightly as he caught Mason's eyes. The DS was trying very hard not to break into hysterics.

'Er, right,' Weedle said. 'Shall we go in, then?'

They followed him, three of them stifling a giggle, the little man sniffling as he walked up the drive.

The third key was the right one and it was stiff. Weedle struggled. They could see his ears turning pink. Then the door opened. They pushed past.

The house had that vaguely familiar, vaguely stale smell of abandonment; faint traces of cabbage, human breath, dust mites and disappointment settling on their lips. It was a little too cold.

'Er, we normally put the central heating on, but . . .' Weedle paused. Only Moira looked at him. 'We usually . . . about two hours a day . . . but we were asked not to.'

Caz was still treading carefully with Mason even as she trod carefully on the stairs. Kitchen and bathroom windows were favourites. She expected one to be unlatched. If Peter Mason was put out by the suggestion that his lot had missed something he was covering it well.

The bathroom was clean but not gleaming. She

looked into the cistern. There was dust on the water but maybe not as much as she had expected. The windows were properly closed and there were no scratches. Moira and the DS were downstairs. She could hear their different voices, the rhythms of their banter as they searched for the break-in. She went through to the larger front bedroom. It was past noon. Number seven obviously got its light later in the day. She looked at the dust.

There was a thin, bacterial coating of grey along the skirting boards. The cheap curtains sagged with a similar sad debris and the off-white cross-pieces of the window casements were delicately settled in the same way. The window-sill, though sprinkled too, looked younger, cleaner, less abandoned. She went back to the doorway. The light-switch was barely dusty. Using her torch, she shone it obliquely across the wall. There was a different shine, an almost perfect rectangle where the wallpaper had been roughly rubbed. Someone covering his tracks.

Caz went back to the window and looked out. There was a slanted view into Amanda Fleet's lounge and into almost all of the bedroom opposite that matched this one. The first five or six feet of the hall would be visible through an opened front door. Caz felt cold. Turning away from the window, she knelt down to study the floor. An area of carpet felt different and there were three small circular indentations as if at three points of a triangle.

He'd been here.

'Sergeant Mason!'

107

'Yo!'

'Could you come up, Sarge?'

'You want me?'

'I'm in the front bedroom.'

'Well, why didn't you say?'

There was a silly leer in his voice but she refused to react to it. Mason wasn't doing himself any favours, but she promised herself to be good.

'I'm in here,' she said when she heard him on the landing.

'Peter's coming!' he cooed. She looked skyward for help.

Caz told him. 'The animal's been here. He's wiped the light-switch and the window-sill for prints. I think he's been in here watching Amanda Fleet. Take a look.' The DS moved to the window. Caz waited a moment. 'If you look at the floor here, you can see where he probably dossed. The cleaner patch there will be where the previous owners had their bed, but here,' she pointed out an odd-shaped flattened patch, 'it's been squashed down much more recently.'

Mason crouched to look.

'What about these, Peter?' She pointed to the circles.

Mason spoke straight away. 'Tripod feet. See, three circles, a point inside.'

'For a camera?'

'Or a 'scope. Could be either. No way of knowing.'

'But we know he's been here. He was watching. At least we know why he's never been seen. The bastard must suss out his victim's habits and their neighbours'. Once he's sure he has an open field, he strikes.'

'Jee-zuss!'

'It's frightening isn't it?'

'Is it? I was just thinking of the flak. We didn't clock his hide-away.'

'Yeah, you did, Sarge. You looked at it this morning, suggested we look at it this afternoon.'

'Oh, I did, did I?'

'You did, Sarge. And I'm very grateful for the help.'

Mason cottoned on quickly. 'That's OK, detective. We're all on the same team after all. And it was good work, you spotting the marks on the bedroom carpet.'

'That was me?'

'Acute observation under pressure. I'm impressed.'

'Why, thank you, Sergeant.'

Mason suggested they adjourned to a pub. He said he didn't fancy any of the ones in Redbridge and recommended The Salmon Leap in Totton. 'You know it? It's not far from the start of the Totton 10K.' He radioed in, asking for fingerprints in the bedroom, bathroom, kitchen and hall. When he told Weedle they'd need his place for another week the estate agent's face dropped, picked up for a protest, then changed its mind. As they were leaving, Moira whispered to Caz, 'Weedle's a collector. Guess what of.'

'Matchboxes?'

'Nope!'

'Cigarette cards, car numbers, First Day issues?'

'Condoms!'

'Condoms . . .'

'Yep.'

'I presume, unused.'

'I didn't like to ask,' Moira said. 'He says he's got over a thousand.'

The Salmon Leap was modern, a sweep of red brick and glass, video games and MTV high on one wall in the bar. The beer was all right, Peter said, and they did great cheap lunches. When he ordered a king-size T-bone to follow potato skins, Caz told him why he couldn't break forty minutes for 10K.

'Same problem as me, Peter, just a different level. When you run, every pound counts. Racing up to eight hundred metres you can get away with a bit of weight provided you've got the power to go with it – Tom McKean and John Regis, for example – but once you're up to the mile and beyond, forget it. If you want to break forty minutes, restrict your diet. You're fat.'

'I'm not fat!'

'Not as far as your DI is concerned, or in the eyes of Joe Public.'

'That's what I said.'

'But for a runner, you are fat.'

'You ever thought of joining the Diplomatic Corps, Flood?'

'I'm right, Peter. What's more you know I am. In a marathon, every pound over your rock-bottom racing weight costs two minutes extra on your time. You take off a stone, and at least two minutes off your 10K.'

The DS lit up a cigar.

'Oh, this isn't real!' Caz groaned. 'How many of those a day?'

'A couple. Maybe three or four on a Saturday.'

'What, and one just before a race? One at the drinks station?'

'Don't be daft.'

'It's not me who's daft, Sarge.'

Moira broke in, suggesting another round. She went off for two more orange juices and a second, near-illegal pint for the DS.

Mason was conciliatory. 'You're serious aren't you?'

'You bet I am!' Caz said quickly. 'Look at me. I'm skinny, right?'

'I'd say pretty tasty.'

'Well, you stick me next to Sally Gunnell and I'm porky, but put me alongside Liz McColgan and I'm a fat cow.'

'Isn't that just a bit OTT?'

'No, it's horses for courses,' Caz said. 'I'm a copper first and a runner second. I did think about doing it the other way round but to really compete now you've got to be full-time. If I was full-time I'd be eight to ten pounds lighter. *Then* I'd be skinny.'

'You talk like an anorexic.'

'Well I'm not, Peter. I'm a realist. There are a few girls out there like me, fringe England runners who have to decide what they want. I'd *love* to be a bit better. I'd *love* to go sub-two minutes for eight hundred and yes, I'd love to blow Kath Bailey and Sue Dilnot away in the Totton 10K, but to do it I'd have to give up the job or my social life. I won't do either.'

'*They* do it.'

'That's because they started off built the right way. They're little boys.'

'Ooof!'

'I don't mean that in a nasty way. I mean they're waifs. I know both Kathy and Sue and they're both really nice ladies, but they are *built* for distance running, there's nothing to them. I'd say they were delicate, tiny little things except that when they race, they're so gutsy. Get up close to them, they are really small. Small bones and good muscles to start with, no body fat to hide it, and then an awful lot of dedication and hard work.'

Moira came back with the drinks. 'You two still prattling on about running?'

'We're finished,' Caz said. 'I just told Peter he should take off a stone.'

'Off where?' Moira said incredulously.

The DS took a thin fold of his stomach in his fingers. 'She's right. It could come off.' He shifted slightly in his seat. 'And I used to have a tight little arse when I was twenty.'

'Well, there y'go Pete!' Caz said. 'All you gotta do now is want to!'

He leaned back, taking a long sensuous drag on

the sweet-smelling cigar. 'Ah!' he said, almost crooning, 'and there, my dear, lies the rub.'

'Being fit's not everything,' Caz decided. 'But not so long ago, being fit kept me alive.' She drifted off, remembering.

Others ran to be fit, they ran to be fast, they ran to be thin. Some ran to be the best or to chase the best. She had run to stay alive. For more than three hours, shuffling, shuffling, refusing to stop, forty feet this way, forty-two feet that, with frost settling on her shoes and cold in her heart. But Caz didn't die, she wouldn't die.

Far off, Moira was talking to the DS. 'White. Six feet two or three, at least two hundred pounds. Fat hands and rough pudgy fingers. Wearing a shooting jacket. Clean-shaven, possibly hairless and bald. Boxer's nose. Blue or blue-grey eyes.'

'What did you get, a photograph?'

'Photographic memory.'

Caz listened, letting herself drift slowly back towards consciousness. She stayed fallow, letting them speak. Moira was talking again.

'We're pretty sure the animal drove an F-Reg ex-Rediffusion van, an Escort, probably bought at an auction. They spray over the logo but only thinly. You can still see the original paintwork. We've got a trace on but we've got nowhere yet. Once these vans hit an auction they could be anywhere and they've probably changed hands a couple of times at least.

'There's a DS Jenny Griffin at Central, Richmond. She's on to some possible new witnesses for us, a couple of conservatory salesmen that were around when the second attack occurred. Oh, and the animal wore a bobble hat. Black and yellow. We haven't even started down that route.'

Mason responded. 'I can think of a few black 'n ambers. There's Newport AFC, Wolverhampton Wanderers and Hull City for starters and Wasps, the rugby side. Newport were a league side that went pop and dropped out of the league. They were Newport County then. They were re-born a few years back.'

Caz woke up fully and cut in. 'If there were only four possibles we'd be ecstatic. But I've seen black and amber on park pitches, never mind all those non-league football teams. It'll be worth checking out Wasps, though. The animal was big 'n' fast and his face had done the rounds. There's a fair chance he played some rugby.'

'I'll ask about down here,' Mason said. 'Some of our lads are into soccer. They might come up with something.'

'It's the hands that get me,' Caz said. 'I've been trying to imagine what Jill Brown described. She said his fingertips were hard and rough, like corns.'

The DS held out his heavy hands, palm up. 'Like these, you mean?' He curled the fingers upwards, and slowly raised them in front of Caz's face. The middle and index fingers were coarsened and scarred.

Caz shuddered. 'Yes. I think so. Where did you . . .? Why?'

'I'm a radio buff.' Mason explained. 'This is from soldering work.' He held the fingers together as if he was holding something between them. 'When you're soldering, wires get hot. After a couple of years, your fingers toughen up and you don't feel the heat any more. I'd make a guess your man was in electronics, something that required a fair bit of soldering.'

'A TV engineer?' Caz asked.

'Good bet.'

'Or an ex-engineer,' Moira said slowly.

Caz expanded. 'Someone who had bought his old van, maybe still did a bit of repair work. Someone who'd have access to people's homes.'

'Oh Jeez,' Moira said heavily.

Mason cut in brightly. 'I can check out the local TV repair companies for you, starting with Rediffusion. Our boys can hit Southampton, Eastleigh, Fareham and Pompey.'

'Cheers, Peter. We got nowhere with Brighton and Chichester when we asked about the van, but we weren't looking for an ex-engineer then.'

'There is another possibility,' Mason said. He was looking at his fingers. 'These are hard because they've been cooked, but they're even worse because I did some karate a few years back. Might your fellah have done martial arts?'

'Oh, shit! I hope not. I don't fancy arresting a gorilla with a black belt.'

'You got some big blokes at Brighton?'

'Oh, yeah,' Caz said. 'Jim Greaves is well over six foot tall and our DCS, Norman Blackside, he's built like Godzilla.'

'What about my Billy?' Moira said.

''Er, no, Moira.' Caz said. She turned back to DS Mason to explain. 'Moira's fellah is about six-three but if he turned side-on and stuck out his tongue, he could do a good impression of a zip.'

The WPC made a little protest.

Caz smiled. 'OK, Mo. I'll be kind. Let's just say Billy's not filled out yet.'

'Well, *I* think he's big.'

'What are we talking about now, Mo?'

'Billy. I think he's *tall*.'

The DS interrupted. 'Shit! I've just realised. Shut up, you two.'

'What?' Caz and Moira spoke together. They sounded girlish.

'The animal. He used a *soldering iron* on these women. He didn't *brand* them. He *burnt* them with a soldering iron. Show me those pictures again, Flood.'

Caz opened one of the files.

'That's what these marks are.' Mason pointed at the colour photograph of Irene Stubbs' shoulder. 'The bastard burnt them with a soldering iron!'

Caz went to interrupt.

'No,' Mason said. 'Before you say it. There are two types of iron. One's for bench work, it plugs in and stays warm. The other kind is an instant one for engineers out on the road. They're called soldering guns. Click and they're hot in a second. The triggers are spring-loaded for safety.'

Caz and Moira were thinking the same thing. '*It clunged.*'

'You're right, Peter,' Caz said slowly. 'It was a soldering gun.'

Mason was pleased. 'I'd go so far as to say that when we find this creep, we'll have a reasonable chance of matching the burn marks to the gun-bit that'll be in his tool-box.'

'Once we find him,' Moira said.

Fourteen

Detectives from one force don't just go blundering around on someone else's patch. There is a protocol to be observed, usually contacts at DCI level or higher, before detectives can conduct interviews of suspects or witnesses away from home. There was a time when the Metropolitan Police had refused to allow an interview on a nasty rape case Caz had been connected with. The suspect avoided interrogation because the Met had him under surveillance for a big drugs bust. She never found out if the villain went down for anything. All she knew was that the locals didn't get him for their rape.

DS Mason short-circuited any territory problems by taking them to see Clive Parker himself. They met in the foyer of a modern blue-white building, in an isolated visitors' office with glass walls overlooking the old Pirelli factory. The DS explained that they were investigating an attempted murder and they needed to make some urgent checks on the entries for recent 10Ks.

Parker was early to mid-forties, well-spoken and

quite helpful – Peter Mason's description. When he came out of the lift to see them he carried a small A4 folder. Caz recognised him immediately; but if he recognised her he didn't show it. More likely he didn't make the connection between the Totton 10K's plucky second placer and the detective now addressing him. Yes, he was still the race director, he said, but he was about to pass the reins over to a chap called Jones who had been the director before him, as soon as everything was ship-shape of course. 'Just tidying up the accounts with the Totton Lions, making sure everybody has received their results, tying things down with the race photographers, that sort of thing.'

'We were hoping, Mr Parker, that you might be able to supply us with lists of runners from the last few 10Ks. Would that be possible?'

'Runners or entrants, Sergeant?'

'Is there a difference?'

'There's quite a big difference, I'm afraid. We get between eleven and twelve hundred entrants but we've still got one thousand finishers on the day.'

'I'm not sure,' Mason said. He glanced at Caz. 'We'd like both if possible.'

'A list of runners I can sort for you quite quickly. Well, finishers actually. The raceday programme will contain some entrants who never actually turn up, and there will be quite a few who enter too late for the programme and still don't run on the day.'

'Addresses?'

'All our entry forms go to our computer man, a

chap called Dean Richard. He does address labels
for us as well as the results on the day. We also send
all the runners' names and addresses to Gareth Boxx
at Boxx Brownie, the photographers. They do our
race pictures. They'll actually be more likely to keep
addresses than Richard will. They have to keep a
check on who pays for photographs and who doesn't.
I imagine that Dean will delete his race files as soon
as he possibly can, to make space on his computer.
I'm not quite sure what he does with the original
entry forms but I imagine he throws them away. He
does most of the races round here. He's very good.'

'Would you have his address?'

He tapped the plastic of his folder. 'In here. Whatever you require. I can give you Gareth Boxx's
address too, home and business, and Ron Jones's
home number. You might want to talk to Jane Bell
and Irene Sandford as well. They both help out with
the race. Irene has been our finish director for the
last few races. My right-hand woman, you might say.'

Dean Richard lived just outside of the city in a small
village – well, more a smattering of houses really –
just off the Southampton-Winchester road. He wasn't
in, but his answerphone said he'd get right back to
them if they left their number after the beep. Caz
put the phone down without speaking.

They didn't get an answerphone when they
telephoned Boxx Brownie but, if they had, they probably would have received a more intelligent response.
Eventually they realised that Mr Boxx wasn't in

today, and a high-pitched YTS male voice said thanks for calling. When they tried Boxx's home number it rang for a while but no machine interrupted. Caz was just about to replace the receiver when a smooth, dark voice broke on to the line. 'Hello. This is Gareth Boxx. How can I help you?'

'Mr Boxx? I'm Detective Constable Flood. Would it be possible to see you this afternoon, Sir? We are making enquiries about a recent local road race, the Totton 10K. We understand you are its race photographer.'

'For my sins, yes.' There was a faint timbre of Welsh in the voice.

'Could we pop around for a chat, Sir? Just a few questions. We are at Portswood Police Station in Hulse Road.'

'Well, you're no distance then, are you, my dear?'

'Then could we—'

'Pop round? I guess so. I wonder, though, could you give me, say, twenty minutes? I'm working with a model and I've not quite finished.'

'Certainly, Mr Boxx. Shall we say half-an-hour?'

'Say what you like, I will be ready in twenty minutes. Goodbye.'

Caz replaced the phone.

'So what's the score, Caz?' Moira asked.

'I'm not quite sure. Boxx says he's just finishing off with a model.'

While they kicked their heels, Mason suggested coffee. Doing a quick sum, Caz thought their caffeine intake was lower than their excesses for an average day, so she said yes for both of them. The DS glanced at Moira to see if she could speak for herself. Moira just smiled sweetly, a passive yes. Mason went off, whistling tunelessly.

'We'll have to check out the other four attack addresses, Mo. See if the animal had similar bolt-holes where he could watch the victims from.'

'I can tell you there were no unoccupied houses on the two Worthing jobs. I'd've remembered, I'm sure.'

'I wasn't suggesting otherwise, Mo. But even if you did miss something, that doesn't make you a bad copper. There's just not enough of us is all. Increase the force by thirty per cent and scrap the Crown Prosecution Service and we'd cut crime in half in a twelve-month.'

'Get rid of the CPS? You wish . . .'

'You don't think we could?'

'Oh, sure we could; but I don't see it happening, do you?'

'Point taken,' Caz said. 'They'll have us paying for our own coffee soon. Did I tell you? I was at a local nick a couple of months ago. I'd just nipped in to see a mate. They'd installed a neat little microwave. "That's nifty," I said. "Oh, that's not for staff," the desk-sergeant told me. "It's marked, 'prisoners only'. Villains mustn't have cold food, no matter what." '

'The pendulum will swing back one day, Caz.'

'You reckon? We've got the Law 'n' Order party in *now*! God knows what'll happen when they move aside.'

'It'll change. It has to.'

'Oh, yeah? One million lemmings can't be wrong.'

'Now you're depressing me, Caz. I need some coffee.'

'You won't have to wait long. Here comes Peter the Great.'

'Don't you like him, Caz? I think he's quite sexy.'

'What?' Caz said. 'You need to do something about your hormone balance, Mo, before it gets you into some serious trouble. If Mason is sexy, I'm celibate.'

'Well you are, aren't you?'

'Only until January the fourth!'

Mason arrived grinning. 'Right, girls! Coffees! And three Kit-Kats, OK?'

'The diet starts tomorrow, does it, Sarge?'

'Something like that, Flood. I could tell you I was carbohydrate-loading for a race next Sunday but it's only a 10K. Down your neck of the woods.'

'Chichester!'

'Bless you!'

'Very funny!'

They drank their coffees. Moira and the DS split Caz's chocolate. When Caz raised her eyes to glower at the WPC she grinned back at her with her big brown eyes and said, 'There's nothing wrong with hips, Caz!'

The DS had some information. 'While I was downstairs I had a word with a couple of the lads. One of them's a referee and well into non-league football. I asked him about teams that wore black and amber. Do you want to know how many there are?'

'Not really. But you're going to tell me, right?'

'Apart from the four teams we thought of earlier, my mate gave me nine teams that sport yellow and black as home kit, another one that's amber and navy blue and a couple more that wear black and amber as their second strip.'

'Shee-it!'

'And that's just the local ones! If you scrub the two Newports, Hull City and Wolves and ignore Southport and East Thurrock, Essex, you're down to ... Hang on, it's on a piece of paper somewhere ... In alphabetical order; Banstead Athletic, Cove, Havant Town, Wokingham, Newbury and Trowbridge, Wilts. On the other side of the M4 you've also got Marlow Town and Slough.'

Caz looked overjoyed.

'To be fair, Slough actually plays in *blue* and amber ... then there's all the little clubs that don't make the league handbooks, and there's Basingstoke and Whyteleaf in Surrey. Their second kit is black and amber.'

'Do me a favour, Sarge.'

'Name it.'

'If you know someone who's into rugby, don't ask him anything.'

'I knew you'd be pleased, Flood. This is what good detective work is all about, eh? Eh?' He bit on a last bit of biscuit. *Her* biscuit.

'Can I scrounge that list, Sarge?'

'Be my guest.'

Caz took the list and asked could they go now?

Then, with a cheeky grin and a suddenly acquired Welsh accent, she said, 'Let's go chat to Gareth Boxx, look you.'

Fifteen

Gareth Boxx had given them a prestigious address in Grosvenor Square, just off Southampton's Bedford Place, on a site immediately behind where the coach station had once stood and was now replaced by offices. They went in Valerie's Daimler, swung right opposite a row of restaurants and rounded a copper statue of Lord Louis Mountbatten. Bedford Place was pleasant enough up to eleven o'clock but a notorious trouble spot after about eleven-thirty, when the home-going restaurantees came face to face with the drunks eating their fish and chips or trying to remove inedible yellow chillies from their doner kebabs. Caz was amazed to see the Mountbatten statue still standing.

'Long roots!' Peter said as they spun past.

Boxx had the largest penthouse in a large, fairly new block, with perfectly manicured gardens, a hissing fountain and three floors between his cave and the noise of the Saturday night yobs. To get to him, they passed through double gates, rounded the building, contacted him through a barking grill and took

a compact lift. The DS smiled as he found himself
unavoidably face to face with the two ladies. He was
still smiling when Caz reached past him to press '3',
her forearm brushing his cheek.

'Hello!' Boxx said, sweeping open his door and
bowing them in. The instant Caz saw him, she
thought, 'He's just had sex!' As she followed the
others into the flat, she wondered where the thought
had come from. A gorgeous smell of roasting coffee
beans wafted into the hall. The DS was leading the
way but had stopped at the door of the lounge. Moira
bumped into his rear, causing a traffic jam. Boxx
waved over them at the sergeant. 'Do go in, please!
There's coffee brewing. Best Brazilian. May I tempt
any of you?'

The reason for the hesitation at the head of the
queue was obvious the moment Caz finally managed
to get through the door. The room was stunning,
nothing less. To the left, a wall raced away vertically
almost twenty feet. From there, a pine-clad ceiling
slashed down towards the outer wall, still nine or so
feet from the floor, where the angle changed and the
sloping wall-roof was broken by five copper Velux
windows.

The ceiling's light brown stripes were broken only
by discreet flush-set spot-lamps. These were on, no
doubt for effect, as they walked in. The lounge must
have been more than forty-five feet long and, central
to it, about one third of the way from the far end
of the room, there was a solid grey-white chunk of
marble, starkly lit, serving as a coffee table. On it,

dumped casually, was a silver Hasselblad camera with a longish lens, a light meter and a small red notebook. From somewhere in the distance, Boxx told them to sit down. Moira and the sergeant obeyed, choosing one each of five low-slung cream leather saddled armchairs but Caz stayed on her feet. 'Do you mind if I stand?' she asked quietly as Boxx came in. 'I've been on my backside most of the day and I could do with stretching my legs.'

'As you wish,' Boxx said.

'I'm Detective Constable Flood,' Caz said formally. She was taking long slow breaths through her nose as unobtrusively as she knew how.

'Black or white?' Boxx replied. He had a plain, simple smile. Neat teeth.

The tall wall to the side of the lounge was bare, except for two gleaming polished oars with painted dark-green blades and gold-leaf inscriptions. One, even from ten feet, Caz could read. There were college names, Queen's, Balliol, Trinity, Christ Church.

Boxx could see her wondering. 'Oxford Eights!' he explained from behind. 'We won the blades because we "bumped" the others, that is caught them, despite a two-and-a-half length standing start.'

The shape of the sharp ceiling made the focal end wall almost triangular. Caz looked at that and said, 'Actually, I was admiring those paintings.'

There were three paintings and they looked like a set. One was eight feet by three, the next, five by about two foot-six. The last was shaped to follow the slope above a two-foot rectangle. All three were grey-blue based and stood out four inches from the wall in deep relief. They were pastel canvases but with brave slashes of colour through the fog that just about said 'Manhattan'.

'It's called *New York Trilogy*,' Boxx explained. 'I actually bought the set from a gallery in Bal Harbour, just north of Miami Beach. The wall needed something special and this was it.'

'It's perfect!' Moira said from one of the low chairs. 'I think I like the little diddy one on the end best.'

'Thank you,' Boxx said. He flashed an economical smile at her. 'I'm a photographer. I appreciate only three things: beauty, drama and class. Those pictures have all three. What do you think?'

Moira was tickled. 'Oh, yes. Definitely. The big one is almost . . .'

'Sexy?'

Moira flushed very slightly. 'I think so.'

Mason asked, 'Did you have the little one done specially, Mr Boxx?'

'Yes. Not even I'm that lucky. It works well, doesn't it?'

'Must've cost you a packet.'

Boxx grinned and coughed. He didn't need to say yes. He brought the coffee over on a large bamboo tray. He saw Moira look curiously at the designs and explained, 'Ah, Singapore, years back. A job.' Moira mouthed an 'Oh!' but no sound emerged. Boxx sat down opposite her. She shifted slightly, then sat forward, bringing her knees tight together and clasping her hands demurely around them. Whether Boxx noticed her nervousness or not, Caz wasn't sure. She had just sat down herself and was glad to be in jeans. What *was* it about this bloke?

Boxx poured the coffee, mumbling that they could sort out their own milk. He took his black, he said. The three police officers all had white. 'Right!' he said briskly, 'That's a little more civilised! Now, how can I be of help?'

He was clever. He looked first at Caz to acknowledge her, then turned to Sergeant Mason once she knew that he was simply following form. On the way, he made eye contact with Moira and she squirmed again. The DS started talking. 'We are grateful for your help, Mr Boxx. There have been a number of incidents involving runners from the two latest Totton 10Ks. We are of the understanding that your company takes photographs of the finish of the race.'

'Yes.'

'We would like to see any photographs of a Miss Jill Brown and a Mrs Irene Stubbs. We can furnish you with descriptions and with their approximate finishing times.'

'Would you have their race numbers?'

Mason glanced quickly at Caz, then looked back at Boxx. 'No.'

'But you have their full names and addresses?'

'Yes.'

'Then we should be able to trace them for you.'

The DS looked pleased and sat forward slightly. 'Perhaps you could explain, Mr Boxx, how your photograph system works?'

'Certainly. I'd be happy to, but do drink your coffee before it gets cold.'

There was a clink of expensive china. Caz watched Moira as she looked over her raised cup towards the photographer.

Boxx continued, 'There are two ways of making money from race photographs. We can either sell the photographs before the race and just take pictures of the runners who have pre-paid, or we can blanket-shoot everyone and mail them after the race on a sale-or-return basis.'

'And you do?'

'A little bit of both. But mainly we blanket-shoot and mail after the race.'

Caz asked, did he get ripped off much?'

'A lot. Many runners receive a finish photograph and just keep it. So we log every person we mail and we log our returns. Stitch us up once and you don't get another photograph. Simple!'

Caz suggested that Boxx Brownie must have an extensive database.

'We do. At the last count we had about seven thousand runners on our files, about half on the black-list. The others are new runners or established paying customers.'

'What about staff?' Mason asked.

'At the labs we've got two full-timers, two part-timers, a receptionist and the company accountant. On race day, we take between three and six people: photographers, loaders, counters and spotters.'

'Spotters?' Caz asked.

'We take as many shots as we can but we make a special effort if anyone has pre-paid. We mark their race numbers with a great big cross. The spotter, usually a youngster, makes sure we don't miss an X.'

'As in "X marks the spot"?' This was Moira, who retreated immediately, faintly pink and awkward.

Boxx noticed but was kind. 'Very well put, Miss . . .?'

'Dibben,' Moira said. 'WPC.'

'That's an unusual name.'

'I meant Moira. Sorry.'

Caz winced, Mo was way out of her depth here. She cut in. 'So, Gareth, if we give you a name, you can tell us if that person is on your database and whether or not they've bought your pictures?'

'And which races they've been in – if we got a shot of them finishing.'

'If?'

'We have a hit rate of about ninety, ninety-two per cent. We're good and we have four or five shooters with long lenses. Nevertheless, in a blanket finish, sometimes you just can't get the shot.'

The DS spoke again. 'How exactly do you get your names and addresses to tally up with the numbers?'

'Two ways. We offer a free servce to race organisers. They send us their entry forms; we do the runner lists and send them back. If the organisers don't want to do that, we get a print-out from the results man and tally everything up after the event. It's slower, but sometimes there's no other way. The Totton 10K we do the hard way but their results chap is superb.'

'Dean Richard.'

'Yes. He's as good as they get. He uses a portable IBM. No one better.'

They finished their coffees. Gareth Boxx offered them more. A meter in Caz's head dinged 'overload' but she still said yes. After Jenny Griffin's flask and Hulse Road's canteen, Boxx's fresh ground Brazilian was ecstasy.

Gareth explained that this wasn't his office. He had a studio here, across the landing, but the business address was where the computers were. No, it wasn't that big a penthouse, he'd bought two. In this one he had a lounge, a kitchen, two bedrooms (he paused for Moira's sake) and a bathroom. Across the landing he had a studio, a second kitchen, two more bedrooms, another bathroom and a super little darkroom.

'It's completely illegal, of course. It breaks the tenancy agreement. The darkroom's not anything like the professional darkroom we have at the office, but it's pretty sophisticated for the bits and pieces I have to do at home.'

Caz suddenly remembered the model. '*Twenty minutes.*' He *had* had sex.

They arranged for one, two, or three of them to come and see him first thing in the morning. He gave them a card with his office address. 'I'm sure you understand, yes? If it's really a problem, I could up-anchor and go into the office today. Trouble is they'll be developing and printing for a race this Sunday-past and we may be waiting around quite a long time . . .'

They said it wasn't a problem. Boxx poured more coffee. When he looked up, it was with his measured smile.

'Tomorrow then? Nine-thirty. I look forward to it.'

Sixteen

When they finally left Gareth Boxx it was getting late, and by the time they had dropped Peter Mason back at Hulse Road it was getting dark. The girls decided that they had a long way to go, so tonight's overtime would be down to the DS. He agreed to pay an evening call on Dean Richard and they set off for Brighton. At three o'clock in the morning Brighton was one hour's fast drive away but if they caught the rush hour they'd be lucky to get back in two.

They rolled from Portswood Headquarters and turned left into Hulse Road. Passing cars already had their headlights on and there was a steady stream of traffic in Banstead Road desperately seeking a traffic jam.

'Not planning anything special tonight, are we, Mo?'

'Seeing Billy.'

'This Tall Billy or Big Billy?'

'Very funny, Caz.'

'No, I'm not. I'm sorry, Mo. Billy's all right. Really.'

They got through Lodge Road lights and on to a dual carriageway out of town. Moira asked Caz when she'd be moving out of the DI's flat.

'As he would probably say, Mo, "soonest". But I'll need to have a chat with him first, and I reckon I owe him a good drink.'

'I thought he looked shagged yesterday.'

'I know, Mo. He runs on adrenaline, nothing else. If he's chasing someone or he's just caught 'em he's fine, but knock him back and suddenly he's running on an empty tank. I worry about him a lot. I don't think he eats his greens.'

'Do you think he'll miss you?'

'I'm not sure,' Caz said. 'I think he likes my company but he likes his space even more.'

'Me, I don't need *any* space. I like people, lots of noise, parties!'

Caz groaned. 'Maybe moving in isn't such a—'

'It's a great idea, Caz! We get on great and the forty quids will be handy!'

'OK. You've sold it, Mo. I'm moving in.'

'Good!' Moira said. 'So what did you think of those two blokes today, Peter Mason and Gary Shoebox?'

'I've told you, Moira. Your hormones are going to get you into trouble.'

'But what d'you think?'

'I think DS Mason is married; Boxx – I don't know, but I think he was screwing one of his models just before we arrived.'

'Why d'you say that?'

'He just was. Take it from me.'

'Well I thought he was *very* attractive. I liked his hair.'

Caz tried to picture him. He was another six-footer (it was her day for bigger men), his hair had been quite short on top, dark brown, but longer down over the ears and at the back, ending in a delicate pigtail with two coloured beads to keep it straight. His face she couldn't remember, just his controlled smile and his eyes, a sort of tawny colour but deep and riveting. He made her uncomfortable, as if he was driven, single-minded. She thought he'd be a real problem on a date, one of those men who'd need a 'no' in writing.

'Not my type,' she said, lying. 'But yeah, I suppose so.'

'Well, *I* fancied him.'

'Moira, you'd fancy absolutely anything. You need treatment!'

'You know what they say, Caz; it doesn't matter where you get your appetite, just so long as you eat at home.'

'Is that one of yours?'

'Billy's.'

'Ah, that figures. A typical man's statement.'

'You don't agree? You really didn't fancy Boxx?'

'Wrong word, Mo. "Fancy" to me means "I wouldn't mind". Gareth Boxx was a bit off-putting. He'd probably be great fun to flirt with at a dinner-party but I think he'd get a bit difficult one-on-one.'

'At a dinner-party?'

'Yes. You know what one of those is, don't you, Moira?'

Moira made a rude noise. 'What about his place, though? Wasn't that really something? He said I could come and look at his studio if I wanted. He said I had a great face for photographs. I wasn't pasty like you.'

'He said I was *pasty* ?'

'Well, what he said was, I had rich skin.'

'I am not pasty!'

Moira replied with a voice straight out of the American Deep South. 'Well, you sure ain't dusky, honey-chile!'

'Pasty! Huh!'

'Oooh, touched a nerve there, did we, DC Flood?'

'Sod off' Caz said.

They were well into the evening traffic-flow and already approaching the lights of Portsmouth. Caz began to react to the day, undoing mentally, and (with an hour's driving left) winding down a bit too early. She pulled out without a proper look in her mirror, only to swerve back in as an angrily blasted horn dopplered past them. 'Fuck me!'

'Not just now, Caz,' Moira said seriously. 'I'm a little tired.'

Caz slowly bit her tongue, one of her tricks for winding herself back up. In two days they seemed to have come so far. They knew what the animal looked like, that he used a soldering iron to mutilate his victims, that he was bald but wore a bobble hat to cover his head. They knew his MO and now they knew he was a watcher. He was careful. But he . . .

'Moira, the animal – if he has the time to watch, where does he get his money from? What does he live on? He can't have a straightforward job, and if he's on the dole, how can he afford his trips out?'

'And where does he hide his van,' Moira added, 'when he's watching from his bolt-hole? Surely if he just parked the van up somewhere, *someone* would notice?'

'So he walks there, or he bikes.'

Moira thought out loud. 'Maybe he runs?'

'Maybe he *races*,' Caz said quickly. 'Christ!'

'D'you mean he could've run with these women, made some kind of choice? He could have run in the Totton 10K?'

'Why not?' Caz said. 'Jill Brown told us she'd run fifty-six minutes. That was the same time as Irene Stubbs. The animal might be running in a race and taking his pick of the women runners.'

'God! It's frightening,' Moira said. There was a real quiver in her voice.

'How do you think *I* feel, Mo? If we're right, I will have run with this animal. I might have brushed past him in the crowd. He might have been stalking *me*! He might have been watching me, stood in the crowd at the prize presentation, watching while I got my prize.'

Moira was working something out. 'If he ran, Caz . . .'

'What?'

'If he ran in the race. If he finished. He might have had his photo taken. Gareth Boxx could have a picture of him!'

Caz flicked her left indicator on and looked for a parking place. As she slowed, faster cars slicked by on her right. 'Oh, nice one, Moira!' Caz said. 'He's big and bald or bloody big and wearing a bobble hat. You're right. If he's run *anywhere* we'll have his photograph! We can even make a guess at his running time, though I find fifty-six minutes, even for a big bloke, a little bit suspicious.'

Moira asked, 'Is fifty-six minutes slow?'

'Nine-minute-miling. It's new jogger speed or people who walk and run.'

'Well, if the animal is very big, maybe fat . . .'

Caz thought a moment. 'Irene Stubbs said he was very quick. He sounds big, like a sprinter. They're not always great shakes over middle distances but I'd still expect him to be quicker than fifty-six minutes. At least sub-fifty, maybe even close to forty minutes.'

'So DS Mason could have run in with him!'

'Well if he did, I'm not telling him, Mo. How about you?'

'Er, no thanks, Caz. You're the boss, remember?'

Caz finally found somewhere to pull off the road. Her body still felt tired but her mind was racing at sixty. She sat bolt upright, seeing him. 'He starts at the back!' she said suddenly. 'He starts with the grannies, the shufflers and the don't knows. He works his way up through the field. He picks a number.

Jesus Christ, Moira, the animal is *selecting* his victims.'

Moira sat quietly, then she mentioned Amanda Fleet. 'She didn't run ...'

'But she *entered*, Moira. I'll bet she entered. I'll bet she watched ...'

'I wish I'd asked Jackie. I wish—'

'Don't worry about it now, Moira. She's raced somewhere. I know it.'

The car swept into the top of Brighton at two minutes to a damp six o'clock. They were at the nick in John Street twenty-five minutes later, after crawling in light rain behind bumper after bumper and blearing red lights. The car park underneath the station was half-full, mainly with detectives' cars. Nothing changed; the lads were working late.

Caz parked Valerie's Daimler and briefly thought she owed it another clean. Moira stretched as they both got out and groaned as she suddenly realised how knackered she was. 'No worries, Mo,' Caz said devilishly. 'We should be away for eleven. You can grab an Indian then and eat it with Billy in bed.'

'Oh, God!' was all Moira said back.

They went through a yellow-painted metal bomb-proof door. Why it was bomb-proof, Caz didn't know; she had never ever found it locked. The concrete back stairs echoed with their passing as they went up, their personal noise relative to the background more significant now than at nine o'clock in the morning. Inside, the nick was probably not much quieter than at the start of the day, but outside Brighton was slowly quietening, winding down towards the week's darkest hour, seven p.m. on a Tuesday.

They dived into a ladies together and came out after swilling their faces with stiff, cold water. Awake, they went upstairs. As they took the last bend on the painted steps they heard the roar of Norman Blackside's voice fifty feet away and through two doors. '. . . give a shit, Tom! No one goes home until . . .!'

They hit the landing. There was a crash of a door slapping back. Then another. Then Tom MacInnes emerged. Red. Steaming. Moving quickly.

'Good timing, ladies!' he said roughly as he strode past. 'War Room in ten minutes. The fifth woman, Jane Daily. She's just died.'

Seventeen

Saint and Greavsie were sitting in the War Room along with two detective sergeants: DS Lindsell and DS Reid. There were a couple of drafted-in DCs and a few uniforms, all of whom Caz knew well enough to nod to. They barely responded to the two women walking in.

'What's up, Doc?' Caz said, but she might just as well not have bothered. Only Jim Greaves responded, and that with a pathetic grunt. The room was so thick with depression you could eat it.

'Coffees!' she said to Moira.

They were back in a rushed six minutes, two minutes before DI MacInnes and the DCS tanked into the room. The squad had thickened up slightly, but more than half of them were still out working or had gone home. The discomfort amongst the lads was palpable; Caz had no idea why. Then she found out. Blackside stepped up to the lectern and stood silently, staring into the room with well-deep black eyes. He loomed even larger as he breathed deeply, raising his shoulders and then his head as he stretched to conquer.

'De-*tect*-ives? Hah!' Then he was silent, glaring, daring anyone to speak. 'Jeremy Avocado,' he said eventually. He held up a huge photograph and paused again, 'Jeremy, ... William, ... Av-o-ca-do.' Hard men were shrinking in their seats. 'Remember him?'

There was no response.

'*You remember him!*

'So he got away. Was it a private plane to France? Smuggled out on a ship? No. The prat holes up two streets away from this nick and not one of you arseholes even sniffs him. And you are de-*tect*-ives?' More silence.

A chair squeaked and Blackside focused in on its occupant, DS Reid. Reid froze and Caz could see his neck redden as he tried desperately to look normal. 'Well now Avocado *is* away. We've fairly reliable information he's out of the country. He drove to Hull once all the hoo-hah had died down and then he got a ferry across the North Sea. *This*, gentlemen,' Blackside waved a small colour photograph at the room, 'is a postcard. The naked bird is *The Mermaid*. She lives in Copenhagen and keeps an eye on the harbour. Guess who signed the postcard.' He nodded to the DI, who stepped forward to speak.

The room almost oozed pain. Only Caz and Moira seemed immune. Moira had been too small a cog in the chase to feel any responsibility and now she vaguely enjoyed seeing a few macho men taking it. Caz had been in hospital, out of it altogether, and secretly she had expected something like this from

Avocado. She wasn't glad he'd got away. The feeling was more like respect for a highly competent enemy. She almost thought 'chivalrous' but the word sounded bizarre.

She was listening to Tom MacInnes talking steadily. They were winding down the Avocado exercise to near-stop. DS Jenkins, a DC and one uniform were to be left on that job, the rest of them were in at seven tomorrow. Now they had Jane Daily to worry about, a rape victim, badly beaten and now dead. DCS Blackside was going hands-on on this one, the DI was saying. He wanted an early result. MacInnes would be his second in command and he had promised the DCS a result for Christmas.

'Where's DC Flood?' MacInnes said. The voice was harsh but as Caz looked up she could see a flickered apology in his face.

She stood up with Moira. 'Here, Sir!'

'Can you come up here, Flood? Put us straight on where we are?'

'Sir!' Caz stood up. She was suddenly nervous and took just one step.

Blackside bellowed from backstage. 'Well, come on, girl!'

She went forward, after the briefest sisterly touch on her arm from Moira. All male eyes were on her back as she walked through and she felt stupid and awkward. She made a vain attempt to walk normally but some low-life smacked his lips anyway and made a squeaking sound as she passed. As she stepped up on to the stage she smiled formally at the two senior officers but behind her back she was showing the finger to the idiot in the audience and to anyone else who thought the cap fitted.

She spoke softly, and said 'Good evening, Sir' past Tom MacInnes to the grumbling Detective Chief Superintendent. Blackside gestured towards the lectern. She turned, biting the inside of her cheek for adrenaline. She looked out into the room and the lads waited. Flood on trial.

'OK. Er, OK.' She coughed once. 'Four rapes! Now a murder!

'My notes aren't quite up to date.' She glanced back at the two officers. 'I've only been back from Southampton for fifteen minutes. Yesterday I was in Richmond with WPC Dibben and one of their own, DS Griffin.'

She was feeling stronger. 'We have an accurate description of a male Caucasian aggravated rapist. He is six-foot-two or taller, very well built, weighing at least two-hundred-and-twenty pounds, but may be heavier. He is clean-shaven, possibly hairless and completely bald. He is known to have worn a black and amber bobble-hat on at least one occasion, this possibly to hide his distinctive baldness.

'There are a number of other personal features we know. The attacker has fat, pudgy hands and coarsened fingertips. He is believed to be involved in electronics in some way, possibly as a television engineer. We have reason to believe our man to be quite quick on his feet and very strong. He also may have done martial arts.

'We are fairly sure the target has used a grey Ford Escort van, F-reg, probably bought at auction. It will have done at least sixty-thousand miles. The van is almost certainly ex-Rediffusion, lightly sprayed over. Their TV engineers tend to hammer their transports so the van should look its age.

'MO. We believe that at least some of the victims were watched for a considerable period of time before any attack and we have positive evidence that in one case the victim was watched from a house opposite. Today we discovered that four of the victims were definitely runners or joggers and three can be traced back to the Totton 10K, a road race in the Southampton area. For those of you who don't know, 10K is six-and-a-quarter miles.

'We have further reason to believe – but we haven't proved it yet – that our man has targeted females running in road races, that he starts at the back of the field among the slower runners, and works his way forward until he spots his chosen victim. As yet we do not know precisely how the victim is chosen nor how the rapist discovers their address.

'The actual attacks have all been very similar. The female is rushed from behind and knocked down as she opens her front door. In all five cases, no one else was at home and we now believe this is because the rapist has studied his victim's movements beforehand.

'The attacks have become increasingly more violent and more frequent. Attack One, the only one not to have been a completed rape, took place in October last year, the second attack was April this year, number three was in September and four and five occurred in the last fortnight.

'This animal', she paused briefly, expecting an objection from behind, 'has progressed from simple rape to add buggery and other sexual offences to his repertoire. Finally, he has been deliberately burning or branding the victims, we now think with a instant soldering gun.

'I'm sorry if that's incomplete. There'll be a full written report ready for the DCS first thing in the morning. Meantime, are there any questions?'

Someone in the back shouted that Wolverhampton Wanderers played in black and amber. Caz thanked him and added, 'And Hull City, Newport AFC, at least two rugby clubs and another dozen non-league soccer sides.'

'Just trying to help . . .'

'It's appreciated. If anyone knows any other clubs, amateur sides and park sides, there'll be a full list on Greavsie's desk, stick the name on that.'

Another voice: DS Lindsell. 'If your man ran in the Totton race, won't he be in the list of runners?'

'*If* he did, yes, Sarge – but any one of eight hundred men.'

'How about we contact each running club and eliminate their members via the club secretary? If the man runs with a club, we will be able to focus in on him pretty quickly. If he's an unattached runner, then we could hit them as our second bet.'

Caz looked out into the room, her confidence still growing, her voice ever stronger. 'I should have said that we have another strong avenue of enquiry which we are intending to follow up tomorrow. There has been a large number of professional photographs taken of the runners in the various Totton races. We have a very good chance of spotting the animal if he indeed did run in the race and finish. WPC Dibben and myself have an appointment with the managing director of the photo company tomorrow.'

The room was now quiet. DI MacInnes stepped up to her side. He whispered, 'Thank-you, Caz', then spoke loudly to the room, his raw accent creeping out against his will. 'Jane Daily died this afternoon. She went into cardiac arrest at sixteen-thirty-eight and was pronounced dead at seventeen-oh-one-hours. She did not regain consciousness at any time subsequent to the rape and battery. It's now a murder. We have one week to get a result. After that, Region comes in. Ah don't have t'tell any of y' how important a result is, do ah?'

Nothing but shuffled chairs. Now Blackside loomed up between the two smaller police officers like a great avenging angel. The lectern light lit him from the chin upwards like a ghoul. He spoke quietly, a bull seal's quietly.

'It's been a long fortnight, *men*, but you are not going to *believe* the next seven days. Before any of you goes home tonight you make sure that your oppos will be in with you before seven o'clock tomorrow morning. There will be *no* excuses and positively no exceptions. The personnel lists are down to DS Lindsell and DS Reid. DI MacInnes and myself will be sharp-ending this one right to the finish. Anyone fucks up this time round, that sharp end is up their arse. Do I make myself *absolutely* clear?'

Eighteen

The Daimler, the smell of leather polish and Valerie, were left in John Street's basement car park. Caz walked home. She needed time to think.

She hadn't spent a dozen nights at Tom MacInnes's gloomy flat. She'd been drunk with him twice, maybe three times; they'd talked about villains, a little bit about life. Tom had started as he meant to go on. Caz was on the couch with her bed-clothes rolled up behind, and a couple of her cases were stacked opposite the bathroom in a tiny cupboard that Tom called his cubby. There was enough room in there to hang her one dress, a track-suit and a couple of jackets. Tom had made everything very impermanent, so why did she feel so bad about moving out?

The rain floated over her in lightweight folds, faintly salten, like cold cobwebs in her hair. She didn't mind the vague cold, and the wet suited her peculiar mood. The street was quiet, almost ill; sullen shops mourning the winter, flickering neons, shuttered doors, the gutters running with drifting streams of thin water, paper debris moving slowly, grabbing at the kerb, fluttering on the hill.

She was bound to go; she had to go. There was a tacit understanding in the nick that the DI had laid out a huge favour when he had put Caz up, but now the rumours were beginning and the jokes were getting heavier and more open. It was time to leave. Sharing with Moira was ideal; there would be no major commitment and the rent wasn't a problem. Their getting on well was a bonus and she'd have company over Christmas. So why did she feel so lousy?

By the time Caz had reached the wide spaces of the Old Steine she was thoroughly wet – the crept-in, chilling wet of drizzle. There was a string of dew drops above her eyes and she rubbed the arm of her jacket across her forehead while she waited to cross the road. Cars slickered by, fithing as spray rayed out from the wheels. Everything seemed to be winter-dark, dirty and soulless. It had been a coolish seventy degrees in Portugal today. Valerie was probably breaking his machine down right now, stripped to his T-shirt and shorts, looking forward to a slow evening, a little grilled fish, some rice, too much wine, a little light conversation. Suddenly she saw a woman there too; laughing, with dark shiny hair, gleaming white teeth, rich brown skin. A flicker of jealousy raced through her as she rushed across the wet street.

In the wrapping rain and darkness, the DI's place could have passed for a Glasgow tenement, sad and hidden in its little side road. When she opened the street door she smelt faint dampness in the communal porch. She shuddered, feeling uncharacteristically sorry for herself. Now her shoes were wet and she could hear them squelch and squeak as she went up the dry stairs. If she hadn't felt so bloody cold, it would almost be funny. She needed to do something, but she really did *not* feel like a run.

She broke through the front door, already stripping off. Her jacket missed the chair she threw it at, partly because she was hopping towards the loo and trying to remove a wet training shoe. The shoe came off and she deftly changed legs, leaving damp impressions of her other foot on the wooden floor. 'Hah! Done it!' she hissed as she crashed through the bathroom door. Her voice echoed awkwardly in the empty room.

She stripped quickly, down to white, almost dry underwear. Her clothes were in a ball as she emerged and she flicked them into the cubby. From her handbag she took a cassette tape, then she looked for Tom MacInnes's stereo. At the last moment it occurred to her to throw the latch on the inside of the door. Tom wasn't likely to be home for another hour but she hadn't quite decided how he'd react if she was working out in bra and pants on his lounge floor when he came in.

The tape was her own compilation, aerobics music: warm-up, stretch, faster stuff, and then grunt music for her stomach and back work. She started with Malcolm McLaren's 'House of the Blue Danube', circling her neck both ways then reaching each arm towards the ceiling to stretch the muscles of her sides. In the soaring, swaying choruses she soared and swung to the ceiling and to the floor in wide sweeps of her arms and with bent and straightened legs. She was feeling a touch better. As McLaren's instrumental finished, she took two hugely deep breaths then stood tall, waiting for the next track, 'Bazooka Jo'. She followed the rhythms of Les Tambours du Bronx, throwing back her elbows at shoulder height, punching out fists and making herself a crucifix, then up high and out wide in an escalating, sexier series of moves. Now she was squatting, taking all her weight on tight, straining quadriceps, still punching, still swinging, getting hotter, loosening up.

Then it finished. She growled.

She did her stomach and back work to David Lee Roth's 'Sensible Shoes', her spine pressed tight into the floor as she reached her elbows to opposite knees, did tight abdominal crunches and knees to elbows with opposite leg extended. She could feel the heat growing in her tightening stomach muscles but she refused to give in and let her back arch away from the floor. It was tough but she survived. She was smiling as she did pelvic tilts. The exercise and the music made her think of Valerie. Everything hurt just enough.

A lot of runners lacked real upper body strength. Caz wanted to be the exception. Her five or six minutes of circuit training – ten press-ups, ten squat thrusts, twenty sit-ups and ten tricep dips – she did to silly music. This tape was 'Monster Mash' and

'Ghostbusters'. Other compilations were even sillier. The silliest and toughest was trying to do a record number of press-ups while listening to John Lennon's 'Cold Turkey'.

But not today. Today, her session was fifty minutes. At the end of it there was sweat on the floor, Caz felt stretched, strong and sexy, and she didn't give a damn about anything. She picked up her jacket, flicked off the door-latch, scampered through to the bathroom and bombed water into a pool of Imperial Leather bath essence. She was singing 'Sensible Shoes' when Tom's key clacked in the lock. She stopped the bath, leaned out to see his face and shouted to him, 'Don't cook, Tom. We're out. My treat and it's already booked!'

Caz emerged from the bathroom's steam after another ten minutes. MacInnes was drinking a Whyte & Mackay. She had spiky damp hair, a look of apology on her face. She smiled softly. 'I hadn't actually booked anywhere, Tom, but it is my treat. Where shall we go?'

MacInnes said nothing but raised his glass; a question.

'Yes, please!' Caz said. As he poured, she suggested Armando's Ristorante. 'You must know it, Tom. We can walk there from here. In the Lanes?'

'I know it,' MacInnes said, 'and you lie far too easily.'

'I'm sorry. I didn't want you to say no.'

'I wouldn't have,' he said. 'You're going to tell me

you're moving out, aren't you? I might as well get a free meal out of it.'

Even Armando's little Italian is quiet at nine o'clock on a winter Tuesday. The DI and the DC sat in a half-lit corner. Caz faced into the room. Tom MacInnes sat opposite her, oblivious of the other diners. The head waiter, Gabrielle, had taken his one night off a week and they were waited on by the owner who knew both of them. Fresh turbot was on the menu. Tom ordered some grilled and Caz matched him. She matched his whisky aperitif too, but then she asked for a bottle of her favourite Chianti Classico Riserva. While they waited for their garlic bread, they talked about the case.

'So what's this man like, Caz?'

'Big, Tom. Very angry. He lives alone. Not poor. He has some money.'

'Is he a runner?'

'He runs but he's not a club runner. If he was in a club he'd be a mixer. This man's a loner.'

'So why ask DS Lindsell to contact club secretaries?'

'Well, I could hardly tell him *not* to, Tom!'

'How big is he? How violent?'

'I'd say huge, Tom. I'd say six-three, six-four, and at least sixteen stone, maybe a lot heavier. Apart from the violence he's shown to the women I'd say he's probably a gentle giant.'

'So he'll come quietly when we find him?'

'I don't think so, Tom. I think he'll fight like shit, maybe even force us to take him out. He's terribly angry about something. He wants to be hurt.'

'Tell me how he does it.'

'He chooses a race. They're advertised in sports shops and in the athletics magazines. He enters in the normal way. He gets there early, has a little wander while it's quiet, then he sits down somewhere to watch the other entrants arrive. Somehow, he picks one from the crowd. Maybe he picks two or three. Before the race, he goes and sits on the kerb a little way back from the start line. Five minutes before the race, the road fills up. There are thin, sharp men at the front, just one or two women. Then there are the cross-trainers, men with heavier frames, obvious muscles, thirty-three, thirty-four minute guys. Then there are the good veteran men, a few more women, then there are the chatterers, the average club men, the good women. He stays sitting on the kerb. Legs pass him. White, pink, brown. He sees feet, trainers, laces. He smells smells. People brush past him now, stepping over his legs. It's getting more crowded. He smells body heat, a waft of perfume. The loudspeaker barks out something. He gets up. He's not quite at the back so he pushes his way out. He feels claustrophobic, more and more angry.

'Suddenly he's free of the crowd. Sunlight hits him in the face. The wind catches his cheeks. He is so relieved. These people! They crowded him, stepped over him, tripped on his feet, glanced down at him, touched his shoulder as they passed. One of them made eye-contact. One of them chose him. He was treated so badly. Someone had to pay.'

The restaurant was warm. Dark grey surrounded

their table. Caz now had her eyes closed. She spoke slowly. Other diners were ghosts in the mist.

'The gun goes off. The racers fly away, one woman with them. Women like me take an extra second to get into their stride. They're with the top vets but will drift back after a mile. People are still walking, watching their feet. The race is fifteen seconds old and those at the back are just approaching the line, shuffling, going from a walk into a jog. He has knelt down; his shoe-lace is undone. He's thirty yards behind the last runner, a little lady with silver hair who can only dream of beating the hour. The crowd are just breaking. He gets up. He gives a sheepish grin and begins to jog steadily after the back markers. He's counting; or he's looking for someone.'

Caz opened her eyes, breathing deeply. MacInnes said nothing. His fingers were over the top of his whisky. She looked into him, her eyes too white, her pupils swollen and black. 'No father,' she said, 'and I think his mother died, summer, last year.'

'What?' MacInnes said.

'No paternal control, it's classic. The father either left or died a long time ago. The rapes look planned, which means we have to move backwards from the Brown attack, that gives us June, July last year. The anger suggests loss. I think his mother.'

'That's profiling?'

'Some of it, Tom. Some of it I just know.'

MacInnes shook his head. 'Don't ever say that to Blackside, Caz.'

There was nothing else to say.

The garlic bread arrived, delivered by Armando's grandson, eighteen and dark with a cedilla of hair on his forehead like a young John Wayne. He crashed into their gloom like a shattering glass, winking at Caz. 'Il Grigio, right?' he said, his accent absolutely English south coast.

'Dark 'n' red,' Caz replied with a smile, just as another diner raised a hand to him.

'Uno momento, Signor,' the waiter said, his arm raised, straight from Naples. He winked again at Caz, poured them both a half-glass, then left.

'How does he know where they live?' MacInnes said.

'I'm not sure, Tom. Maybe he follows them home from the race.'

'Perhaps,' MacInnes said. 'But he'd have to be bloody good and pretty lucky to do it without being seen and without losing them.'

'Well, how else could he know?'

'He has their addresses,' MacInnes said flatly.

'Before he picks them?'

'Somehow.'

'Every race is slightly different,' Caz said, thinking hard. 'The Totton takes entries on the day. They charge a pound extra for the privilege. They have big tables laid out with entry forms and lots of pens.'

'He could simply watch someone filling in their form?'

'I guess so, but it seems a bit unlikely. I'm sure I'd be aware if someone was trying to read my address.'

'Just a thought . . .'

'Jill Brown and Irene Stubbs wouldn't have

entered on the day. The Running Sisters had arranged a trip down there. They'd've entered early to be certain of a place.'

'What about the other three?'

'Can't say yet, Tom. I have a feeling that Amanda Fleet may have entered and forgotten. That happens when people enter early. She said she'd never run in a Totton but DS Mason from Shirley told me she'd entered.'

'So if he gets their address from the race he must be . . .'

'Intercepting their mail?'

'A postman?'

'Or has access to computer records?'

'The race director?'

'I met him yesterday. He's about five-nine and he has his own hair.'

'Who else?'

'There's the results man, a chap called Dean Richard. I know him from races. He's well off six feet and he isn't bald. DS Mason was going to see him last night.'

'And?'

'There's the race photographers. A company called Boxx Brownie does Totton. I met the owner yesterday, chap called Gareth Boxx. He's a six-footer with a pig-tail. I'm over there tomorrow. We can check out the staff then.'

The fish came, lumpen, thick white flesh, a skein of buttered brown. It was so soft it fell away from their forks, a puff of flavour escaping. Caz took a mouthful; the moist white gently lifted from the bone and squeezed into the curve of her fork. She closed her lips on ecstacy. This was very serious food. She smiled at Tom.

Nineteen

It was an absolute black out over the sea. Caz woke to the insistent bree-bree-bree of her runner's watch alarm. She let it burr, reminding herself that this was Wednesday, it wasn't even half-past five yet and she was going out for a long run. She could feel the poisonous remains of last night's amber and red drink, and once again she thought about giving up drinking and going for the national squad. She could feel air bristling round her face, morning cold; but she suddenly said, 'Sod it!' and rolled herself upright and on to the floor. She was still in last night's underwear and it occurred to her that she was turning into a slob. 'Come on, Flood,' her self-coach whispered. 'Get yourself awake, stretch, get out there and kick some arse.'

Green light from a clock radio flickered numbers on to her face as she stood tall, then took a quick, deep breath and tiptoed into the bathroom. In there, she pulled the short string of Tom MacInnes's shaving light and looked into the mirror to assess Kathryn Flood, eight hundred metre runner, 2:00:03.89 best, now running 2:15s at the height of summer. 'You need a kicking, Kathryn Eff,' she said quietly. 'A pull through with a Christmas Tree, a month as a vegetarian and a fortnight's winter training in Lanzarote with Linford Christie.' She cleaned her teeth and splashed cold water into her face. When she looked up again she was pink.

Ten minutes later Caz was going out through the street door wearing a bright yellow 'Sub-4' thermal top and calf-length grey bottoms. She had white gloves in her waist-band and an orange-yellow reflective waistcoat in her hand. Ten miles and back to the flat for six o'clock was her intention. Her brain had suggested eight miles in the same time and she had to politely tell it to mind its own business. Wednesday was a tempo run and a schedule is a schedule.

She set off gently without too serious a stretch. After three minutes, she picked up the pace to something around seven minute miling, and headed out of town along the high cliff road past Roedean school. Seven minutes later, she was another mile away, hearing her own breath on an empty night, ducking her eyes from the only car to pass coming her way. Below her, the sea was darkly silver; faint, white-topped waves visible occasionally where land-light drifted out or clinking yachts reflected on to the water.

Now Caz knew exactly why she ran. Blood coursed through her, her legs swishing economically as she muscled smoothly east. Her head had now cleared and as she reached her half-way point she thought about last night.

Tom MacInnes had told her that moving out was utterly sensible. She knew straight away that he had wanted her to stay. He explained that DCS Blackside was aware of the situation and sympathetic to it. He also told her how the DCS and those that he conferred with had suggested that Caz should now find her own way in the world. Would she be waiting until the weekend? he asked. Yes, Caz had said.

'Maybe we'll eat out Friday,' he suggested.

'I'd like that,' Caz said.

She was running back towards Brighton now and as she breasted one rise she saw the lights of the town and the amber glow above it in a dark purple sky. The beauty of it made her run that fraction harder and she put in a good six-and-a-half minute mile.

When they had got back from Armando's, Tom had asked her to pour two Whyte & MacKays. He had actually said, 'Make mine too large and make yours a small one.' He put a vinyl on his old stereo – 'Rhapsody in Blue' – and they talked into the small hours listening to that and a series of classical LPs, most of which Caz vaguely recognised but couldn't name. Tom had told her she was a Philistine and that she should get herself properly educated but then, in the next breath, slightly darker, he decided, 'Ah, maybe not, lass. We can't know everything.'

He had asked her about her boyfriend. When was Valerie coming back? She said she didn't know exactly when, or exactly what their relationship would be anyway. He slugged more whisky as he said he understood.

'Did you know I was married once?' he said quietly. 'I was still on a beat then. Ma wife's name was Elizabeth. Lizzie MacInnes. When we divorced, she went back to live in the islands. She married a crofter who still spoke Gaelic. I never bothered after that. I'm celibate, Caz. Have been for fifteen years.'

He had looked so small then, so frail. She had felt deeply bad about leaving him on his own. He had poured another big whisky and got up for his bed. As he left he told her he was retiring within eighteen months. Unless the drink got him first.

She wound down over the last half-mile, stuttering to a halt by the pier. She stopped to stretch her calves, leaning on white railings, then stretched her quad muscles with the railings as support. She heard the wet chimes of six a.m., heard the swishing of the sea. Tom's flat was three hundred yards away. She walked there, letting her sweat cool in the breeze.

Twenty

Caz had been in work forty minutes when Moira got in ten minutes early. She had finished working with Holmes and had already got a print-out. The two of them were in Valerie's Daimler heading out of town by twenty-five-to-nine.

They met DS Mason at a drive-in McDonald's in Southampton's Shirley High Street. He said he usually ate his breakfast there. Caz didn't even bother to mention his 10K time. He talked while eating an Egg McMuffin followed by Hash Browns. They drank coffees that made Jenny Griffin's flask seem OK.

'This Dean Richard guy should be in the force,' he told them. 'He's got a database that MI6 would be proud of and he can play around with it to produce whatever information you need. I've got a list of Jill Brown's races and times. If she gets any quicker she'll be beating me soon.'

'She's trying to get her weight down,' Caz explained.

Mason missed the sarcasm completely. 'Your Mrs Stubbs ran once, in the Totton just before she was attacked. And I checked Amanda Fleet. She was on his computer. She signed up for the Seventh Totton 10K but never ran it.'

'Three from five,' Caz said. 'We should've run the other names too.'

'I did,' Mason said quickly. 'I had a word with intelligence. Your murder victim – Jane Daily – she ran in the last Totton, the first Sunday in October. The other one – Jackie Engels? – she's never been in a Totton but she did run in the Victory Five at Portsmouth. That was two days before she was attacked.'

'I *knew* they were runners!' Moira said.

Caz didn't even bother to laugh. 'So, it's definitely runners being attacked.'

'And a runner doing it,' Mason said.

Caz looked right at the DS, her face brimming. 'Then we'll have the bastard soonest!' She stumbled when she heard her MacInnesism slip out and she glanced at Moira.

Moira was eating half of one of the hash browns and hadn't noticed. She had her mouth full when she spoke. 'Maybe Boxx will have a picture of our Duncan Goodhew. That'll give us a number, name and address.'

'If only life was that easy,' Caz said. She drank her coffee. It tasted like the Solent on a bad day.

Boxx Brownie had small premises close to the back of town centre, a stone's throw from another Mac's and not far from Debenhams. The tiny reception area was covered from floor to ceiling with photographs; one wall with standard wedding scenes, soft-focus muted shots of couples, pretty page boys in silk, another with industrial Cibachromes, and a third with good quality black-and-whites of fledgling stars still wide-eyed, looking for their big break. The receptionist was better looking than anyone on the wall. She said good morning. 'Welcome to Boxx Brownie. *Now you can rest. We shoot the best.*'

'Is that the company motto?' Peter said with a gleam in his eye.

'Oh, no,' the receptionist said, smiling back. 'I make a new one up every day. I'm doing marketing at tech.'

'It's really catchy,' Peter said. Behind him, Moira made the sign for wanker.

'Thank you. *Put you at your ease. Always here to please!*'

'Brilliant!' Mason said. 'Here to see Gareth Boxx?' The girls were cringing.

'*Must be the Fuzz. I'll give Gaz a buzz.*' She smiled, a Pepsodent smile.

Moira and Caz exchanged bemused glances. DS Mason was in raptures, already thinking of one hundred and one rhymes ending 'uck'.

'Will he be long?' Caz asked sharply. She caught the receptionist's eyes and with a severe look said, 'If your answer rhymes, you're under arrest.'

'I'll just buzz through,' she said.

Peter was still entranced. '*We'll be at a loss if we can't see the boss!*' he said. The little secretary grinned all over and sat forward, offering her red-bound cleavage to him. There was a distinct possibility that Mason was going to become delirious.

Caz whispered from just behind his right ear. '*Keep an eye on the clock and a lid on your cock*!'

The intercom crackled. 'Ah, Mr Boxx! Inspector Mason and his help to see you . . . Send them straight up? Yes, Sir!' She leaned away from the intercom and looked up, eyes only for Peter. 'It's through that door there, first left and just up the stairs. Mr Boxx will be waiting at the top.'

They left.

Gareth Boxx was waiting as promised. He was dressed in low-slung designer jeans with a wide leather belt, and a white, long-collared shirt. A silk cravat was knotted at his neck and dangled loosely down his chest like a gypsy. He looked vaguely 'sixties'. 'Good morning!' he said, smiling. 'Some decent tea?'

They went through to a small room. There were three chairs on their side of a four-by-two desk and no room to even pick up a cat, never mind swinging one. 'Small is beautiful,' Boxx explained. He looked at Moira. 'Beautiful as in small overheads, as in profitable.'

The walls may have been cream underneath but they were almost perfectly covered with work: glamour shots, women with dilated pupils and pouting lips, hunky men with perfect bodies, some Hasselblad proofs with two-and-a-half inch squares laid four by three, various certificates, one *Sun* front page. In frames were a couple of beautifully moody moors scenes, prize winners with *Wuthering Heights* clouds etched black across the sky.

Mason looked at them admiringly. 'Red filter jobs?'

'And then burned in some more in the darkroom,' Boxx said.

'Very gothic,' Mason said.

'D'you like them, Peter? That one was a Canon AE–1, thirty-five mill, HP5, shot with a twenty-eight mill lens. That one there I did with an A1 and a standard lens. I've got lenses now that cost ten times what my complete kit cost in the good old days, but my early stuff is still the best.'

Peter stood to look closer at the moors shots. 'The integrity is excellent.'

'Bog standard paper too. The enlarger was Czechoslovakian. I think it cost about a hundred quid.'

'I've got one of them at home.' Peter said knowingly. 'For my competition stuff I use the club's kit, but I only do thirty-five mill. I'm just a poor copper.'

'I used to be poor too,' Boxx said. 'But then I decided not to be. I ended up with this place, a modelling business and a bit of work for the nationals.'

'Is this *Sun* front page you, then?'

'Fergy showing too much leg, yeah. That was up in Romsey. She was opening a swimming pool.'

'Nice bit of leg,' Peter said appreciatively.

'That was the least revealing shot I took,' Boxx said casually. 'I was lying on the floor with a five hundred mill lens set up, waiting for her to get out of her car. I got a couple of her breakfast but the paper wouldn't go with them.'

'I like it,' Peter said. 'How'd you get in with the *Sun*?'

'Er, could we . . .?' Caz squeezed in a word. She showed a patient face.

'Oh, I am sorry,' Boxx said to Caz. 'Professional pride. I quite forgot myself.' He spoke again to the DS. 'Ask me about the *Sun* later.' Then he looked at Caz, properly this time. He smiled. 'You know, you've got an interesting face; nice bones. Have you ever modelled?'

Caz bit. 'I'm not a bit too pasty, then?'

He remembered. 'Well, nothing that make-up couldn't sort out, toot-sweet.' Caz folded her arms. 'No, really,' he said gently, 'you've got your own look. I'd call it pinched beauty.'

Moira shifted in her chair and Caz felt a little rush, a silly victory. She was trying to think 'bollocks' but she heard herself saying thank you to Boxx.

'No problem. I only say it like it is. Beauty, drama and class, remember?'

Caz smiled. 'Yesterday you said Moira was beautiful.'

Boxx protested. 'But she is, Caz, she is!' Briefly he sounded like a gesturing Frenchman. 'Moira is a classically beautiful woman – look: good eyes, good bone structure, great lips.' He spoke to her now instead of about her. She was blushing painfully. 'You must know you are beautiful, Moira.' He looked back to Caz. 'But sometimes beauty is not enough. There needs to be something else, an imperfection, a difference, some uniqueness. Your friend is beautiful, you are attractive. Tell me, which would you rather be?'

Caz didn't answer. The photographer's directness was intrusively intimate and she felt disturbed. She knew what he meant but she didn't like him understanding her so well.

DS Mason changed the subject. 'The, er, lady runners? We were hoping . . .'

'Oh yes,' Boxx said casually, as if he hadn't just fondled the two women. 'Of course. You've got their names and dates of birth?'

The firm's computer was in another room, this one splashed with some great finishing shots from races, eyeballs-out veterans, winner and second neck and neck. They found three references to Jill Brown. They had pictures of her in two Tottons but had missed the one in the middle. They had Irene Stubbs coming in and breaking fifty-seven minutes with a huge smile on her face and her hand raised in triumph. Seeing their lit faces, Caz felt a little surge of anger against the rapist and, for some reason, against Gareth Boxx.

The photographer used an intercom and called for someone called Sally. Sally barked back and he gave her some neg numbers. Minutes later she was barking again. 'We've got a print of Brown, I'll have to do you one for Stubbs.'

'Quick as y'can, Sally. All right?'

'You know I'm doing the specials for Drapers, don't you?'

'Just do it, Sally. Now.' Loud. He sounded suddenly ruthless.

'Thanks for that,' Caz said.

Boxx waved at her inconsequently. 'It'll be half-an-hour. What else d'you want to know?'

'There is something else, but I'm not sure if you'll be able to help us.'

'If you don't ask, I definitely can't.'

'We were wondering about characters. People that stand out. The very small or the very tall, people in silly outfits, that sort of thing . . .'

'Wondering what?'

'If you or your staff would remember individuals. If you had a description, might you be able to say if a person had run in one of your races?'

'Say "thinnish, in running kit", you're dead. How distinctive is this person?'

'Tall, six-foot-two to six-six, very big and heavy, probably completely bald or wearing a bobble-hat which might be black and amber.'

'A man?'

'Unless you know of any twenty-stone bald women about six-foot three.'

Boxx looked deliberately blank. 'Nothing comes to mind. The only name that rings my bell at the moment is Quasimodo.'

'It's not a problem,' Caz said. 'It was a long-shot, anyway. We'll get him the hard way. It'll take longer, that's all.'

'Get him?'

'We'd like to talk to someone with that description, yes.'

'Your rapist?'

'A material witness,' Caz said.

'And you think this big guy has run in one of my races? The Totton 10K?'

'Perhaps.'

'He's a suspect?'

'We can't say that, Mister Boxx.' She was unconvincing.

'You think he's your rapist!' Boxx hissed.

Caz stiffened and spoke formally. 'We have a description of a man whom we would like to interview, Mister Boxx. And we would be grateful if you could check your records. If necessary we would like to work our way through any photographs you have on file.'

'You don't mean that!' Boxx said.

'I'm afraid we do.'

'Twenty thousand photographs; fifty, maybe sixty thousand negs?'

Caz thought, 'shit', but said, 'A mere bagatelle, Sir.'

'What about my business? If you take my negatives and prints, I'm stuffed. What about the loss of trade. Will I be compensated?'

DS Mason interrupted. 'This is a *murder* enquiry, Mr Boxx.'

Boxx turned. 'I thought you were looking for a rapist. I read—'

Mason stopped him. 'Miss Brown and Mrs Stubbs were sexual attacks, but we now have two further assaults to check out with you. We are particularly interested in Mrs Jane Daily who ran in the latest Totton 10K.'

'I can look . . .'

Caz spoke up. 'Mr Boxx, does your company photograph the Victory Five?'

'Yes, we do. And the name is Gareth.'

'OK, Gareth. Then we're also looking for a Mrs Jackie Engels. Her address is in Worthing. She ran forty-two minutes in the Victory.'

Boxx went back to the computer, muttering that they could have asked him earlier. He found Engels' file and a short one on Daily. He buzzed Sally with two more numbers. She was now in a foul mood. He turned back to his guests.

'But we don't appear to have anything much on your Jane Daily, I'm afraid. If she did run in the Totton we may have got her, but the shot could have been poor – a hand in front of her face, poor focus, something like that. If you can get her finishing time, we can work off that. She might be in a shot of someone else who was just in front of her or just behind.'

Caz asked, 'Can you list names that finished around a time?'

'Not directly,' Boxx said, 'but I can ring Dean Richards or look up the times in the various results booklets. I get most of them sent to me.'

There was a light rap on the door and a callow

youth entered, looking embarrassed, almost to the point of fear. This was Timmy, Boxx's YTS trainee. According to Gareth Boxx, he made good tea. 'Timmy's a bit nervous,' Boxx explained. 'He was done twice for nicking cars when he was fourteen, but I thought I'd give him a chance. Anyone who can hot-wire a Cortina ought to be able to look after a photo-lab. He's all right. Aren't you Timmy?'

'Yes, Mr Boxx,' the boy said. 'Can I go now?'

'On yer bike then, Timmy. Go give Sally a hand.'

As the boy left, Boxx shouted after him: '*Darkroom lights*!' He turned back to his guests. 'The first week he was here, he tried too hard. He walked into the darkroom and we lost a film. I was going to sack him on the spot but he was like a lame dog. In the end, I just couldn't do it! I chewed his balls off, though. He won't make that mistake again.'

The tea had been made with filtered water; real tea (not bags), and there were cups on the tray, not the usual mugs. There was also a bowl of sugar and a jug of milk – definitely not the typical industrial offering. Boxx said it was his one weakness. Tea and coffee should start out with the very best ingredients, be made correctly and served decently. 'Timmy may never end up as David Bailey,' he said flippantly, 'but he'll know how to make good tea.'

Moira poured and Boxx spoke with a softer, more placatory tone. He was thinking, couldn't he come to some arrangement with them about the photographs, something that would suit both sides? 'My staff and I know half the names and three-quarters of the faces of the people in our races. We also know how to look at a negative and see the print. Thursday is a quiet day. Today and tomorrow we could sort out all the negs and prints. If you don't want to take our word for it, we could at least pre-sort and make things a bit quicker for you when you eventually start your search. Maybe you could do the work here? We could put a room aside.'

Mason said he didn't see a problem. Caz said she'd speak to her DI for approval. 'Great!' Boxx said. 'The four of us and Sally could blitz the whole lot in forty-eight hours. What d'you say?'

'I say we'll get confirmation as soon as possible, Gareth.'

They were gone at twelve o'clock with two good pictures of Jill Brown – the slightly looser-fleshed version just before her attack, and a sharper, firmer, feistier one a year later. They had a victorious seven by five starring Irene Stubbs, and one of Jackie Engels finishing on the running track at Mountbatten Stadium alongside another woman sporting an equally wide and satisfied smile and, more importantly, a blue club shirt. As they were leaving, Caz and Peter shared recognition of the club colours: 'Portsmouth Joggers!' They had an address of Jackie's running partner too, courtesy of a promptly paid bill and an asterisk on Boxx's computer. It was time to ring in.

Twenty-One

Peter Mason was going for a pie and a pint; the girls decided to skip. They had left Gareth Boxx with the job of producing photographs of all the runners from five minutes before to two minutes after the finishes of Jill Brown, Irene Stubbs and Jane Daily. There would be numbers, faces, names and addresses but, Boxx explained, many of the people around them would be the same; most runners were fairly consistent with their times.

They were in reasonable spirits driving back. The investigation still had legs and they didn't mind working with DS Mason. True, his brain was in his trousers, but that was the male norm, so they were fairly comfortable with the fact. 'Hard in the cock, soft in the head,' Moira said matter-of-factly as if the single sentence summed up men and women. When Caz asked if that referred to Moira's Billy as well, Moira said, 'Oh, let's not start all that again.'

They were parked at John Street just after half-past two. They went upstairs, checked in and picked up their messages, all boring except for one mysterious 071 number for Caz to ring, ASAP. She stuck the Post-it on the back of her hand as they went through.

The War Room was almost empty, one DC writing with a dry marker on a huge white board, a civilian typing in one corner. When they asked, the DC said they were hitting Worthing with everything and DI MacInnes had gone to Rediffusion's HQ to talk about their vans. On one wall were pictures of Jill, Irene, Amanda Fleet, Jackie Engels and Jane Daily. Above were harsh titles: ASSAULT, RAPE, RAPE, RAPE, MURDER. Below the pictures were cautionary notes about the living victims' right to anonymity. There was an artist's impression of the animal – an ox of a man, as big as Blackside but ugly, evil, with his mashed, bald face and pudgy rough fingers. He had a striped hat in one hand. When Caz looked at him, she could feel him, see the whites of his eyes.

Moira went to get them coffees while Caz nipped along to see the DCS. His door was open when she got there and he waved her in before she knocked. For once there was no bull-horn 'Come!' to shatter the calm. 'Five o'clock!' he said loudly into the phone as he put it down and looked up. 'Flood!' he then said amiably. 'Take a pew.'

Caz laid out the facts so far, clearly and precisely. She explained that by ten tomorrow morning they would have a couple of hundred photographs and a five-to-one chance of the animal's address. Then she explained that she needed two days unless they hit lucky early on. 'To look at all Boxx's stuff, Sir. We expect him to have one or more shots of the rapist.'

Blackside fed her questions. Exactly what was the race connection?

'The attacked women were all runners, Sir. Four had entered the Totton 10K road race, three actually ran in it. The three that ran all clocked similar times and were attacked soon after the race.'

Were they followed home?

'We think not, Sir, but we can't rule that out. We think maybe he had access to names and addresses. DS Mason is talking to the Royal Mail this afternoon but he says his house is on the same round as Clive Parker and he's never had a gorilla for a postman.'

Who was Clive Parker?

'I'm sorry, Sir. The race director for the last four Totton races. They run it twice a year.'

A suspect?

'No, Sir. Totally wrong height and looks. Got a steady office job. Couldn't get to the crime scenes even if he wanted to.'

She went into more detail, explained about race photography, about the results computers, Dean Richard.

Him?

'Looks quite like Parker, Sir. And he works down in Poole, nine to five. Hasn't missed a day's work in seven years.'

'And it's not Postman Pat?'

'We're checking, Sir, but we don't think so.'

When Caz got back to the War Room, Moira was

waiting for her with two plastic mugs of mid-brown. She had her shoeless feet up on Greavsie's desk and was innocently showing a lot of leg. The dry-marker DC was having trouble concentrating and Caz gave Moira a nudge. As her legs swept down from the desk-top she revealed even more and grinned, just a little sheepish. A fax machine beeped.

Caz went over. The shiny sheet of paper had 'DI MacInnes' scribbled across the top, the name followed by a series of car numbers. On the bottom he had written, 'These are all the Foxtrot registrations. Echo, Golf, Hotel to follow.'

'Here we go, Mo!' Caz said. 'You grab E-G-H and sit on them. I'll take this lot through to control and call up the Owner's Index on the PNC.'

Moira yelped. 'Hang on a minute, boss. There's more F's coming through.'

In fact there were forty-six ex-Rediffusion Escorts all originally with F Vehicle Registration Marks. Two had been bought by company engineers as transport for the wife; three had been written off in crashes. The rest had been sold through an intermediary at ADT Car Auctions. They produced thirty-six addresses, most north of Manchester, four in Wales, ten either in London or South of the M4. There was an address in Woking, another in Basingstoke, one in Esher. Two more VRMs had been listed as stolen.

Caz wrote out a slip for Intelligence and instructions for each relevant force to check out the owners of each pinpointed van. She was going to get the orders signed off by the DCS but, before that, she asked the computer for a cross-check with the Suspect Vehicles List and another linking the thirty-six owners with the Criminal Names Index. There was an ABH last known in Watford, and an Indecent Assault. Woking. The ABH was down as five foot ten, the IA from Woking was six foot two. Shit!

She ran down the hall to Blackside's office, knocking and bursting in without thinking. The DCS was picking his nose. 'Sir!' she said, not even noticing. 'I think we might have found him. Peter Edwards, aged twenty-eight, address in Woking. He's six-feet two, got an F-Reg ex-Rediff van and was done for an Indecent Assault in 1989!'

Blackside had something rolled up between two fingers. 'Picture, Flood?'

'I came straight away, Sir. I'll go back and call it up.'

She left, faintly pink, went back to Control and called down Edwards' record. He had been done in November 1989 for molesting a teenage girl at a bus stop. She read his description – six-two, fifteen-and-a-half stone, but that was three years ago; a borderline possible. He'd had hair then, too.

She went back to Blackside's office, more controlled this time, and gave him the fuller details. Blackside told her to action the other addresses through Control and then get as many of the door-to-door lads pulled in as soon as poss. He looked at the faxed photograph. Caz was just about to go.

'Flood?'

'Sir?'

'Did you look at this bloke?'

'Only quickly, Sir.'

'Is it him?'

Caz took the picture. She felt it. She looked into Peter Edwards' eyes. He looked back at her, grey, black and white, unmoving. She stared. 'No, Sir.'

'I didn't think so, either, Flood. But we'll hit the shit anyway.'

'Yes, Sir!' Caz said. She left to do her job.

Control radioed out and a block of DCs and PCs squawked back, fighting for air space. Door-to-door on a wet December afternoon isn't exactly fun, and being told to finish early and get back in was the police equivalent of winning the pools. She heard Billy Tingle's voice, DS Reid, DC Bramshaw, then she heard Greavsie asking if it would be all right for him to stay out just a bit longer as he wasn't quite soaked through yet. The desk-sergeant never flinched. 'Thank you, 089. Message passed to DCS Blackside fifteen-thirty-nine hours.'

'Cheers, George,' Greavsie said. 'I'll be there for four o'clock.'

By four o'clock, Blackside had arranged for local beat PCs to check every one of the ten southern addresses. He wanted to know who lived there, was he a big bloke, was he bald? The locals were warned not to go directly in, simply to suss out the van owner and his house. Meanwhile they were going to go in on Edwards mob-handed.

The lads were all in by five-past four, the

grape-vine rampant from Caz to Moira to the white-board DC and then virally through the crowd. By the time Greavsie had arrived, the word was that a six-foot-six Ed Petersen, bald Swedish sailor, was holed up in a hotel in Southsea, probably armed, possibly with hostages. The liar who had started that one was idly picking at his nails with a pen-knife.

Blackside strode in at ten-past, a gruff nod to DS Lindsell and then up on to the stage. He stopped at the lectern. Everyone shut up except Greavsie who was just coming to grips with the Petersen details. There was an awful double-second while everything focused on the talker. The man near to him looked away, red-eared.

Jim realised, a second too late. Blackside bellowed. 'Greavsie! You arsehole! Shut the fuck up!' The DC flinched, his shoulders ducking. He looked up, red-faced. 'Right!' Blackside said, his voice still booming. 'We may just have us our lad. Either way we soon will have.' Every face looked to the stage.

Brighton sent three cars, ten men, plus Caz and Moira. They were meeting two more cars, a DCI and three detectives from the local station. By six-fifteen they had men ready in the back gardens both sides of Edwards' house, cars both ends of the street. The grey Escort van was parked outside the terrace, its tax out-of-date, two bald tyres, and dirty windows. Caz and Moira were in the back of Greavsie's Sierra as it backed slowly up to the van. Greavsie was wound right up. So was Moira. Caz could only manage 'vaguely interested', having already decided that Edwards wasn't their man. When Blackside's Scorpio screamed into the close seconds later, she sighed. When three beefy DCs piled out and ran to the front door, she groaned. They knocked, the door opened. The DCs moved quickly. Then Edwards appeared, struggling, shuffling, an apparently broken leg encased in dirty plaster. End of drama.

Edwards was brought out, seedy, sunken eyed, scowling. His shirt was stained with some unknown food, his dark hair lank and dirty. The hair was bad enough, but the dirty scribbled-on cast on his leg, even worse. Blackside was now out of the car, half-way down the path. He turned away in disgust.

'Book the little shit!' Blackside bawled, waving his arms. 'Book the twat for something, anything – for being ugly. I don't care what, but book him.' He started walking back to his car, then he turned again. 'And check out that fucking plaster cast. I want the signature of the artist or he's locked up!'

Blackside walked to Greavsie's car, anger red across his face. He smiled darkly at the driver. 'They're going to need a hand in there, Greaves,' he said. Jim looked up. Blackside leered at him. 'Go sort 'em out, will yer? I'll drive this back. Make sure you get my car back to Brighton fer nine o'clock.'

They were back at John Street for eight o'clock to find an anxious Tom MacInnes by the station sergeant's desk, twitching, waiting for the news. Caz nodded discreetly to him, then pretended to be doing something important. The DI tilted his jaw into a question mark and the DCS shook his head. 'Nothing doing, Tom. Edwards was a little toe-rag but he wasn't the one we wanted.' He waved for the DI to follow him as he walked towards his office.

Moira looked tired and was miming 'Drink?' when her Billy came through. 'Oh, hi-yah, Bill,' she said demurely. 'Caz and I were just going over to the Grapes.' Built in was, 'Are you coming?'

'Great!' said Billy. The three of them booked out and left.

'So how's life, Billy?' Caz asked, being polite as they waited at the bar.

'Twenty-two days without a ciggie!' he said proudly.

'Sent all your clothes to the dry-cleaner's yet?'

'What for?'

'When you start to notice the cigarette smell, Bill, yer getting better.'

'Oh, I notice,' Billy said. 'I just haven't got the money for the cleaning.'

They sat down. Moira had bought the drinks: orange juice for herself, a whisky and ginger for Caz, a pint of bitter for her boyfriend. She was disappointed about Peter Edwards. 'Don't be, Mo,' Caz said. 'At least we'll have put the fear of God into him. That should slow him down a bit.'

'I was just sort of hoping that we'd found him. And that we'd get the collar.'

'A pat on the back, maybe.'

Billy spoke. 'A couple more black 'n' ambers for you, Caz. Esher Rugby Club and a Sunday football side called Wasps who play in the Camberley League.'

'They on Greavsie's list?'

'Yeah, I put 'em on this afternoon.'

Esher. There was a Rediffusion van logged for Esher . . .

'You sort out that urgent personal, Caz?'

Caz was thinking. She looked at Moira. 'What?'

'You had a message, Caz, remember?' Moira explained. 'Ring this number – very, very urgent. You stuck the Post-it on the back of your hand.'

'I'd forgotten,' Caz said. She was still thinking about Esher. She fumbled in a jacket pocket, coming out with pens, a packet of three, a spare hair-band and some loose change. In the other pocket was her warrant card and the yellow slip. She read the 071 number and the message. 'In your interest you ring us. Urgent!' There was a contact name, D. K. Snow, and an extension. Caz swigged her whisky, took a five-pound note from her purse and passed it to Moira. 'Get 'em in, Mo. I better go use the phone.' It looked like Moira was going to protest, but Caz got her retaliation in first. 'Five minutes, Mo. Is all. Talk to Billy.' With that she was gone.

The phone wasn't exactly private, a small cream machine on the end of the lounge bar, but this was the best time to use it; the day shifts had finally crawled home to their wives, those on lates were still working. She leaned defensively against a wall, dropped 50p into the slot and punched digits.

'News International.'

There hadn't even been one ring. Caz wasn't ready.

'News International,' the voice said again.

She recovered. 'I've been asked to ring a D. K. Snow.'

'Which paper?'

'What?'

'D. K. Snow. Which paper? Do you have an extension?'

Caz spelled out the number.

'That's a *Sun* number,' the disembodied voice said patiently. 'Putting you through.' There were about three bars of the middle of some awkward classical piece. Before Caz could recognise it, it broke and someone said, 'Features.'

'I'm trying to get hold of a D. K. Snow.'

'Debbie's gone home for the day. Can I help?' The voice sounded light and friendly. Red hair, Caz thought. Then she thought, 'Gotham City, Jimmy Olsen'.

She was smiling, but Jimmy Olsen wouldn't know. 'My name is Caz Flood,' she said. 'I'm from Brighton. I got this message to ring. It said it would be in my interest.'

'Is Caz Kathryn? The good-looking policewoman that landed that plane in the sea? The Girl Who Saved Brighton? You must be. I'm Debbie's evening cover, Dick Charge. The paper would like to do something on you. We were getting worried. We thought maybe the *Mirror* or the *Star* had got to you. Listen, can I call you back?'

Caz looked down at the phone. Across the top was a piece of dirty paper taped down well, but fraying at the edges like an old Elastoplast. 'This phone doesn't take incoming calls.'

'No problem. I'll give you a number. Ring it in five minutes and reverse the charges. I'll bell Debbie. She'll be expecting your call.' He rattled off an 081 number, then repeated it. Then he asked if Caz had a pen. 'Oh, silly me!' he added before she could speak. 'You're a police officer; you're probably taping everything I'm saying.' Caz managed a little laugh. He wished her good luck and put the phone down.

Caz walked back to Moira and Billy. She picked up her whisky and looked vacantly at Moira.

'Well?' Moira said.

'Well what?'

'Well, what was the mystery number?'

'The *Sun*,' Caz said. 'Apparently, you're looking at The Woman Who Saved Brighton.' She drank her whisky – most of it, Moira had bought a double with her money – then she leaned back, loose-muscled, wondering what Deborah Snow was going to have to say for herself. The earlier whisky had blunted her body's needle-points; this one was hot in her belly and buzzing out through her. Caz felt all right.

'So what's the *Sun* want with an anorexic dipso?' Moira challenged.

'Caz ain't anorexic!' Billy said quickly. Moira flashed brown eyes at him. He wilted and muttered, 'Well not really . . .'

Moira still looked daggers. She told Billy to get some more drinks in.

As he got up to escape to the bar, Caz told Moira she didn't know what Snow wanted. She was going to ring them back in a couple of minutes, she said, and why was Moira being so horrible to Billy?

'I wasn't being horrible. I was just keeping him in line.'

'Keeping him in line, Mo? I'm surprised you haven't got a ring through his bloody nose!'

Moira was unrepentant. 'I only gave him a smack because he fancies you.'

'Everyone fancies me, Moira. *Except* Billy. If he drooled any more over you, you'd drown. You know that.'

Moira grinned. 'It's nice to make sure, though, isn't it?'

'No,' Caz said.

'What d'you mean, no?'

'I wouldn't want that much power. Power corrupts, remember?'

'You'd rather *not* have it?'

'I'd rather not need it.'

'Yer mad. What's the alternative?'

'Equality?' Caz suggested weakly.

'We'll never have that. We take what we can, when we can. For every DCI Lank there's three Billys. I like my Billy.'

'Pussy-whipped is too accurate a phrase,' Caz said. She stood up.

'Some of us, it's all we got,' Moira said.

Billy was coming back. Caz got up to go to the phone. As she passed Billy she touched him on the shoulder sympathetically, sighing quietly. She waved back at Moira without looking and went through to the lounge.

Deborah Snow took the call, interrupting the operator's standard spiel. Immediately she spoke as if she and Caz were age-old friends.

'Dick Charge said that you prefer to be called Caz. Great name! I was *so* impressed by what you did, landing that plane. One up for women, eh?'

'I just aimed for the softest thing I could see.'

'Oh, I'm sure. They told me you were modest. We need to meet.'

'Why, exactly?'

'We'd like to run a special on you,' Snow said. 'I've seen your picture; you're pretty. We've got an England runner, glamorous, who does something incredibly brave ...'

'I got my England vest when I was seventeen!'

'You've run for England, yes? That's good enough for me!'

'And I wasn't brave. I had no choice.'

'We'd like to offer you quite a lot of money.'

'What for?'

'Your story. An extended interview. Some photos. You know, you could do the image of policewomen a power of good. Half our readers think WPCs are all butch.'

'Dykes, you mean?'

'Of course, I—'

'Exactly how much?' Caz said sharply.

'Twenty-five thousand pounds.'

'No.'

'Thirty-thousand.'

'Yes. You know what I cannot talk about?'

'Of course,' Snow said. 'Anything *sub judice*. Explicit police procedures. The attitudes of your superiors. The conduct of other officers. That's standard crap. We deal with it all the time.'

'Thirty thousand? That's pounds?'

'Yes.'

'Who do I have to sleep with?' Caz asked.

'Hah-ha!'

'I've always wanted to buy an MX5. What's the tax on thirty thousand?'

'Twelve K.'

'I could get an MX5 for fifteen.'

'We could get it for you. Plus the three thousand. When can we meet?'

'I've very busy on a big case,' Caz said. 'But we can talk in the evenings or on the weekend. It depends how urgent this is.'

'The contract's urgent, like tonight is urgent. We could talk this weckend.'

'Are you serious?'

'About the weekend?'

'No, about me signing up tonight.'

'I'm ten minutes from the M23,' Snow said. 'I can do Brighton in an hour and a bit. The contract is drawn up already; all we have to do is sign.'

'I can have an MX5 . . .' Caz said dreamily.

'We have to meet first,' Snow said.

'OK,' Caz said. 'I'm in a pub called the Grapes of

Wrath, next door to John Street police station. I'm with some friends having an after-work drink. You can find me there.'

'I'll be there by ten o'clock.'

'Have you eaten, Deborah?'

'Not yet.'

'Well there's this brilliant Italian I know. We could . . .'

'Good idea, and it's on the paper.'

'I'll see you later, then.'

'OK, Caz. Do they run a tab in the pub?'

'A slate.'

'Well, stick this evening on the slate, Caz. The paper will pick the bill up.'

Caz said thank you. Before she said goodbye she told Deborah to expect a big bill. Snow chuckled and told Caz not to drink too much. 'Hasta la vista!' she said, then she put the phone down.

Twenty-Two

Deborah Snow was sharp. She arrived at ten o'clock sharp, was sharp when she spoke, dressed sharp for power, and had angles and sharpness in everything she said and did. She was long-faced and had long dark hair, a thin pointed nose and an angled chin. She was not good-looking but she had that elusive 'it'.

When she entered the Grapes she didn't pause as she cut another angle through the tables and then through the crowd at the bar. She was one of those people who always gets served before you, and within a minute she had turned away holding four glasses and a dark green bottle. She looked round, the bottle at chest height, spotted Caz's corner and swept across the room. Click, click, click, she eye-balled each of them, then she sat down, swishing into her chair and clacking the bottle on to the table.

'Cheers!' she said, the glasses still a spray in her fist.

Caz leaned over and took two. 'Deborah Snow, I presume?'

Snow put the other two glasses down, one in front of Billy, one in front of Moira. She took out some business cards and handed them round. Moira read hers out loud.

'That's right, features editor,' Snow said. 'Do you read the *Sun*?'

'I read my fellah's,' Moira said quietly.

'Good enough for me!' Snow said. She looked at Billy and picked up the bottle. 'Would you care to do the honours, er . . .?'

'Billy.'

'Yes, please?'

Billy removed foil. The bottle was cold and damp with condensation.

'How did you get served so quickly?' Caz said. 'I didn't even know they sold champagne in here.'

Snow smiled. 'My assistant rang ahead for me while I was on my way. He asked for two bottles of good champagne and told the landlord it was for the newspaper. The chances are they had to send out for this; it's good stuff. They probably stuck it in the freezer to chill it quickly!'

'And four glasses?'

'I rang from my mobile, a while after Dick had rung. The reception is not staggering north of Brighton is it? Your landlord was pretty accommodating. It might just have had something to do with a couple of sixty quid bottles of champers. I told him who I was. He said you were with two friends.'

'You don't mess about, do you, Deborah?'

'Nor you, I'd guess.'

Billy finally managed to get the cork undone. He had the bottle angled underneath the table and was thumbing it furiously, his cheeks bulging. There was a loud pop and an excess of spluttering foam as he said 'Shit!' and brought the bottle out hurriedly. There were three instinctively raised glasses in front of him half-filling as champagne rained down between them. All three of the women had moved back from the wet, leaning their arms forward towards the drink. In unison, they said a sarcastic 'Cheers!' to Billy. Billy was pink. 'Done this before, have you?' Snow said.

Caz introduced her friends.

Snow was polite and gave them measured smiles. She turned back to her prize. 'You said there was a good restaurant?'

'In the Lanes,' Caz said. 'Not far from where I'm stopping.'

'Soon as possible, then,' Snow said quickly. Her eyes flickered just enough for Caz to get the message. 'There's another bottle behind the bar, Billy,' she said tersely. 'That's for you and Moira. I have to whisk Caz away from you now. Have a good night.'

'Cheers!' Billy said. He stood up awkwardly to shake her hand, banging the table with his knee.

'Billy!' Moira said, her head still lowered. He dropped, almost to sit down again, but his arm was still extended.

Deborah Snow reached out and clamped his hand firmly. 'We meet again . . .' she said. She nodded to a flushed Moira.

They left together, Caz leading. Even as they went through the door Snow was trying to take control. 'This Italian restaurant sounds quaint but I'm stopping at the Grand. I booked two late meals there if you'd prefer.'

Caz could feel slippery rocks under her feet. 'No thanks,' she said firmly. 'I've had enough culture shocks for one night. If it's OK with you, Deborah, I'd rather my simple little Italian.'

'Absolutely no problem,' Snow said. 'My car is over there.' She pointed at a white Toyota Celica. 'You say it's not far?'

Caz hadn't booked and even Gabrielle's favourite customer had to wait five minutes for a table to be cleared. They stood at the bar sipping malts. Caz was thinking she could get used to this, the mellowness blooming through her. Debbie – she had insisted on being called Debbie – was asking gentle questions about the final moments before the micro-light had crashed. This was all off the record, she said, she was just curious on a personal level. All Caz could remember about it now was the sense of farce as she presumed she was just about to die. 'At the time, it just seemed impossibly funny,' she said. 'I remember people looking up. I wanted to wave to them but I couldn't let go of the controls.' Debbie nodded profoundly as Caz chattered.

They had little time to wait. Gabrielle came to them, crooning '*Mia cara*!' to Caz in his deep, sexy voice. He led them to a table near the kitchens, pulling back Debbie's chair as Caz sat down unaided, already ordering garlic bread.

'Multi-tasking!' she grinned to the reporter.

'Smell that garlic!' Debbie said with a mock grimace. 'I'll stink tomorrow.' She looked up at the round waiter and past him at the dark kitchens. Now she grinned. 'But I'll bet it's worth it!'

Twenty-Three

It was inevitable and Caz predicted it; the conversation on the way down to Southampton in the morning was dominated by questions about the woman from the *Sun*. Moira would not stop.

So what was it all about then? What did they want to know? When was it all happening? When were they doing the photographs? Did she have to go to London? How much?

Caz told her.

'*How* much?'

'Thirty thousand quid.'

'You're taking the piss!' Moira said.

'Never over money.'

'Yer rent's just gone up.'

'No it hasn't,' Caz said. 'The money's already spent.'

'Oh, come *on*!'

'They're giving me a car.'

'Don't be silly.'

'I'm not being silly. When Debbie told me how much, I said I'd be able to buy an MX5. She said it'd look quite good in the photos. Said they'd speak to Mazda and get me one in a few days.'

'There's a waiting list for them, isn't there?'

'Not if you're going to get free publicity.'

'I don't believe it.'

'I find it all hard to believe myself, Mo, but there's a contract in my bag . . .' Caz sounded dreamy. 'I fancy British Racing Green, a wooden dashboard, wire wheels, a nice stereo . . .'

Moira sighed. 'All right, I get the picture. So when exactly did you sell your soul to the devil?'

'I didn't!' Caz said.

'And you don't have to pose in the nude with John Major?'

'Nope!' Caz said. 'But I might have to sleep with the chief constable.'

'Why's that?'

'To actually get my hands on the money. It's against policy.'

Moira let out a long, drawn out 'Oh!' She was slightly bemused. 'For a minute there, Caz, I thought you were going to do something immoral.'

'What *me*, Mo? Do you think I would?'

They parked at Hampshire Police Divisional Headquarters in Hulse Road and went to look for Peter Mason. He was in the staff canteen with a second mug of tea and an empty dinner-plate in front of him. When he spoke he still had his mouth full. He was grinning. 'Bacon buttie! Even better than a Mac!'

The three of them bummed a lift down town and

were dropped off in Hanover Street, yards from McDonald's, the helpful PC presuming that Peter was on his usual. Caz grabbed the DS's arm before he could even think about it and they scampered quickly downhill, past travel agents, a building society, Dillons bookshop and an open park. As they crossed the road opposite Debenhams, Caz was talking about Peter Edwards.

'He was a real slime-ball. The place was a tip. The Chief Super was so pissed off he wanted him done for something, anything. Far as I know they did him for his van: no tax, three bald tyres, no brake light. There was a girl in the house too, maybe underage. Greavsie was trying to check it out but they couldn't get hold of her parents. Nice, eh?'

'Jack the Ripper!' Mason said.

'What were we supposed to do, Peter? *Not* go?'

'I don't suppose you had much choice.'

'No, we didn't. They'll have clocked all the van addresses by now. We left too early, so I'm not sure what's happening. But presumably all the owners came out clean; otherwise Blackside or MacInnes would have put the block on us coming down to Southampton.'

'Give it until lunchtime,' Mason said. 'You can bell Brighton from Boxx's place. With a bit of luck we might have some pictures by then.'

Moira spoke up. 'And addresses. If the animal entered races he must be on the computers some-where or in one of the race programmes. If he is, that's just leg-work. We just talk to 'em all.'

'*If* he used his real name and his real address,' Caz retorted. 'Anyway, Pete Lindsell is working on that, I'm keeping way out of it.'

'Surely this guy wouldn't have been that stupid,' Mason said. 'Not stupid enough to give his real name and address?'

'Why not?' Caz said quickly. 'He might have presumed we would never make the connection between the victims and their running. He might just be a nutter and not be thinking things out.'

'You don't really think that, do you?'

'No. I think he uses a false identity.'

'So how does he get his number?' Moira asked.

'On the day,' Caz said. 'He must enter on the day!' She stopped.

Serial offenders almost always dirtied their own nest first, committing offences in or near where they lived. If they got away with their early crimes they often 'matured', moving further afield and applying more sophistication to their plans. If the animal had used his real name or address for the seventh or eighth Totton 10K he had taken an unnecessary risk. But he *might* have been less careful when he entered the sixth, and did he enter the fifth? Caz was trying to remember. Didn't the Totton mail-shot previous runners? Yes! So Dean Richard must have runner lists from earlier races. The Totton sent out an entry form for their next race with the results from the current one. Did that mean Richard could select runners from *any* Totton 10K?

'Hey, Caz!'

Caz looked up. Peter and Moira were twenty yards ahead, waiting to cross the dual carriageway behind Debenhams. She raised her arm, distracted, pausing long enough to cement the thought, then, sprinted quickly to catch up. She was breathless with adrenaline.

'Peter. Do you have Dean Richard's telephone number at work?'

'Why?'

'Do you have it, Peter?'

'Yeah, I have it,' Mason said testily. 'What's the problem?'

'There's no problem. I think I might have thought of a way out of some work!' She pointed at the Debenhams building. 'I'm going for a coffee, you coming?'

Twenty-Four

Caz and the DS sat down while Moira queued for three coffees and a tea-cake for Peter. Caz looked up into Peter's face. She could see the red beginnings of annoyance flushing his cheek. She quickly became a woman, smiling, touching his hand as she apologised sweetly.

'I'm sorry, Peter. I know you're the DS. It's just you've been so friendly, so nice, I'd sort of forgotten. My head is spinning. Give me a chance to explain.'

Her sex was just another weapon but she was annoyed at herself for using it. She glanced at her hand, then up at the sergeant's face and pointedly back at the table, slowly breaking contact with him, beautifully ambiguous.

Mason was dead. He smiled. 'That's all right, Caz. You're a bright young copper.' He lifted his hand as if it was tingling. 'Maybe you're just a touch over-keen?'

Caz grinned widely. 'Only a touch, Sarge?'

Moira came back and sat down. Caz began to explain while they drank their coffees. 'The animal is targeting races, especially this one. It's not impossible that he has used his real name and address for the sixth, seventh and eighth Tottons, but I'd bet my career he hasn't. But *beforehand*, say in the fourth or fifth he may well have used his own name or his real address.'

Moira frowned. 'Why?'

'Because he wasn't a rapist then. He probably wasn't even planning, *then*.'

'So what good is that?' Mason asked.

'We look for someone who ran in the fourth or fifth Totton, maybe the sixth, and *didn't* run in the seventh and eighth. If I'm right, the animal won't be on record for the last two races. If he is, it'll be under a false name. We need to get hold of Dean Richard. Not only can he give us that kind of information but he can tell us roughly what the runner's time was. You can be virtually certain that a man as big as this one wouldn't break forty minutes. If we make the cut-off at, say, thirty-eight minutes, I reckon we're pretty safe.'

Mason looked uncertain. 'What sort of numbers are we looking at?'

'Not that many. First off we can discard all women, about a third of every race. And we can drop anyone faster than thirty-eight minutes and slower than fifty-eight. Our man is very likely to be an unattached runner. He's a loner, so it's very unlikely he'll be with a club. DS Lindsell's talking to the club secretaries anyway, so we can leave that to him.'

'So, numbers?'

Caz was now very animated. 'We ask for men who ran in the fourth, fifth or sixth Totton 10K but then *didn't* run in the seventh or eighth. We should also look at names entered in the last two races but not the other three. One of them ought to be false. If Richard can tell us whether they're late entries or not, even better.'

'So, *how many*?'

'Excluding the fast guys, the women, the over forties – maybe only twenty names, maybe even less.'

'Why exclude the over forties?' Moira asked.

'If we draw a blank, we could look at them, but serial rapists are almost always in their late teens or twenties. Leaving the vets out shortens the list.'

Moira looked puzzled. 'Vets?'

'Veteran runners,' Caz explained. 'Men become vets at forty, women at thirty-five. It makes them competitive again. At thirty-nine a good male runner finds it hard to compete with the best twenty-five year olds. A year later he becomes a vet and suddenly he's a fast newcomer!'

'What about the Rediffusion vans?' Moira now asked.

'What d'you mean?'

'The addresses.'

'Presumably they've all been visited by now, but we could cross the list with Dean Richard's one. You never know, we might get lucky.'

Peter Mason broke back in. 'OK, OK. I'll get hold of Richard now. We don't need to go to Poole. I warned him yesterday that we might need him. He can leave work and be in Southampton before lunch. That do yer?'

'Almost,' Caz said. 'But before we go to Boxx's, what happened at the sorting office last night?'

'Do you ever take a breath?' Mason said.

Caz shook her head.

'I went down there about half-six. There's a Customer Liaison man, a chap called Lawrie Jamieson. When I got there he was just about take a bunch of little kids, beavers, on a tour. I tagged on for the ride. It was quite interesting.'

'So what did you find out?'

'Always post your letters first-class and never put loose change in the envelope.'

'Loose change?' Moira said quietly.

Mason glanced quickly at her. 'It screws up the machines. They recover forty quid a day in Southampton!'

'Our villain?' Caz asked.

'They call the sorting office the "MLO". That's Main Letter Office. Vans arrive at the back door with sacks from post boxes. They get hooked up on a sort of conveyor, then they go inside to be sorted into letters and parcels, first- and second-class deliveries.'

'Go on.'

'There's a hell of a lot of noise and quite a lot of activity. From what I saw, most of the sorting machines were made by Toshiba. The first machine chucks out oversized letters and turns all the others round so that the post code is front and bottom. It's quite fascinating.'

'Our villain?' Caz said.

'No way he could pick up specific addresses early on.'

'How about later on?'

'Well, the envelopes come out of one machine and they get put in big plastic boxes. Some business letters can be automatically coded with little blue dots to represent the post code but a few have to be spotted by human operators as does all the private mail.'

'How do they do that?'

'If I hadn't seen it I wouldn't have believed it. There's a great long row of people, mostly blokes. They sit at a machine, and as the letters go by one-by-one, they type in the post code as they read it off the letter.'

'What about letters without post codes?'

'The operators know most of the local ones and virtually all the first threes, the numbers that indicate the town. They're incredible, and they work at a hell of a speed. They're expected to get through two thousand letters an hour and mistakes count against them. They don't make many.'

'Doesn't all the noise distract them?'

'I asked that,' Mason said. 'They were wearing ear-defenders, I thought, but in fact they were stereo head-phones. They get a choice of music or they can bring in their own. I thought they looked a bit like battery-chickens, but they all seemed happy enough.'

'Could any of them lift Totton 10K mail?'

'No way.'

'So who could?'

'Well, those workers produce letters with blue dots on that other machines can read. The next stage is all done automatically, breaking the mail down into local post, neighbours and the rest. The "rest" is the rest of the UK. That gets broken down into six major districts. There's no way there either.'

Caz was faintly exasperated. 'Any way *at all*, Peter?'

'Hard to say. There's one big machine that sorts the local and neighbour stuff out into smaller batches. The settings get changed every half an hour or so for different jobs. At the right time you just might be able to nick letters, but you'd have to hang around for the right moment and know exactly where to look. Not only that, but there are big-brother type watchers who prowl about on catwalks up above the machines for security. I'd say highly unlikely.'

'Is that it, then? What about postmen?'

'Ah, that's the bit I haven't mentioned yet. Y'see, I went to the sorting office, the Main Letter Office, where letters come *in*. The MLO. It's down the docks next to Parcel Force. Where we needed to go was the *Delivery* Office.'

'The Delivery Office?'

'Yeah, in the High Street. Below Bar. Right opposite Habitat.'

'Opposite Habitat . . .'

'That's right, Caz. You know, you're very quick when you try.'

'So what happened when you went there, Peter?'

'Where?'

'Where they do the deliveries! The Delivery Office.'

'I haven't been there!'

'What?'

'Well, at the Main Letter Office, the real rush is in the evening and up to midnight, sorting out all the collections. At that time there's nothing to do at the *DO* because all the letters are still at the *MLO*. Got it? The night shift at the DO start getting stuff from the MLO at about eleven o'clock but the real activity there doesn't start until about half-past five in the morning.'

'And you went there this morning, right?'

'No.'

'So you're going tomorrow morning?'

'Not exactly, Caz. You are.'

'Oh cheers, Peter.'

'Not at all. I figured you'd be over here anyway. I cleared it with my DCI and he'll've spoken to Brighton by now. You're single and it's your case.'

'*My* case!'

'Well you know what I mean, Flood. You did get us this far.' He smiled. 'You got somewhere to stay tonight?'

'Why, are you offering?'

'I could be. You can bet your legs you won't get expenses for a stop-over.'

'Me *and* Moira?'

Peter swooned. 'That's my unfulfilled fantasy.'

Caz snarled. 'If I'm getting up at half-past four it's gonna stay unfulfilled!'

'I'm supposed to be seeing Billy tonight,' Moira said slowly. 'We were going to meet up in the Police Club and then go on for a curry...'

'Ah, love,' Mason said with a mock syrupy voice. He looked into Moira's eyes. 'Moira, your story has touched my heart. Please accept my most sincere sympathy. It's true, is it not? A policeman's lot is not a happy one?'

Moira looked up at the DS, her black hair shining, her dark eyes deep and warm. Her lips were faintly moist and she parted them with a delicious smile. Mason smiled back.

'Get fucked,' Moira said.

'Get fucked, *Sergeant*,' Mason chided.

'Oh, I am sorry, Sergeant,' Moira said. She was still smiling. 'Go get fucked, *Sergeant*. Preferably with a bent stick.'

Twenty-Five

They left and walked across to Boxx Brownie's cramped offices. Moira was walking slowly at the back, muttering about Billy and threatening mutiny. Caz had to remind her that shit shifts were all part of being a copper.

'But I only joined for the uniform!' Moira said.

Boxx's dizzy receptionist was ready for them with her extra-white smile and a couple more two-liners for her inspector. Peter had been practising, ready for the morning, but was trying to hedge his bets now that he knew there were two more women in town overnight. Moira was still scowling over Billy and not taking much notice, but Caz thought everything was predictably pathetic as the sergeant tried to line up something for the weekend while keeping his options open for tonight. She was regretting the brief touch in the coffee-shop. She didn't and couldn't fancy Peter. Why did every male copper think every WPC was available? Why did they say and do things to women on the force that would cause riots if they tried it out of uniform?

They went upstairs to escape the rhyming blonde, Peter a little behind as he had a quiet word before he followed. Gareth Boxx was waiting for them, smiling, his piercing eyes quickly assessing Caz, then softening for Moira. Moira looked away quickly.

'I see the Sergeant's quite taken with Mandy,' Boxx said. A wide smile.

Caz smiled thinly. 'Can you blame him?'

'I suppose not,' Boxx said slowly. Then dismissively he sighed. 'But Mandy wouldn't be much of a challenge . . .'

He was still smiling but Caz was not amused. 'We've got half a million photographs to look at, yes?'

'No.' Boxx was still smiling. 'It's not quite that bad. I've narrowed it down to about four thousand. There's coffee and orange juice laid on and I've booked La Lupa for one o'clock.'

Caz was surprised. 'La Lupa?'

'A little Italian. I hope you don't mind. It's on me.'

Peter Mason came up the stairs, clumping into the conversation. 'Did I hear someone say La Lupa? Great place! Right on!'

'I think that's a yes,' Caz said.

Gareth Boxx took them into a cutting room. There were two long tables, a large single-bladed guillotine and two smaller ones with wheeled cutters. The walls were again plastered with photographs, but with no obvious theme. One that stood out was a raging fire, a pier blazing in evening sun, black smoke curling skyward. Boxx saw them looking.

'That was Southampton, six months ago. Lucky shot. I was at a friend's place in Bugle Street a couple of hundred yards from the fire. I heard the bang, looked out and saw the flames. I ran down to the fire in my socks with my mate chasing after me and carrying my shoes! I couldn't get very close, but I got that shot from the Town Quay with a long lens. Dramatic isn't it?'

'Bit of a tint,' Peter said.

'It was a news shot, not a composition.'

'I saw it on TV,' Moira said.

'That's why there's a tint. I rushed the film down there. They turned out six by eights for me in twenty minutes. It was on local TV after News at Ten.'

'Oh, yeah, I saw it,' Peter said appreciatively. 'And the front page of the *Echo*, wasn't it? The End of the Pier?'

'Well remembered, Peter. I earned twice on that one. A hundred and fifty quid, I think. At the time it was better than a kick in the head, but not exactly a Fergie exclusive or a close-in on a bank robbery.'

'We all dream of them,' Peter said.

'I don't dream,' Boxx said heavily. 'Dreams are for tossers.'

Peter looked faintly put out. 'What's that supposed to mean?'

'Whatever you like,' Boxx said sharply. 'You get the big shots by being ready; by going to where it happens or where it might happen. Always carry a camera, always have a spare. Make your own luck.'

'But there's still luck, Gareth.'

'Maybe, but didn't Gary Player say, "the more I practise the luckier I get"?'

The DS huffed. 'Sounds like you should have been a war photographer.'

'I'd've liked to,' Boxx said gently. 'Beauty, drama and class, remember? Who wouldn't want to capture the instant of death or the face of a killing machine? What could be more dramatic? What could be more beautiful?'

'Beautiful?!' Caz said suddenly. 'There's nothing beautiful in death, there's nothing exciting. That's for Hollywood. Go to a motorway crash and smell the stink! Go to a post-mortem . . .'

Boxx was calm and didn't react. 'You're talking about the dead, Caz, I'm talking about the instant of dying or the moment of killing – the crossover, the focus on one final thing; the killing or being killed. Nothing artificial.'

Caz was thinking of a little girl; a police sergeant burning to death. She felt sick. She lashed out. 'Gareth, you don't know what you're talking about!'

Boxx smiled calmly, those eyes softening again, as if on cue. 'But I do, Caz. I'm sorry if you're upset, but I know *exactly* what I'm talking about. You are disgusted by the dead, but I'm not talking about the dead. I'm not talking about the waste or tragedy. I am talking about that split-second, that moment when the bullet hits, when the body loses the soul. Nobody has ever got that picture, they are always a

215

thousandth of a second too late.'

Caz went to speak, silent anger making her feel ill. Her fists were clenched.

Boxx stopped her, looking deep into her face. 'We don't agree. I'm sorry. I won't raise the subject again.' He smiled softly but Caz felt insulted. Somehow Gareth Boxx had slipped inside her guard and touched her. She was hopelessly off-balance. She didn't know if the feeling in her gut was anger or panic. 'I need the loo,' she said awkwardly. 'Where is it?'

'Downstairs,' Boxx said. He touched her arm. 'It's next to reception. Mandy will show you.' She pulled away. He turned to Peter and Moira. 'Right! Maybe we should start on these pictures.'

As Caz went down the stairs, she forced herself to calm down, breathing deeply and walking deliberately. Behind her she heard scraping chairs and then the growing murmur of the others' conversation, slightly embarrassed, stuttering to restart in the difficult first moments of her absence. She didn't like being so disconcerted by a man. She didn't like being out of control.

'Fuck you, Boxx!' she hissed as she banged through the toilet door.

Twenty-Six

When Caz got back, Peter and Moira were working steadily through piles of six-by-four colour pictures, quickly eliminating large numbers. Gareth Boxx was working more methodically with strips of developed negatives against the plastic white of a light box, occasionally muttering 'ah-hah' as he worked, and putting film aside. Caz sat between Moira and the DS, feeling superfluous. She coughed, then she asked if Peter had rung Dean Richard yet.

'While you were in the bog,' the DS said. 'He's coming here at two o'clock.'

'Oh,' Caz said. Peter slapped another dozen pictures from left to right.

Gareth spoke absently without looking up. 'I should've explained earlier. The photos you've got there are all from races in Hampshire, Sussex and Surrey. I thought that would be enough for starters. The problem we've got is that these are shots of runners who haven't bought from us or have failed to pay up in previous races. If your man bought his pictures then we'll have to find him through these

217

negatives. I'm sorting out six-footers. I'll get Sally to run off some contacts as soon as we have enough.'

'Which races are you looking at?' Caz asked. Her voice wavered slightly.

'I'm half-way through the Eighth Totton 10K. One big guy, a couple more round about the six-foot mark.'

'Do you have the Fifth, Gareth?'

'Yes, but—'

'Can I take a look? The others seem to be doing well enough without me.'

Boxx put down a film after another few seconds examination. He passed her a black file with a little over thirty Perspex folders clipped inside. 'Take your time,' he said. 'Don't discard anything unless you're sure what you're doing. If you're in any doubt, just ask.' She took the file, sucking on her teeth. 'And try not to touch the negs, eh? They pay my wages.'

Caz bit her tongue. 'I won't touch the negs.'

She started at the front of the folder, then realised that the sheets of film were filed in finishing order. She replaced the first sheet and flipped to the last, pulling it out. Against the dispersed light she saw big gaps between runners, runners approaching the finish clock alone, the real slowies, the stragglers, little ladies finishing just outside the hour. Brown-orange figures crossed the finishing straight behind these determined joggers, the reversed images of thin men, already showered and on their way home.

The second sheet was full of first-timers, nine- to ten-minute-milers and those who had gone out too fast and had to walk. Her eyes hurt her already, the non-colours making her concentrate far too hard. There was a shot of one tall figure, heavyish. Caz put it aside and moved on to the third sheet.

She was on the fifth sheet when she heard Boxx say, 'Coffee, anyone?' She waved a yes, absently, staring at the film in front of her. She rubbed her eyes, concentrating on the amber outline of a lumbering figure in the celluloid. The man was tall; very tall, very heavy. She looked at the figure's head. A woollen hat. She could feel her breath. Her stomach burned and her throat thickened.

'Does anyone have a magnifying glass?' she said.

Twenty-Seven

Caz stared at the brown-green half-inch of evidence, locking on to it as though fearful it might escape if she looked away. Someone touched her arm, Peter. She knew it was Peter when he spoke. 'Magnifying glass?' He pushed against her arm again. Harder this time.

Under the distortion of the lens, Caz could see him – huge, with big hands, almost as big as Blackside. He towered over another man in the finishing straight as he cruised in somewhere around forty-five minutes, a respectable time for someone so large and heavy. Even in negative, she could see he wore full-length running tights and a long-sleeved top. With the hat as well he must have felt very warm; but seeing him, knowing him, made Caz cold with hate. 'I have you, you shit!' she hissed at the inert plastic. It was only when she spoke that she realised her teeth had been clamped tight together. Opening her mouth gave her a brief, sudden pain.

She turned to Boxx. 'Gareth, how quickly can we see a print of this?'

* * *

Four of them squeezed into the darkroom, the sharp smell of fixing chemicals commented on by the women but hardly noticed by the men.

'You get used to it,' Boxx said.

The room was a deep red, glowing from the dark-room safety-light, but Caz could still see his smile. 'I'll run off a very quick black-and-white first,' he said. 'Then we'll give your negs, and the ones I've pulled out, to Sally. In half-an-hour we can be sitting down with a dozen eight-by-tens in full colour.'

'Can you really do that?' Caz asked. 'Make a black-and-white print from a colour negative?'

'Oh, yes,' Boxx said confidently. 'The quality varies a bit and you lose outlines sometimes, but you do get a likeness. A colour negative has layers and is designed to throw colour, not shades of grey. Something blue might look like something red when we print a black-and-white, but it's worth doing.'

He had slipped the negative into a mounting frame and this now clicked into the body of a large, expensive-looking apparatus. A button was pressed and the animal appeared below, flat and lifeless on a smooth white board.

Gareth Boxx adjusted something on the body of the enlarger, muttering, 'Sharpening up ... the image ...' When he was satisfied, he blocked the light and the board below returned to a dull white ceramic, almost grey. Moira and Caz were fascinated but Peter was admiring the equipment.

'Just have to get some paper ...' Boxx said.

'I thought it had to be completely dark all the time,' Moira said slowly.

'Only while you load negs,' Mason said. 'You develop a keen sense of touch.'

Gareth opened a plastic container and removed a black plastic envelope. From inside, he took a large piece of paper and laid it on the enlarger base. A frame clipped down, holding the paper flat. Then he opened the lens cap, flooding blue-white magical light downwards. Then the light stopped. Nothing had happened; the paper was still paper.

'Doesn't the . . .?' Moira muttered.

'Patience, sweetheart,' Gareth said.

'No clocks?' Peter said. It was more of a statement than a question.

'No need,' Boxx smiled. 'Not for this, anyway. I can time anything from five seconds to ninety in my head.' He went to the first of three trays of liquid and dropped in the paper. After about two seconds he turned it over with a pair of tongs. He chuckled. 'Come and take a look at this, Moira. This is the sexiest moment in photography.'

From white, the paper hesitated, then seemed to discolour. Faint blushes of grey appeared, then blacks, then lines and shapes and then, so eerily, a man, *their* man, the animal, the pig who had slammed into five women's lives and nearly wrecked them all. They watched in awe, then suddenly Gareth was shushing them out of the way, lifting the paper from 'DEV' and into 'STOP'. 'Him, yes?' he said smugly as he lifted the paper into the third tray.

'I think so,' Moira said, very slowly.

'It's him,' Caz said. 'No doubt at all.'

'Great stuff!' Boxx said, almost laughing. 'Well, once he's washed off and dried, he's all yours!' He went to a sink and dropped the photograph into a huge cream drum. A tap opened and the drum began to move, water leaving though small holes as fresh liquid poured in through another. He turned to his guests. 'OK, let's go have a word with Sally. We'll get her to bang this lot through the machine and see what else we've got.' He flicked on a light and turned to leave. The detectives hesitated, looking at the slowly turning drum. 'Oh, come on,' Boxx said, glancing in the same direction. 'He's not going anywhere!' He opened the darkroom door, harsh sudden daylight making them turn away. He led them out. '*Sally!*'

They knew who Sally was, but until she slapped into the cutting room, none of the detectives realised that they'd never met her. Previously she had just been the bark on the other end of the intercom, now she was a large woman in a white coat with a shock of bleached hair and a good line in back-chat.

They were drinking their coffees. She asked which one was hers. Boxx answered. 'None of them, Sally. Can you put these negs through the Gretag?'

'Any chance of a coffee first?'

Boxx looked like he'd been here before. He sighed. 'A quick one.'

'A quick one's fine!' Sally said. She looked at Peter and winked. 'You all right, mate?'

'Oh, I'll get your print,' Boxx said, almost as an

aside as he got off his stool. 'Sally, keep our guests happy for a couple of minutes, would you?'

'No problems, Captain!' Sally said. She grinned as Boxx left the room. She waited fifteen seconds before turning to the women.

'So what d'you you make of *El Presidente?*'

Moira looked surprised. 'Sorry, what?'

'Oh, come on, love. Has he given you the stiletto look yet, followed by the warm "I really need to be loved" look? Hell, I could write a book about his techniques. In the year I've been here, I've seen him try every trick in the book plus a few originals. Our Gary likes to win. He usually does.'

Moira was looking uncomfortable, so Caz cut in. 'D'you always talk about your boss like that?'

Sally looked surprised. 'Why not?'

'Well, for starters, you might get yourself the sack.'

'I should worry!'

'Don't you?'

'No, not at all. I'm good at my job and old Boxy understands me.'

'What's that one about with friends like that I don't need—'

Sally finished it for her. 'Enemies!'

'Yes.'

'I'm not his enemy,' Sally said flatly. 'But I'm not his friend either. Gareth wouldn't fancy me – he likes model types – but if he did fancy me, he wouldn't get near. He is definitely *not* my type.'

'So what's your type, Sally?'

'Safe. Normal.'

They could hear footsteps. Normal? What a funny thing to say.

Boxx was at the door. There was a peculiar, quick smile on his face like a snake stretching in the sun, then it was gone. He looked at them all then sneered, just for Caz. 'It is absolutely *not* true. I deny everything.' Now he managed a dark smile. 'You must understand about Sally. She's only been out of the hospital for eighteen months.' The smile broadened to include the eyes. 'Some of what Sally says may be a little less than the *actualité*. She tell you about the dog? It's a lie. I have never eaten a live dog. I don't even *like* dog.'

'Yes he does,' Sally protested. 'Medium rare.' She stood up.

'OK. OK. Now be a good girl and bugger off, Sal. The Gretag?'

'I'm going.'

As Sally left, Boxx moved as if to smack her backside but she stiffened and dodged him, a cold look on her face. She was going through the door when Boxx complained loudly, 'You just can't get the staff . . .'

His assistant didn't even bother to reply but she left, head up. There was a second's awkward silence, then Boxx spoke triumphantly. 'Your man.' He waved the photograph.

'Let me see!' Caz said, a little too quickly. Her voice was an octave too high. Boxx waved the black-and-white image. 'He's a handsome bastard.'

They crowded round the largest cutting board.

With four of them staring, even the twelve by ten inch shot was only just big enough. Moira's arm was resting on the huge curved guillotine blade and it moved beneath her. Almost absent-mindedly, Boxx moved it back into place and locked it. He smiled at Moira. 'Better safe than sorry, eh?'

As they continued to stare he gave them the runner's name.

He should have been big and he was – very big. But he should have been ugly and he should have looked evil. He was no male model, but Leonard Copthorne Burke, aged twenty-nine, unattached runner, time of 44:53, looked wholesome and friendly, with a broad 'I've just run a personal best' smile breaking out across his face. He looked the kind of gentle giant who wouldn't hurt a fly.

Caz immediately thought of the simple migrant worker in *Of Mice and Men*. 'Lennie,' she said.

'Who?'

'Lennie Small,' Boxx said before Caz could answer. 'An idiot.'

Neither Peter nor Moira looked any the wiser.

'I'll explain at lunch', Caz said. 'If we get a chance for any.'

Gareth Boxx was loving his executive moment. He said 'And' very loudly, and waited for them to turn round. The three of them had 'And what?' written all over their faces. Caz was faintly annoyed that she let Boxx play with her like this. 'And ... I can give you three addresses, a list of his races and probably a dozen colour photographs of him, spread over the last three years.'

'Is that now?' Peter said. 'As in immediately?'

'His details are on the computer, next door. Sally is doing those other shots already, but now we know who he is I can pull out every shot we've got of him.'

Twenty-Eight

Leonard Copthorne Burke had run in the Fifth Totton 10K. Boxx Brownie had sent him his beaming photograph on approval. One week later they received a postal order for £3:95. They had sent the photograph to an address in Esher.

When L. C. Burke ran in the Sixth Totton 10K, he looked as though he had something weighing heavily on his mind. Two weeks before the attack on Jill Brown, his finishing time was two minutes slower than his April race. There were no raised arms this time, and his face looked cold and hard. Sally Pitt had mailed him another seven-by-five colour print. It had come back marked 'not required'. L. C. Burke still had a good credit rating with the firm.

There was no Burke in the Seventh Totton 10K, but Lionel B. Clarke came down the finishing straight in forty-nine minutes plus odd seconds. Sally hadn't mailed this particular photograph. Unfortunately the runner's raised hand had obscured his face and the shot was ruined.

It was a bright Spring day for the Eight Totton

10K. The runner wearing 747 and clocking fifty-oh-three had used the name Bill Leonard. He was looking left at the crucial moment and that shot was binned too. Bill Leonard and Lionel B. Clarke had given the same address in Southampton's Ocean Village. Had Sally or Tim sent out the photographs, the envelope would have been returned, 'Not known at this address'. They were both entries on the day.

But they still had the Esher address. Adrenaline flew. Caz was straight on the phone to Brighton, while Peter Mason got on the radio to DI Denham at the police station in Shirley. The Sergeant had the better of the luck.

'Dave, yeah we've clocked him. Yeah, Esher!'

Brighton Control was barking something about DI MacInnes being tied up. Would Caz wait? She told them it was urgent and listened to Peter.

'You what? Oh, Shit.... When?... Fuck!' Peter clicked out.

Caz heard, 'MacInnes!'

She said 'Sir!' automatically.

'Flood. You heard yet about Burke?'

'No, Sir. We were just ringing you with his name.'

'Where did you get it?'

'The photographs, Sir.'

'You have photographs?'

'Yes, Sir. They're pretty good. We've got one other address and a couple of aliases, Lionel Clarke and Bill Leonard.'

'Your animal was one of the Rediffusion addresses. A little close in Esher. He left months ago. No one knows where he went. He lived with his mother until she died of a heart attack last year.'

'And Esher Rugby Club wear Black and Amber . . .'

'There's a full-scale door-to-door going on up there now. DC Saint has gone to the rugby club, but we already know Burke was a very big chap. He went bald when his Mum died. A neighbour said it took less than a week.'

'Have we any idea where he might've gone, Sir?'

'No. His next-door neighbour suggested Portsmouth. Someone else said Southampton. There's nothing very definite yet.'

'We've an address in Ocean Village, Southampton, Sir, but I think it's duff.'

'You still with DS Mason?'

'Yes, Sir.'

'Put him on.'

Caz handed over the phone. She suddenly realised that she'd been sweating and the handset was clammy. Peter took it without comment. For the first time in five minutes Caz remembered Moira. She was still slowly sorting through photographs but was now sitting up attentively, trying to pick up snippets of information.

'DS Mason'. . . . Yes, Sir. DI Denham. Yes, Sir. . . . Unlikely, Sir. The names are AKAs. . . . Yes, Sir. Within the hour. . . . Yes, Sir.'

Peter put down the phone. 'Your DI says to tell you well done. He wants Southampton to check out the Ocean Village address mob-handed just in case.

He wants you and Moira to stay here and pull every photo Boxx has got and any other addresses or names.'

'Charming!' Moira said.

'You'd rather a trip down the village?'

'I'd rather a pizza at La Lupa's,' said Caz.

'Make that two!' Moira said.

Without Peter they were a little slower. After a while, the various images of runners began to blend into each other – so many grinning personal bests, so many drained, tottering athletes, so many neck-and-neck finishes between same-vest rivals or club versus club. There were so many shapes, so many small, lightweight flyers, so many chunky forty-minute men, so many less firm, less young, so many women. When Caz found a picture of herself – she was not too pretty at the end of a hard 10K – she felt odd, as if the image was of someone else, some distant, even dead person.

But they found him again, once more as himself and once more as Lionel Clarke. Sally printed off two eight-by-tens of each picture with young Timmy helping out on the Gretag. Neither Caz nor Moira could hide how impressed they were by the grey and white Swiss machine. In six minutes, start to finish, the Gretag could turn a tiny piece of brown plastic into a large, clear shot of a killer. Timmy explained that negative 'dry-to-dry' took only thirteen minutes and that on a good day he could go from film cassette to prints with a lot of spare time in the half-hour. As

231

he said, fifty thousand quid was cheap!

Peter Mason had taken a set of photographs to Southampton Central for distribution to various forces. Caz and Moira had a second set and now two more still shots. It was half-past twelve.

Gareth Boxx was passing the door as Caz decided to break.

'Gareth, are we still on for La Lupa?'

Boxx spread the fingers of his hand indicating five minutes. Caz smiled as he disappeared, her earlier anger long gone, transferred back to Leonard Burke.

Twenty-Nine

La Lupa formed the ground floor of an office block, opposite a Bottoms Up and a few doors away from Habitat, across the road from the Post Office. It wasn't Armando's, with all its craziness and dark atmosphere, but it was wide open, light and airy, with quick service and cheerful, chatty waiters.

'Great for hen parties, I've been told,' Gareth explained. 'There's a second room the other side of the bar. It takes about fifty covers.'

'I hate hen parties,' Caz said quickly. 'The only thing worse than a big group of drunken men is a group of drunken women!'

'Oh, I quite like them . . .' Moira said.

They ordered pasta, three times spaghetti carbonara, and Boxx bought a bottle of Frascati. Just enough, he said, to help the lunch along without taking off the edge for the afternoon. They chewed breadstick, waiting for the meal, and Gareth questioned them about Leonard Burke. How would they find him now that he had left his previous address? Would it be easy? Would they find him soon?

Caz explained, it all depended.

'It depends on a lot of things. We may get his national insurance number, his bank accounts or his credit cards, and trace him that way. Or he might subscribe to a magazine. Then we could get him through his previous address. On the other hand, if he's gone and he keeps his head down we may lose him, at least in the short term. We'll be looking for help from the general public or a bit of luck on a door-to-door. It's hard to say.'

'What's your best bet?'

'His behaviour patterns. Once we know what kind of bloke he is – what he likes, what he eats, where he spends his time – then we can guess at what he might be doing now.'

Boxx was surprised. 'You know what he's like already. He attacks women!'

'But he also eats, sleeps, dreams, buys clothes. We know he bought a car, a van. We know he has a soldering iron. He's a rapist for less than one per cent of his time. We catch him through the other ninety-nine per cent.'

'I don't understand.'

'Neither do I,' Moira said.

'Try this, then,' Caz said, sitting forward and slightly more upright. 'A man does something awful like rape. That's a brief, transient thing. Even if it's the most important thing in his life, it's still not the most common attribute he has. If we look solely at the rape, he might be hard to find.'

The food came. It was steaming.

Caz continued. 'Say he's a vegetarian and we know he's in Hampshire. We know what he looks like and what he eats. We question the staff at every vegetarian outlet and *maybe*, just maybe, we find our man.'

Moira looked up, fork and spoon poised. 'Is the animal a vegetarian, Caz?'

'No, Moira! I don't know. I didn't say he was a veggie. I said, if he *was* a veggie we'd have another way of finding him.'

'Oh!'

'Oh, eat your pasta, Moira!'

Caz ate. Occasionally she spoke. But the conversation was nothing – trivia. She managed to produce stock answers to the sentences that were aimed at her without ever truly engaging her brain. While she was thinking, it occurred to her that these petty rebounds probably didn't make her look all that exciting to the proprietor of Boxx Brownie. It might have mattered, but right now she was thinking about serial rapists, *catching* serial rapists.

There was that line in Casablanca: 'Round up all the usual suspects.' Even now that was a typical police ploy. A sexual offence, no problem, speak to the known offenders.

Serial rapists were on a continuum towards killing – and if they weren't caught, serial killing. But when you looked at the ones that *had* been caught, the ones that hit the headlines as they scurried one step ahead of the law, their true nature was so often *not* public. If they *had* previously offended, there was a good chance that their offence was *not* sexual – burglary and common assault were favourites. There were good arguments for analysing the types of rapes and from that, predicting the history of the rapist, but still the force relied on that vague quality, 'experience.'

Someone, somewhere had once said that a disguised man still casts the same shadow. Norman Blackside had once said that serial killers signed everything they did.

'What d'you reckon, Caz?'

She was miles away. 'About what, Moira?'

'Staying over at Gareth's flat tonight?'

Caz was still thinking about Blackside. She came back into gear.

'At Gareth's?'

'Yeah, Guh-ah-ruh . . .'

'Piss off, Moira.'

'Gareth says we could stop at his place.'

Boxx interjected. 'Across the landing, actually. You remember, there are two spare rooms there . . .'

'I remember, yes.'

'Is that yes you remember, or yes you'll stay?'

'Yes.'

'Excellent,' Boxx said. He gave Moira a wink and smiled at both of them. His smile was the one that Sally had called, 'I really need to be loved'.

They were back at Boxx Brownie for five-past two; for Dean Richard, five long, long minutes after he had arrived. He was sat in a corner, nervously smiling and clutching a plastic cup of coffee. He looked blitz-krieged and desperately relieved to see them.

Gareth Boxx handed over the keys to his second flat and offered them the use of his office before disappearing. The women led Richard away. He still seemed a little nervous and continually pushed light-brown hair back from his forehead. When he spoke of Mandy there was a little tremor in his voice.

'Everything she said rhymed. It was a little, er ...'

Caz felt wicked. *'We should have been back, but lunch was too slack ...'*

Richard looked in pain. 'Oh, no. I mean, er, really ...'

Caz grinned then apologised. 'I'm sorry, Mr Richard. My little joke. Thank you for coming. I believe you've already met our colleague, DS Mason?'

'I know him from races ...'

'Did he explain what we wanted?'

'Not exactly. Just something about race entries ...'

Caz explained. Richard replied. For that kind of information they would need to go to his place. He was sure he could help but it might take a while.

'I live on the way to Winchester. It's hardly a village, more a—'

Caz came in quickly. 'A smattering of houses, really.'

'Er, yes, I ...' Richard looked at her oddly.

Sweetly, Caz said, 'We left our car at the station. Could you give us a lift?'

Thirty

Caz used to play a game with a psychologist friend at university, trying to predict the cars owned by various people. Double-glazing salesmen drove Cavalier SRi's, nurses drove Fiestas, bookmakers had big Jags or BMWs and their managers went round in Sierras.

The friend did her third-year thesis on the Psychological Correlations Between Choice of Vehicular Transport, MMPI scores and the F-Scale. She got the first that Caz just missed when she proved the relationship between personality and transport, even after she had discounted economic factors such as availability and economic resources.

'Basically, Caz, some people wouldn't be seen dead in a Porsche, only Italians buy Fiats, train-spotters drive Ladas or Yugos, and Hooray-Henrys tootle round in Range-Rovers or thrash about in things with wire wheels.'

Caz was forced to ask, 'And second-hand MGB's?'

'Promiscuous. Even slaggish. Student doomed to failure, probably . . .' The friend's name was Cynthia.

She had actually said that the MGB was more of a woman's car than the MG Midget, usually indicating a woman thrusting her way into a man's world. Caz said 'bollocks'. Two years later she was a copper.

'So how do you like your Metro, Mr Richard?' she asked.

'What? Oh, it's fine. It's, what, economical.'

'And before this?'

'What, oh, I had another Metro. And before that, an Allegro.'

Caz thought, 'No cars then?' but instead said, 'Is your place far?'

'What, Oh, not far, no.' He crunched a gear. 'We, er, turn here.'

The house was pleasant, small, two-up, two-down, studiously clean, neat and laid out for one. The kitchen was wiped and pine-fresh and the lounge-diner vacuumed and dusted. There were two books on the dining table and another dozen or so on a small bookcase. A largish IBM portable PC was on a small desk with two piles of race-entry forms beneath heavy glass paper-weights. There was a bulky dot-matrix printer on a bespoke stand to the right.

'Race HQ!' Richard said. He suggested tea or coffee as he flicked on his machine. Moira offered to make it, and Richard sat down in front of the monitor as it swelled into life. 'So what do you want to know?' he said confidently.

Caz sat down. 'First off, we would like to find out all the races run by a Leonard or Lennie Burke.'

'Middle initial?'

'C'

'And how far back?'

'To begin with we'd just like two years. Later on, we might want more.'

'No problem.' Richard said. His hand flicked quickly over the keyboard. Caz watched the screen. A logo flashed by, then a query form appeared. In 'surname', he typed 'Burk' followed by two dots, then he pressed the enter key. The screen went blank, then a counter appeared rushing madly through hundreds into thousands.

'Right,' Richard said. 'First off, I'll pull out all Burkes, male and female. We can filter out anything you don't want later.'

There was a double beep-beep.

'There are seven,' Richard said a few seconds later. 'Leonard C. Burke; Lionel Burke; and plain L. Burke; Ann & Sandra Burke – I know them, they're racing twins from Romsey in their mid-fifties – and there's David Burke and Les Burk without the "e" on the end. Which ones do you want?'

'Can you give me the latest address for all seven names?'

'Ann & Sandra too?'

'Yes. They might be related to our man.'

'OK.'

'I'll give Moira a hand with the teas,' Caz said. Richard was already shaping the query. As Caz left the room, the printer burst into life.

They were sat with their coffees – well, Red Mountain actually, as near as they were going to get. Caz had some computer print-out on her lap and a chocolate Hob-Nob biscuit in her mouth.

She spoke with difficulty to Moira. 'Leonard, Lionel and L all came from the Esher address. David Burke is from Pompey.'

'That's right,' Richards said. 'He's a good super-vet, fifty-two years old and still breaks thirty-eight minutes. Very thin.'

'Scrub David, then,' Moira said quickly.

Caz continued. 'Les Burk, no "e", is down as age twenty-eight, no estimated time, and an address in Fareham.'

'And another one in Richmond,' Richard said.

'This is going to be a nightmare!' said Moira.

'No it isn't,' Caz said. 'Let's start again. Dean, can we look at finishers and their times?'

'Of course.'

'Right! Then let's go!' She wiped crumbs from her lips and stood up.

The database had nine thousand, four hundred and eighty-one names.

'Nothing faster than forty-two minutes.'

Six thousand, two hundred.

'Nothing slower than fifty-two minutes.'

Four thousand, eight hundred and eighty-eight.

'Scrub under twenty-fives.'

Four thousand, one hundred and twelve.

'Scrub over thirty-fives.'

Nineteen hundred and eleven.

'Were any of our unknown Burkes with a club?'

'No.'

'OK, no club runners.'

Eight hundred and seventy-seven.

'No women.'

Four hundred and ninety three.

'We know Burke ran in the fifth, six, seventh and eighth Totton 10Ks. Take out anyone who ran elsewhere on those dates.'

'It'll take a while,' Richard said.

They waited. Three hundred and twelve.

'Take out anyone with an address in the last year that's the same as it was more than eighteen months ago.'

Seventy-six names.

'More coffee?'

'Please, Moira.'

'Yes, please.'

'Can you add some priority fields, Dean?'

'How many?'

'Say three – one for finish time, one for name, one for address?'

'Easy!'

'Great!'

'Anything else?'

'A print-out of that last seventy-odd?'

'My pleasure.'

The printer began to sccripp.

'So where d'you want these coffees?' Moira asked from the door.

Dean Richard knew seven of the remaining names

by sight, dragging the total number below seventy for the first time. Caz was pleased to see Lionel Clarke and Bill Leonard had been caught in the net along with another forty-eight minute man, Larry Copthorne. While Dean added the three other database fields, Caz wrote 1s, 2s and 3s on the paper on her lap. Forty-four minutes through to forty-eight minutes got a one, the quicker runners got a two, along with the slower, forty-eight plussers. In the name column she gave 1s to Burke, Breck and Brack as well as Clark, Clarke, Leonard and Copthorne.

Caz gave 2s to any other surname beginning with B, 3s to the rest. Two 2s she upped to 1s when she realised that the initials were L. B. and L. C. B.

She was miles away when she heard the computer man speak. 'Done!' Dean said. 'Now what do you want to do?'

Dean Richard made a happy and helpful taxi-driver, dropping Caz and Moira off at Hulse Street. At the computer in his home, he had been in control and his confidence had soared from his earlier diffident self to someone very much stronger and self-assured. Only slowly was that confidence waning, and he chatted comfortably all the way into Southampton. His quieter nature was betrayed just briefly when he finally said goodbye. Once more, the car met the personality. 'What, oh. I hope everything is, er . . . Well, goodbye then . . .' He was trying quite hard, and both the policewomen gave him their very best smiles. When he drove away he was pink.

'Right!' Caz said briskly as the car prutted away. 'Let's get indoors and play with these names.' She was waving paper and a small computer disc.

'D'you think Peter will still be there?' Moira asked.

'I should worry?' Caz said with a look.

'I was just . . .'

'You were, weren't you?' Caz said.

Thirty-One

Peter Mason *was* there. Moira's eyes widened when
he said hello. Caz got on the phone to Brighton but
the DI and Billy Tingle were out. She left them both
messages. Yes, Moira was saying, they *were* stopping
in town tonight, they couldn't get expenses for a
hotel. They didn't fancy starting from Brighton at
four o'clock and Gareth Boxx had lent them a key.
Caz groaned. She made another mental note to talk
to her oppo about her hormones. She looked at
Peter's face. It had gone from interested, through
friendly, to predator in about a quarter of a second.
In a split second less, Moira had gone from innocent
abroad to sacrificial lamb. Caz went for a half-hearted
go at him. 'Presumably you'll be going home to see
the wife, tonight, Peter?'

'What? Well actually, she's away at a friend's.'

'So, let me guess, Peter. You're looking for company.
We're supposed to be eating out tonight, are we?'

'Well, it'd be—'

'Nice?' she said, faintly sarcastic. 'Three not a
crowd then?'

'Isn't Gareth coming?' Mason asked. 'I thought – with the key, you know . . .'

'Know what, Peter?'

'Well I just thought . . .'

'You presumed.'

'I just thought,' he insisted. 'If we were all in town . . . We could . . . Well, we could make up a four. Get something to eat, maybe do a club or go to a casino.'

'You did, eh?'

'Well, yeah. No strings or anything. Just mates out on the town.'

'I hate casinos,' Caz said.

'So do I. How about a club?'

'Too smoky. Too many boy racers and bimbos.'

'Quiet coffee back at your place?'

Caz corrected him. 'Boxx's place.'

'There, then.'

Moira got in quickly and said, 'Why not?'

Caz was thinking, 'Oh, Moira.' They had no clean clothes and that was the first 'why not' of fifty. That was what she thought. She *said*, 'OK, Peter, you win. Seven o'clock, Boxx's place.'

Caz was quiet as she drove the Daimler round to Grosvenor Square. The projected night out had made her think again of Valerie doing his thing out in the winter sun. The unwanted image of someone dark-lipped and sultry with designs on his body had flashed back into her consciousness. She was annoyed at herself for allowing the thought and even more annoyed for agreeing to go out with Moira and the DS. But then Moira probably would have gone anyway ... and Moira wouldn't handle ...

Her anger slipped out into words. 'But it's got nothing to *do* with you, Flood!'

'What?' Moira said.

'Nothing,' Caz said. 'I was just thinking about something.'

There were large, black wrought-iron gates into Osborne House. Moira swung them back and Caz drove the Daimler through. There was something about hiding behind gates that said money, power, maybe superiority. They parked in the visitors' slot and walked round the back of the building. The few cars that were parked there were expensive, starting at Porsches and working down, but only as far as nice BMWs. The Ferraris were probably garaged. Even with security gates, you couldn't be too careful.

This time they didn't need to call Gareth Boxx on the security intercom. Moira flourished the key and grinned, just a little childishly. Caz told her to stop dicking about. 'Fer God's sake, Dibben. Let's get in!'

Boxx's note was pinned to their door. It said, 'Why eat out when someone will cook for you?' When they looked at *his* door, another note said, 'When you like, after seven.' Moira was grinning again.

Caz reacted. 'No way, Mo. You couldn't be more wrong.'

They went in, not sure what they would find. Moira

looked like a child, with wide, white, expectant eyes. Caz told her to put it away.

Boxx's main penthouse had been expensive, classy and sexy. The guest penthouse was expensive-ish and still sexy, but only faintly so. The huge lounge doubled as a studio but most of the photographer's various bits and pieces were stacked behind a black lacquered Japanese screen. The word was functional. Caz thought, 'Danish'. The furniture all looked pine; primary coloured futons folded up on sprung wooden frames.

Instead of the grey marble block in his flat, this lounge had a six-foot-square low table, some kind of bright yellow wood, pinish but not actually pine. A lamp with a fawn shade fell from the clad ceiling and hovered, absolutely central above the table, an inch from its surface. Boxx had left an ice bucket with two bottles of wine on the table, Sancerre and a dark Spätlese, Mosel-Sahr-Ruwer. One sharp drink, one sweet. Was that a bottle each or a spread bet? Either way, they were both suitably impressed.

Off the hall, there was a small pine kitchen where everything was squeezed away out of sight. The surfaces were shiny, some kind of pine-look melamine and absolutely spotless. Inside the cupboards, spices and tins were lined up neatly: artichokes, bambooshoots, beans, carrots. A-B-B-C. To the right of the cupboard was spaghetti, tomatoes, water chestnuts ... There were very few dried goods, presumably because this flat was less used. The room was almost too clean. The neatness made Caz think of *Sleeping With the Enemy*. She smiled lightly but said nothing of it. 'Let's do the tour!' she said.

They were like kids in a toy shop. One: darkroom. Two, three: bedrooms. Their host had arranged everything. Laid out for them were twin beds covered with neutral linen and decked with fresh towels, a set each. On the pillows two T-shirts. When they picked them up they could see they were printed with an advert for Boxx Brownie – a huge, red eye with a camera lens instead of a pupil and a splash: 'Boxx it. Keep the moment for ever.' Gareth had left a note – they might want something fresh to wear . . .

Moira seemed pleased, but Caz felt herself vaguely disquieted – invaded. Violated was far too strong a word, but it was the first one she'd thought of. She still hadn't worked Gareth Boxx out, and she didn't like that one bit. The more she thought about him, the more confused she got. In some ways he was frighteningly attractive, but something about him, that she hadn't yet been able to define, repulsed her.

Moira was saying something from the en-suite bathroom. She was sing-song, virtually crooning. 'Oh, bloody hell, Caz. Come in here and see!'

Caz followed the voice into the bathroom. In there was yet more pine and a lot of mirrored glass. The pine was the wall of the two-seater sauna, already baking, and the duckboard placed between that and the bath. The bath was something half-way between a conventional soaker and a tall Japanese tub. There were three steps up to it and one long step down inside, making a rounded enamel seat. There were no conventional taps, just buttons on the wall and a hole in the bath's side. On another pine table nearby were two jugs, again oriental. They were next to a sink, presumably meant to be filled and poured on to the occupant of the peculiar bath. On a long shelf were odd-shaped glass jars full of pretty coloured oils. The loo and bidet were conventional. The place was spotless. It gleamed like a show-home.

'How are you supposed to bathe in that?' Moira said, bemused. She waved at the tub. 'Do you stand up in it, sit down or what?'

'I'm not sure,' Caz said. She was trying to remember something she had read once. 'I think you sit in there or stand up and someone soaps you down. Then they pour the water over you out of those jugs.'

'Ohhh, sexy!' Moira said.

Caz explained further. 'I think the woman bathes the man, honouring him.'

'You what?'

'I'm not sure, but I think it's the nearest Boxx could get to a traditional Japanese tub, the ones geishas use to wash their men.'

'I don't know what you mean.'

'Neither do I,' Caz said. 'For sure. But I think it's good that we're here together.' She managed a little smile, but she still felt like she was standing on one leg in a gale. Boxx, you bastard! she thought. When was the last time she had read up on approach-avoidance behaviour; on catastrophe theory? She asked a question of Moira. Hormones aside, what did she think of Boxx? Moira was slow to answer, still looking around.

'Moira?'

'Sexy ain't it?'

'What is?' Caz said.

'This place. Everything. Being away for the night. You know.'

It was Caz's turn to be obtuse. 'Know what, Moira?'

'Don't tell me you don't fancy Gareth.'

'Like a gazelle loves a leopard, sure.'

'So you do, then?'

'Let's go and break open the wine.'

Caz turned and went out of the bathroom. There was a faint flutter in her breathing as she went past the beds. She made herself think of Valerie. She saw a micro-light curving in the sky, but then that bloody woman again. What a bitch!

'So how much?' Moira said in the lounge. 'How much do you fancy him?'

'Piss off, Moira. I fancy *you* more than Boxx. This is a bloke who thinks dead people are beautiful, remember? I don't fancy him, right?'

'That's good, 'cos I don't either.' Moira was being sarcastic. 'Or Peter Perfect. So we can stay in and be nuns together, yeah?'

'You could fit in that bath face down, Moira.'

'Oh, boss, are we getting touchy?'

'No.'

Moira softened. 'I wonder what Billy will be up to tonight?'

'Do you care, Mo?'

'Of course I do!'

'Why?' Caz asked.

'Cos he's my bloke. Don't be stupid.'

'*I'm* being stupid? Moira, you—'

Moira cut in quickly, a different colour to her voice. 'It's only talk, Caz. I don't really mean anything. I just like blokes coming on to me, don't you? Nothing has to happen, does it? We can just have a good night out, can't we?' She corrected herself. 'I mean, in.'

'Yes.'

'So everything is all right, then?'

'It's not a game, Moira.'

'What?'

'Sex.'

'Of course it is.'

'Oh, Moira, fer fuck's sake! You need to grow up fast or you're going to hurt yourself. You said all men are rapists, remember?'

'Yes, but . . .'

'But what? They're not? They are?'

'Not Peter or Gareth.'

Caz was twisting a corkscrew into the bottle of Sancerre. She was getting angry. 'Moira, there are nutters out there: sickos, blokes like Burke. They rape. They kill. But we're not talking about them. They're animals. They don't care what you look like or how you behave. They're sick. But what about ordinary blokes, blokes like Peter Mason, blokes like Gareth Boxx, blokes like your Billy? They're ordinary men. It's their *job* to fuck. They're bull males. You can't wave your red rag at them and then complain if they charge at you.'

'What are you saying, Caz – that we can't dress nice, look nice?'

'Here we go. "I dress for myself. It means nothing", yeah?'

'Something like that, yes.'

'Oh, Moira. You know that's ridiculous. Where are the glasses?'

Moira presented two long, thin champagne flutes.

Caz sighed. 'Let's go sit down, Mother Teresa.'

Thirty-Two

Moira took a single mouthful of the cold Sancerre and said it was far too sharp. 'I fancy something like Liebfraumilch,' she said. 'You know, like Blue Nun or Black Tower.'

Caz threw her the corkscrew. 'Try the Spätlese. If that's not sweet enough, you're dead.' She smiled divinely; all the more Sancerre for her.

They were sat on two of the folded futons. Caz's was a royal red, Moira's was blue. Caz smiled again at her friend. 'Moira, you've got a problem. You're a bit of a prick teaser.'

Moira looked up from her struggle with the bottle, chastened, red, ready to argue. 'How can you say that? I thought we were friends.'

'We are, Moira. But even friends can be bloody stupid.'

'I don't know what you mean.'

Caz sighed softly and took a deep breath. 'That's the worst bit, Mo. You probably don't.' She looked up. Moira looked hurt. The cork was still in the bottle. Caz spoke softly to her. 'Moira, trust me, you're an accident that's just waiting to happen.' She leaned over and took the bottle from her. As she spoke again, she wrenched the cork free.

'How did you and Billy start out, Mo? Can you remember?'

'We had a drink in the station club.'

'He fancied you?'

'Oh, yeah, straight away.'

'How did you know, Moira? Did he say?'

'No, I just knew.'

'If he didn't say, how could you know?'

'Well . . .' Moira hesitated. 'Well, from the way he *was*, you know, smiling, saying nice things. He asked me for a drink, didn't he?'

'But he didn't say anything?'

'Not the first couple of times. Later.'

'So you worked out that he liked you, that he fancied you, from the way he acted, from how he behaved.'

'Yeah.'

'And he knew you liked him, at least a bit, from the way *you* acted, from the way *you* behaved?'

'Well, yeah . . .'

'So you can give people, give *blokes*, a certain impression, without saying anything? They can read you, what you do?'

'Yeah. I'm not stupid, Caz.' Moira's face was darkening.

'No one's saying you're stupid, Mo. But we all do stupid things. This morning I calmed Peter down by just touching his hand. Now, tonight, he's round here and I could have to deal with it. My touching him was deliberate, even if it wasn't conscious. It was a mistake. Luckily, he thinks you're a better bet than me. I think I'm off the hook.'

'Does Peter fancy me?'

'I've no idea,' Caz said. 'Probably. But he thinks you fancy *him*. And he probably thinks he has a fair chance of getting somewhere.'

'But I haven't even—'

'Done anything? So who's Sexy Rexy?'

'I was just joking.'

'Of course you were, Moira. If you half-fancied DS Mason you wouldn't give off signals would you? Just like Billy didn't or I haven't with Gareth Boxx.'

'You said you didn't fancy Boxx.'

'But you thought I did.'

'Well, the way you've been acting. And you got too wound up far too quick earlier today. Yeah, I think you fancy him.'

'And Boxx will read the same signs, won't he? So, maybe now you can see why I didn't really want to stop here tonight. We've got a key. I presume Gareth has too.'

'So why *did* you stop?'

'Because *you* were stopping, and because I like going near the edge. And because I *do* fancy Boxx; I loathe him too. That's what fascinates me. I'm trying to work out something inside *me*.'

'So would you . . .?'

'What, Mo? Fuck him?'

'Well, yeah, I suppose that's what I mean.'

256

'Five years ago, I definitely would have. I tried a few bastards then. But now, no. He'd have to do something very special to persuade me. No, I wouldn't. Even if there wasn't Valerie.'

'I'd almost forgotten Valerie.'

Caz moved. 'We need to freshen up and I need to speak to the DI.'

'Does that mean I get first try at Gareth's tub?'

Caz managed a real grin. 'Moira, be my guest.'

Thirty-Three

There was a good chance that Tom MacInnes wouldn't be home, but Caz rang there anyway. He answered second ring. 'Hello, Caz.'

'How did you know it was me?' Caz said.

'Recognised the ring.'

'Oh, right,' she said. 'D'you want to know about our rapist?'

Caz gave the DI the aliases used by Leonard Burke, followed by probables to be checked out in the morning. She explained about the last seventy names, most of whom were certainly innocent. But those tagged with priority one, she added, they were a little more interesting. 'Burke doesn't seem to have invented names that are all that far from his own, Tom. It's possible that the false addresses he's given may be cousins to the real one, maybe anagrams or mixtures of real and false.'

'So what are you going to do with them?'

'Moira Dibben and I will be going to the Main Delivery Office at half-five in the morning to check

out all the Royal Mail. We should be finished for
half-seven. We'll check in at Hulse Road first thing
after breakfast and start eliminating the genuine
names and addresses then.'

'Can't we help this end?'

'Doubt it, Tom. Most of the addresses are in
Portsmouth, Southsea and Southampton. There's one
or two up the M3 but we're well on top of them. DS
Mason will be giving us a hand. We should be finished
by twelve.'

'OK,' MacInnes said. 'Ring me at John Street
before nine-thirty and fax across your suspect
addresses. You know we've got absolutely nothing to
do.' The DI had the faintest of chuckles in his voice,
but Caz thought he sounded lonely. She was a little
softer when she spoke again.

'We still on for that meal tomorrow night then,
boss?'

'Tom,' he said.

She said goodbye and put down the phone.

It was twenty-past six and Caz hadn't even thought
about her bath. The second bathroom in the flat had
become Boxx's darkroom, so it was the Japanese
tub or stink. She went through to where Moira was
luxuriating and humming some tune. The tub was
neck deep in foam, and the water was so hot that
Caz could see her mate going red beneath her brown
skin.

'Come on, Madonna. I want five minutes in there!'

'But Caz, it's—'

'Yes, probably illegal. Come on!'

Caz had ten minutes so she grabbed the front-door key and nipped down to the car. There was nothing worse than bathing and then re-dressing in dirty clothes, so she jogged round to check the boot of her car for spare gear.

She hadn't come prepared but it wasn't unusual for her to have running kit packed away, just in case. She couldn't remember, but when she opened the boot she discovered a complete outfit, all Asics, all blue. There were long, soft woollen bottoms, a medium long-sleeved sweatshirt splashed with the Asics logo, socks and trainers, a large T-shirt and, rolled inside, the *real* prize – fresh underwear. It had been a long day.

When Caz returned, Moira was still in the bath, still humming, but she was out two seconds before Caz had finished filling the threatened jug of cold water. Caz threw her one of the towels and went through to the lounge. Now she had made her point, she told Moira that she had ten more minutes. Caz was going to work out. Mo made a feint towards the bath but Caz shook her head.

'Don't even think about it, Dibben.'

Boxx had a top-endish Sony midi-system spread along one wall on another low pine shelf. It wasn't *high*-fi, but it was pretty good for a guest room. No wires showed, not even the mains. Then she saw the plastic enclosures hiding them, tacked underneath the wood.

Above the stereo shelf, exactly the same length and perfectly aligned, was a purpose-built cupboard, pine of course, one CD deep, but only a quarter full. Caz looked in. There was one U2, a Simply Red Japanese import, a Chris Rea, a couple of Led Zeps double CDs, and about a dozen heavy-metal bands: Metallica, Iron Maiden, INXS, Pil, Nirvana . . . She took out Rea's *Road to Hell*, knowing that the four-four beat of part two was good for working out.

She kicked off her shoes and jeans while the rain-fall and radio introduction to the first track trickled on, and by two minutes seventeen seconds of that she had rolled her shoulders, stretched her sides and loosened her neck. At two minutes forty-five, Rea began to sing. Caz stretched towards the ceiling, first with both hands then further still, with each arm in turn. The warm up was a total of four minutes fifty-three seconds.

Road to Hell Part II was another four minutes and thirty-three seconds. To the beat, she forced twenty fast press-ups followed by thirty stomach-crunches, then she went back to the press-ups, then crunches again. She stopped counting movements once the pain came, but kept pushing herself until the end of the track. She stopped then, dripping with sweat, reached up and selected track ten. For the next six minutes she stretched her hamstrings, quads and back, finishing by stretching tall and relaxing on the floor. A total of fifteen minutes, twenty-seven seconds. When she finally stood up, she felt great, like someone else, a pumping heart on elastic. Moira applauded lightly from the door,

Caz shook her head. 'You've got no idea, Moira. This you should try.'

'I'd rather ten extra minutes in the bath,' Moira said.

'Fit is sharp. I want to be sharp tonight.'

'Does that mean you don't want another drink?'

'Don't be stupid, Mo.'

'Oh, good. Where d'you want it?'

'In the bathroom,' Caz said. 'Did you clean the bath?'

'Of course. And while you were bruising your bum I ran you a fresh one. It's waiting for you. Am I a wonderful person or not?'

'Pass,' Caz said. She grabbed her kit and padded out of the room.

As Caz slipped down into the tub she could hear Simply Red. Moira must've changed the CD. The water was oily and smelled of flowers. It was delicious; sensuous. Moira tapped the door and brought in another tall glass of Sancerre. Caz took it. Then she sipped a little of the light wine and ooohed.

She suddenly remembered some Basingstoke runner giggling in the showers after a hard cross-country. The runner had said that bathing after a hard race was better than sex. Caz closed her eyes and thought about it. She thought about her body, then drank some more wine. It was close.

When Caz came out of the bathroom, her blonde hair loosened. She was wearing the Asics stuff and shuffling in padded white socks.

Moira was sulking. She moaned about Caz's fresh clothes.

'You know what they say, Mo. Be prepared.'

'What are you, a boy scout?'

'No, Mo, just careful.'

Before Moira could say anything, there was a loud, intrusive buzz. She looked at Caz, a brief flash of what looked like mild anxiety.

'That'll be the DS,' Caz said calmly. 'Must be an intercom somewhere.'

'In the hall,' Moira said.

'Well, we'd better let him in then, hadn't you?'

'Can't you?' Moira said.

Caz went out. She pressed a button.

The wall crackled. 'It's Peter.'

'Come on up. Boxx's landing. We're the door opposite.'

She pressed another button. There was a distant burrp. She went back to Moira, who still looked worried. Caz smiled. 'Keep your cool, cherub. It's not *that* bad. Just remember, big animals have momentum.'

Thirty-Four

When they opened the door, Peter Mason greeted them with a big grin. He was in grey slacks, black shoes, a navy blazer and a white T-shirt. If the girls had been betting on his dress-sense, they both would have come second. Peter had chosen 'cool'. It was smack on seven o'clock.

To be polite, they dragged him in and he drank half a glass of Moira's Spätlese. Then they told him they were eating next door. Peter eased back in his chair.

Caz told him not to get too comfortable. 'We said we'd go round at seven.'

'Oh, right,' Peter said.

When Peter had arrived, Boxx's door had been firmly shut. When they went out this time, it was ajar for them. They went in, heading for the sound of music and the smell of freshly-cut vegetables.

Gareth Boxx leaned a head back from his preparation and shouted them through to the lounge. He was wearing a plastic pinnie with the torso of a pink woman on the front in black underwear. He smiled affably. 'I'm cooking Thai,' he said. 'Come on in.'

Caz had forgotten the splendid lounge, the ceiling, the art on the end wall. Whatever Boxx was, he had the ultimate bachelor flat. She made an effort to mentally separate the man and the decor. As usual, Moira was open-mouthed. Caz pointed to her own lips. Mo closed up. There was more wine in another bucket, this time on his marble table.

As Caz saw it, Boxx shouted again. 'There's wine chilled on the table; a bottle of Sancerre and another bottle of the German. Just help yourself.'

'Got a beer?' Peter shouted.

'Out here. There's a selection. Take anything you want.' Caz noted that he wasn't in the least surprised by Peter's presence.

When Peter went through, they followed. Caz was carrying the bottle of Sancerre. She was curious. She wanted to see Boxx at work in a kitchen.

Moira was wearing the Boxx Brownie top, and when she walked into Boxx's kitchen he grinned. 'Didn't fancy yours, then?' he said to Caz.

'It's nice. Thank you,' Caz said, slightly muted. 'It didn't go with my Asics, that's all.' She could hear her voice. She sounded lame.

'Whatever . . .' Boxx said. He turned back to his cutting board.

'The beers?' Peter asked.

'Oh, sorry, Peter,' Boxx said quickly. He was back to lightweight again. 'Under there. Take what you fancy. I'll have a couple of Becks.'

'Right on!' Peter said. Another black mark for dialogue.

Peter came out with the two Becks and a couple of Grolsches. It figured, Caz thought; only a DS, stroke pratt, stroke medallion man, stroke boy racer, would ever even *think* of drinking Grolsch. Why fight for half an hour to get into a bottle of lager? Blokes!

'Ooh, could I have one of them?' Moira said.

'The Becks?' Peter said.

'No, the one with the funny top.'

Caz turned quickly to Boxx's handiwork. 'You're a serious cook, Gareth?'

'Whenever I can, yes.'

'Where'd you learn? That looks like you know what you're doing.'

On a large rectangular rosewood board were neat piles of cut vegetables, spring onions, topped and tailed, all of identical length, red-tinged Spanish onion cut into minute segments, red and green peppers in half-inch slips . . .

'I spent some time in Malaysia,' Boxx said softly, just to Caz. 'And a year in Thailand. A girlfriend once told me that food preparation is like foreplay. You can't take too much time over it.' He wasn't grinning. He turned to the sink to rinse the knife. It gleamed as he twisted it in the water. 'You cook?' he said.

'Some.'

'But you're always rushed, right? Never time to prepare properly.'

'I try; weekends mostly. With a friend round or

something.' Caz felt vaguely heady. She swigged a major chunk of her Sancerre.

'What about preparation?'

'I don't know. Every meal is different. I'm not a scientist. You look like you count peas. Me, I just wash 'em, cut 'em and chuck 'em in. There ain't nothing that I don't know about stir-fry.'

Moira cut in. She still hadn't figured out the top to her Grolsch. 'You never eat in, Flood. You live in Italian restaurants.'

Caz looked at Boxx as if she'd been caught lying. His tawny eyes were soft. They said, 'Take no notice, we understand.' She knew it was a technique, but her brain was arguing with her body. She smiled back, a similar message, her head's little voice echoing, 'Watch your step, Flood.'

'Moira,' she said sharply. 'We are talking about *food*, here; Armando's is food. Vindaloos don't count.'

Peter took Moira's bottle and sprung it open. 'What about Kuti's?' he said as the top phipped.

Boxx spoke. 'He's got a good point, Caz. Kuti's is Bangladeshi. Last year it got two rosettes from the RAC. There's only two three-rosetters in the whole country.'

Caz waved an open hand. 'I must be prejudiced, then. I think maybe it comes from my days as a student. I just can't see Indian meals as anything but a cheap night out after too much lager.'

'Oh my,' Boxx said. 'You *do* need educating.'

'Maybe. But it takes a long time to live down a

reputation. Eating Chinese out used to mean *el cheepo quickie*. Now they have gourmet oriental. It's still Chinese but now they call it Mandarin or they call it Cantonese.'

Peter laughed. 'The Thais have started out with the right attitude, then. They're expensive already, and as for that green curry stuff, jeez.'

'I'm serving some of that tonight,' Gareth said. 'Why, do you not like it?'

'Like it?' Peter said. 'Do I *look* like a man with a stomach?'

Thirty-Five

'So tell me, Detective Constable Flood, have you got your very bad person yet?'

They were seated round a large dining table dealing with Gareth's perfectly prepared display. The soup ('hot water waved at a chicken') was gone, and a serry of dishes waited for them down the centre of the table.

'Very bad, Gareth? This man is a *killer*. Try evil. Try sick. But "very bad"? It sounds like you're trying to be funny.'

'Not at all,' Boxx said. There was no apology in his voice. 'I was being polite with my guests. Personally, I can't manage to care very much about the guy, but I presume all three of you do.'

'It's our job,' Peter said bluntly.

'It's more than that,' Caz said.

Boxx waved at the rank of shallow bowls. 'Thinly-sliced beef, bamboo shoots, oyster sauce. Sesame toast; pork and ginger; lemon chicken. That sauce is pepper, quite hot. That one is sweet 'n' spicy.'

'What's the green stuff?' Moira asked.

269

'Green curry.'

'Yeah, but what is it?'

'Very, very hot and there's lamb in it.'

'You should try some,' Peter said. 'A little.'

Caz watched as Moira tentatively took a smidgeon of what looked like green mud off Peter's spoon. She turned back to speak to Gareth Boxx. 'From your photographs, and the addresses that went with them, we now know where the rapist *used* to live. It looks like he moved either just before or just after he started his attacks. My colleagues at Brighton will be trying to find out where he moved to when he left.'

'And he lived where?'

The green curry was beginning to work on Moira. Her eyes were watering and she was spluttering as she reached for her drink.

'Esher,' Caz said, looking across.

Moira slurped some more wine.

Caz leaned towards Boxx. 'I'm amazed at you, Gareth.' She wasn't yet quite angry. 'Do you really mean you don't care there's a serial rapist out there? Someone who has murdered at least one person and might do so again?'

'Why?' Boxx said calmly. 'It's only one more in a line. How can I be concerned about people I don't know? What's the point? You are concerned because it's your job, but what does it really mean to me? Why *should* I be concerned?'

'Human decency?'

'Why is it decent to pretend to care? Do all the "decent" people go out at night and walk the streets

to protect women? Do they campaign against por-
nography? What do they actually *do*? People *say* they
care. But what they mean is, "Hey, let's talk about
that rape, that murder, that air-crash." They have to
pretend concern. If they simply admitted that the
drama excited them they would be frowned on,
wouldn't they?'

Caz stiffened. 'Jesus, Gareth!'

Boxx remained calm but insistent. 'You're doing it
already. I'm being honest. I'm telling you I don't
have any particular feelings about a few strangers
in Brighton and you're damning me as a heartless
bastard.'

'Yes!'

'Well, you shouldn't.'

'Why shouldn't I?'

'Because it's false. It's bullshit. Everyone is
interested in death. Do you know how many people
are killed every day on the roads? Fifteen! We could
do something about that. But do we care about the
killed, the maimed? Do we really? Drop the speed
limits to fifty and you can halve the road deaths
overnight.'

'I spent a year scraping people off roads, Gareth.
Don't try to tell me that it isn't horrible. You don't
know what it's like.'

Boxx stared at her. 'Oh, but I *do*, Caz. I do.' His
eyes were firm and definite. 'I know what life is like.
I know what people are like. People are essentially
shit. You just have to accept it. When you accept it,
things improve. You do the best you can with

whoever floats by on the surface . . .'

The others were silent, watching Caz and Gareth at war. They heard Caz hiss, 'You what?'

'I think you heard me the first time, Caz.'

'How can you equate road deaths with murder?'

'Road deaths *are* murder. Every politician knows it. Every thinking turd.'

'Road deaths are accidents, Gareth!'

'No they're not.'

'You're so experienced,' Caz sneered. 'How long were you in Traffic?'

Boxx ignored it. 'What about drunk drivers?'

'Forget them, the rest.'

'Forget them?' Gareth countered. 'That's just it. You can't. Tell me, if we discovered tomorrow that halving the speed limit would eliminate road accidents, what would happen?'

Caz felt battered. 'I don't know.'

'Yes, you do,' Boxx said. He was in for the kill. 'They'd ignore it – argue with the evidence, anything. But would they do it? No bloody way! No government could pass it and none would try.'

'And you call that murder?'

'Yes. It's a conscious choice to let other people die for the sake of speed, for the sake of the economy.'

'I think that's a sick thought, Gareth.'

'No you don't, Caz. It's written all over your face. You kill people every day. I kill people every day. Nobody damns us because the deaths are accepted. Fifteen, maybe twenty dead a day is the going rate, that's all.'

Peter looked away from Moira for a moment and asked, did Gareth really believe that?

'Of course I do!' Boxx said. His face was lit up like a missionary. 'We can build safer houses if we want to. We can build safer cars, safer roads; and trains and planes and kiddies' toys. But *they* don't *sell*. Travelling slow doesn't sell. People don't want to pay to save other people's lives. Accidents happen to other people, everyone knows that.'

'What's this got to do with rapists and murderers?' Caz said.

'Everything. You could light every street, you could put four times as many policemen out there. That would make the world a safer place wouldn't it? But who would pay? Face it, Caz. Shit happens. It's a fact of life.'

Peter had cut in now. 'We all know shit happens, mate. So do the girls. We're coppers.'

Caz watched, fighting down something. Gareth was tense. Sprung. What she hated most was knowing he was right.

He came back quickly, almost breathlessly. 'That's it, Peter, we watch all that shit on TV news and read about it in the paper because it *excites* us! We love it, don't we? Don't we? We all need drama. Biafra, Clapham, Lockerbie, we *live* off it, for Christ's sake!'

'I had a friend in the Clapham crash,' Peter said softly.

'So you felt different, right?'

Peter stiffened, his hands poised on the table's edge. 'Yes,' he said. 'She was killed.' He spoke deliberately, as if daring Boxx to say something wrong.

Gareth merely smiled. His voice lowered. 'That's OK, Peter. I understand your selfishness. It's good. This one disaster directly affected you. That's perfectly understandable. It's only when it comes home to us, when it comes close, that drama becomes tragedy.'

Peter looked as if he ached. 'She was an ex-copper,' he said dully. His words came slowly, but he fixed Gareth with a stare. 'We went back a long way.'

Boxx sounded sympathetic. 'I know, Peter. But the trains are just as fast, aren't they? They run just as often, don't they?'

'You know they fucking do!' Peter snapped. 'What are you trying to say?'

Gareth smiled. 'Someone did something wrong. No one went to prison.'

'British Rail got fined.'

Gareth smiled again. 'The taxpayer paid the fine!'

'That's just the way it is.'

'Remind me,' Boxx said slowly. 'It was what, thirty-five people, right?'

'Thirty-six,' Peter said.

'So if I kill thirty-six people by doing something wrong, I get fined and someone else pays the fine for me?'

'If you say so.'

'But if I kill one person in a fight, I go to prison. How many would have had to die at Clapham for someone to have ended up behind bars? Fifty? Eighty? What's the going rate?'

Caz suddenly felt massively tired. The wine was gone. She waved an empty glass, then asked if she could say a word. There was a charge in the air, dark and thick. 'Do you mind?' she said. Both the men said no and their shoulders dropped. Peter's hands waved at her. Caz took a breath. 'It doesn't matter. If it's not going to change, it doesn't matter.' Gareth moved as if to speak but Caz spoke again to pre-empt him. 'As one turd to another, Gareth, can't we stop this?'

Boxx sagged and waved, but he said OK.

Caz said thanks. 'Can I get badly pissed now?' she asked flatly. 'Is that OK?'

'That seems like a fairish idea,' Moira said.

'OK,' said Gareth. He was utterly relaxed. 'What does everybody want?'

Thirty-Six

There are only so many ways of getting pissed, but there are different kinds of pissed. Moira was used to the frivolous, giddy journey with a bunch of mates; through blurred to silly and on to being sick. That was the kind of atmosphere that could get you drunk drinking Coke.

Or there was the drinking craftsman approach, where you were alone in the crowd, studiously downing whiskies or vodka; where the taste didn't matter, the people were incidental, and anything said was responded to by your autopilot head. You were sober that way, just angry, until at the end of your night, you tried to stand and you realised someone had removed your spine.

And there was this kind of drinking – calculated, menacing, challenging the glass, the bottle, the amber poison of the Scotch; there was tonight's kind of drinking – joyless, quiet, where everyone knew they were taking poison but that if they didn't talk about it, it wouldn't hurt so much. It was the kind of getting drunk that Valerie called 'bad drunk'. The kind of

drunk he said he'd be if he ever put a pistol in his
mouth. This was the kind of drunk Caz wanted to
be.

They hadn't quite stopped arguing. Peter had
wanted to blame the BR Engineering Management
for Clapham. Moira had tried to say something about
the ordinary blokes, the engineers, doing too much
overtime. When Gareth then spoke it was very carefully, no longer confrontational. He said that the
engineers had to live and if they'd been unavailable
for work, they would have soon discovered which list
they were on. He said that the foremen were given
a job they more or less couldn't refuse. He said that
pressure had come from a management itself under
pressure to update the signal mechanism and all that
had come from a government desperate to straighten
out British Rail and turn it into cash. 'And then, of
course, there are all those blue-rinses who will vote
them back in and the commuters who'd do anything
to get to Waterloo two minutes earlier.'

When Caz said 'Stop!' this time, it was stop. Gareth
had stood up, left and returned with a tray, glasses
and an assortment of bottles. The room suddenly felt
colder. When he put the tray down, he put it on the
floor near Caz, sat near her on the thick carpet, put
his hand on her thigh, waited for her to look into his
face, let the lock hold on for two complex seconds,
then he said sorry.

Caz looked back at Boxx, trying to decide on
something. She nodded slowly. Gareth passed her a

thick-based glass. She chose the Glenfiddich and asked if there was any ginger. She was waiting to snap back when sacrilege was mentioned but nothing was said. Boxx took the vodka.

They had met at seven o'clock. They had eaten by eight. By nine o'clock they had fought and had stopped. By ten they were lip-numbed drunk and by eleven o'clock they were alone.

When Moira and Peter creaked upright some time around ten-fifteen and Peter had made some mock-slurred statement about a club, Caz had just looked up, her eyes the neutral side of cold. In the morning she'd remember that she had said 'momentum' to Moira. She would forget for a while because the word had been wasted.

Moira was the first kind of pissed. She was out of control and Caz didn't give a shit. It was like watching someone walk off a cliff with a smile on their face. Caz wondered if she did care, or was Moira just one of the day's fifteen. Caz was dying herself, working at it. When she thought about Moira, her temporary little death didn't seem to matter much. As Moira left, yards behind Peter, Caz whispered, 'Don't cry in the morning.'

Thirty-Seven

Later, Gareth fucked Caz. Then *she* fucked him. It
was dark, desperate, and technically sound. They
fought in a bed with navy sheets, Caz wanting to
throw herself back at him hard, damning, cursing,
hurting, trying to pretend that Valerie didn't exist.
When Gareth slipped down between her legs she
looked up at the ceiling lined with a street shadow
and thought professionally about the sensations,
marks out of ten. She had been hot with neither
passion nor lust and she knew it. When she realised
why exactly she had done this to herself she asked
him to stop.

'I have to go now, Gareth,' she said firmly. For a
second, he continued. She grabbed at his hair. 'I'm
going *now*,' she said.

She squirmed free, smelling her own musk and
another, sharper smell – distaste. She stood at the
side of the bed, a black shadow across her face. Boxx
looked as though he was about to speak.

'I'm all right,' she said quickly. 'I'll wash next door.'

When she looked at his face, it was tainted a faint

279

purple by a trick of the light. 'Had to be done,' she said. 'Didn't it?'

'I thought so,' Boxx said.

'And you have a big dark secret, right?'

'Bigger and darker than you could handle, Caz.'

'There you're wrong, Gareth.'

'We'll see,' he said.

Then she asked him if he had any Elton John.

'Most of his stuff. Take what you want.'

'And the rest of that bottle?'

'Be my guest . . .' Gareth said.

'Thanks.'

She was naked when she left him, her clothes rolled in a bundle round her underwear. She found Elton's Love Songs, a glass, the bottle. She went to the Japanese tub to wash, to soak with 'Blue Eyes' on repeat. She had worked out that she did love Valerie but she found it impossible to cry.

Thirty-Eight

The early morning alarm call was booked for four-fifteen. It came too late to save Caz the dreams she had feared and too early for the alcohol in her to have faded to anything approaching legal. She woke, still drunk, unhappy and wanting to hurt someone.

The flat was somebody else's, with a somebody else's smell and a somebody else's electric feel. She had given herself an hour, less the time Moira would waste, and the seconds it would take to eat a couple of slices of toast. As she rolled out of bed she groaned, thinking of Valerie, willing a postcard from him, a message, his early return.

It wouldn't be very nice outside; dark, sprinkling cold and winter slippery. There would be no one on the streets but she had to get out and run. She felt round in the dark and found her work underwear from yesterday, slipped into that and then into the blue Asics shorts, her legs up in the air. She took the Boxx Brownie T-shirt and pulled it over her head then slipped into some soft white socks. When she padded lightly from the bedroom, her Asics racing shoes were in her hand.

Moira was on the lounge floor, on one of the bright futons. It looked like it had been dragged drunkenly off a chair, the bedroom too far to make. There was a bottle tipped over near her sleeping body and a small sea-stain, once froth at the bottle's mouth. Moira looked terrible, lilac eye make-up and mascara a mess on a face left ugly by her open mouth.

Caz picked up the bottle and gently pushed at her friend's jaw. Moira rolled and muttered down deep in sleep. Her face looked sweet but run with tears. Caz pulled the blanket up and slipped away.

Outside was sharply dark, a peculiar neoned cat-cold morning. The cold hurt and Caz was glad of it. She started to jog, quite lightly, feeling the bite of the cold in her nostrils, in her throat. With no time spare, she circled the building once, then headed for a multi-storey car park a hundred yards away.

Its slopes meant pulsing muscles, pain, cleansing.

She went in, past black and yellow striped barriers, through the random smell of piss and night. One light only shone on each level, making the floor shine amber as she flapped very quickly past.

There were eight floors. By four, she felt her quads, by six they burned, by seven they screamed. On the last half floor, white and frosted, she kicked again, one push through the fire, knee-lifting to take the very last ramp, taking the burn. She stopped, heaving, by a rolled red fire-hose, the city black and loam beyond her. She rested ten seconds then started to jog back down.

On the second climb she shaved a second off her time. At the top she looked out at clocks and roofs, allowing herself thirty seconds.

On the third run up she was slower, and on the fourth, without a rest, she ran the fastest time of all. The cast hands of the clock on the white tower of the civic centre clunked on to ten-to-five. A minute later she was jogging from the car park and across the road to the flats.

Her body had been rushed through. Caz felt close to whole, but she knew that last night would not fade as quickly as the drink. The dark around her wrapped her mood but she knew there was nothing to do but wait for time to pass. She went in. She used the lift and stared at herself in its mirror. The doors took seconds to open, leaving her too long with a clear look at herself. She went in to the flat. Moira was about to experience fall-out.

Caz flicked a kettle on. The clack was followed by a rush of taps. The kitchen brightened, then there was the click of spoon on mug. Now the lounge lights, harsh, followed by a quick dash of noise, Caz calling Moira back from the dead as she filled the bath.

Caz bawled through. 'We have to be gone in twenty-five minutes, Mo.' She was already naked, pouring bath oils. When she heard nothing, she shouted again. 'You can have my water.' She was stepping into the tub. 'Come on, Dibben! We've got work to do!' A noise came back. Moira was awake, cursing about DCs. Caz sounded painfully alive. That was close to the truth. Flood was human again. Just a little darker, maybe. Maybe empty, but still going.

Caz was still gently broiling when Moira scraped through. She stood at the door, forlorn. Caz looked up to see her mate and made a vague sarcastic remark. Moira looked about to cry and turned to the sink.

'There aren't any toothbrushes,' Caz said. 'Looks like Gareth Boxx is not perfect after all.'

'But I need to—'

'Use toothpaste and a towel, then.'

'I . . .'

Moira was pathetic. Caz put a finger roughly to her own teeth to explain. 'Like this, you know . . .'

'Oh, Caz . . .'

'Don't drink it if you can't think it, Moira!'

'OK,' Moira said.

Caz asked if she was all right.

Moira said of course. Then she asked if Caz would be long in the bath.

'I'm about ready,' Caz said, pulling out an arm and staring at it. 'What kind of pink would y'call this?'

'Lobster,' Moira said. She sounded flat. Too flat to talk back to.

'You're not a happy bunny, are you?' Caz said. When Moira failed to reply she pulled herself upright and stepped out. They were in too much of a hurry for a proper chat. 'Twenty-five past is the latest, Mo. You going to be ready?'

'I'll be ready,' Moira said. As Caz went by her, a

little instinct flashed awake. She thought about asking was everything all right, but when she turned Moira was already sliding downwards into the oily water. Caz turned away.

Moira's long sigh sounded like a valve letting steam. Later, Caz thought; we'll talk next time our feet touch the ground. Moira had allowed herself to sink gently beneath the water. The end of her sigh turned to bubbles but Caz was already gone.

Thirty-Nine

They were away on time but only after gulping down over-milked coffee. On their way down the stairs Caz was still eating honeyed toast. Moira was quiet.

They were little more than a mile from the Central Delivery Office and they swished there gently through early-morning streets, past the old city's walls, darkened offices and unattended bus stops.

'Not exactly busy is it?' Caz said quietly.

Moira huffed. They turned right and crossed the High Street near a bomb-ruined church. Suddenly there were people.

'This busy enough for you?' Moira said.

The streets were full-parked, double-parked, vans and lorries competing for illegal roadspace. Burring and whirring between them were yellow-decked fork-lifts, large men and scurrying boys. There was a faint smell of discarded vegetation and diesel. Boxwood crates spilled cauliflower and oranges. It was another world, a night-world, bizarre and oddly exciting. Caz sniffed the air, reacting, but Moira was neutral.

They parked on double yellows and walked

towards the activity. It was five twenty-eight and not a postman in sight. As they rounded the last corner and stepped carefully between crates, a woman cycled past, her navy uniform with piped red peeping from beneath a waterproof.

The woman chirped at them both, 'Guh mornin'!' Automatically, Caz said 'Good morning!' back. The woman was wobbling the bike through the debris. She raised a hand and waved back at them as the bike turned right, disappearing through a gateway. The greeting had brightened Caz's mood. 'That's where we want to be,' she said brightly to Moira. She was pointing at the blue gate.

'I can read,' Moira said. God, Caz thought, she was in a *wonderful* mood.

Caz walked ahead, following the bike's little red light.

DS Mason had told them that their contact at the Delivery Office would be a man called Pete Jackson. As they turned into the still empty yard, a dark-haired, light-faced man in civvies waited to greet them at the top of a concrete ramp. 'Mr Jackson?'

'The one and only!'

'I'm DC Caz Flood. This is WPC Dibben.'

'You're just in time.'

'We are?' Caz said. 'For what?'

'To beat the rush,' Jackson said.

He waved for them to join him. As they did, he said, '*That* rush . . .'

Moira turned to look first, a half-second before Caz, just as the first of the morning postmen entered the yard, a scattering, like early-leavers at the end of a football match. Caz thought, 'Where did they come from?', but before she or anyone had a chance to say anything, the stutter of people became a trickle, them the trickle a steady flow. They were mostly men, but there was a fair sprinkling of women, all in navy-blue and red, but most with an extra top, gloves and a scarf.

'My people,' Jackson said with a little sarcastic grin. 'Family, every one of them.' The two policewomen turned. Jackson was grinning. 'Mother-in-law . . . ugly sister . . .' He was gesturing vaguely at the stream of bodies. As they arrived at the ramp he began to acknowledge each and every one. There was George, a Frank, two Sheilas and a Clare, 'Chivvy', Jack and Smiler, and then a stream of names and back-chat too rapid-fire even for a quick policewoman's ear. Someone, just as he had passed, decided to ring back a tongue-in-cheek version of 'Always Look on the Bright Side of Life', and all those following took it up, rocking and rolling 'barrupp, barrupp, barrupp' as they went through flapped rubber doors.

'Don't you just love 'em all?' Pete said. Then, as there was still a question on Caz's face, he added, 'There are two special buses for early-morning workers. They pick up all over town; arrive five-thirty.'

The group banter of the troops outside the letter office had broken down inside into chattering cliques of threes and fours, or pairs of good mates talking about last night's telly or the match. Pete Jackson led them in. He was chirpy but very slightly awkward, not really knowing what two coppers wanted on his little patch.

'I got a phone call from Lawrie Jamieson saying you'd be coming in but I must admit I was a bit surprised. We've got our own checking system here and I wouldn't have thought your lot would be interested in someone nicking postal-orders.'

'You're right,' Caz said. She was looking into the expanse of the sorting office at a classic case of organised chaos. 'We're not looking for petty thievery; it's something else.'

'You'll tell me when you're ready I suppose?'

'Correct!'

'OK, let me show you how everything works.'

They walked slowly, like tourists at an exhibition, Jackson their guide.

'These alleyways are called roads; we've got three, South, East and West. There never was a North. Mail comes in from the Main Sorting Office in "local" bags, but sorted for just one of the roads.

'Over here . . .' he walked quickly away from the central activity . . . 'those bags are sorted by people like Jim. Mornin', Jim. Jim's been here all night. He'll be finishing in half an hour. He takes the South's letters and splits them up into the various walks.'

'Walks?' Caz asked.

'Postman's round.'

He moved on again to an area with a rack of open-topped sacks.

'Packages are pulled out and dumped in these, a

sack a walk. Each walk has a few boxes. The postman empties the boxes and sorts the letters out.'

Caz nodded. 'Can we see that?'

The three of them cut through the sacks past inquisitive eyes and a jokey, bantering crowd of post people. They were working with a peculiar rhythm, throwing parcels and large envelopes with an odd, floating gesture that seemed incredibly accurate. Jackson saw them looking and answered them before they could ask the question.

'You're looking at their arm action? It comes naturally. A few years back they had these industrial psychologists come in to see if they could improve efficiency. They took weeks trying t'figure out a better distribution method. Every newcomer does too; but this way's the best, believe me.'

They got to the head of one of the roads, a long parallel line of thin tables backed by grids of box upon box that Jackson said were called frames.

'The postman grabs all the mail that's been sorted for his walk. He comes down to his frame and then puts the letters into the actual addresses. This is Maggie. Mornin', Maggie.'

Maggie, the cyclist, had a shag of bright yellow hair and a twinkle in her mid-fortyish face. She never looked away from her clockwork efficiency but she still knew who they were. 'If you're looking for work, luvvies, don't bother. The only good thing about this job is the hours.'

'Finish twelve-thirty,' Jackson explained. '*Some* people like it.'

Caz looked at the frame, a grid of tall thin slots with street names below and numbers, one for every flat, every house, every office, on a round. Some of the addresses were written in a beautiful copperplate hand, with thick and thin strokes of a delicate pen. Jackson explained. 'We used to have two chaps, all they did was write and re-write the street names when walks were altered. We use a computer now.'

Moira finally spoke. 'What do they do now, wedding invites?'

'One's retired. The other chap's still here. He works as a cleaner now.'

'Well, *that's* a step up!' Moira said.

Caz asked if they could see the frame for the Northwood Estate. Clive Parker, the race director of the Totton 10K, lived close to there.

'That'll be S–62,' Jackson said. 'Chivvy Johnson's walk.'

Chivvy Johnson did not look like Caz's stereotypical image of a postman. As they walked through to his frame, Pete Jackson told them that Chivvy was renowned for his pipe, his placid nature and his low centre of gravity. He also told them that Chivvy did shopping for half-a-dozen OAPs and had tea with one or two if he thought they were lonely. He was short, solidly fat, dapper enough to be a bobo doll, with a great, grey-white beard topped by a pristine curled moustache. His eyes were wet and serene. He looked like someone who read Proust in the afternoons and fell asleep the moment his head hit the pillow. For a fleeting second, Caz envied him his peace.

'Chivvy. This is Detective Constable Flood and WPC Dibben.' The postman held out his hand. 'The officers would like to know more about your walk.'

'And what would they like to know?' He spoke of them but looked straight at them. The blue of his eyes was almost lilac.

Caz flashed a quick smile. 'We're not sure, er . . . Chivvy?'

'Bob.'

'Could you just tell us about your round, Bob. Your walk? Are you familiar with a race called the Totton 10K?'

'My walk is nothing special. I've been doing it for thirteen years. I do the Avenue and Northwood. The Totton 10K is the first Sunday of April and the first Sunday of October.'

'You know it well, then?'

'I know its mail!' he said.

'Which is?'

'Well they must get seven, eight hundred letters in the last month before the race, most of them in the last couple of weeks. After a while, you get used to it. I even band them up separately.'

'Band them up?'

'When yer getting your walk up together, you band up – stick lacky bands round chunks of yer round. I band up the Totton 10K stuff on its own. It does the organiser a little favour. When he gets his mail it's already sorted into personal and race stuff.'

'And do you sort all your mail?'

'More or less. If the night-shift's slack they sometimes do you a favour rather than sit around, but ninety-eight, ninety-nine per cent is down to me.'

'Thank you, Bob. You've been most helpful. It was nice meeting you . . .' Caz offered her hand again. The postman's second handshake was as warm and secure as the first had been; like his eyes. 'What a nice man,' she said to Pete Jackson as they headed towards the canteen.

'Very reliable,' Jackson said.

'Definitely not the villain we're looking for!' Caz decided.

Jackson laughed. 'If you're after villains I can give you an alphabetical list, but none of them work here.'

'OK,' Caz replied. 'Can we talk about it over coffee?'

Forty

'What we need, Peter, is some way a villain can get hold of specific mail. What we're actually thinking of is the entry forms for the Totton 10K.'

'You don't suspect Chivvy?'

'Definitely not,' Caz said.

'So what d'you want again?'

'You're a villain, Peter. You want to get at the mail that goes to the Totton 10K. How would you do it? How could it be done?'

'You've been to the Main Sorting Office?'

'A colleague has.'

'Well, you probably know it's just about possible to nick one-offs like pools envelopes for the postal-orders inside, but it's not easy to target anything significant. And there are one-way windows overhead with supervisors behind keeping an eye out.'

'So that's out?'

'I'd say. If your thief is regular, he'd be caught.'

'So we're back to this place.'

'Again, there's a thousand ways to nick *a few* letters but none to keep it up for very long.'

'Does that happen very often?'

'What?'

'Letters being nicked?'

'It happens,' Jackson said. 'A postman notices a lot of cards to a kiddie, guesses it's birthday time and lifts a few cards in case Grandma has sent a tenner. You'd be surprised how many people still post cash. If they didn't, then the few bad apples wouldn't have cause to steal letters.'

'So how d'you pick up on that?'

'You can't until you get complaints. But once you do, as soon as a round gets iffy you can send in test letters and see if they arrive. We always catch them in the end. People have got to trust their postmen.'

'Do you vet people when they apply for the job?'

'We have our own investigators, the same people that eventually catch the ones that go wrong. We'll take on people with a criminal record, but not if they've lied about it.'

'So, this round,' Caz asked, 'how could it be got at?'

'The night-shift, cleaners, the postman, his opposite number if he has one and maybe the postman or woman on the walks nearby.'

'The walks?'

'The nearby frames. Someone on S–60 might manage to lift something from S–62, but it would be pretty hairy trying to do it. That's what line managers – supervisors – are for. Odd behaviour sticks out usually. Because the everyday, normal activity is so smooth, it has a rhythm. If someone is doing something abnormal a super can just sense it.'

'But it could be done?'

'I guess so, but not long term. And anyway, if someone was nicking entry forms and cash, they'd be getting complaints at the race HQ wouldn't they? That would bring in the investigators. I don't see how your crook can be nicking stuff. We would know.'

They finished a second coffee, the usual abysmal stuff. Caz wondered briefly about what she was doing to her stomach. She excused herself and stood up to stare out of a window, down into the hall. She thought about letters, cards, parcels, junk mail, names, addresses. race-entry forms, people . . .

She saw only the tops of people's heads, their shoulders, their rhythmic, smooth, repetitive motions: letter in a slot, parcel, letter in a slot. She felt her stomach turning over. If Burke wasn't getting access to computer programmes then he had to be getting access to the mail. He *had* to be getting access to the mail. But Peter Jackson said it couldn't happen. So how was something that couldn't happen happening? She turned away from the window.

'Peter, could you tell me about the delivery rounds? What happens when the postmen and women leave here?'

There was little that Peter Jackson could tell them but he told them anyway. He told them how postmen sometimes took a quick tea-break around six. He told them how the most senior postmen had first option on the available rounds, and how the newest arrivals were firstly reserves and then got the grottiest, coldest, most miserable walks.

He told them about women out in the dark early mornings and how a postman or woman is usually seen as neutral, part of the landscape. Just once had a postwoman been attacked. She had screamed and her attacker had fled.

They were back downstairs and still strolling when Peter told them how postmen did blocks of flats with an assistant, often a woman. He told them how the woman would jam open the lift and guard the postbag while her colleague walked that floor. Acceleration, he explained, meant driving a van out and dropping off the various postmen at the beginning of their rounds. 'Up together' was when a walk was fully banded-up and ready to go out. Postmen were not allowed to band up until after the hooter went at six-thirty.

They were standing by a pile of filled postbags. 'And that's about it, ladies. I can't think of anything else to tell you.'

Caz asked if she could just wander for a minute. Something was niggling at her and she wanted it to come out.

Jackson hesitated. 'I'm not really supposed to . . .'

Caz looked up, smiling.

'But seeing as you're both coppers. I guess . . .'

Jackson walked slowly away. Caz watched him go then shook Moira awake by saying, 'Come on!' They started at the beginning of the letter sequence again, watching the packages being sorted, the walks being topped up, then the individual letters finding their ways into their personal slots.

A few postmen nodded and said hello now that the supervisor was not with them. Caz said hello again to Maggie and then to Chivvy Johnson. Caz was searching for something, something that was vaguely nagging at her. She had wandered around waiting for the thought to solidify but it stubbornly refused.

'Haven't you had enough yet?' Mo said. She slumped down, still miserable, sitting like a great lump on a pile of fat mailbags. She was moaning. 'They get a measly hundred and sixty-five quid a week for forty-one hours of this. In the wind and rain. What do they do it for?'

Caz put her foot on to canvas. 'Some, it's all they can get; but most it's because it fills the morning. Like Pete Jackson said, they've got writers, footballers, people who play in rock bands. It's the rent paid but without work getting in the way of life.'

'What d'you mean?' Moira said.

'It's a job, Mo. Keeps you fit but doesn't get in the way. No stress.'

Moira was sullen. 'Well, it's not my idea of fun!'

'But being a copper *is*, right?'

'Did I say that?'

'No, Mo, you didn't. Now you tell me it ain't so.'

'It ain't so.'

Caz didn't believe that Moira meant it but she kept the conversation going. 'Would a bacon butty help or will it just make you think of Billy?'

    'Both.' Moira said.

    'Let's go, then.'

Forty-One

They didn't speak as they left through the back door. Pete Jackson waved a distracted goodbye and then they were gone, out through the rubber flaps and back into the tail-end of the wholesale grocery show. When they turned into the street, almost every lorry was gone and the street had reassumed its placid middle-of-the-night dampness. Caz was amazed, but had no one to tell. Moira with a hangover was bad news.

In the High Street, almost opposite Habitat, there was a tiny caff called Hasty Tasty, a top-end greasy spoon which probably made ninety per cent of its income before most normal people arrived at work. Caz dragged Moira in there and went to order. At the last minute, on grounds of health and fitness, she opted for a poached egg on toast rather than the butty, but even as she went to sit down she realised that she was conning herself.

The dripping bacon her body would deal with, but the two bottles of wine she'd had the night before would do a little more damage. For the one hundred and eighteenth time, she briefly thought about a year

300

off booze. Just once, before it was too late, she thought, she wanted to find out how fast she could run.

Moira was saying something. 'Did you have a paper round when you were younger, Caz?'

'I'm sorry, Mo, what? I was thinking about last night. I drank too much.'

'When I was fourteen, I delivered papers. How about you?'

Caz was amazed. 'What the hell made you ask that?'

'Those postbags. It just reminded me of humping newspapers around.'

'I used to deliver the evening papers and the Sundays,' Caz said. 'I hated the Sundays. With all those magazines and things, the bags were too heavy. I used to have to go back to the shop for a second bag.'

'I used to hump both bags,' Moira said. 'At the start of my round it was incredibly heavy but it soon got lighter. I just didn't want to have to go back, so I took the grief at the beginning.'

'You were a hero, Moira.'

'No, I was just a big, strong girl.'

'And now you're a delicate flower?'

There was a flicker of a smile on Moira's face, but it went almost as quickly as it had come. 'You're beginning to understand me, Caz.'

'Oh, God! I hope not!' Caz shot back.

They ate and were away by half-past seven. The

roads were still quiet and every traffic light was red, making the morning even slower. Caz had been thinking. 'I've just realised, Mo. We've got nearly seventy names to check out but if we go back to Boxx Brownie they can eliminate most of them on their computer. If Boxx has them on file, we can check the pikkies and eliminate them from our enquiries. What d'you reckon?'

'Seems sensible.'

'You could go up to Hulse Road, Mo. Start some of the house checks with Peter. I could go to Boxx's place for when he opens. Yeah?'

'Couldn't we do it the other way round, Caz?'

'What, you go to Boxx's?'

'I'd appreciate it,' Moira said. 'I just . . .' She was close to tears. Caz finally clicked. She glanced across at her friend. There was only one thing that made a woman that upset – that deep-down 'I can't get it out' upset.

'Oh, shit, Mo,' Caz said softly. 'What have you been up to?'

Forty-Two

They were in Bedford Place, only thirty or so seconds away from Hulse Road. Caz put her foot down as the lights changed, ignored the next left turn and headed for the Avenue. She couldn't believe that she had been so obtuse – the lounge, the mascara, Moira's refusal to react . . .

She turned up the Avenue, crossed a junction and headed for Southampton Common. A huge pub called the Cowherds was on the left. She pulled in there. By now Moira was crying freely.

'D'you need a cuddle, mate?' Caz said softly.

'No,' Moira said. 'I just need to talk.'

Not far from their car was rolling green; the sort of place Caz might run on a bright spring morning. But not now.

'I really liked Peter,' Moira was saying. 'I didn't mind having a few drinks with him, even a few too many drinks. He's a bit older; there's a bit more about him than Billy and he is sort of sexy in a mature way.'

Once these trees and bushes, these acres of grass meant that civilisation wasn't advancing. Now this hemmed-in splash of forest *stood* for civilisation.

'But he's married. I told him when we went out. He took me to some place called the Concorde Club on the way to Eastleigh. We had a few more drinks and we danced a bit. I danced up close because I liked him á lot. I could feel that he was interested, you know. When you're that close, a bloke can't hide it, can he? But I said I couldn't do it because of Billy.'

Two hundred yards away was an old public convenience with an odd Victorian slate roof. It was a classic cottager's cottage. It would stink of piss and crude pictures would be cut into the toilet doors.

'When we left, Peter was so nice. We kissed a bit in the car. That was sort of OK, and I thought I had him under control. I liked kissing him and he kissed well. We'd had a good night out and I thought this was like a reward.'

Some people were so desperate for sex, so hidden, so closeted, so unable to reach out that even a seedy toilet on the edge of a dog-turded park was . . .

'I thought he might try it on. Well, blokes do, don't they? He was big and he didn't give up straight away but when he thought he wasn't going to get anywhere he said he'd take me back to Boxx's place.'

But Caz could run herself into bloody pain. Run past places like that public toilet. She could drive herself until the pressures inside built and burst. She could wash away almost anything.

'When we got back, you were asleep. Peter came in for a quick drink. He said just for ten minutes. When he started kissing me again and trying it on, I tried to stop him. There was a part of me that might have wanted to do it but I kept thinking about Billy and I kept thinking that Peter was married.

'But it still happened. I tried to stop him but it happened. Peter did it to me. I was too drunk. I didn't feel anything much. He didn't use a condom. He made me, Caz.'

'He raped you? Are you saying Peter *raped* you, Moira?'

'He made me, Caz.'

The word is rape. The act is rape. The act is aggravated sexual assault. The offence is sexual intercourse against a woman's will. Caz told Moira.

'Moira, Peter *raped* you. That *is* what you are saying?'

'Is it?'

'Yes.'

'It is?'

'Yes.'

'Oh, Caz. What can I say to Billy?'

When you tread in dog-shit nobody blames the dog. They just know you smell and they don't want you bringing the shit indoors. When a WPC accuses a fellow copper of rape she is bringing it indoors. Never mind what happened, think of the smell. If he didn't put a gun to your head, and you got pissed with

305

him . . . If you went out dancing, dancing close . . .

Didn't he have a hard-on? Didn't you arouse him? You knew what he was like when you went out with him. You dressed like that – would you say you looked sexy? Oh, and it was sort of a foursome? You left the other two together and the pair of you went out. You were already drunk? And now you say he *raped* you?

'Moira, did you try to stop him?'

'All the time, yes.'

'You said no?'

'Yes.'

'Peter knew you didn't want to have sex?'

'YES!'

'He made you do it?'

'YES!'

'He forced you?'

'He forced me.'

'Did Peter actually threaten you? How did he make you?'

'I don't remember exactly. He just didn't stop. I was trying not to, and Peter took no notice. He just did it.'

'You were forced to have sex?'

'Yes. Peter forced me. I was raped.'

Forty-Three

'Have you thought about it, Moira? Have you thought about what you want to do?' Caz turned. The car creaked as she moved to speak. She felt heavy, as if the seriousness of Moira's news had somehow physically changed them both. Then Moira spoke.

'I don't know, Caz. I don't know what's best.'

A jogger swung past the car, running smoothly but taking it fairly easy. He was fairly light-boned, good heel-lift, wearing Reeboks; a Southampton City runner. As he passed, he glanced across at the two women then he picked up the pace.

'Caz, I don't want Billy to know.'

They waited. The runner was moving quickly away, kicking hard up a shallow incline and into the park. The car settled. Moira stopped crying. Far off a clock chimed. It was seven forty-five. Moira spoke very softly, with something that sounded like guilt tingeing her voice. She looked after the runner and deep into the trees, anywhere except at Caz or into a mirror.

'Oh, Caz,' she said.

'What?' Caz said gently.

'Caz, I don't think I *can* do anything.'

'I know, Moira.' Caz started the car. Before she drove off she took a deep breath.

Forty-Four

When they left the pub car park, Caz turned the Daimler away from the town and headed up the slight hill of the Avenue past the University and then out towards the A33. On the outskirts of town, she went left, following a sign for Romsey, wasting time and trying to think.

Caz wasn't certain about her own position if she sat on the information Moira had given her, but at least Moira had reported the rape within twelve hours to a police officer. There would be no medical evidence of penetration or of physical hurt and, anyway, Peter Mason would be sure to admit to intercourse. He would only dispute consent.

Moira had been pissed and happy to go off with Peter. At best, she would have a one-in-fifty chance of getting the Crown Prosecution Service to bring the case. If it got to court, her chances were then about one in five.

Two hundred and fifty to one was pretty lousy odds even if you were doing something for all women. They were lousy odds if taking them ruined your career and lost you your fellah.

But all that didn't stop Peter Mason being a rapist. All that would never give Moira back whatever it was she thought she had lost.

And all that didn't sort out the rest of this investigation. It didn't solve the immediate problem of who should work with whom.

They were approaching Romsey. A hairpin left immediately after a bridge turned them on to a one-track, mud-slicked road. Caz asked Moira the obvious question. Could she work with, speak to, sit in the same car as, the man who raped her last night?

'If you can't, Moira, we've got a hell of a lot of bullshitting to do.'

'I can't,' Moira said. 'He'll—'

'It's OK, Mo. Can't is enough.'

'What'll we do now, then?'

Caz swung a bend. 'I don't know yet. I'm still working on it.'

The road wound back towards Southampton and eight-thirty. On the way they had to negotiate a flooded stretch of road before coming to an industrial estate and the M271. They took the road marked 'Docks'.

They decided that Moira had food-poisoning. They would go to Boxx Brownie's first and Caz would ring the DS and put him on hold. If they cleared up the sixty-nine names at Boxx's they might not need to go to Hulse Road at all. If they did, Moira could stop off at a pub and Caz would go in there on her own.

'How does that sound, Mo? Peter will wonder a little bit, but that's just tough. I figure he'll be happy to keep his head down, so I don't see him creating about protocol or throwing his rank around.'

Moira blew her nose. Caz took that to mean OK. They drove towards town centre.

Boxx Brownie's reception was open. The cute receptionist, Mandy, was there, instant smiles and ready to issue her poem of the day. Something in the air stopped her though, and she merely said good morning. Caz felt a trace of guilt and said something nice about her hair.

'Had it done yesterday,' Mandy said brightly. 'D'you like it?'

'On you, it's great,' Caz said. 'Is Gareth in?'

Boxx wasn't in yet but his assistant Sally was. When they met at the top of the stairs she stared at the two detectives for a long second as if trying to make a decision. Caz explained about their list of names.

'No problem,' Sally said. 'We've got a pretty nice D-base system here. You've got your names on disc?'

'As ASCII.'

'Still no problem. Can I have it?'

The sixty-nine names were reduced to eighteen in forty-four minutes. Sally imported their ASCII file, converted it to a D-Base format one then cross-linked it to their database. Meanwhile, Gareth Boxx had come in. Sally broke off to make him coffee. 'How we doin'?' she said.

Five of the eighteen names they had left were known aliases of Leonard Burke. They were drinking coffee while they talked about the last thirteen. Boxx had breezed into the cutting room, nodded to Caz and Moira (he acted as though last night had never happened), and asked if he could help. When Sally said they were on top of things he said fine and left.

'He's in a funny mood!' Moira said.

'I've seen it before,' Sally said heavily. She caught Caz's eye and looked away quickly.

The thirteen names weren't anywhere on Boxx Brownie's system but it wasn't impossible that they might still be traceable at another photographers. Sally excused herself to try a couple, borrowing a print-out of the shortened list.

'At least this is going well,' Caz said once she'd left. 'How are you feeling, Mo?'

'I'll live,' Moira said.

'One pig at a time, eh?'

'Maybe they're all pigs, Caz.'

'What d'you mean?'

'I was just remembering that talk I went to in the summer. The one at Brighton University. They said all men were rapists. I told you. We had a row about it. You said it was stupid. You said not to generalise.'

'Let's not fight now, Moira. We might need each other.'

Moira looked suddenly pensive as if she was wrestling with a problem. Her voice sounded slightly strange. 'Caz, we're going to catch Burke, aren't we?'

'Yes!' Caz said.

'It's just that, forgetting the murder, Burke is a rapist, yes?'

'Yes.'

'And Peter is. Peter raped me . . .'

'What are you getting at, Moira?'

'Well, even though Peter . . . even though he made me, I can't help thinking that what Burke did is much worse. Is that because he's done it more than once, or is it because he hurt them as well?'

'Them?'

'Rene, Amanda, Jackie, Jane Daily . . .'

'The law says it's the same offence, Mo. There's only one kind of rape.'

'But that's not true is it, Caz?'

'What's not?'

'Peter is not like Leonard Burke. He just—'

'Peter *raped* you, Moira.'

'I know he did, but . . .'

'But he didn't? You *didn't* try to stop him? He *didn't* force you?'

'No he did. He did, but . . .' Moira was thrashing around desperately for the right words, almost as if she was looking for a way to excuse Peter. 'What I mean is, if I was on a jury, I wouldn't think that what Peter did to me was the same as what Burke did to Irene Stubbs.'

'Read your law, Moira.'

'I know it is, *officially*, Caz. But me and Peter, what Peter did, it sort of *happened*. I should have seen it coming. I was a bit to blame.'

'You were not, Moira! No woman *ever* is to blame for being raped.'

'I think I was.'

Caz snapped. 'You were *not*, Moira!'

Moira flinched. Then she sat forward, suddenly stronger as she spoke. 'Can't *I* decide, Caz?'

Caz was uncomfortable. 'What do you mean?'

Moira spoke firmly. 'It was *me* who was raped, Caz.' She was speaking slowly now but with a new-found strength. 'Can't *I* decide whose fault it was? Would you mind? I mean, is that all right with you?'

Forty-Five

Sally came back, clicking loudly in the corridor and cracking open the door with a flourish.

'Bingo!' she said as she came back into the room. The women's conversation was instantly suspended but not forgotten. Caz was seeing Moira for the first time, and seeing something of herself for the first time. Sally had just saved her. She had stopped Caz telling Moira that her rape belonged to all women.

'You've got five of these aliases, right?' Sally said. 'I took thirteen names with me and all bar three were on Mike Nixon's system at Reading. They do the same as us. I rang two other race outfits. Neither of them had these three either.'

Caz grunted. 'So we're left with eight names and five are definitely Burke.'

'Correct! Not bad for seventy-five minutes work, eh?'

'It's better than that,' Caz said. 'It's not far from brilliant! Could I use your phone?'

She was put through to Tom MacInnes and he said

good morning with a touch of affection in his voice. 'Good morning, Tom. We're down to just three spare names.'

'Are you going to tell me them now or fax me?'

'It's only three names and addresses, Tom . . .'

'OK, fire away. And how was the Post Office?'

Even as Caz started to speak, she was seeing the pattern. The first name was Vincent Pink. The address was Brayfield Towers, Southsea. The second was a Leonard Brayfield of Magnolia Terrace, Eastleigh. The last name and address was E. Lee Vincent, 17, The Terraces, Pinkney Hill, Bucks.

'The bastard's playing silly games with us!' she gasped.

'Not for much longer,' MacInnes said. 'So, how did it go down at the sorting office, Caz?'

'I'm not sure, Sir. I was with one of their line managers, a chap called Peter Jackson. It's possible to nick the odd letter but, according to Jackson, there's no way someone could consistently steal forms. That pushes us back to the computer men but I'd bet my wages they're clean as a whistle.'

'Why would Burke need to *steal* entry forms?' MacInnes asked.

'To get the addresses, to—'

'Caz?'

'You mean he only needs to—'

'Look at them, yes!'

'Jees!'

There was a long silence, both of them thinking. The open line between Southampton and Brighton buzzed.

'OK, Caz. We've got our eight anagrams, addresses and names. Burke is either playing games or he's incredibly stupid.'

'So do I get them to work on, Tom, or do I have to figure out the letters?'

'You and Dibben have the letter end, Caz, you're already into that. The DCS and me can play silly buggers in Brighton with the addresses.'

'Right!'

'I reckon Blackside is going to love you, my girl.'

'I'm sure.'

'Ring me every half-hour from half-past ten on.'

'No probs, boss.' She waited.

MacInnes spoke again. Very carefully. 'So it's how does Burke get to *read* the mail? You got that, Caz?'

Caz put the phone down. When she'd done it she stared blankly. She was still looking at the phone as she spoke to Moira. This was silly. If they hadn't been able to figure out a way for the animal to *steal* letters, why was the job any easier now? Now they had to think of ways for him just to *read* them.

'The DI says Burke isn't nicking letters, Mo. He's just taking a peep and borrowing a few addresses for his notebook. Any ideas?'

'The old steam job, you mean? Boil a kettle?'

'Maybe.'

Sally laughed. 'Like looking at the boyfriend's love-letters!'

'Right!' Caz said. 'But how is the question. If we get to how, we've got where. If we figure out how, Burke could be banged up today.'

'More coffee?' Sally offered.

'Why not?' Caz said. Then she looked across at Moira. It had been a strange morning. Caz's day had started at four-fifteen. It was barely ten o'clock and she was feeling peckish already. She had made a mistake passing up on that bacon butty and Moira had hardly touched hers. They'd been talking about . . .

'Mo, what were we talking about in that caff?'

'This morning?'

Caz blanked her.

'You mean this morning! I don't know. Running? You wouldn't have a bacon butty because you said they were fattening.'

'But what were we *talking* about?'

'Paper rounds,' Moira said.

'We both did Sunday deliveries . . .'

'And the bags were bloody heavy.'

'You used to manage two, Mo. You said. I used to go back to the shop.'

'For your second bag.'

'J. C. Bugger, Moira!'

'What?'

'How many letters does a postman carry?'

'Lots, I guess.'

'But Moira, how many *bags*?'

She went straight to the phone.

Forty-Six

'We call them pouches,' Peter Jackson said. 'Every postman has a first and second pouch. A van takes all the second pouches and drops them off at a pre-arranged place on the postman's round.'

'D'you mean behind a bush or something?' Caz said.

'No. It would be at a shop or with a member of the public.'

'And how are they chosen?'

'The drop-offs?'

'Yes.'

'The postman sorts out his own. The second pouch has a special tag. They are worth 42p when they get redeemed. We've got one paper-shop in the middle of the business area does very well, thank you. Four or five quid a day just for being open at the right time.'

Caz's hand was beginning to sweat. She was measuring her words now. 'Peter. Does Chivvy have a second pouch?'

'Of course.'

'And where is his drop-off?'

'A sheltered housing scheme for oldies in North-wood Road, called Brayfield Mansions. The pouch gets left in the warden's office.'

Brayfield! It felt like an arrow hitting home.

'And how long would the pouch be there? Is it specially sealed?'

'How long? It varies. Probably less than an hour on average. And they're not sealed, just tied up. But if anyone ever started lifting letters from a pouch we'd know straight away. That's the first place we'd look.'

If they were stealing letters, Caz thought, yes. But if they were steaming open race entries, copying names, selecting . . .

'Peter,' Caz felt giddy, 'I don't suppose you know the name of the warden at Brayfield Mansions?'

'It used to be a middle-aged woman, I think her name was Mary something. Something like Copstun or Colthorne, something like that. She died quite suddenly eighteen months or so back. I don't know who the warden is now. Chivvy'll know, though. He should be back in anytime.'

'We'll be there in five minutes,' Caz said.

Forty-Seven

Northwood Road was only two streets away from
Hulse Road police station. The thought that the
animal had gone to ground that close, freaked out
Peter Mason. Everything had changed with their
news, including the intention to protect Moira's sensi-
bilities. She had to come along. When Peter saw her,
he said a broad 'hello', not even a whisper of doubt
in his face.

Moira stone-faced him.

They got on to Brighton. Norman Blackside came on
the phone and said they had just decided that Burke's
real address might be Brayfield something. They had
been just about to start working through their Kellys
when Flood had rung.

The DCS went straight through to Winchester after
their call to brief the Assistant Chief Constable. The
ACC pulled out an Armed Response Vehicle, a
House Entry team and a couple of dozen foot sol-
diers and dogs. A mini-bus full of woodentops was

now banged up in the car park of the County Cricket Ground and two unmarkeds were thirty yards either side of the target building. So far no one had seen Burke or knew if he was in the warden's flat.

Someone thought to ring Social Services. The night warden was down on their list as Lionel Copthorne, the day duty was a man called Field. No one seemed to have a clue what either Copthorne or Field looked like.

The office had a breakdown of the residents as of June that year, but no one knew if there had been any comings or goings in the past six months. The wag at the Social said something about pouring them in at the top as they fell out the bottom. The DC this end of the phone call told him he wasn't funny.

The ACC was apparently very unhappy about an armed siege that might involve pensioners. He was *en route* from Winchester now and wanted nothing to happen until he got there.

They decided to use a water-board van to suss the place out. Two DCs drove up dressed in Southern Water overalls and tipped out some kit into the road. The older one then went and knocked on the warden's door to warn him that they were going to lose their water for an hour.

The day warden wasn't there. They knocked four more doors before getting a coherent answer. No, Mr Field was over the other side fixing one of the porch lights. When they found him, he was up a step ladder screwing back a glass cover and grunting. One of the detectives smiled up at him. 'Mr Field?'

Field's first name was Frank. He was sorry to be so vague, he said, but he'd had to do the sleep-in duty last night and one of the residents had got him out of bed at three o'clock in the morning. The night warden had had to shoot off, he said; something really urgent, a death in the family. 'His cousin came t'see him yest'day. An uncle died sudden. Lenny ast me could I cover for him for a couple of days. I said o'course.'

'Does Lenny live here?' the detective asked.

'In the spare room, backuv the office, yeah.'

'Could we just see?'

'What for?' Frank said.

They showed him their warrant cards. Frank was surprised. They weren't after Lenny, surely? Lenny was the biggest, softest bloke you could ever hope t'meet. All the old ladies loved him. They asked Frank, would he mind, but they needed to see Lenny's room? Frank gave them the key but he warned them. 'I reckon yer've got yer wires crossed if yer checkin' up on Lenny. Got a heartuv gold, Lenny. D'never do anythin' illegal.'

The DCs radioed in as soon as they'd opened the door. The suspect had done a runner alright, but there was enough evidence in his room to sink the Belgrano, including photographs. Burke wasn't coming back. He'd left them a message. Was that Brighton DC, Caz Flood still there? She was? Well they didn't want to be alarmist or anything but *her* picture was there too, a big one. And her address was pinned beneath it.

Forty-Eight

Tom MacInnes and Norman Blackside arrived just after one o'clock. Caz had spent the best part of the morning in the canteen under strict orders not to leave the building until her DI and DCS had spoken to her. Someone had managed to slip her a copy of her picture and a few Polaroids of Burke's squalid room. She had stared at those, at herself finishing a race, and tried unsuccessfully to work things out. What she found strange was that the race photograph suggested Leonard Burke had been stalking her. She found it hard to believe. She trusted her animal instincts. She was certain that she would have sensed Burke if he had been out there.

Gradually she was winding herself up. She had been cheesed enough when they kept her away from what she thought was going to be Burke's arrest. She had hidden the photos away and now she was getting a little bit more than slightly pissed off. By twelve-thirty she was ready to tear the arms off anyone who so much as smiled in her direction.

She had been downing extra-strong machine coffees and brooding over Peter Mason. He was over at Shirley Nick now, and Moira was down town pretending to be tidying up things at Boxx Brownie's. God, when that creep Mason had smiled at them this morning! She was thinking of different ways to hurt him when DI MacInnes walked in.

'Flood!'

The DCS was following. Caz stood up.

'Good morning, Sir!'

'Afternoon, actually, lass. Tek a seat.'

The DCS came in. He nodded. 'You OK, Flood?'

'Fine, Sir, I'm just sick to death of coffee.'

He sat on the edge of a table, hunching, trying to look smaller. Caz smiled briefly but couldn't sustain it.

'We have a situation, Flood.'

'Yes, sir.'

'Question is, what do we do about it?'

Forty-Nine

Considering that she was discussing an animal who had maybe been stalking her – a multiple rapist and a murderer – Caz was surprisingly articulate and clear-thinking. She wasn't at all sure why.

Burke had had her photograph. Was it one he'd taken, one from the local press, or a Boxx Brownie type of picture taken at a race? Caz told them that she thought she already knew. The DI said that it would be checked out.

Burke had also had her address, the address of her flat in Brighton. At least he hadn't been so close-in that he knew she had moved in to the DI's flat.

'Which suggests he's picked up on me like he did with the other women,' Caz said. 'From a race entry form. Probably from the Totton 10K.'

'Seems that way,' Blackside said. 'You might well have been one of his targets a few weeks ago, when the two women were attacked in Worthing.'

'Unless he's picked up on me since then, Sir. Since I became part of the investigation?'

'How's that possible?' MacInnes said. 'We don't put adverts in the press . . .'

'I'm thinking out loud, Sir.'

Blackside spoke again. 'We can't discount that possibility, Flood, but it seems much more likely you were one of three runners that Burke had picked out from the Totton road race. You were in hospital when the other women were attacked. Maybe he clocked your place and when you didn't show, he tried elsewhere.'

Caz shuddered. 'Do you think so?'

Tom MacInnes said it was the most logical explanation.

'I guess so, Sir.'

'And if you were back there now, lass, he might still be watching. He might be waiting for his chance.'

'So if I went back, we could catch him? I'd be the bait?'

'It's a thought, Caz. If you—'

'I don't think I could go back to the flat, Tom. Not after—'

Caz and the DI had slipped into using first names. The DCS seemed either not to notice or not to care. 'No one's asking you to move back in, Flood. Not if you don't want to.'

'But if Burke has already sussed my place out. He'll know I'm not there.'

'That's true,' MacInnes said.

'So even if I went back, we'd have to somehow let him know . . .'

'That's tricky,' Blackside said. 'I don't see how we can fix that.'

Caz sat up. 'Neither do I, Sir. But I know a woman who can . . .'

The deal Caz struck was a good one. First off, a team of professional house cleaners would be hired to strip out everything damaged or soiled and put her flat back as it was before her burglary. That was in hand by two o'clock.

The second part of the deal involved Debbie Snow and the *Sun*. Caz had been stewing for days now, trying to work out how she was going to turn her new-found fame into a Mazda MX5. She well knew that clearance from above was absolutely essential for anyone to be allowed to talk to the newspapers. She also knew that they virtually always prevented money changing hands unless it went straight to charity and not into a policeman's pocket.

But the publicity would be good for the force, she explained. After all, she was 'The Girl Who Saved Brighton'. Debbie Snow was keen to do her story. They could take her picture outside the flat and make sure the piece got into the Southern papers. Then Burke would know. When he came for her, half a dozen hairy coppers would be waiting for him.

Blackside wasn't sure if he could swing it on the money.

'Why not, Sir?' Caz said, excited now. 'It won't hurt anyone. Everything will be cleared before it goes to press.'

Blackside wasn't convinced. 'I'll do what I can.'

Caz smiled. 'And we get Burke too, Sir. It's perfect!'

'I don't know . . .' Blackside said again.

'You do, Sir. It all makes sense. Who loses?'

'Burke, I hope!'

'But no one here. No one on the force, Sir. I get my flat back, we catch a villain, we're all happy.'

'I don't see the Chief Constable wearing it.'

'I do, Sir. It's gotta be worth a try. He can only say no.'

Blackside tried to smile. His face changed shape but it wouldn't have been fair to say he actually smiled. 'OK,' he said. 'Meanwhile, you keep to public places and you watch your step, right?'

'Of course. Sir. But we already know Burke's MO. He attacks from behind and on the doorstep. I'm not that worried. If you're happy, I'm happy.'

'What are you up to this afternoon?'

'I need an hour's personal time, Sir. Then I was off back to Brighton.'

'OK. Tonight you'll be at Tom's place?'

'His sofa, Sir.'

'His sofa, right.'

Blackside turned to MacInnes. 'Tom?'

The DI rose.

They left. The DCS was muttering, 'The Girl Who Saved Brighton? Jesus!'

Caz watched their backs. One they were gone, she punched the air. She looked at the clock. It was ten-past two. She left, dropped a note for Moira at the front desk and went out, looking for Peter Mason. She had to make sure that he knew, she knew. All men? Maybe not. But this one? He was a pig.

Fifty

Caz had rung the station at Shirley. She had collared another DS, the only one in. The DS told her that Mason usually took a late lunch and spent it in a snooker hall called Q-Ball. A few of the lads had a game there, it was only a couple of minutes from Hulse Road in a panda.

When she went in she was stopped at the door. She flashed her warrant card and a thin, cold smile. She went straight upstairs, through maroon-painted double doors and into the snooker room.

There were six tables, all being used, but no Mason. The room was heavy with light blue cigarette smoke curling up into the lights. A couple of guys muttered something about a woman being there. She ignored them, went to the bar and ordered a Bells and Dry.

The barman served her. As she took her change she said 'Same again.' Then she heard Mason's voice, round a corner, on the other side of the bar. She slugged the first double and squeezed the glass tightly in her fist. Mason was laughing. She thought she heard him say 'scored...' Then he laughed again.

Now she thought she heard him say 'pussy'.

She took the second drink, left her change and walked slowly round the bar. Peter Mason was on a tall stool opposite a guy that looked like another plain-clothes. Behind them was another lounge, this one with just two tables and a slightly better decor. This time she did hear him: '. . . know what I mean?' She was behind him, feet from his stool. Suddenly his bald head looked pink and gross. He was still laughing and his mate laughed too. Then Caz lost it.

She had to be quick. She moved forward and pulled at his collar, hard, backwards, tipping him and the stool towards her. As he went, Peter tried to call out 'What the fu—?' but he was already crashing hard into the floor. There were cigarette butts where he landed. 'You lying fucking animal!' Caz shouted as he hit the floor. Then she looked up. His friend was moving.

There was a rack of snooker cues to Caz's right. She had one of those in her hand before the friend had even managed to stand. Suddenly it was snapped, its splintered middle spiked and dangerous. She put the jagged wood into Peter's cheek, inches from his left eye, shouting at the friend, 'Don't fuckin' *move* or I'll take his eye out!'

She looked down at Mason. He was bewildered, not frightened, but he knew enough to stay still. 'You fucking shit, Mason!' Caz shouted. 'Strutting around here, boasting about scoring with Moira. You arsehole! You didn't *fuck* Moira, you *raped* her! You're a shit.'

The friend was now standing. He was trying to talk calmly. Waving exposed palms at Caz. 'Hey, hey, OK.'

She looked at him. Her face was red and ugly. 'Who the fuck are you?'

'I'm no one,' the friend said. 'Just a bloke in a snooker hall.'

'If you're a mate of this shit, then you're an arsehole too.'

'OK, I'm an arsehole. Now why don't you put that down?'

'Fuck off'

'You must be Caz Flood,' the man said. 'Caz, this ain't a great career move.'

'Fuck you, pal!'

'You are Flood, right?'

'If you don't sit down, I'll take his face off'

'OK, OK.' He sat back down. Caz looked at the man on the floor.

'I thought you were an all right, ordinary guy, Peter, but you raped my mate. How could you? You come near her or me again and so help me I'll castrate you!' There was a spot of blood on Peter's cheek. Caz could feel tears of rage and frustration welling up inside her. She pulled back the broken cue, threw it to the side and walked away. There was no movement from the DS or his friend. As she went through the doors, there was a sudden rush of voices. She didn't look back.

Fifty-One

Moira and Caz drove back to Brighton in near silence. Caz had got used to the specialness of the Daimler and now, in this mood, it was just another car. The motorway slicked grey underneath them and away behind, the car's wheels drumming, a grey sea off to their right across a wave of mudflats. Too much had happened for one day. Now Caz was acutely depressed.

It was knock-off time when they got to John Street. They went in, logged their return from Southampton then booked themselves straight out again. There was a note for Caz saying that cleaners were already at her flat. She could move in tomorrow but not until her protection had been slipped in first. She felt heavy and tearful but she had given up on letting go. She simply left work and went home.

Home was Tom MacInnes's slightly depressing flat. She got in, left the curtains drawn, grabbed a drink and crashed on to the sofa. When the DI came home two hours later she was gracelessly sprawled on the upholstery, the empty glass beside her unconscious body. He dropped a travel rug over her legs.

Caz was dreaming about Mason. The snooker cue was a barbed harpoon, ripping into his face.

MacInnes saw her discomfort, saw his DC thresh and turn on the settee. He could do nothing. That was why he slipped away to soak in a bath.

In the morning she would feel different.

Fifty-Two

Caz woke to the sound and smell of spitting bacon. She groaned awake.

Tom MacInnes shouted through from the kitchen. 'Is that you awake, Caz? I was beginning t'think you were sickening for something!'

'What time is it?' she said.

'Seven o'clock.'

'I must've dozed off.'

'In the morning, Caz!'

'You what? Oh Christ!'

'You'll live,' he shouted. 'I shoved a pillow under your head between tosses and turns. You were still out cold at the end of *News at Ten* so I threw a duvet over you and went off t'me bed.'

She was leaning in through the kitchen door. 'There's no need to shout, Tom. I'm here now.'

'And dressed too,' MacInnes said. 'I'm amazed.'

'Very funny, Tom. Do I have time for a bath?'

'Five minutes.'

'That's enough.'

'Take this with you,' MacInnes said. He was

holding a tall glass of freshly-squeezed orange juice.
'Ta.'

'I thought you were looking a little bit peaky, Caz.
Figured you'd be needing the vitamins.'

'You're not far wrong there, boss.'

'Right then. Piss off and have that bath. You've
got four minutes now.'

'I'm gone! I'm gone!' Caz shouted. She was already
turning. As she left, MacInnes called after her. 'Oh,
and Norman Blackside cleared your newspaper story
with the CC. I'd've told you last night, only . . .'

But Caz couldn't hear him. She had already shut
the bathroom door. Water was running and she was
undressing.

'. . . You get t'keep yer money too. Flood, you must
be doing something right.'

Fifty-Three

Blackside's eight o'clock morning call in the War Room seemed strange to Caz. She'd missed a few by being in Southampton and this one seemed most definitely to be muted compared to the usual. She sat on her own. When Moira came in, she was with Billy. They seemed to be OK.

The DCS strode in as normal, with mighty steps to cross the floor and take the stage, his voice boomed just as effectively, but somehow things weren't quite the same. Afterwards, Caz decided it was because they had just had half a victory and no one was quite sure if they were doing well or badly.

'So we've firmed up on the serial rapist. The name on his birth certificate is Leonard Copthorne Burke and to date we've had seven AKA's and nine different addresses.

'Burke was working under the name of Copthorne as a sleep-in warden in a crinklie depot, just a couple of hundred yards from Hulse Street Headquarters in Southampton.'

There was a flurry of muted laughter.

'Forensics will be spending a bit more time in Burke's little den yet. They'll be there all day today. So far we've got pictures of the rape victims and a picture of Jane Daily. Burke also had a picture of one of our own on his wall . . .'

The rumours were right. Everyone turned to look at Caz. She tried to smile but she looked slightly pathetic.

'Burke has done a runner. We don't know why he suddenly decided to fly the nest, but he has. Our best chance to catch him is to chain a goat in a clearing and wait.'

A couple of chairs moved.

'The goat is DC Flood. We haven't got a clearing so we'll have to use her flat. And we're going to flush out the creep by using the papers. Flood is going to be famous and our man is going to come looking for her. Any questions?'

Saint called out from the back. Did they have any idea why Burke had suddenly decided to do a runner?

'None yet,' Blackside said, 'but we're looking at it.'

Would there be overtime to cover DC Flood's back?

'No. Split shifts or time off in lieu.'

There were no more questions.

'DS Reid will have your assignments for today. There'll be a list of Caz's back-up teams and times up very shortly. Don't go out until you've read it.'

Then the DCS was gone. As soon as he'd left the room, the lads buzzed round Caz. They were talking about the film *Stake Out*, and the sex scenes between

Richard Dreyfuss and Madeline Stowe. There was going to be no shortage of volunteer guards. Caz cringed. She was rescued by Tom MacInnes as he poked his head into the room and shouted, 'Telephone call, Flood!' She looked out from the mêlée and caught his eye. He grinned at her predicament and added, 'It's Deborah Snow!'

She took the phone call in the charge room. Deborah was excited. 'I've been speaking to your Chief Super. It seems he's given you a free hand to speak with us.'

'Hardly, Debbie. The usual rules apply. They're being nice to me because we need a little favour from you.'

'Which is?'

'When can you get down here?'

'Down here? You're joking. I'm phoning from the Metropole!'

'You're not hanging about, then?'

'I already told you, Caz. You're a good story. You can knock the tabloids for our use of language but we're all pros. We don't dick about!'

'I'll speak to my DI. Be there in an hour?'

'Do you fancy breakfast?'

'Only if the Metropole does bacon butties, Debbie.'

'I'll check.'

Caz went to say 'Don't bother', but the *Sun* woman had already put down the phone. She nipped round to see MacInnes.

Fifty-Four

Caz walked in to see Tom MacInnes with a broad smile on her face. It lasted about a second and a half. The DI was standing behind his desk. So were DCS Blackside and DS Mason. MacInnes asked Caz which did she want first, the good news or the bad news?

'Is there good news, Sir?'

MacInnes let Blackside speak. 'The good news, Flood, is that you haven't done anything in the last twenty-four hours that could put you on a discipline charge. The good news is that there's nothing you've done recently that could lose you your job.'

'And the bad news, Sir?'

'You will be working with DS Mason until the Burke case is closed.'

'But, Sir!'

'*Flood!*' Blackside leaned forward, his face closing on Caz. She could smell his breath; it was dark and manly with distant peppermint and even more distant garlic.

'Read my lips, Flood. You have just run out of lives. You will be working with Detective Sergeant

Peter Mason as of now, until the end of the Burke case and for exactly as fucking long as I think fit. Can you read my lips, Flood?'

'I can now, Sir.'

'Then say hello to Sergeant Mason. You've got a new boss.'

Caz glared but only with her core.

Mason felt it.

She said, 'Sergeant? I'm supposed to be meeting Debbie Snow from the *Sun* at the Metropole. It's been cleared. Will you want to come?'

Blackside leaned forward again. Caz didn't fancy him but in his closeness she could feel a strong sexual power. He smiled. 'That was *very* good, Flood. Now fuck off and sort yourself out.'

'Yes, Sir!' Caz snapped obediently. She looked at Mason. 'Sarge?'

'Outside, Flood.'

'Yes, Sarge.' She turned, clicked her heels and left. Peter Mason shook hands with Blackside. Then the DI. Then he followed Caz.

Caz walked stiffly ahead down the corridor. She could feel Mason's eyes burning into her back. She wanted to scream. She turned, ready to lash out. Instead she used her tongue.

'So how did you manage this one, Peter? Funny handshake crowd is it? You a Mason, Mason?'

'My DI insisted.'

'Your DI!'

'Yes, Flood. He was the guy you called an arsehole

341

yesterday. He could've taken your fuckin' head off but he didn't. He could still have you off the force in half a day.'

They were face-to-face across the corridor. 'Hey, *you're* the rapist!'

'My DI isn't deaf, Flood. If you went, I'd be gone too and Moira wouldn't exactly come out the other side squeaky-clean either.'

'Don't start threatening Moira.'

'I'm not. Where is she?'

'I think she's working Holmes. I haven't seen her this morning.' Caz suddenly sagged. 'Shit. I don't want her bumping into you.'

'Where can we go?'

'Down the back stairway,' Caz said. 'The garage.'

'A drive?'

'I've got to go to see Deborah Snow.'

'And we've got to talk.'

'The stairs are this way, Sergeant.'

They left in Mason's Cavalier, Caz directing. As they swept down on to the Old Steine, Peter sighed. He was about to speak, but Caz spoke first.

'Let me guess. Moira wanted to sleep with you, right? She was willing. As far as you were concerned it was just an average leg-over. Now you want to tell me you never forced her.'

'I never forced Moira, Caz. I've never raped anyone.'

'Fuck off, Sergeant. I saw Moira in the morning.'

'*Detective*, Moira Dibben and me went out, we got

pissed together, we danced a bit, we ended up neck-
ing, we fucked around a bit then we went back to
Boxx's spare flat.'

'And you raped her.'

'Then we had sex.'

'You forced her to have sex.'

'Bollocks, Flood!'

'You raped Moira.'

'We had sex. Her problem is the morning after.'

'She said you raped her.'

'She said.'

They had arrived on the seafront. Out off the shingle
beach the channel looked choppy. Whitecaps leapt.
They stopped opposite Deborah Snow's hotel. Caz
felt cold. She had to go in.

'I don't know how long I'm going to be, Peter.'

'It doesn't matter.'

'I could be hours.'

'I'll wait,' he said.

Fifty-Five

Caz went in to the glassy Metropole reception. She would have asked for Deborah Snow but then she saw her getting up from a chair. There were at least half a dozen newspapers on the coffee table in front of her. Caz could see some heavies as well as the *Mirror* and the *Sun*.

'Caz!' Debbie said. There was a huge smile on her face. '*Great* to see you!'

Caz asked about the papers. What was it? It was OK to write for the masses, but actually to read the stuff . . .?

'Poor disillusioned fool,' Debbie said.

'I can see you've got a *Guardian* and a *Times* there.'

'Research. I read all the time.'

Caz was unbelieving. 'But you don't actually read the *Sun*, do you?'

'I most certainly do,' Snow said indignantly. '*And* I like it!' She waved, and an immaculate waiter came over almost instantly. 'Two coffees! Thank you!' She turned back to her guest. 'When I was sixteen I saw this competition. The finalists were supposed to get the chance to be journalists. All you had to do was write your life story in no more than seven hundred and fifty words. I had a go. I reached eight hundred words and my fifth birthday.'

'What are you saying?'

'Journalism takes real skill. A good one-liner is as intelligent as a *Times* editorial; sometimes it's better. We're competing with TV, for Chrissakes. We have about five seconds to make an impact. It's a fast world out there.'

'Yeah, but the *Sun* . . .?'

'Some great front pages – covers that have made history. One or two MPs knocked over . . . we do all right. There's tit on page three; so what? There are sixty million tits in Britain. We just show them two at a time. Not that the public *want* tit, of course . . .' Debbie sighed. 'Fancy brekkie?'

As soon as they walked into the restaurant, the *maître d'* was at Deborah's side. She asked for a window seat. They could see out across Kings Parade and into the filthy sea. Caz could see Peter Mason's Cavalier, Peter's face a blur, this by a trick of the light. She looked away. They had coffee and talked.

A waiter came over. Debbie whispered quickly while Caz looked out again. Then she said, 'More coffee, Caz?' and asked about her father.

When the waiter came back, he had a silver platter in each hand. Beneath the first was an earthenware dish containing lumpy porridge – just right for

Debbie. Beneath the other (the plate gleamed), was a neatly-cut and presented sandwich, white bread and butter, thinly sliced pork fried in animal fat until crisp and served with a light tomato-based sauce. There was a garnish of parsley and tomato on the plate, but the meal was still . . .

Caz gasped. 'A bacon butty!'

'Well, you said.'

'But I was only joking. I've eaten already. I'll be gross!'

'Don't worry about it,' Debbie said. 'You'll burn it off.'

Caz grinned and nibbled.

'You were saying,' Debbie said again, 'your father was shot?'

The interview finished around twelve. At two-thirty they would meet again and walk up to Inkerman Terrace. The photographer was due in Brighton at lunchtime; no, not from the paper, Debbie said, they used an agency – one of their regulars. Debbie gave her a little cheek-peck kiss as they parted. They would shoot a lot of stuff if that was all right with Caz; formal, glamorous, stuff in uniform, some shots in running kit. Yes, it was a bit cold, but something on the sea-front would be *g-r-reat*. Caz said her nipples might show through the running vest. Perfect, Snow said. She would be sexy but hidden away. Was that OK? For an MX5? Caz thought. For an MX5, naked across the bonnet was OK. She smiled. 'Well, if you think it's *absolutely* necessary . . .'

Caz went out and picked up Mason. They drove back

towards the nick. He said that whether she liked it or not, at some point she was going to have to listen to his side of the story. If he had to tie her up and gag her she was going to have to fuckin' listen. The cold of the car had made him angry. 'Jesus, Flood! Why do women want it both ways all the time?'

'You raped Moira,' Caz said flatly. 'You let me know when you're going to try to justify it. I'll be all ears, but it won't change a thing.' He clanged a gear and swore. She sneered. 'You're a rapist, Sergeant.'

They parked underneath John Street and got out. Caz said she had to go upstairs to see the DI. Mason said fine, he'd come along.

They went up the back stairs. Caz was wondering how long it would be before they bumped into Moira. She didn't know if Moira had said anything to Billy about their night out, or worse. She was jumpy and itching with unresolved tension. She needed a run or a fight.

'You're enjoying this, aren't you?' she said to Peter as they clacked up steps.

'Don't be so fuckin' stupid!' Mason said.

They went in to see DI MacInnes. He looked up at their faces and asked if everything was all right. Caz fumed but Mason said they were getting there. 'Right!' the DI said quickly. 'Just to let you know the score. Your place is spotless, Caz. Apart from a slight smell of paint you wouldn't know we'd been in there. There's a couple of DCs next door in Trevor Jones's, and DS Reid is drinking coffee in your kitchen as we speak.'

'Thank you, Sir.'

'Oh, and I swapped out your mattress and your pillows. As far as you're concerned, it's a new bed.' He reached under the desk. 'And this is for you, too.' He was embarrassed as he brought out a large, pink soft toy. A piggie.

'It's Vincent!' Caz said.

'Ah think it's a cousin, actually, but at least you've got something t'...'

Caz held the pig. She spoke softly. 'Thank you, Tom.'

'Yeah, right...' MacInnes said. He coughed. 'Right! Blackside'd like to see you for one o'clock. We'll have finalised your security by then. The two of you go get yerself a pie and a pint. Back here for then.'

Caz hesitated. 'I was wondering, Sir...'

'About WPC Dibben?'

'Er, yes, Sir.'

'Day out. Driving the CC to Bramshill. She'll be there tomorrow, too.'

'Thank you, Sir.'

'So you two go an' talk. Have a pint, eh?'

'Sir!'

They went across to the Grapes. Peter got whiskies. Caz insisted on paying her half. He ordered a curry. Caz said she didn't want anything. They sat down in the lounge bar.

'Will you give me a *chance* to speak?' Peter said softly.

'Say what you like.'

'Will you hear me?'

'I've heard it all before, Peter.'

'Jesus!'

She looked cold. 'I *know* what you're going to say, Peter. I've arrested rapists. I've been there in the interview room with the tape running when they swear on their mother's grave that she wanted it. Even when the woman's vulva is bruised, her vagina has been ripped – even when her face is cut and she has a black eye. Then it's, "well she likes me being a bit rough".'

'Caz, Moira Dibben wasn't hurt. She had no bruises. We had sex; not very good sex. We were pissed. She shouldn't have, I shouldn't have, but that's all it was, a couple of coppers at it.'

'You made her.'

'What the fuck does that mean?'

'You forced her.'

'I didn't.'

'Did Moira try to stop you?'

'Yes.'

'Did you stop?'

'No.'

'So you raped her.'

'No, I was persistent. I tried it on a few times. She didn't just say yes but she didn't get up and go either.'

'Did she say she couldn't?'

'I've told you that, yes.'

'She's got a boyfriend.'

'I'm married!'

'Chicken Curry?' A twenty-year-old barman with a stupid grin on his face stood there. 'Chicken Curry?'

'I know what it is!' Mason said. 'Stick it there!' He pointed at the table. The barman grinned but the DS was not amused. 'And just what d'you think is so fuckin' funny?'

The barman ducked away quickly, his palms raised. 'Nothing mate. Sorry, OK? I've just got that kind of face.'

'Well fuck off, then,' Mason spat. He turned back to Caz. 'As far as you're concerned, Flood, I'm a rapist. If I am, I'll be that for the rest of my life.'

'Yes.'

'So why won't you give me five real minutes to speak. Why won't you listen? Are you so certain? Or is it that you're afraid that you might be wrong, you and all those other bullshitting women who reckon sex is always cut and dried?'

'It is.'

'What?'

'Sex. Cut'n'dried. No always means no.'

'If you really think that, you're not off the same planet as me, Flood.'

'I really think that.'

Mason stared at his curry. The cooling outside edge was already skinning. 'I just want five minutes,' he said.

Caz said OK but all her decisions had already been made.

He pulled his meal towards him with an action that looked like he had to force down a few forkfuls

of the food on principle, even though he had absolutely no appetite. He looked up but neither of them
wanted eye contact.

'I'm half-married, Flood. I've got a daughter, seven
years old. Pretty soon she'll be talking about boys,
then she'll have periods, then she'll be coming home
late. She'll be the target for every spotty lad with a
little bit of balls.'

He took two fast mouthfuls of curry and rice. Then
he wiped his mouth with his hand. 'I know what
she'll go through. I'll try to tell her what blokes are
like, really like. I'll tell her because I'll still remember
what I was like.

'But she'll go to parties. She'll end up dancing,
drinking, trying a smoke. She'll half-remember what
I told her or what her mother has told her. We'll
have said to be careful, not to screw around, not to
get into situations she can't handle. It would be nice
to think she'd be sensible – that the very first time
she really fancies some young buck her hormones
won't take over – but why shouldn't they? She's a
person, not a principle.'

Caz stared. A grain of stained rice was stuck to
Mason's lip.

'So, your lot say, "We know what we want, we
come out up front with it. If we want a man, if
we want sex, we just tell him. No always means no
because yes means yes." I'm thirty-six, Caz. That
clear-cut situation has only happened to me twice,
once with a DI who told me she didn't like being
groped while she made her decisions, the other time

with my missus. I was a virgin when I asked her to marry me. She said OK. Then she took me upstairs and fucked me on her Dad's bed.'

Caz was heartless. 'I'm still listening, Peter. But to what?'

'Maybe I don't move in the right circles, but the women I meet *don't* always make it clear. I'm an average horny bloke. They know it. They play on the fact. Sometimes I think "I'm in here", and I get it wrong; but most of the time, I get it right. Maybe she's saying yes in her own particular fashion, maybe she isn't, but a straight yes is so bloody rare it's not worth arguing about. The women I date make you jump through hoops, Flood. It's all part of the game.'

'What's this got to do with you and Moira?'

'Everything! Moira behaved like maybe half the women – girls – I've slept with. My marriage is name-only. Anyone who goes out with me knows that. I'm hunting. So Moira kept trying to cool me down? They all do! If she had just wanted a quickie the first time I tried anything I'd've been surprised. You *expect* resistance. It's part of the fun. It's par for the course. Half the reason that there's so much sexual grief out there is because of the games we play.'

'But Moira resisted. In the end you forced her.'

'No. I did *not* force her. I overwhelmed her. *She* gave in. I never threatened her, I never pinned her arms down, I never got her so pissed that she didn't know what she was doing. She put up a fight but it was a token fight. All she ever had to do was say no.'

'She did say no!'

'What would you do if you said no to a pass and the guy didn't think you meant it?'

'I'd say no again and make sure he knew.'

'And if Moira didn't?'

'She was still saying no.'

'No she wasn't. I've heard *real* noes. They bring you up short. The woman changes. She moves. She snaps. She pushes you away. For any average decent bloke, that kind of no is crystal clear. When a situation is screaming yes, a thousand yesses, you have to make your no stand out. Moira wanted sex. She just wasn't sure about her boyfriend in Brighton. Did she actually say that I raped her? That I bullied her, forced her?'

'You made her, forced her, ignored her noes. You raped her.'

'And that's what she said? She actually woke you up and said that I had raped her?'

He made me, Caz.

Moira, Peter raped you. That is *what you're saying?*

Is it, Caz?

Yes!

It is?

Yes!

Oh, Caz, what can I say to Billy?

Caz looked up. If anything, there was pleading in Peter's eyes. She hesitated for maybe a second, then she put a lid on it. 'I don't remember the words,

353

Peter, but I saw her face. I saw her tears. I think you raped Moira. You can talk about it forever, but it won't change a thing. Moira's going to live with it, maybe Billy too. She isn't going to report it because she can't. But she thinks she was raped. I think she was raped. You were there. You were her rapist. You're a pig.'

Peter looked as if he was cold. His eyes were dark and distant as if he had just pleaded for his life and lost. There was something desperate in there and a flash of pity threatened Caz's resolve. She stood up quickly, saying she was getting the drinks in. Yes, she said, she'd get him one. She looked down at his plate. 'Eat yer curry, Peter. You might as well. Life goes on, doesn't it?'

She went to the bar. She knew Peter wasn't looking at her. When she came back he was quiet. They both drank doubles.

Fifty-Six

They walked back to John Street. DCS Blackside was in the War Room with Tom MacInnes, Saint, DC Greaves and George Lindsell. Up on the wall was a diagram of Caz's building, the streets around it and her flat's interior. A little shiver went through her.

As they entered, Blackside stopped speaking for a second, nodded to them, then continued. 'Access to Flood's flat will be across the fire escape from Jones's flat and from Karthoum Terrace, across the gardens here and up this ladder. We've made an arrangement with the couple in number twenty-eight. There's an empty house, number twenty-four. There's a possibility Burke may try to use it if his MO's anything to go by, so we'll be keeping a low profile in the hope that he just steps in.

'If Burke goes to pattern, Flood is at greatest risk the moment she opens her door. Ideally we'd want men in the street but there's no way we can do that without frightening him off. As well as having a man inside Flood's place and the others in Jones's flat, we'll have

355

the team out back and an ob unit opposite in number thirty-six.'

Caz spoke. 'How long would it take for the guys to make it to my door, Sir?'

'We reckon from upstairs, down, out and across the road is at least twenty-five seconds.'

'That's too long, Sir. Burke could've whacked me and got me inside by then.'

'Yes, Flood. We're still working on that. But don't forget there'll be one of ours *inside*.'

Blackside began speaking to the men again. 'What concerns me most is that this Burke seems to know what he's doing surveillance-wise. He seems to case the streets pretty well and choose the quietest moments to attack. We can't even put dummy workmen in the street without scaring him off. Our main weapon has to be Flood herself and the guy on the inside.'

Caz interrupted again. 'How long can we run this for, Sir? What do we do if Burke doesn't show? He may be a bit cleverer than we think. The day you put a stop to my back-up might be the one he's waiting for.'

'Your reporter is getting pictures today, right?'

'Yes, Sir.'

'Will they make tonight's papers?'

'Brighton, maybe, Sir, but probably not. Tomorrow's the better bet.'

'And the nationals?'

'Just the *Sun*, Sir. They can get me on page one tomorrow morning. They're going to lead on the coming story, The Girl who Saved Brighton and all

356

that . . . We've promised them the Burke capture as an
exclusive.'

'Oh, we have, have we?'

'It was the only way we could get them to rush, Sir.'

'Whatever happened to public-spiritedness?' Blackside said.

'It flew off with Community Policing.'

They weren't there much longer. Caz was shown the
rosters, told who would be where and at what time.
MacInnes offered her an anti-stab vest, something to
be worn under her jumper. Caz said she never wore
jumpers. MacInnes barked and said she did now.

But she still had to work with DS Mason. He was
going to start dropping her off at lunchtime and again
at five-thirty. They were to make a show of his leaving.
He would drive down to the front, park and wait.

'DS Reid will cover days, seven through to seven.
DS Mason will be your night-watchman. He'll come
over the back gardens twenty minutes after he's dropped you off. He'll be kipping in your front room. If you
talk, put the TV on loud. It's just possible that Burke
listens in.'

Caz asked, were they still out looking for Burke or
was this it? Blackside told her that there was an army
still looking for him and that every Escort van in
Hampshire was being stopped and checked. Fairly soon
there would be complaints, he said, then he grinned.
'But that's what were here for, isn't it – complaints?'

Fifty-Seven

Debbie Snow would be waiting by now, clicking her heels in the entrance to the Metropole. Caz told Mason she had to go. 'I'll drive you,' he said.

She suggested that it wasn't necessary. He'd had his say, she had had hers. She didn't want his company, and wasn't the feeling mutual? He accused her of being unprofessional. Even if it was temporary, he was still her oppo and if anything happened to her, it was him they'd talk to first.

He told her, 'I'm just doing my job now, Flood.'

They used his Cavalier again. He drove steadily without speaking. When they got to the Metropole he parked badly and stepped out with her. Debbie Snow came out wearing a long, almost ankle-length cashmere coat. It looked about a thousand quid's worth. The doorman stepped forward to speak about the car but Mason quickly barked 'POLICE!' Deborah Snow offered her hand. He shook it, then they got in the car.

It was not a great day. There was a noticeable cutting wind and the sea still looked threatening.

Around the base of the pier, white spray exploded and fell. When the DS came out of the car park he spun the car very quickly out across the road, slotting sharply in between two other cars. One blared his horn. Mason acted as if he hadn't heard.

'Do you always drive like that?' Debbie Snow said.

'I'm a professional,' Mason said. 'And that was perfectly safe.'

They turned into Inkerman Terrace. To Caz, it looked strangely barren. There were cars outside her flat so they parked opposite. Caz saw the lace curtains twitch in Mrs Lettice's front room. She spoke quickly to Mason and to Debbie Snow, saying she just wanted to say hello.

'That's my next door neighbour,' she explained. 'She's a nice old dear. She'll have been worried about me. I'm just going to see how she is.'

'We've got time,' Debbie said. 'The photographer hasn't arrived yet.'

When Caz stepped out of the car, she really noticed the wind for the first time. Sometimes, when the European weather fell in a certain way, Brighton seemed to be a channel for a vicious wind piping straight down from Russia. She raised a hand to the hidden Mrs Lettice as she ducked across the street.

'Mrs L! How are you? Did you know? I'm just about to move back in! Just thought I'd say hello. See how you are.'

'I'm well, thank you.'

'I had my place redecorated after the burglary.'

'I saw you in the paper.'

'Did you?'

'They said you might get a medal. You were away for a while?'

'The decorating, Mrs L. You know . . .'

'I suppose you'll be back to borrowing milk again now?'

'Probably, Mrs L.'

Caz slipped away. She would have liked to have given Mrs Lettice a hug, but they were too many generations apart. Instead, they said a polite little goodbye and before Caz had reached the bottom step, Mrs Lettice had silently closed her front door. Caz looked up as a large white van pulled into the street. So did Mrs Lettice, taking notes as usual. Caz didn't see her, just the flick of her boiled-white lace curtains and her tan shape in the dim background of her front room. Debbie and Peter broke out of the car.

The van pulled up, two faces blurred behind a rainbow-sprayed black reflective windscreen. Caz dipped to see the faces as the doors opened. She noticed the T-shirt first, the red eye, the penetrating lens, long frayed-knee jeans – Timmy YTS.

Gareth Boxx dropped down from the driver's side. There was sunlight in his face. He squinted as he said hello. 'It seems', he said, 'that we are destined to meet.'

Fifty-Eight

Debbie Snow explained as they stood at the steps of Caz's flat. Gareth Boxx was one of two South Coast freelancers they used. He was good. He'd tried to break in to the paper a few times, but it was his shots of the Southampton pier fire that had finally got him noticed.

'Do you remember it? It was this summer. A mystery fire. One heck of a blaze. Gareth's shots of it were superb.'

'Did the pictures go national, then?' Mason asked.

'No. We bought them, but a big drugs-in-athletics scandal broke a couple of hours later. By the time there was room for Gareth's picture, it was old news. Still, he broke through, so it wasn't so bad. He's had one front page already.'

Boxx waddled up to them with two aluminium cases. He seemed to feel the need to apologise. 'That was the picture of Fergie. It pays the wages.' He shrugged. 'Same as race photography. But one day' – he turned to watch Timmy pull a long silver case from the van – 'one day they're going to buy the

361

picture from me that makes them bin the druggie . . .'

'Maybe,' Debbie said.

Peter, Debbie and Caz went upstairs. Caz's door was open and Jack Reid was waiting at the top of the stairs. He was wearing a shoulder holster that held a short-barrelled Smith & Wesson. As soon as he recognised them, he grinned. Debbie looked at Caz, her eyes wide. 'That's to do with the favour,' Caz said.

Inside, the flat was impressive. Caz was definitely not complaining. The spring-clean done by Maids was superb and the quick-flash decorating was seamless. The television and stereo had been put back in their original, carpet-denting positions, and someone had left a massive bouquet of flowers in the corner where her soft-toy piggies used to live.

'Nice place,' Debbie said quietly.

'Thanks,' Caz said. 'I had a burglary here about a month ago. The animal made such a mess of the place I was going to move on. But . . .'

'We should be able to get some nice shots in here. Gareth can probably get some moody ones of you with the light coming through the window.'

'If you say so,' Caz said, distracted. 'What's that smell? I can smell garlic.'

Jack Reid came out of the kitchen with a plate of hot bread. 'The DI's idea,' he said. 'When you've got a house up for sale you should always be cooking fresh bread as the punters arrive. Tom says it makes a house a home. I don't know how to cook bread but

I got these twenty-minute bake things in Sainsbury's.'

'Oh, cheers, Jack!'

'And we got you a coupla bottles of nice plonk,' he said, smiling again. 'They cost three-ninety-nine each so they should be pretty good.'

'What's it called?'

'I dunno. It's in the kitchen. It's red.' He went out, leaving the garlic bread. Seconds later he shouted through. 'Er, it's California. Ernest Gallio Cabber-Nett-Soh-Vigg-Non.'

Caz shouted back, 'Stop pretending to be a pleb, Jack, and bring a corkscrew through!' Suddenly she realised she felt good. She was home. She had been scared to come back but she'd been wrong. The boogie man had gone.

Peter Mason didn't notice the change; Debbie Snow didn't notice; Jack Reid was clattering about in the kitchen and he couldn't notice, but when Boxx came in with his cases, he noticed straight away. With his photographer's eye he saw the spark that had returned to her, a spine stiffened. Caz Flood was suddenly taller, brighter, sharper.

He didn't know why she was different, only that she was different. Caz knew, though. Animals were stronger on their own territory, birds braver in their own nests. She was home. She had somewhere to sally forth from. Something like singing electricity hummed in her. She suddenly knew the photographs were going to be brilliant!

'Who fancies a drink?' she said.

Caz was already crunching into drooling garlic bread. The others grabbed a chunk each. She was so happy to be back she oozed joy like the bread oozed butter. When Jack Reid came through, one bottle, five glasses, the corkscrew, she jibed at him, 'And how long d'you think that's gonna last, Jack?' He went back for the second four quid's worth. She shouted again. 'And we'll need another glass for the boy!'

Gareth and young Timmy began arranging things while Caz and Debbie talked on the sofa and the two detective sergeants conferred by the window. Jack Reid had started out by saying that the best laid plans of mice and men gang aft a-gley, though he had phrased it slightly differently. 'Blackside's gone and got his arse about face,' he'd said. 'You were supposed to move back in here tomorrer, not today. I didn't get here until one o'clock and half the lads are tied up elsewhere. We won't have the surveillance teams sorted out until the morning.' He had been tapping his gun when he added, 'Still, I've got my big stick signed out, so we should be all right, eh?' Now he chatted quietly to Peter Mason and took quick glances down into the street every other minute.

Caz spoke to the reporter while Gareth Boxx and his assistant clattered efficiently round them, setting up their equipment. Every now and then, Caz would look up to see Boxx listening and smiling. Whenever she noticed him, he grinned and went on with his work.

'There's a serial rapist out there, Debbie. He's attacked five women. The last one, Jane Daily, has died. We know the rapist's name and what he looks like but when we raided his last known address he'd skipped. My bosses think I'm on the rapist's list. There was a photograph of me on his wall and he had this address. We're hoping he'll come looking for me. Then we can nab him.'

'So what's this favour?' Debbie said.

'This place got turned over by a sicko burglar, at the tail-end of the Avocado thing. I had a few days out of it in hospital, then I bunked up with my DI. I've been away for three weeks. We think this nutter may have been watching the house while I was away. He'll know I've left. We need to tell him I'm back.'

'So you want photos? The house, the street? Slip something into the story?'

'Yes. It's got to be done right, though. One, it mustn't be obvious and two, I don't want every wierdo wanker who reads the *Sun* working out where I live!'

Snow laughed. 'You're saying one wierdo is enough?'

'Absolutely!' Caz said.

Gareth and Timmy had set up a white sheet opposite a window, and a camera on a tripod with shortened legs was pointing up towards a chairback. They had stopped, waiting for Caz, and the young lad was sipping his wine, trying desperately to look cool and sophisticated. Boxx was faintly amused.

Debbie Snow called him over and explained the

dual purpose of the shoot. He seemed to take it on board very quickly. 'I thought we'd get some dark, moody shots over here,' he said. 'We can make you look strong and determined and if you can act, we can do a few vulnerable ones. The lighting's great.'

'What about my clothes?' Caz said.

'What you've got on will do for now; then, if you've got a jacket, something a bit more macho, that'd be good. D'you have a housecoat?'

'Yes. It was a present but I never wear it.'

'That'll be good for the "Ms Alone" picture. When we do that, maybe you could wet your hair?'

'One step at a time, Gareth.'

When Boxx eventually went to work he was quick and efficient, balanced and composed. Occasionally he touched her, tilting her head, moving her hair, altering the line of her shoulder. It was probably only fourteen or fifteen hours since they'd been in bed together. Though Caz could still feel some electricity in his touch she couldn't believe his neutrality, even coldness. Even worse was her own coldness towards him. He worked. She wasn't listening deeply but he was coughing out photographer's clichés like 'give me angry, Caz', 'give me sad'. She felt detached, looking on. She felt like she was in a play.

She thought she was ignoring him but he seemed more than happy with the shoot's first stage. She began to wonder who he was taking pictures of. After the leather jacket shots ('Oh, hard! Hard!') and the housecoat ('I'll just loosen this. Now, Caz – you're low, you're weak, look down.') she asked for another glass of wine. Then Boxx asked about the running shots.

Debbie woke up to speak. 'How about it, Caz? Do you have any kit here?'

Caz changed into her red and white striped club top and black shorts, but when Debbie insisted that the shots would be outdoors, she went back into the bedroom and swapped the shorts for a pair of scarlet Lycra running tights. Vanity stopped her putting Helly Hansen long-johns on underneath the red nylon. She still had a good shape, and if they were going to take pictures of it she was going to look her best.

They went out, took a dozen shots outside the flat and then went on down to the sea-front. Caz was wearing a black Frank Shorter Goretex top. She jogged ahead, but when she felt the full force of Siberia screaming along the boulevard, rather than tootle half-a-mile for a warm up, she huddled into the doorway of a tiny, isolated sweet shop and waited for them to bundle after her. The weather made the session short but Debbie had been right. The cold made her nipples rise up. Caz hurt, but then she thought, if this story is the Mazda, my tits have just paid the road-tax.

They wrapped the shoot up quickly. Timmy started refilling the van while Gareth struck some sort of deal with Debbie. The paper would develop the shots to save time but they were still his. The best shots would be in the papers tomorrow and they'd fix it so Caz got a set of prints. The *Sun* would run a teaser about The Girl Who Saved Brighton in the morning but the main article would be held back for a week or so.

Then Debbie said she had to think about getting back up to London. She would go by taxi from the flat via the hotel for her gear. When the cab arrived, they swapped perfunctory hugs on Caz's doorstep then Caz turned to ask Gareth when was he going.

'Oh, I'm not,' he said, smiling inanely. 'Seeing as I was down here on *Sun* money, I thought I'd bang out some local shots to keep.' His smile was about the same when he asked if she could put him up tonight.

'What about Timmy?' Caz said.

'Off back on the train, I'd say. He's had his adventure.'

Caz wanted to say no, but she knew that Gareth had put both her and Moira up. There was no way she could decently refuse.

'OK,' she said. 'The spare room.'

'That's what I presumed,' Boxx said.

Her smile was thin. 'As long as we understand one another.'

Gareth smiled back, then the smile dissolved quite quickly. His face was flat and lifeless when he spoke again. 'I think we understand one another, Caz, don't you?' She looked up at the windows and Gareth followed her gaze. Mason and Reid were staring down at them from behind the curtains. Caz could just see the butt of Jack Reid's gun.

'Is it all right if I leave the rest of my camera stuff with you for the afternoon?' Gareth said.

'I might be out,' Caz said. 'But I guess it'll be pretty safe.'

'You mean with Clint Eastwood guarding it?'

'Yes.'

'So, it's all right, then?'

'Yes, Gareth. You can leave your stuff.'

Boxx was ready to go. He leaned closer to say goodbye. Up in the cab of the van, Timmy shifted. Boxx grinned quickly. 'I think the boy must be on a promise,' he said. 'Never seen someone so keen to catch a train.'

'Goodbye, Gareth.'

'Goodbye, Flood.'

Boxx stepped on to the flattened mudguard of the van and swung up into the cab. The door slammed. The diesel choked, flobbed twice, then bundled into life. The van chuggered into gear and edged out from the kerb. Then Boxx's head re-appeared through the open window. He looked benign. Caz was still. He shouted down to her, 'I presume you're gonna let me buy you a meal tonight?'

She said, 'Why not?'

'See?' Boxx said. 'We *do* understand each other!' The van went up the street to turn around. On the way back down, Boxx looked straight ahead. Caz was already inside. She had things to check.

Fifty-Nine

Little things can be important. When Caz went in she suddenly thought about the mail. There wasn't any. She ran up the stairs shouting.

Jack Reid spun round too quickly as she came through the door. 'It's in the kitchen,' he said when she asked. 'And do us all a favour next time. Knock!'

She went through and found her letters. There was the usual shit, half a dozen brown envelopes, one a bill with red writing, a letter from an old Uni' mate, and a couple of postcards. One yellow envelope informed her that she had just won at least £150,000 in a draw.

One of the envelopes was a race entry. The Victory Five. She'd missed running in that event while she'd been in dock. There was a second one, scheduled for the first Sunday in January: the Stubbington 10K, an ultra-flat run near Fareham. She always clocked good times in that one, including her personal best of 34.01, but it was always too windy and, for some reason, even though she regularly collected prizes, she never enjoyed the race. She took her race number from the envelope, a red 948, and pinned it up on the wall.

She could hear DS Reid and DS Mason in the lounge. She went through to find her handbag. While she was opening it, she suggested tea. They said OK. She went out to make it, carrying the Polaroids of Burke's room and a folded picture of herself. These she pinned up on the wall, next to the Stubbington number. Then she sat back and stared, thinking.

There was a glass of red wine left in the second bottle. While the kettle boiled she knocked it back. She kept looking up at her picture, thinking. She was in club kit and it looked like she had just blown away a Southampton Road Runners vet, a Scotsman. His name was Andy something. The clock wasn't in the photo but she remembered her time. She had the photo somewhere else. It was a Totton 10K. She'd run 34:40, her second-best-ever-time.

She went back through and asked Jack to finish the teas. Then she picked up the phone. She waited, then she asked for Forensics. The guy she wanted was out.

Over their teas they discussed the coming stake-out. As coppers, they all knew that protection was mindlessly boring with the occasional tense moment. Only one protection job in fifty actually involved real violence. Someone once said protection was like flying an airliner, hours of boredom sandwiched between two or three minutes of solid anxiety. For Caz, it was different. She thought she had finally worked out when Burke would come. As long as it was on her own turf, she welcomed him.

She changed the subject back to photography. Jack Reid was a fairish amateur and had got a 'highly commended' in a national police competition. Peter Mason had heard about his success but he had managed to forget it. He didn't thank Caz for reminding him. He wasn't greatly pleased that one lucky shot of Jack's out of a thousand could beat anything he ever did. All *his* stuff – moody, broody and technically clever – should be picking up commendations all the time. He kept winning local stuff, he said, but nothing in the bigger world. He wasn't really joking when he said that sometimes he thought about keeping pigeons.

'Perhaps you're trying too hard,' Caz suggested.

'What d'you mean?'

'Trying to take winning shots instead of simply taking good pictures until the big one pops out.'

'And you know all about it, I suppose?'

Caz was curious, she said. How much did photographs age? Did machine prints last longer than good studio jobs or were they all much of a muchness? Would Peter be able to tell when a print was made, just by looking at it? Could he tell if a print had been run off recently? Would all those wonderful Ansel Adams pictures eventually turn yellow?

'Pictures that are old now were taken a long time ago,' Mason explained. 'The paper was poorer in the forties and fifties and the developing processes are much better now. Today's pictures will last for a long time. It would be pretty hard to tell if a picture had been recently printed but if you gave me two, I could tell you if one was significantly newer than the other.'

Caz finished her tea. 'I could do with a run,' she said. 'I feel cooped up.'

'Don't be silly,' Jack Reid said.

'Just a short one, Sarge, the length of King's Parade and back. I'm a runner; I'll freak out if I don't get my legs moving.'

'No.'

'Let her, Jack,' Mason said. 'I can follow her in the Cavalier. It's wide open space and Flood is pretty damn quick on her feet. This Burke character isn't going to attack her on the bloody *prom*.'

'I still don't think it's a great idea.'

'Think about it, Jack. It's what she'd do on a normal day. Things should look normal. We're trying to coax this animal into the open.'

'How long will it take you to run three miles, Caz?'

'If I warm up before I go out, about twenty minutes.'

'Twenty minutes?' Reid said enviously. 'It takes me twelve to do the one-and-a-half of the fitness test!'

Caz grinned. 'Well, normally, I'd be quicker, Sarge, but I've just had half a bottle of wine and a cup of tea.'

'Very funny, Flood,' Reid said. Then he added, 'Be careful out there.'

'As if I wouldn't, Sarge.'

It was almost six o'clock. Caz was still in her running kit. It was covered up with an Asics track-suit. She stripped off and went out on to the stairs. At the top flight she turned round and stepped backwards down on to the third stair. Mason and Reid were watching, their arms folded.

Caz stood with her left arm up on the banister for balance, then with her right she leaned across and pressed 'start' on her stop-watch. With the beep she began to step up on to the top flight, left-right, down-down, counting one-two-three-four with the move-ments. Both the men were looking quizzically at her, so she explained, already huffing. 'It's lifting the body against gravity! Very tiring! Four minutes of this . . . is bloody hard! Quickest warm up I know!' She was already gasping. 'It's – called – the – Harvard – Bench – Test.'

Peter Mason left just before Caz, waved, got in his car and cruised away. When Caz came out seconds later, she was flushed and wet. She did a quick ham-string stretch on her steps and then set off at a good pace to the bottom of the street. As soon as she hit the sea-front she crossed the road, skipping between a line of stationary cars. Then she took aim at the town and went for it at around six-minute-mile pace, counting lampposts. She could feel the wine and whisky in her system.

Running hard into the wind was peculiar, her own movement taking away the awareness of the air moving and replacing it with an invisible cushion for her to continually push down. The resistance of the air was quite incredible, increasing with the square of its speed added to hers. It was like pushing a giant pillow while tied behind by elastic.

She looked for Peter's car but failed to notice it. It didn't concern her. Even if the animal appeared out of nowhere, he was very unlikely to be able to overpower her and carry her out of sight. Nevertheless, she flicked her eyes both right and left as she ran, looking for something, anything, a cue, something to put her defences into a full red alert. She thought she was 'condition orange' at the moment – feeling fairly high on the possibility of danger but not really believing it was about to happen. She still thought she knew when Burke was going to come.

At the Dolphinarium, she gasped and turned. As soon as she was facing the other way, the wind's howl and rush changed into an odd, warm pressure on her back. Unfortunately, on the return journey she wouldn't reap the full benefit of the reversed wind-pressure. Her forward speed of ten miles an hour was now subtracted from the wind in her back. Still, her return mile was at 5:20 pace, and it felt really fast. Half-way back, she saw the DS, stuck in the traffic and bawling into his radio. She thought it really funny. He looked pink and angry.

When she reached her street Mason was just turning the car round. She jogged to a halt. Stopped and turned, she could feel the wind again, cold and angry on the side of her face. She walked across the road.

Sixty

Caz could have jogged up the street but she walked. Between the houses it was still cold but at least she was out of the wind. She decided that Peter should have squeezed himself out of traffic by now and U-turned back along the front towards her. She reckoned he was just yards away on King's Parade.

Fifty yards from her front steps she bent down and tied her shoelace. Her ears buzzed with the wind and the effects of her run. She sniffed the air. There was something. She felt for it but it had gone. She shook her head.

Every one of Caz's arteries, every arteriole, every capillary; in her legs, in her arms and in her back were loosened, charged, filled and ready, pumped with bright red blood, thanks to her run. Her lungs were mucus-freed and deeply opened, readied for great effort by the sharp work she had already done. Now her muscles were tensile and at their maximum strength.

Caz knew that all this was chronic, warmed to by her recent activity. And this power was *without*

adrenaline. In seconds, endorphins, the runner's mor-
phine, would begin to wash down through her head,
her reward for working out, a free, no side-effects high.

She passed Mrs Lettice's window and got to her
own steps. Without looking back, she tensed, feeling
for the sound of movement. There was nothing. She
sat down to stretch her hamstrings, leaning forward
to hold her flexed feet one at a time. She strained
towards the 'p' of pain, not doing too much, then
she stood to lift her heel towards her rear, kicking
slowly into her buttocks, stretching her quads.

And that was when Leonard Burke grabbed her.
Not from behind, not with a sudden rush, but from
beneath her, from the bowels of her house, from the
basement – a massive, dirty hand clamped around
her calf and then him, this gross, evil, pug-faced man
climbing the railing, climbing, pulling her leg against
the metal, grinning at her. Knowing.

His slap caught the top of her head as she went to
scream. It had been aimed at her fragile jaw but she
had ducked. It hurt her dully, separating her for a
vital second from action. Far off, she thought she
heard blue-white sirens as she screamed, *'Reid!
Reid!'* loudly, desperately, as she flailed at Burke.

He was above her now, tip-toed, edged on to crum-
bling concrete, lifting her captured leg, still grinning,
still silent as he pulled her. Caz punched, slapped,
scratched; every blow aimless and pathetic. She had
no base, no place from where she could project her
power, her lifted leg dreadfully neutralising every
self-defence trick she had ever learned.

Your legs, Flood! Use your legs! Let him have *the left!*

Let him *give you power*!

She stopped resisting Burke, suddenly, absolutely, surprisingly. She went *with* his pull, climbing up on the sudden split second of his surprise, only one split moment from defeat. But as she rose, she kicked out, straight into those teeth, the face, once, twice, bloody. His arm came up. More blood. His grip on her leg loosened. She kicked again. Then he fell back. Into the stair well. She was still shouting, '*Reid! Reid!*'

She heard the Cavalier first. She heard the gear missed and the wheeing, screaming engine as it raced up the street. She heard the lump as Mason jumped it up the kerb, and then she saw Peter's face as he slammed the car into the railing and Burke's bloody, climbing fists.

The flat door opened at the same time as Mason burst out of the car. Burke was roaring like a trapped animal, like a bear at bay down in his pit. DS Reid was shouting at Caz to get out of the fucking way. He had pulled his weapon, shaking with rushed adrenaline, holding the pistol double-handed, crouching now, pointed at Burke's chest.

Reid shouted, 'Stand Still! Armed Police Officer!' The gun wobbled. Then Burke rushed the steps, still roaring, one arm hanging like a flapping shutter. Reid let one round go but then lowered the gun as Burke came out, straight at Peter Mason.

Mason stood his ground, then, at the last moment,

stepped slightly to one side. He struck the rapist once, his truncheon smacking sickeningly into Burke's already shattered arm. Burke screamed and his rush stuttered. Then Mason hit him again, again on the bloody arm. Burke fell to his knees, faint. A blurred second later he was face down and handcuffed, conscious again but groaning, squirming away from the pain and towards Caz. Blood dripped from his face and from his useless arm. Reid rose and held the gun a foot from his head. He was waving Caz past him, up the steps, out of the line of fire.

Cars bounced into the street.

Sixty-One

It was a big capture and the atmosphere at the station was very different. Everyone was fired up by the arrest; everyone wanted to see into the cell. No one wanted to go home early off days and as the night-shift got wind of the collar and came in for a look-see, the place got more and more cluttered, more and more manic, until the custody sergeant finally lost his rag and told everybody to piss off out of it. Even then the corridors echoed with loud noises, the stories just taking off. The best one so far was that Flood had deliberately shot the geezer in the balls.

They had dragged in the Police Surgeon and a second doctor to cover his back. Burke was still under restraint; so big that no one fancied taking off his cuffs. The quacks were pretty certain that his arm was broken. They gave him a sedative so the cuffs could be removed and arrangements were made for an ambulance to come down from Brighton General. Casualty already knew that their next patient would be accompanied by four lumpy uniforms. Burke would be X-rayed, put back together and then ship-ped straight back to John Street. Blackside was already getting confirmation that they could keep him in the cells once his arm was fixed.

DS Reid was writing up his 'Discharged Firearm' report, the arrest report, and about fifteen other forms. Peter Mason was ploughing through his forms including his explanation of 'necessary force'. Caz hadn't started her forms. She was in with Tom MacInnes.

Their door was shut. MacInnes' voice buzzed behind the glass. 'You can't keep getting away with this sort of thing, Caz. You were dead lucky. If DS Mason had been a bit slower, you could be dead now and Burke could be gone.'

'No, Sir. Burke just arrived a bit early, that's all. I'd figured he was coming at changeover. We'd've had him then.'

'You're kidding yerself.'

'I knew Burke was coming, Sir. He wasn't going to get away.'

'So what the fuck happened, Caz?'

'Nothing, Sir. He was just a bit earlier than we expected and a bit stronger than we expected. I was wondering whether he might be on something . . .'

'The doctors will find out soon enough, but I don't reckon so. I just think we have ourselves a complete nutter. You were dead lucky, Flood.'

'He wasn't that clever after all, was he? Not with the van.'

'No. DS Mason spotted it three streets away. He radioed it in and then he chased after you. Couldn't you have at least carried your radio?'

'I didn't think Burke was stupid.'

'What about that radio?'

'I can't run properly with it, Sir.'

'That's an excuse for getting killed?'

'No, Sir. It's just a fact. I told you already, I thought Burke would be coming an hour later. I'd worked it out.'

'Well now, you unwork it out, Caz. You had no reason to believe you were in any danger until the morning, not until after the newspapers were published. Nevertheless, when you went for your run you agreed that DS Mason would shadow you in his car. You got that?'

'Yes, Sir.'

'And you carried your radio when you ran, but it's a bit iffy occasionally. You were going to report it in the morning.' MacInnes paused. Some of the tension seemed to drop from his shoulders. He pulled out a drawer and waved a wee dram. Then he asked Caz just what he ought to do with her.

Caz said, 'Promote me?'

MacInnes nearly wept. He filled two cups. 'Drink yer whisky. Flood. Then get the hell out and do yer paperwork. I said the day you joined us you were a mistake. You didn't *have* to prove me right.'

Sixty-Two

Caz sat at the same table as Peter Mason while she did her paperwork. He said nothing, other than acknowledge her arrival. She worked with a Biro and cursed bureaucracy, the Crown Prosecution Service and the Conservative government. Then she finally gave in and said thank you.

'I was just doing my job, Flood.'

'I know,' Caz said. 'Thanks for doing it well.'

'Fuck off, Flood.'

'You probably saved my life, Peter.'

'Reid did that.'

'Maybe,' Caz said. Then she asked if she could buy him a drink later.

'Why?' he said. 'Feeling guilty are we?'

'I just wanted to say thanks.'

'If you want to do that, you can give me a lift to Southampton in the morning. You might remember, I've written off my motor.'

'Where are you sleeping tonight?'

'I was booked into your flat.'

'That's still on if you want it.'

'Not scared I'll try to rape you then?'

'No, Peter.'

'So why the gesture, Flood?'

'Because of Burke, I guess. And maybe because Moira was a little bit right. I can't forgive you for what you did to her, but she's right, what you did *isn't* the same as what Burke did.'

'My, we change our tune quickly, don't we?'

'No, Peter. You're still a rapist.'

'But it's all right to kip on your settee . . .'

'If you came near me, I'd kill you. You know I would.'

'Do I? How were you doing with Burke?'

'Enough not to lose,' Caz said.

The paperwork, their joint burden, quietened them. Later, they drifted away. There was another whisky in the Grapes, a taxi down to and along the sea-front and then, after they'd climbed the stairs of her flat, a couple of glasses of Caz's best Chianti.

She had walked up the stairs ahead of Peter and she realised she'd had no feeling of danger. There was no hair risen on her neck, no bile even threatening in her stomach. She could hear a distant voice asking her but how could she have gone there alone with a man like that? Peter sat on her sofa. Caz was at the far end, her new, pink Vincent tucked between her knees. She looked at Peter. She drank some more wine.

They broke a second bottle, more *Il Grigio*, stuck some slow music on. Peter toyed with his glass. He said that when Burke came for him, he didn't move because, deep down, he wanted to be hurt.

'But my body took over. I didn't decide to step aside, it just happened. Then I was just hitting him. I wasn't going to stop until he went down.'

Caz was reflective. 'I don't remember all that much about the arrest, Peter. I remember kicking him in the face. His teeth were covered in blood. I didn't think he was going to get up after he fell into the basement.'

'That was his anger,' Peter said. She poured more wine. He looked up. 'In the end it was surprisingly easy, wasn't it? Do you think Burke had finally lost control? D'you think that was why he suddenly made mistakes?'

'I don't know,' Caz said. 'I think – ' She was about to say something about Gareth Boxx but the phone rang. 'Jeez!' she said. The noise raifed through the house like a knife through skin.

'Shall I get it?' Peter said. She nodded.

'Hello?'

It was the station duty officer. MacInnes and Blackside had just been called out. There was another body. A woman had been found in Chichester, dead about twelve to fifteen hours. She had been raped, but there was no semen. She had the burn mark on her arm.

'MacInnes will be here for us in two minutes,' Peter said.

They stood outside, waiting for Tom. The wind had

fallen but the night was wrapping in, wet and sullen. They were sobering up fast. When the DI's Sierra flipped its lights into the wet street they were huddled together against the damp. They got in.

'Burke was back at John Street at half-past-nine. He said he didn't want a solicitor but we gave him one anyway. He knew we had him for the attack on you and he confessed straight away to the other five, plus another one that went wrong, some lass from Southampton. He never said a word about this sixth woman.'

'What do we know about her, Sir?'

'Surname Ellis, mid-twenties. Found dead, head injury and stabbed. All Burke's usual signs plus the burn mark, but no semen, according to the doctor. It was an isolated farm, not Burke's usual territory. There were Goodyear tyre marks in mud at the scene, same as Burke's Escort.'

'We were a day too late,' Peter said.

Caz felt sick. 'No we weren't.'

They were swinging left on the Old Steine. Tom MacInnes had just said he was surprised about this last attack. 'Burke just came straight out with everything else, a classic get-it-off-the-chest merchant. Why the fuck he wants to sit on this last one is a mystery to me.'

Mason spoke, his hand on the dash as MacInnes swung the car hard. 'Do you think he's finally over the edge, Tom?'

MacInnes spat out of his window. 'Edge?' From the back seat, Caz briefly saw his face. 'Edge of

Beachy fuckin' Head, if I had my way!'
   They were at the station. It was one a.m.

Sixty-Three

They woke Leonard Burke. He was calm, quiet, slow-spoken and apologetic. No one was taking chances, and his good arm was handcuffed to a desk. The DI asked him, what else did he have to tell them? He said, 'Nothing.'

Blackside and MacInnes were sitting opposite him, a solicitor called Gordon to his right. The interview door was open. Peter Mason and Caz watched, Caz half-hidden, fascinated, trying finally to understand.

'The last one, the blonde one. I didn't want t'do that. But he said she was bad, that she was after me. He said it would be just one more, then he'd show me how to stop. He took my picture.'

'Who said, Lennie?'

'The Vulture.'

'Who's the Vulture, Lennie?'

'God.'

'Did you kill Mrs Ellis, Leonard?'

'Who's Mrs Ellis?'

'Where were you this morning, Lennie?'

'Walking round Brighton. I went to the arcades. I like the lights.'

'Which arcades, Lennie?'

'On the pier.'

'Tell us about God, Lennie. Tell us about the Vulture.'

'I can't.'

'Why can't you, Lennie? We're your friends.'

'You're not my friends. You can't trick me. He's told me about you. I know all about you. The Police are very bad.'

Blackside took a turn. 'Hello, Lennie. Do you know who I am?'

'No.'

'I'm Norman.'

'I'm Lennie. Are you a policeman?'

Blackside glanced quickly at the solicitor. 'No, Lennie, I'm not.'

'What are you then?'

'I can't say,' Blackside said. He shook his head sadly. 'I'm not allowed.'

'You're very big, Norman. You're big like me.'

'That's right, Lennie. We're the same.'

'I'm an Avenging Angel.'

'I know,' Blackside said.

Burke looked confused. He tilted his head. 'So, you . . . are you?'

'I can't say. I mustn't say. I'm just like you, Lennie.'

'Have they got you too?'

'I'm afraid so, Lennie.'

'The Vulture will come. He'll rescue us, Norman.

He can do anything. He knows everything. Where you go, what you do. He has a thousand eyes.'

'I can do things as well, Lennie.'

'What things?'

'I can make all these people go away.'

'Can you?'

'Yes. Do you want me to?'

'Yes.'

Norman Blackside pushed back his chair. As he stood, he remained slightly bent. Then he rose dramatically up to his full height, threw out his arms and roared, '*Go! In the name of God, Go!*'

Caz had heard the DCS bawl out errant coppers before, but this time when he shouted, his voice rushed out of hell, actually hurting their ears and making the solicitor flinch. He was waving his arms in a camp stage gesture at the solicitor and Tom MacInnes, bellowing again, '*Go! Now!*'

MacInnes stood. Gordon stood. They left the room together, the DI holding Gordon's elbow and steering him out.

'OK, Lennie,' Blackside said. He lowered his great bulk, then he leaned forward and looked directly into Burke's face. There was low, dark power in his control. 'It's just you and me, Lennie. Do you know who I am now?'

'Yes,' Burke said.

'Shall I shut the door, Lennie?'

'Please.'

Blackside came to the door slowly – strutting, huge

and majestic. Caz and DS Mason had given way to the DI and Colin Gordon. The solicitor looked lost. Blackside smiled and whispered to him, a strange look in his eyes. 'Don't you worry yourself about PACE, Colin. Lennie Burke is off the planet. I just want to check him out on Ellis. Five minutes, OK? The tape is running.'

Colin Gordon nodded weakly. Blackside smiled again as he closed the door.

Sixty-Four

Blackside came out after thirty-five minutes. His eyes were staring and stark. Caz, Peter, the DI and Colin Gordon had been watching through the 'one-way' front next door. Blackside was sullen and frustrated.

He spoke to MacInnes. 'He didn't fall for it, Tom. He'll talk about all the attacks except Ellis. You saw him. God's still into him for that one. He thinks I'm the Archangel Gabriel, but he won't roll over for Chichester.' He turned to the solicitor. 'Are we all right on this one, Colin?'

Gordon shrugged.

'Fer fuck's sake, Colin. You're not going to be a pain over this?'

'My client – the Police and Criminal Evidence Act –'

Blackside cut him dead. 'Yer fucking *client*? For Christ's sake, Colin, he's a fuckin' *Martian*! This isn't going to court, so why worry about PACE? Burke's booked into Broadmoor, not Dartmoor. Now look, Colin, it's one o'clock in the morning. All we want to do is clean this thing up.'

The solicitor made an attempt at not being intimidated. 'You must see it from my point of view, Norman. The interests of my client . . .'

'Interests? He kills people!'

'My client's rights . . .'

Blackside was daggers. 'OK, Colin. If you want to be here all night. You tell me about your clients rights. And when you've finished, then you tell me how we can get him to come clean on the Ellis killing.'

'Well, I would like to talk to Leonard again. He says he was in one of the arcades this morning.'

'He also says he talked to God!'

'Nevertheless . . .'

Blackside gave up, exasperated. He turned to Tom MacInnes. 'Time for a chat, Tom?'

MacInnes was still looking through the glass at Burke. Burke was staring into space and muttering, shaking his head. MacInnes nodded absently.

'Right, then!' Blackside said. He glanced at DS Mason and Caz. 'D'you think you could rustle up some coffee, Flood?' She looked. Blackside flashed her a faint smile. 'It'd be appreciated.'

'No problem, Sir.' she said. 'In your office?'

'Soon as you like, Flood.'

'Yes, Sir.' As she left, she squeezed Peter's arm, a 'come with me'. They went out together.

The canteen was wound down, an urn fizzing slightly, a few seedy cakes on offer, with currants sticking through icing.

'Fancy one, Peter?' Caz said.

'Will it soak up the booze?' he asked.

'Guaranteed,' Caz laughed. 'They're famous for it. It's the currants.'

They went to sit down. Caz hadn't got Blackside's two coffees. When Peter suggested that wasn't the greatest idea, she said, 'Why? They'll wait.'

The room was very quiet, like a station waiting-room at three in the morning – lights, the smell of past footsteps, their own stomachs.

'Fucking hell!' Caz suddenly breathed out. 'I am *so* tired.'

'Hard day,' Mason said. 'Not including Burke. If it's any consolation, I'm fucked too.'

Caz laughed. 'I don't remember that? When was that?'

Peter was staring. He looked into her face. Her eyes were raw and red with tiredness but the hostility to him wasn't there any more.

'When did I rejoin the human race?' he said quietly.

'I don't know,' Caz said. She seemed soft, almost childlike. 'Sometime when we were round at my flat, I guess. I'm not sure. I just . . .'

'What?'

'Peter, why did you say you wanted to be hurt? You said that when Burke came out of the basement at you, you didn't want to move out of the way. You said, deep down, you wanted to be hurt.'

'You, Caz.'

'What d'you mean?'

'You told me I was a pig.'

'You've heard worse.'

'You made me think about my wife, my nipper, the things I've lost. I'd got used to fucking around, but something you said made me feel . . .'

'Guilty?'

'It's not guilty.'

'It's . . .?'

'I don't know. Going nowhere. Useless. I'm a bloke. I fucked Moira because she was there, Caz. You think I raped her. I didn't, but I might as well have.'

Caz sipped some coffee. She didn't want to reply too quickly. 'Some women would call you a rapist, Peter.' She paused. 'Maybe you are, maybe you aren't, but there ought to be another name for it, for what you did. You abused Moira. What did you say, you "overwhelmed' her?'

'I don't remember.'

'You said you overwhelmed her. Doesn't that imply force?'

'A kind of.'

'Isn't "a kind of" still force?'

'Maybe. I don't know. No, it isn't. It's like the DCs, like Blackside, the way he can control a room. It's force of personality. Persuasion.'

'I know a gang of people who'd call that coercion, Peter.'

'Would you?'

'I might. But I wasn't there. I guess there's a line somewhere. The trouble is, the line moves. Your line and my line might not be in the same place.'

'You're telling *me* that?' Peter said quickly. 'You remember I once slept with a DI?'

'You said.'

'I think I told you – she was one of the few women who just came up front and went for it. We were on a course, in bed the first night. We were having a drink. I asked her, didn't she like the seduction bit, then? She told me to look up "seduce" in the dictionary. I did. Among other things, it says, "to lead astray, to corrupt". What's a bloke supposed to do, Caz?'

Caz broke away to get four coffees. She came back with them on a plastic tray and flicked her head at Peter to follow her upstairs. They went together, the DS leaning past her at every door to push it open. Each time he did she smiled lightly at him, a tiny thank-you. They were half-way up the back stairs when she remembered Gareth Boxx.

'Oh, shit!' Peter said. 'It's my fault. Gareth rang the station to let you know he wouldn't be in town tonight after all. I was by the desk when the call came in. I said I'd tell you. With all the steam around Burke, I clean forgot.'

Caz was in a forgiving mood. 'Not a problem, Peter. My memory's even worse than yours. Gareth was supposed to be stopping over at my place tonight and I'd totally forgotten about it. It's just as well for him that he did cry off. He could've frozen to death outside my front door by now!'

'You've got some of his gear, haven't you?'

'Various bits 'n' pieces. Thinking about it, I don't

really know why he left them. He had his van. He could have put it all in there.'

'Wasn't he in a bit of a hurry to get to the railway station with his YTS lad?'

'He said he was on a promise.'

'Well,' Peter said. 'That'll be it, then.'

They were at Blackside's door. Caz knocked. She'd had another thought.

'Peter, why d'you suppose Boxx thought I'd be at John Street?'

Sixty-Five

Blackside and MacInnes had got tired of waiting for their coffees and had broken out a bottle, one of Blackside's special malts. When Caz and the DS came in, they were on their third or fourth 'just one' and Blackside had mellowed enough to crack some news with them.

'Colin Gordon says Burke is still insisting he had nothing to do with the death of Mrs Ellis. I've told him to wait, we're pulling in the key-holder for the arcades on the pier.'

He offered them a drink.

'Your good DI here has persuaded me that there's at least a one per cent chance that Leonard Burke *didn't* kill Mrs Ellis. She was killed between nine o'clock and twelve o'clock this morning. Burke was at your place well before six o'clock. He told us that he hid in your basement around lunchtime. We believe him. DS Reid was at your flat from one o'clock and he was in and out from then until you arrived. It's not impossible that Burke killed Ellis and then drove straight to Brighton, but it's very

tight. There was a road block just outside Arundel
from nine this morning until five this afternoon and
we've had pandas cruising all the back roads looking
for the Escort van.' He grinned and tried his whisky.
Then he waved the two junior detectives into chairs.
'Of course,' he said as he continued, 'the time of
death might turn out to be wrong, then we're back
in business but, hell, we're up, and I can't sleep. Let's
drag a few key-holders out and put my mind to rest.'
He sat back and grinned. Mason and Flood were
drinking coffee and the malt. 'So' he said. 'While
we're waiting. How are you two getting on?'

Caz and Peter both said 'Fine, Sir' at the same
time.

They were so perfectly tuned that Blackside asked
Caz, 'What about you, Flood?'

'We're getting on fine, Sir.'

'Good,' he said. 'Either of you two got anything to
say about this?'

Caz asked, was there any chance of another
whisky?

'You nervous, Flood?'

'Not exactly, Sir, but I could kill another drink.'

Blackside nodded at the desk. MacInnes picked up
the bottle and swung it across to Mason. 'Yeah, you
as well,' Blackside said. 'It's only thirty quid a
bottle . . .'

The DS said thank you and leaned to top Caz up.
Then Caz said that something was worrying her.

'What?'

'Burke did a runner, Sir. He got on his toes just as

we were about to pick him off. The other warden at Brayfield Mansions said that Burke's cousin had come to the shelter because some relation had died.'

'An uncle.'

'But why should Burke have suddenly got cold feet? He never used his Southampton address. Why would he think we were on to him? Who was the cousin? Someone warned Burke off. The question is who and why.'

Blackside smiled patronisingly. 'Any suggestions, Flood?'

'Yes, Sir, but if you'd give me a bit of rope, first.'

'Drink your malt.'

'Thank you, Sir.' Caz took another sip. She fancied slugging it back but she didn't think the DS would be too impressed. 'Could I just ask, Sir – there was no semen with Mrs Ellis, is that right?'

'Tom?'

MacInnes spoke up. 'None. We've had a fax in from the pathologist. There was no sperm because whoever raped Mrs Ellis wore a condom.'

'That breaks with Burke's MO.'

'Correct,' MacInnes said. 'So does the stabbing, the situation and the time of day. The other attacks were urban and planned. This one wasn't either.'

'It's a copy-cat?' Peter Mason said hopefully.

'How?' MacInnes said. 'We've never published any details of the attacks.'

'Then what?'

Caz stood up. 'Then either Ellis *is* down to Burke, or whoever tipped Burke off has decided to have a try himself.'

'To tip a villain off you've got to know he's a villain,' Blackside said. He sounded mellow, maybe even tipsy.

'So what does that mean?' Peter said quickly. 'Family? Someone close?'

'There is no family,' MacInnes said. 'Not even an uncle. Leonard Burke was alone in the world.'

'No one saw this "cousin"?' Blackside asked. 'Are we quite sure?'

'No one,' Mason said. 'Frank Field was shocked rigid by what they found in Burke's room. He couldn't have been more eager to talk. When this "cousin" turned up, he was over the other side of the site doing maintenance. Burke came over to ask him to cover while he was away. Field never saw anyone.'

'Door-to-door?'

'DI Denham and Bob Scott, Sir. Most of the residents were having their afternoon tea. The rest were asleep or out for the day.'

'So what's left?'

'Either a close friend or someone involved in the investigation.'

Caz was pacing about. 'Close friend? No way, Peter. Not unless Burke is a complete one-off. Serial killers and rapists don't have close friends. If they are protected, it's by family members, usually the wife. If someone else is involved he's an accomplice.'

MacInnes was still waiting for Caz to come out with what she knew. He pushed a little harder. 'We were pretty damn sure there was no accomplice on the first five attacks, Caz. There's not been a shred of a suggestion that someone else was involved.'

'I know, Sir. There wasn't.'

'So?'

'It's someone involved in the investigation. Some-one we've involved. Someone who knows Burke or has found out who Burke is. Someone *we* told.'

'Who?' Blackside said.

'Gareth Boxx, Sir.'

Sixty-Six

The dramatic pictures of Burke's attack on Caz filled four of the first six pages of Saturday's issue of the *Sun*, pushing the glamour shots of The Girl Who Saved Brighton out to page nine. They were award-winning photographs: the man, a known rapist, huge, pug-faced, with white, screaming eyes; the slight woman fighting for her life on her doorstep; the police marksman, the crashed car, a detective sergeant, one Peter Mason, overcoming the maniac.

The story was by-lined, 'By Deborah Snow, a *Sun* exclusive'. It was Deborah Snow, *Sun* features editor, who had received the anonymous package from a motorbike courier. The unmarked envelope she had been sent had contained brief notes, some prints, a private letter and a reel of film. The undeveloped film had been shot in Chichester.

After the photographs from Chichester had been developed, a high-level conference was called quickly. It was decided that, for ethical reasons, the photographs could not be published. Deborah Snow's article dealt with the ethics of the Burke-Flood shots.

She explained in her text how, during her short but intense personal relationship with Caz Flood, The Girl Who Saved Brighton, she had grown to like and empathise with this truly brave young woman. She had felt *forced* to highlight the incredible stresses on Caz; the incredible pressures that the modern-day police woman had to withstand.

Three sets of photographs were mentioned and viewed by a coroner's jury at the Southampton inquest on Gareth Berwyn Boxx.

A Detective Inspector Simon Denham (Shirley, Southampton) gave evidence to the Coroner's Court. He explained how, in the early hours of Saturday morning, he had led a squad of detectives to arrest a man in Grosvenor Square, Southampton, and how they had found the man already dead, hanging from his balcony above a rose garden. The Detective Inspector further explained how an SLR camera had been set up to capture the man's final milliseconds. Prints of this film were shown to the court.

The quality had been a little lacking. An expert explained that, even at seven frames a second and lit by high-powered strobe lighting, approximately ninety per cent of reality is missed between frames.

There was no shot of Gareth Boxx passing from life to death. The set-up was technically poor. It was probably rushed, said the expert. All that was left was his note to one Detective Constable Flood. The letter was detailed, printed on Boxx Brownie letter-headed paper. Across the top of each A4 page was the catch-line 'Boxx it – Keep the moment forever.'

Gareth Boxx explained about his dreams, a life, the one absolute and finally perfect photograph. He was sorry, he said, but he had worked out where Lennie Burke was the night the detectives first came to see him. Burke was quite sick, he said, but he was easy to control. Burke had thought that once the photographs were taken, everything would get better. He had told Boxx he didn't really want to do it again. Jane Daily had been an accident, he said.

'But I convinced him. I had so many photographs. He thought I was God. "Just once more, Lennie," I told him. "Then I can help you. I can sort you out."

'I went wrong with the photo to begin with, didn't I? I re-printed that one of you finishing the Sixth Totton 10K. But Burke was in the race, too, wasn't he? I knew you would eventually work it out. Burke couldn't have taken your photo. You guessed about the pier fire, too, didn't you? And when I turned up at your place – that really was coincidence, Caz – you were just different. When you told me I could leave my camera gear with you, there was something, something in the way you acted. I thought you might have already guessed but I wasn't sure; not then. But you knew I'd arranged with Lennie to call on you just after seven, didn't you?

'I would have dealt with Sergeant Mason. He wouldn't have been that hard to surprise. We were mates, weren't we? And you'd invited me round for the evening. One quick smack with something heavy and goodbye protection . . .

'It wasn't you, really, Caz; you were just a rose, a vase, a piece of still life. I couldn't think of you, the prize was too fantastic. The final acts of a serial rapist turned murderer, all captured on film before he killed himself? I would have made Time-Life.

'I'd figured on black-and-white and colour shots. I had a video as well; it was all ready, but Burke couldn't wait, could he? I thought I had complete control of him but I didn't. I'd hidden him and his van at an isolated place I know near Chichester. I went back to check him in the morning but he wasn't there. I was going to burn the van but he'd taken it and gone.

'I didn't go looking for the woman, Caz. She found me. That was fate. I was looking for Lennie when she came over to see what I was doing. Rape wasn't something I'd ever really thought about until we met, Caz. But then Leonard Burke and I found each other. It was just one more experience, I suppose. The murder had more going for it, but even that wasn't all it's cracked up to be. I thought there'd be a lot more passion in it. I took some photographs after and I sent the roll of film to the *Sun*. Then I went to Brighton to wait.

'If I could have got to Burke first, I would have, but he wasn't playing any more. The shots that we had planned for inside your flat would have been fantastic, but there you are. Lennie was an idiot. He just couldn't wait.

'I hadn't planned on him attacking you when he did. But I'm a professional, Caz. Always carry at least one camera. You never know what might happen, do you? I'll never actually see the prints, but they'll be front page, I know that. By the way, I thought you put up one hell of a fight. These days the papers like feisty female stuff, but where *did* you learn all that Kung Fu?

'I did think about you, about what Burke would do. But then I thought about the evening that you spent here. I've been dead for a while, Caz. What happens to me next is not that important. But when you were here, you killed me again. What does that make you? You are beautiful, Caz. You've got class. And if Burke had been patient – if those coppers hadn't been around – you'd have had your drama, too, wouldn't you? At least I got my photos.

Hasta la Vista, Baby!
Beauty, Drama and Class, Caz. Remember?'

Epilogue

On the 3rd of January 1993 the weather on the south
coast of England was forecast to be cool and dry but
high winds were expected on or near the coast. At
eleven a.m. it was forty-two degrees Fahrenheit in
Stubbington, Hants. In Portugal it was a cool sixty-
six.

Two police officers, Kathy Flood and Peter Mason,
were standing together beneath the start banner of
the Stubbington 10K. They were cold – just like the
other nine hundred and fifty runners – and huddled
down away from the wind. Peter Mason was feeling
trim. After three weeks of a restricted diet, just one
sherry over Christmas, one twenty-mile run and then
some tough eight-hundred-metre reps, in his words
he was feeling tasty. He had lost nine pounds.

It started to rain as the race hooter went and Caz
hissed her last order as the front runners shot away.
'Not too quick over the first couple of K's, Peter.
Keep it for the second half.'

They went past the first kilometre marker in three
minutes and forty-seven seconds. Peter Mason was

immediately worried. Too fast! Caz told him not to panic. The second K was 3:52. The third was 3:53. Now they were rolling sweetly.

At half-way they clocked 19:32, and Peter said he was working very hard. At five miles he'd achieved a personal best, and was suffering, hurting to maintain the pace. With one kilometre to go their stopwatches read 35:38 and 35:35 respectively. Caz had pressed hers when the race started. Peter had pressed his as they'd crossed the start line.

The last quarter of a mile of the race sent them round a roundabout. With a hundred and fifty metres to go they both knew Peter was sub-forty minutes. When Peter saw the clock, he kicked hard, leaving Caz for dead. His time was 39:03. Caz had run a slow 39:10.

In the finish funnel, there were five other runners between the DS and the DC. Caz was trying to shout something ahead but Peter was too busy punching a clenched fist into the air.

When, in the mill of bodies getting drinks, she eventually caught his arm, Peter turned round. There was a woman with him, sweet-faced with dark brown curls round her head. 'Hey, Caz!' Peter said. He was grinning like a schoolboy. 'This is Ann – the Missus.' The woman nodded.

'Who was the first lady?' Caz asked. 'What was her time?'

'I wouldn't know,' Ann said. 'This is the first time I've ever been to a race.'

'Jane Harrop,' someone shouted casually. 'Thirty-five twenty, I think.'

'Oh, G-r-reat!' Caz thought. 'I just blew a hundred and fifty quid.'

Peter was covered in sweat but his eyes were bright and shining. 'Hey,' he said, 'I got a PB today. How did you get on?'

Caz smiled at the woman then grimaced at the DS. Then she said, 'You are an arsehole, Mason.' She waved a hand, turned away, and went to the showers to sluice down. While the soap suds were still rolling over whatever hips she had she compared this feeling and sex. It was no contest. She dried off, got dressed, went to the car and drove up to Gatwick Airport.

She had a flight to meet.